# *blink*

Andrea Badenoch lives in Newcastle.
She is also the author of *Mortal* and *Driven*,
both available in Pan.


Praise for *Blink*

'Shockingly atmospheric and evocative'
Jake Arnott

'Badenoch brilliantly combines atmosphere,
suspense and emotion' Helen Dunmore

'Compelling . . . A book I was reluctant to close'
*The Times*

'A gripping, atmospheric story . . . Excellent'
*Manchester Evening News*

'Wonderfully atmospheric and brilliantly plotted.
Badenoch is a talented writer of suspense' *Irish News*

'Brilliantly creates an atmosphere of emotion and suspense'
*Newcastle upon Tyne Evening Chronicle*

'The brilliantly constructed plot unravels at
a tantalisingly thrilling pace that keeps you intrigued
until the very end' *Metro North East*

# *blink*

ANDREA BADENOCH

PAN BOOKS

First published 2001 by Macmillan

This edition published 2002 by Pan Books
an imprint of Pan Macmillan Ltd
Pan Macmillan, 20 New Wharf Road, London N1 9RR
Basingstoke and Oxford
Associated companies throughout the world
www.panmacmillan.com

ISBN 0 330 39283 2

*to Steve Manchee*

# Acknowledgements

Friends and colleagues have been generous with their memories and their expertise. I would like to thank Esmee Slattery and Bernadette McAloon for recollections of their Durham childhood, Roger Forsdyke for police procedure, Carl Keifer, Martin Leichter and other members of the Kodak Camera news group on the Internet for information on the Box Brownie, Alison Grant for her knowledge of film, Rick Morgan for details about surveying, Julia Darling and Margaret Wilkinson (amongst others) for their helpful comments on early drafts.

Any mistakes are mine and all anachronisms are deliberate.

Finally, I am indebted to my agent, Jane Conway-Gordon, the Royal Literary Fund and to staff at the Northern Centre for Cancer Treatment for support during the difficult months when this novel was in progress.

# Extract from *The Amateur Astronomer* by Patrick Moore

A total eclipse is among the grandest of Nature's displays. As the Moon sweeps on, the light fades, until at the instant the last of the disk is blotted out the atmosphere of the Sun leaps into view. There are the magnificent red prominences; there is the glorious chromosphere, and there is too the 'pearly crown' or corona, a superb glow surrounding the eclipsed Sun, sometimes fairy regular in outline and sometimes sending out streamers across the heavens. It is a pity that the spectacle is so brief. No total eclipse can last for more than eight minutes, and most are much shorter, so that astronomers are ready to travel to remote parts of the world in order to make the most of their limited opportunities . . .

It may be of interest to say something about the last European total eclipse, that of June 30th, 1954. The early stages of the eclipse were well seen. Five minutes before totality, everything became strangely still, and over the hills we could see the approaching area of gloom. Then, suddenly, totality was upon us. The corona flashed into view around the dark body of the Moon, a glorious aureole of light that made one realize the inadequacy of a mere photograph . . .

It was not really dark. Considerable light remained, and of the stars and planets only Venus shone forth. Yet the eclipsed Sun was a superb sight indeed, with brilliant inner corona and conspicuous prominences. The two and a half minutes of totality seemed to race by. Then a magnificent red-gold flash heralded the reappearance of the chromosphere; there was the momentary effect of a 'diamond ring', and then totality was over, with the corona and prominences lost in the glare and the world waking once more to its everyday life. In a few minutes, it was almost as though the eclipse had never been.

# The Center for Extreme Ultraviolet Astrophysics
## UCLA Astronomy Department,
## The University of California

The fresh-faced young reporter from the men's magazine was bored. He was bored and disappointed. He sat opposite the woman in the white lab coat and unfashionable eyeglasses and, as she continued to speak, he could feel his mind switch off. Science, he knew, was over his head. He'd come for human interest, gossip, *celebrity*, and instead he was getting this drone of techno-babble. And not only that. She was frumpy and middle-aged. She wasn't worth a visual. He'd have to call and cancel the photo-shoot. There was no way his editor was going to make space for *this* babe in her underwear. 'Excuse me, ma'am,' he interrupted, a little hesitant. She was, after all, famous. Her sky rocket and then her telescope had both been on the cover of *Time*. She'd received some big-shot prize in Sweden then shaken hands with Al Gore one day, George Bush the next.

'Excuse me . . .'

'Call me Professor,' she said. To his alarm, she winked. She adjusted her glasses and stared at him. 'I know.' She opened a drawer. 'I'm sorry, of course you don't need all this preamble. It's all in the press pack.' She handed him a glossy folder. 'You've come about the most important thing, haven't you?' She smiled. 'My telescope.'

The reporter was way out of his depth. He normally covered the studios. He capped and uncapped his pen. 'I'm not a science correspondent, ma'am. I'm . . . I wanted to ask you—'

She continued as before. 'There are actually four telescopes within the Extreme Ultraviolet Explorer, all orbiting the earth on the same satellite. Out there, beyond the earth's atmosphere there's three scanning telescopes operating within a completely unexplored wavelength of light, in low-density interstellar gas which we call a bubble. This bubble is transparent to extreme ultraviolet radiation.'

The reporter felt his heart sink.

'The fourth instrument is a deep survey spectrometer,' she continued, 'which images very different sources.'

Impatiently, he spoke above her. 'I haven't come to talk about your telescope!'

Silenced, she looked surprised. 'No?'

'No.'

She raised her eyebrows. 'You don't want to hear about my white dwarfs and my hot young stars?'

The reporter shifted in his seat. Momentarily interested, he decided after a split second that she was joking. He tried to smile.

She was completely serious. 'My cool stars with hot coronae?'

He shook his head.

She stood up. The fluorescent lighting hit the lenses of her glasses and gave her an eerie, blanked out look. 'Well then, young man, why are you here wasting my time?'

The reporter swallowed. He adopted a more ingratiating tone. 'I've come to find out about *you*.'

'Me?'

'Yep, that's right.' He opened his hands wide. 'Maybe, let's say, how it all started. Where you started and how you came to be here, doing what you do, here in the golden state by the sundown sea. Or your background, say, or your hobbies. Your love-life.' He looked at the floor. The pale, opaque discs of her eyes were unnerving. 'Or childhood. Yes, childhood. You know. The personal . . . angle.'

There was a lengthy silence. The reporter pocketed his pen and notebook, stood up and moved towards the door. He muttered, 'OK, I know. I've blown it.'

'Stay!' she ordered. She crossed over to her notice board and stood for a moment, examining it, her back to him. She turned to him. 'Come here.'

He went and joined her. She was very small, and looking at her from above he could see her thin brown hair was peppered with grey.

'Look.'

His eyes moved over the University term dates and details of faculty meetings.

'See this?' Her arm was upraised. She was directing his attention to a coloured postcard, which showed a rusty winged figure on a hill. 'This is the Angel of the North. It's a very large metal artwork in the north-east of England.'

He was bewildered. 'It is very fine.'

'My mother sent me this picture. I haven't seen the Angel myself, because I haven't been back there for a number of years.' She paused. 'And you see this?' She pointed to a letter, framed and behind glass. She took a handkerchief from the sleeve of her coat and polished it. 'This is a letter from John Glenn.'

'Ma'am?'

'John Glenn.' She sounded exasperated. 'The first American to orbit the earth.'

'Yes, yes, sure.' He took out his notebook and pen and wrote *John Glenn*.

'Major Glenn took the trouble to answer a letter of mine, forty years ago. Here, as you can see, he wishes me well in my lunar observations and my ambitions to be an astronaut.'

'An *astronaut*, ma'am?'

She looked up at him. 'You asked me how it all started.' Still meeting his gaze, she thought for a moment, then sighed. 'It started with this.' She turned back to the notice board and tapped the glass with her fingernail. Then she reached up again and pointed again to the postcard. 'And *where* did it start? You want to know where it started? It started right here.'

# MONDAY

Kathleen walked gingerly down the coal-strewn track towards the pond, her wellingtons slipping on the loose stones. It was windy and her coat collar was buttoned against the early morning cold. Over one shoulder she carried a bulky camera case on a strap. Under her other arm, she held a flat rectangle. This was a long-playing record which she'd borrowed without asking her Auntie Joyce. It was called *Twist With Chubby Checker*. Her Jack Russell terrier trotted ahead. His name was Nosey and his eyes and ears were alert with excitement.

Kathleen was a slight figure on the monochrome slope and her little plaits blew behind her like micetails. Dying fireweed, its cotton puffs recently shed, stirred stiffly at the sides of the path and dust eddied on the faces of the pit heaps, which rose in steep high mounds on all sides. Below, the surface of the water was uneasy. The sky was an unbroken grey and the sullied landscape was colourless and bleak.

Beyond the pond, a lonely house came into view. This was her destination, the home of her school friend, Petra. Surrounded on all sides by mountains of waste from the pit, it resembled an outpost, a place of grim survival. Smoke puffed from its squat chimney and was immediately carried away. A light shone from between half-closed curtains. It looked desolate and unwelcoming.

Kathleen approached the pond. She watched the wind form oily ripples, which rolled then broke, sluggishly. The dog sniffed the air then barked. Here, nothing grew, not a blade of grass, not even fireweed. Polluted by the mine, the once legendary sweet waters had for decades been thick and lifeless. Formed in a natural fissure, the pool was deep – some said bottomless – but it was scummy now and stank of coal.

Kathleen's eyes narrowed. She stopped and peered through her spectacles. What's that? she thought. Still clutching the LP she took off her glasses, breathed on the lenses, rubbed them on her coat, then replaced them. In the distance, on the water's edge next to an ancient, ruined barn, something shone red. It was bright and startling. The dog barked again. A beachball, Kathleen decided, or maybe a lost umbrella. Intrigued, she left the track and walked towards the barn, which tottered on the far shore. Her feet sank into the black mud, leaving oozing footprints. 'Nosey!' she called, as he raced ahead, his tail erect and quivering. As she neared the red blotch, she could see it wasn't round at all. Now it looked like fabric. It's a bedcover, she decided, blown off Petra's mam's washing line. It was caught between two rotting posts, which emerged from the shallows like broken fingers.

She drew alongside the barn. Nosey was running to and fro, by the water's edge, yapping furiously. She caught her breath. She could see it clearly now – the red cloth was a jacket.

Kathleen was afraid but curious. She laid the long-playing record on the ground, unfastened the heavy case and took out Da's old Box Brownie. She steadied herself, holding the camera firmly upright at waist height, in order to take a portrait shot. The wind was blowing against her and she leant forwards, balancing herself. Peering through her spectacles, down into the viewfinder she trapped the exact image and with her right thumb carefully pressed the device on the side that released the shutter. There was a loud click as the mechanism moved.

Carefully, she returned the Box Brownie to its case, then stepped into the foul pond, the cold filling her wellingtons. She waded forwards. She was scared. I've got to see what this is, she thought. The icy coldness rose up her thighs. The skirt of her coat floated then dragged. She lifted her feet from the slimy bottom to stop them sinking. She grasped one of the posts. The discoloured water was black on the surface but a few inches underneath it was a rusty orange, which was both malodorous and dense. She looked again. Above the half-submerged red jacket there were floating tendrils of short blonde hair. She took off her glasses and rubbed her eyes. She saw what was unmistakably a rigid hand, an arm. She polished the spectacles on her shoulder and put them on again. She was reminded of posed plaster mannequins she'd seen in shop windows on her rare trips to town. Her heart turned over and she grasped the sodden jacket, tugging it hard. This freed the stiff figure from its mooring. Grotesquely, it turned over and reared up. It was a dead body. A drowned person. It had a yellowish-cream waxy face and eyes that met hers and stared. She gasped. Its hair was stuck down, its mouth was open with water streaming out. Its lips were drawn back in a frozen grimace from which teeth protruded. She cried out and released it. With a gentle splash it sank below the surface.

Kathleen stepped back, unbalanced. She staggered then fell at the pond's edge. Nosey barked hysterically. Soaked and filthy from her chest downwards, she struggled to her feet. One of her wellingtons came off and was lost. She struggled for breath in uneven sobs, picking up the camera, then half running back to the track. The dog overtook her, excitedly. She turned to look behind. The body was no longer visible but she knew it hadn't been a bad dream. She moved her short-sighted gaze upwards to the pale cloud. There was no break in the flat canopy, not a sliver of blue, not a single bird. Nearby, a hidden train shunted and rattled. Her sobs steadied to a heavy, even rasp. She tried, but failed to remember some religious words. 'Gloria,' she managed to gasp, after a moment. Recovering her voice she shouted loudly 'Gloria!' This wasn't a prayer directed at a godless sky. It was the name of her auntie. Her Auntie Gloria was lifeless, waterlogged, dead. She lay drowned in Jinny Hoolets pond.

Kathleen hammered on the side door of the isolated house of her friend. 'Mrs Koninsky!' she yelled. 'Petra! Help!' She banged with both fists.

Her friend peered through a gap in the curtains. The electric light made her sallow and suspicious. She opened the door. 'Where's the records?' she demanded. 'Where's Chubby Checker? Where's Del Shannon and Neil Sedaka?' She was wearing baby-doll pyjamas and, over the top, a stained dressing gown.

'Phone the police,' Kathleen muttered, leaning in the entrance, water forming a pool at her feet. 'Phone the doctor.' Dismayed, she realized as she spoke that she'd lost her Auntie Joyce's LP somewhere near the pond. She pushed past Petra into the dim scullery where the pot-bellied stove smoked and gave off practically no heat.

'You're all wet,' was the reply. 'You're dirty.'

With uncustomary boldness, Kathleen walked through and opened the door into the hallway. The Koninskys were one of the few families in the area with a private telephone. 'Where's your mam and dad?'

'In bed. Don't you know what time it is?'

'There's a body in the pond.'

Petra's mouth fell open into a silent 'O'. 'Is it a man?' she whispered after a few seconds. 'Is it a man in a raincoat?'

Kathleen ignored this. She picked up the smooth black

handset and listened, tentatively, to the tone. 'What d'you do with this? What d'you do again?'

Her friend grabbed the receiver. She wanted to take charge. 'Nine, nine, nine,' she said with authority. 'I'll do it. We need to dial nine, nine, nine.'

Later, wearing only Petra's unwashed dressing gown, Kathleen stood on the edge of the bath and looked out of a small top window, which was wedged open. Below, the police had put up a screen, which blew like a sail in the wind. Two Alsatians were being led from a van, parked on the hard surface of the track. One uniformed constable was measuring the ground with a tape, another stood hands on hips, his helmet pushed back, gazing across the impassive pond.

'Let me look now, let me look,' insisted Petra, from the landing. 'It's my turn!'

They had been told to stay inside. Kathleen ignored her friend. She was aware that her hands, her knees were shaking. My Auntie Gloria has been murdered, she kept thinking. Someone has done this to her. She's dead.

It was hard to take it in. It felt like a dream, but the scene outside was more than real. It was in sharp focus with stark definitions. Let me wake up, she thought, remembering Gloria's father, Da, and her boyfriend, Billy. Poor Da, she thought. Poor Billy Fishboy. It'll be even worse for them. She tried to imagine both men crying and wringing their hands, but this was impossible.

She craned her neck as the flashing lights of another police car became visible on the road at the top of the hill. She blinked and wondered what the adult Koninskys were doing. They'd disappeared as soon as they'd heard the news. They were nowhere to be seen.

*

Behind the building, unobserved, Marek Koninsky chopped kindling wood. The sound of his axe rose above the wind and the shouts and barking dogs at the water's edge. He was wearing a fine white linen shirt, which was baggy and stained damp at the armpits. His tie and the jacket of his suit hung on a nail. His whole upper body rose and fell rhythmically. The logs split and peeled apart in rapid succession. He worked desperately, his arm flailing and his black hair falling forwards into his eyes. He seemed determined to ignore the growing hubbub near the front of his house. Not even the ambulance siren, as it careered down the road from the village, swerving left on to the track to Jinny Hoolets, distracted him from his efforts.

Marek Koninsky was a stranger. He had moved to this black and lonely place, with his family, eighteen months before. He was a surveyor, which meant it was his job to assess the seams in the mine for future coal. He spoke English in a formal, accented way and when sober he had exquisite manners.

Marek, it was said, had been educated at a Polish academy but had left his country during the war. Little was known of his history, except that he kept moving, as if pursued by demons, enemies or a guilty conscience. The miners feared him because they thought he would close the pit. As well as this, he was known to inspire envy amongst all the men in the village because he was exceptionally handsome and tall. When he first appeared there was a kind of communal shock. No one had ever seen anyone like him before. He resembled a film star or possibly a dissolute aristocrat with his handmade clothes and his dramatic, sensuous features. His eyes were almost as black as his hair. His top lip was a full and perfect cupid's bow. He moved in an elegant, self-conscious way and he was broad-shouldered and lithe. Girls, women, housewives, mothers – all peered at him from doorways and from behind curtains, mesmerized and confused by their fascination, their unspoken, shameful desire.

Nadezhda Koninsky leaned in her front porch, smoking a cigarette. She was wrapped in a shawl and her woollen stockings were rucked and loose. Her fine blonde-grey hair was caught up in an untidy bun. She seemed frail and a little disorientated, shaking her head in bewilderment. She coughed as she inhaled. A police officer approached her and asked her to boil a kettle for tea, but then he backed away nervously when confronted by her peculiar, detached stare. She lit one cigarette from another, throwing the dog-end into a heap that had accumulated within the porch. After a while, in a heavily accented monotone, she began reciting prayers.

Nadezhda was rarely seen in the village. She paid to have her meat, bread and groceries delivered. No one, except the Catholic priest, ever spoke to her and it was widely but wrongly assumed that she knew no English. She seemed much older than her husband and a little strange. Her garments were mismatched, her gestures theatrical and her frequent praying created the impression that she talked to herself. She was sometimes described as mad, but this wasn't true. She was lonely and depressed. Nobody knew her background and because she was foreign and isolated at Jinny Hoolets, there seemed no point in bothering with her.

Up in the village, Billy Fisher, or Billy Fishboy as he was known, pulled shut the door of Gloria's flat. News travelled fast in these parts and he'd learned of her death not long after the police were called. He stood in the entrance and looked around, furtively. He pocketed the key. In front, the wide cobbled area between the shops was deserted apart from a few housewives with shopping bags whose heads were bent against the wind.

Two boys ran past dragging a bogey that was made from old pram wheels. A dog yapped at their heels. They didn't look at him. He was fashionably dressed for the weather and he eased his long, fitted raincoat together, fastening one button but leaving the belt undone. Around his neck he carried a German camera on a strap. Inside his coat was a sheaf of enlarged glossy black and white photographs poking from an envelope. He pushed these lower, out of sight. He tried to swallow his anxiety, his distress. He smoothed his hair in a habitual effeminate gesture. He couldn't help this even though he knew it was widely copied in a mocking way that was both accepting and cruel.

The black, poisonous scum of Jinny Hoolets pond filled his imagination. For a moment he could see it, smell it. It was treacle-dark and stinking. 'God in Heaven,' he whispered. He looked left and right, with his protruding, fishy eyes. Noting that the coast was clear, he stepped from the shadow of Gloria's doorway. The dog stopped in its tracks and turned, growling. Nervously Billy picked up a stone. He disliked all dogs. 'Go away,' he called. He took aim but the animal ran off in pursuit of the boys.

Looking neither to the right or left, Billy set off briskly towards his own home on the far side of the village. Believing he could actually taste the polluted pond water himself, he spat into his handkerchief. 'God in Heaven!' He was a young man who normally never used strong language.

As Kathleen continued to tremble and stare out the bathroom window, Petra held Nosey, Kathleen's dog, under her arm. She was on the landing outside the door. The dog struggled a little because he didn't like her. She clamped him harder. 'Stop it!' she whispered, urgently. 'Keep still, you little bastard.' With her free hand she groped in her pocket. She had two cigarettes and a lighter, which she removed. It was made of gold with a single diamond in the centre and yesterday she'd stolen it from her mother. She flicked it open, creating a small flame and this she moved towards the dog's front paws. He wriggled frantically and freed himself, falling at her feet. Before she had time to back away he bared his teeth, bit her ankle then raced away down the stairs.

'It's my turn!' shouted Petra again, to Kathleen. She was angry. 'Get off there will you, and let me have a look!'

'I'm coming,' Kathleen replied. She felt dazed.

'It's my house and I'm older than you!'

'I'm coming.'

As they crossed in the bathroom, Petra said, 'A funny man's been hanging around here. D'you think I should tell anyone?'

Kathleen didn't reply. She returned to the scullery downstairs. Her clothes were still damp but she put them on anyway. She pushed a foot into her single wellington and located the square case containing Da's Box Brownie. She called for Nosey but he didn't appear. He'll be all right, she thought. He knows his way home. She ran a tap, rinsed a glass and drank some water. The sink was stained brown and there was dirty crockery piled up. She noticed clots of dust in the grey net curtains. She glanced around. The room was sombre and the worn linoleum was scuffed and grubby with bits of trampled food. 'Goodbye,' she called loudly and went outside, limping on her one-stockinged foot.

Mrs Koninsky, still praying fervently, still smoking, stepped aside to let her pass. Kathleen paused and looked at the ambulance, which was perched near the top of the track, its driver clearly unwilling to negotiate the steep, rough slope. Its siren was extinguished but its light was still flashing. Over by the barn, a burly older man wearing a trilby and a coat wrote in a notebook. He had a red face and earlier he'd spoken briefly to

Kathleen. He was nice, she decided and he seemed to be in charge.

Just then a stretcher, carried by two ambulance men, appeared from behind the flapping screen. Mrs Koninsky, oblivious, her eyes half closed, chanted the Catechism. Kathleen's heart began to race. Oh no, she thought. She removed Da's Box Brownie from its case and turned the film advance key on the left-hand side, counter clockwise, to wind on the film. She tried to calm her shaking hands. She counted to five then checked the little red window at the back – it said 'two'. This was a new film and she had seven pictures left. She held the camera sideways, waist height, to get a landscape shot. She squinted behind her spectacles and tried to stay as still as possible. She wanted another picture. She wanted to try and preserve something of Gloria.

The Jack Russell appeared and began barking at the approaching ambulance men, who, uncertain, stopped and stared at him. Nadezhda came out from her reverie.

'Nosey! Away!' Kathleen shouted. 'Go home to your Nana!'

The dog turned and barked at Nadezhda instead. She stepped back into the porch, fending him off with exaggerated hand movements, as if she were miming.

'Nosey!'

The dog lolled his tongue at Kathleen as if he were smiling and trotted off up the track.

The men proceeded to carry the stretcher towards the ambulance. As it came nearer, Kathleen saw that the body was covered in a white Aertex hospital blanket. Its feet were sticking out the end, toes erect, its legs stiff in death. As it passed, Kathleen took a deep breath and steadied herself. She centred it in her viewfinder and took a photograph. Gloria was still wearing her black patent court shoes, Kathleen noticed. They were the latest fashion with a thick heel rather than a kitten stiletto. Kathleen was suddenly very, very sad. 'She only just got them shoes,' she called out to Mrs Koninsky. 'She loved them. She got them from Dolcis, in Newcastle. She drove up there specially in her car. They cost her forty-nine and eleven.'

Later, inside the house on First Street, in the dim warmth of Nana's gleaming kitchen, a pot bubbled on the range and the air was scented with turnip. The banked-up fire cast shifting shadows around the walls. Nana's long body rocked energetically and her knitting needles clacked. She was in her usual place, at the side of the hearth, cushions heaped behind her to ease the pain in her joints. Her chair creaked, the old wall clock ticked and the coals shifted contentedly in the grate. Her wireless played quietly.

Kathleen sat, half-hidden on her cracket, that is her low wooden stool, in a dark alcove. Her hands were folded over the camera in her lap. She'd stopped shaking but her shoulders felt rigid, her legs tense. She was motionless, watching, listening, trying not to attract attention to herself. She'd put her damp clothes in the laundry basket in the wash house and she was wearing her school uniform. She had almost nothing else, except pyjamas. Her glasses occasionally glinted from the gloom of her corner, but Nana and Joyce ignored her.

Nana had lived in this colliery house all her life. Her father was a hewer and then her two husbands both worked at the mine, so there had never been a reason to move. The house was old, underlit and damp but she kept the place spotless, despite her arthritis. She never changed anything unless, of course, it was worn out. She sat in her mother's chair, slept in her parents' bed. She cooked the same plain food she had always eaten, with a fixed menu for each day of the week. She washed on Mondays, ironed on Tuesdays. She said the only thing that needed changing was the calendar, and even this barely varied – it was always a scene of Ceylon, provided free by Rington's Tea. Nana was set in her ways. For the last three years she had never been outside.

Nosey, the Jack Russell, was asleep against the fender, his little legs twitching as he dreamed of ambulance men or possibly rabbit hunts across the fields. Joyce, Nana's daughter, leaned over the table, her hair dishevelled and russet in the light from the fire. Her uniform was partly undone revealing the line of her cleavage, the mound of her breasts. Her little pillbox hat was by her elbow. She heaped sugar into a cup of tea and stirred it vigorously.

Joyce was unmarried and at twenty-eight was considered by most to be on the shelf. Unkind gossips in the village referred to her as 'desperate'. She'd been let down by a sailor when she was twenty or thereabouts and then there'd been further disappointments. She didn't earn enough money to leave home but in any event she would have stayed with her mother. It wasn't the custom in the village for unmarried women to leave their families. The only person who'd ever done this was Gloria.

Joyce was bitter about her status and her humdrum existence but hadn't given up hope of meeting Mr Right. She was attractive in a blowsy way, but overweight and untidy. She had rarely travelled beyond the rows, except to occasional dances down in Stanley or trips to the seaside, which usually happened once a year.

'She always did as she pleased,' said Nana, ruminatively. She rocked more furiously for an instant, then suddenly placed both feet on the mat and stopped. She bent down and tickled the dog's ears and he stretched and sighed. She patted him gently and laid her knitting aside. 'As if this family hasn't been dragged through the mud enough already.'

Joyce sighed. She spoke softly. 'Suicide's so horrible. And there. Imagine choosing to go in there.' She slurped tea from her cup.

Nana stood up abruptly, grasped her stick and lurched towards the sideboard, her long legs stiff and unbending. She was a bony woman, and tall. She had a long, horsy face and one of her eyes was cloudy and blind. She retrieved two glasses and a chipped cut-glass decanter half full of amber liquid. This hadn't been touched since Easter. She poured an inch into each glass and handed one to her daughter. 'We'll be the talk of the neighbourhood.' Awkwardly, she sat down again, hooking her stick on to the mantelpiece. 'Well she's gone.' She thought for a minute. 'She can't get above herself any longer. She can't spread any more rumours about us.'

Nana was a domineering woman, despite her infirmities. At one time she'd been a central figure in village life; treasurer of the Labour Women's Guild, organizer of the Industrial Section at the flower show, a tireless collector of milk-bottle tops for Guide Dogs for the Blind. She'd been famous for her war work. However, she'd never been popular. The villagers looked backwards and they had long memories. She'd always been treated with suspicion. Now, middle-aged, housebound and neurotic, never seen in public, her firmness and rigid character found expression in negative ways. She was bullying and condemnatory.

Kathleen didn't move but there were tears welling in her eyes. She tried to swallow but her mouth was dry. Poor Gloria was a nice person, she thought. She remembered an expression often used by her teacher at school, always about herself. 'You've got a very good brain.'

That's it, she mused. Gloria had a very good brain. She watched Nosey's little heart beating as he groaned and rolled over without waking. He placed his head on Nana's slippers. Gloria was a brain-box.

Joyce pushed her tea aside and swallowed her whisky in one gulp. She picked up a chocolate biscuit and hiccoughed gently.

'Poor bloody Gloria.' There was a silence. The clock struck the half hour. 'I know we were stepsisters, but I'm not pretending. I never liked her and that's all there is to it. Not even when she was little.' She ran her hands through her luxuriant hair and shook her head and began to fasten her overall. She was about to leave for the local cinema where she worked as an usherette. She placed her pillbox hat on the back of her head. 'Mind you. Da will be upset.'

Kathleen listened attentively. Nana knew she had discovered the body earlier, but she was unconcerned about the shock. 'I've told you not to go near Jinny Hoolets,' had been her angry response. 'It's deep and dangerous. Why can't you do as you're told, for once?'

Nana thought for a moment. 'No,' she said reflectively, 'like her? Neither did I. She chose to move out of here, didn't she? She thought she was better than us and she laughed at us behind our backs.'

Kathleen pictured Gloria's neon-lit salon, with its row of overhead driers, its pink ruched curtains. She'd been a hairdresser – the only one in the village. She'd been planning a refurbishment. She had big ideas, plans. She was ambitious. She'd wanted a string of salons.

'That pond was clean once,' Nana said. 'It was covered in birds. Not that I can remember, mind. Da showed me a picture in a book.' Da was Nana's second husband, not Joyce's father. She sipped from her glass as if she was drinking medicine. She grimaced, changing the subject back again. 'Liked her? Why should we have liked her? She ruined your chances with that nice Mr Dobbs.' She put down her glass and picked up her knitting. Her gesture implied that she had nothing further to say.

Joyce stood up and pulled on a wide, old-fashioned fur jacket. Her uniform strained against her hips. 'All those shoes she had,' she said spitefully, reminded by Nana of her jealousy for her stepsister. 'Those stupid little pinafores. Lipstick pale as chalk. That bloody beatnik black. Not much good to her now, are they?'

Kathleen's dismay was suddenly replaced by anger. She stood up and stepped into the pool of light in front of Nana's chair. 'Poor Gloria's dead,' she said simply. 'And she didn't kill herself.' The tears that had been threatening to flow now spilled down her cheeks. She took off her glasses, rubbed her eyes then put them on again. 'She had no reason to.'

Reprimanded, Joyce was immediately sharp. 'Yes, and you'll be dead,' she said, 'if you don't find my Chubby Checker long player. It'll be coming off your pocket money for years.' She opened the sideboard, poured herself another finger of Nana's whisky and downed it in one quick movement. It was rare for her to drink. She was upset. She put the glass on the table.

'All right, Kathleen?' added Nana, aggressively.

Kathleen said nothing. She looked her aunt in the eye. There was a brief silence before Joyce relented. Conciliatory, she reached out with both hands. 'Come here, pet,' she said, softly, but Kathleen only scowled and took a step backwards. Joyce shrugged and left the room.

At that moment, the easy, melodic singing on the wireless was suddenly cut short. There was a brief silence then a serious voice spoke clearly. *We interrupt this broadcast to bring you a special news bulletin.* There was another pause, a crackle and a moment of electronic distortion. Nana was holding her knitting close to her eyes. Her concentration was undisturbed. She was counting rows. 'Ninety-eight,' she whispered, 'ninety-nine, one hundred. One hundred and one . . .'

The newsreader continued. *President J. F. Kennedy has today announced the discovery of Soviet nuclear missiles on the island of Cuba. They were spotted and photographed by reconnaissance aircraft. Cuba is approximately ninety miles off the coast of the United States. There is concern that these missiles may be positioned in order to target major American cities.*

Kathleen moved over to the set and placed an ear next to the grille. She listened carefully.

It was explained that the communist dictator Fidel Castro, who seized power in 1959, ruled Cuba, and he was a close ally of the Soviet Union.

*President Kennedy addressed the American nation today.*

Kathleen prepared herself for the familiar flat, lazy monotone. He sounded confident. *Any missile launched from Cuba against any nation in this hemisphere will bring a full retaliatory response upon the Soviet Union.*

'Two hundred and fifty,' muttered Nana. 'Two hundred and fifty-one . . .'


Joyce was in the damp passageway, exchanging her slippers for stilettos, adjusting her hat in the hall-stand mirror. Kathleen waited for her to slam the door, then went upstairs to the airing cupboard. Her coat was still damp but she put it on. She jammed her feet into her school shoes and tied the laces. Silently, she went out. I wonder where Da is, she thought. It was still early but the afternoon had faded to a grey October evening. The colliery headstock was drawing up pitmen at the end of their shift. He'll know about Gloria by now. The street lights at that moment flickered and came on, dimly. Kathleen paused for a second and blinked. She stood on one leg and stretched her arms into the air, trying to relieve the tension in her body, but she wobbled, unable to balance. I feel awful, she thought.

Da was fed up with his daughter recently, she remembered. Every time Gloria's name had been mentioned in the last few weeks, he frowned, or sighed. I wonder why?

\*

The deputy had called Da away from the coal face. The news was broken loudly to him, underground. The deputy had to shout in his ear because of the rattle of the conveyor belts, and he used very few words. Da put down his tools. His mate Jonty Dickinson, known as his marra, was concerned, but he was not allowed to accompany him to the surface because this only ever happened in the event of injury. Alone, Da trudged the long, dark distance back to the shaft, the solitude briefly enabling him to release his emotions. His metal-toed boots rang out, the lamp on his helmet shone a narrow beam and tears streaked through the dust on his face. He stepped into the cage and came up to bank between shifts, knowing he would lose pay.

Now he stood in his work clothes, black from head to foot, his soft cap clutched in both hands, his head bowed. He was tall for a miner, over six feet, but the bright tiled cleanliness of the mortuary, with its high ceiling, seemed to diminish him. He was sad and hunched and helpless as the trolley was wheeled towards him. The blanket was drawn slowly from Gloria's face, revealing its pallor, its staring expression, its ghastly, toothy grin. Da shuddered, stepped back and closed his eyes. The attendant muttered something consolatory. He looked again, but this time at a chain around his daughter's neck. It was entwined with a strand of debris from the pond. 'Is that . . . Is that . . . ?' he stuttered.

The mortuary attendant was calm but helpful. 'Yes, sir?'

'Is that a silver coin? On a chain around her neck?'

Carefully, the man lifted the jewellery. A little pendant swung between his fingers. It was a two-headed sixpence, made into a necklace, which Da had given Gloria three years ago, on her twenty-first birthday. He'd told her it would bring her luck.

'It's her,' said Da, his voice a dull sigh. He was numb.

The blanket was gently raised.

Da filled in some forms, his coal-covered hands smudging the paper. He firmed his cap back on his head.

'Next of kin?' asked a lady in the office as he handed her the details.

'She was my daughter by my first wife,' he said simply. 'We came up together from Cornwall, thirteen years ago, when her mother died ... she was only young then ... a child ... when we came up here.' He stopped for a moment, letting his voice steady. 'Me, I came up for the work.'

The woman looked at him without emotion. 'Are you the next of kin?'

'Yes.'

'Then sign here, please.'

Da's Box Brownie over her shoulder, Kathleen set off down the street where the neighbours had already drawn their curtains against the coming night. These people don't care, she thought. Gloria was like me, she wasn't really one of them, so they just turn away, pull their curtains together, close off their minds. She remembered something dismissive Gloria had once said about the villagers. 'There's no beauty in their lives.'

She cut through a lane to the cobbled centre of the village. All was quiet; the shops shut up for the day, except for the hair salon. It shone brightly, tragically, its neon lights aglow, with two police cars parked outside. A broad constable filled the entrance. Her auntie's name, in pink, bold writing glowed on the fascia board above his head. It said Hairdresser of Distinction. Kathleen glided unnoticed to the plate-glass window and peered in through the nylon drapes. A group of officers, one the big man in the hat and overcoat, sat around, incongruously, under the dryers. They were drinking tea from Thermos flasks. A young one had placed his helmet in a basket of plastic rollers, which stood on a stand. Another leaned casually against a basin.

*

Gloria had rented the salon soon after leaving her training course in Tynemouth. She gradually built up trade, not least because she was a good listener and a bit of a laugh. As well as this, she gently suggested new styles and experimented with new methods. She understood what women wanted but also what suited them. She was a good hairdresser. She remained an outsider in the community but in her salon she was respected. Some travelled distances on buses or trains in order to entrust her with their perms, colours or sets. She specialized in weddings. These had made her famous, in a small way. Every Saturday two or three brides arrived in housecoats and slippers, all jittery and talkative. They came from the whole of Durham and occasionally beyond. They clutched their head-dresses or bunches of artificial flowers, sometimes even their veils. Gloria always managed to combine these with their hair in a most attractive way. Within three years she'd bought the business and the lease on the building and moved into the flat above the shop. Even though she was still only twenty-four years old she'd decided to revamp the interior, making it more contemporary. She imagined pine, chrome and sleek lines. She was going to rename it Scissors Unisex and had plans to take on an assistant.

It'll never happen now, Kathleen thought sadly. It'll stay old-fashioned, like everything else here. She sighed. Gloria had been one of the few people in the village, perhaps the only one, apart from herself, who was truly connected with the modern world. She'd looked towards the future with excitement instead of dread. This was why Kathleen admired her so much. Gloria had believed in progress. She'd believed in things getting better. Now there's just me, Kathleen decided. Realizing this, she felt tears again come into her eyes. She rubbed them hard.

Joyce stood at the back of the cinema and yawned. Her tray of ice creams was clipped to the harness around her neck, ready to be illuminated in the interval. It was a good house tonight, with only a few centre rows unfilled. She stared at the screen. Cliff Richard sang and danced energetically for the umpteenth time, partnered by a thin young woman whose short hair and cut-off fashionable capri pants reminded her of Gloria.

'Bloody Gloria,' she whispered, without regret, and thought about the impact of the death in the village. She hoped there would be a brief scandal that would quickly burn out. She knew people would have trouble believing that her stepsister had been in despair. She'd laughed such a lot, even if sometimes her laughter was unkind. This made the notion of suicide seem bizarre and out-of-character. On the other hand, she was still seen as an incomer and, in these parts, this could account for almost anything. She tried to picture Gloria deliberately wading into the scummy shallows of Jinny Hoolets pond, intending to kill herself. It was impossible. The well-groomed hairdresser had hated the cold, she'd hated getting dirty. She had no time for self-pity or negative thoughts of any kind. 'Bloody Gloria,' Joyce repeated, pushing these observations aside. She wasn't a reflective person.

At that moment she noticed the new man from the Co-op Butcher's stand up and leave his seat. He was alone and reasonably good looking, even if he was a teddy boy. It's his day off, she thought. He walked up the aisle towards her. She moved under the 'exit' light and adjusted her stance, thrusting forward one hip. She raised a hand to her hair. As he passed on his way to the gents, she parted her newly painted lips in a winning smile. He winked then brushed against her arm, as she shone her torch for him.

Nana was upstairs in the house in First Street, going through her husband's pockets. His best suit was on the bed, as was his sports jacket and his second-best trousers. All she'd found so far were some minutes of a union meeting, a wage slip and an old wallet, which contained his library tickets. She felt in the back fold and produced a photograph of his former wife with Gloria as a child. This she tore into shreds, throwing the pieces into the air.

She examined his shoes, his shirts, his waistcoat. She found an unfamiliar tie, which she rolled into a ball and stuffed into her pinafore, intending to burn it on the range. She found his slippers and taking a half-filled glass from the bedside cabinet, poured water into each. She sat on a hard chair next to the window and looked out into the street. She squinted with her short-sighted eye. A young woman approached, leading a reluctant toddler by the hand. She stopped opposite Nana's front door, hesitated, then bent down to adjust the little boy's clothing.

'Hah!' said Nana aloud. 'Hah!' A new one, she thought. It makes a change from that hussy from Jinny Hoolets. That foreigner. Here's another one, a new one. Come to see him and make secret signals to him from the street. With difficulty, she stood up and leaned against the glass. 'You're wasting your time, whore!' she shouted.

Unaware, unhearing, the woman continued on her way.

'That's right, get away! He's not even here, is he? His sainted daughter's gone and drowned!'

Kathleen slipped round the back of the hair salon, located the key, quietly unlocked and pushed open the rear door. She stepped unseen into the tiny storeroom where Gloria had sipped Tizer and read fashion magazines whenever business was slack. At this moment there was a rumble of inappropriate laughter from the men. Kathleen took a deep breath. The smell of the perming chemicals reminded her unbearably of her aunt. Her heart started beating fast. Gloria, she thought. Oh, my poor

Auntie Gloria. She peeped into the salon. She realized that Nosey the Jack Russell was snuffling at her feet. He'd followed her. *'Go home!'* she whispered, fiercely.

The older, thick set man had put his cup on the floor and was writing again in his notebook. Kathleen followed his gaze. He was copying some words, inscribed large on a wall mirror. The script was wobbly and written in what looked like dark red lipstick. Kathleen glanced down at a jar of combs in disinfectant and two oversized bottles of shampoo, then stared up again. *'I was trapped,'* the message read. Then there was something rubbed out and below, less legibly, *'Now I'm free!'*

Kathleen closed her eyes and opened them, but the words were still there. That's not Gloria's writing, she thought. Without knowing why, she eased Da's Box Brownie from its case. Her hands were steadier than they'd been earlier. She wound on the film, and turned the camera upright to portrait position, pointing the lens at the mirror. The words wouldn't fit in the finder, so she stepped backwards. She knew the glare from the lights would be problematic. As she pressed the lever, releasing the shutter, Nosey burst from between her legs and ran forwards, barking joyously, crashing open the door. One policeman threw his tea in the air as the little dog clamped his jaws around the hem of the burly man's regulation trousers.

'Nosey!' said Kathleen, horrified, stepping forward, as the policemen jumped to their feet and began swatting him, pointlessly. He released the trousers and grabbed the edge of the overcoat swinging briefly above the ground, before letting go and running outside.

Kathleen's cheeks burned. She put her camera away, too shy to look up. 'I'm sorry, mister,' she murmured, 'he's a bit . . . he thinks you shouldn't be here.'

The big, plain-clothes man motioned the others away. They went out to the cars. 'It's Kathleen, isn't it?' he asked. 'We met earlier.' His voice was kind. 'What've you got there then? A camera?'

Kathleen nodded, her eyes still downcast. She took a deep breath. 'Our Gloria didn't kill herself, mister.' She pointed at the mirror.

'Who says she did?'

'That's what people are saying. My Nan. Auntie Joyce. My friend Petra Koninsky. Everyone.'

There was a brief silence. 'We're keeping an open mind,' the burly man said eventually. 'Is there anything you want to tell me, pet?' He sat down again and in a relaxed gesture, picked up his tea. 'You must be very shocked.'

Kathleen nodded, then struggled to meet his gaze. 'What's your name?'

'I'm Detective Inspector Glen.'

Kathleen absorbed this. 'Like John Glenn? The spaceman?'

'Yes, I'm John Glen too, but only one "n".'

Kathleen pursed her lips, appreciatively.

'You like John Glenn, do you?'

She nodded.

'You want to talk about Gloria?'

'No.'

'Well, if you change your mind, I'm down at the police station in Quaking Houses.'

Kathleen swallowed. She felt a wave of certainty. She spoke in a rush. 'She was going to do this place up. She had plans. She was going to make it . . . ' She hesitated.

'Yes?'

'Unisex.'

The Inspector looked puzzled.

'That means men and women all together.

'I see.' He sounded offended. 'All together.'

'She showed me a picture. It was like a sort of cabin. It was called Norwegian Wood.'

'I see.'

'I mean' – Kathleen spoke more confidently – 'she wouldn't go and kill herself, would she? She said rollers and setting lotion are finished.' She paused. 'She said she was a hair *stylist*, not a hairdresser. She was planning on moving into blow-drying. Like Vidal Sassoon.''

The Detective Inspector appeared mystified.

'It's the latest thing. In the hair styling world.' She paused. 'My Auntie Gloria was a hairdresser of distinction.'

He stood up. 'How old are you, pet?'

'Twelve.'

'If there's anything you think I ought to know, you come and see me, Kathleen. Our inquiries are continuing.'

Kathleen shouldered Da's Box Brownie. 'Will do,' she replied, almost smiling. She hesitated, making a joke. 'Roger. Mission control over and out.'

He grinned. 'Friendship Seven. Roger. Over and out.' He touched her camera case with one finger. 'Cheerio, pet.'


Back at home, Kathleen discovered that Joyce was still at work and there was no sign of Da. Nana knitted and rocked in her chair, as if she'd never moved. Nosey lapped some water then settled near her feet. She was listening to *Sing Something Simple* on the wireless. The volume was up loud and every so often she would join in, with odd emphases. 'You are my sun*shine*,' she insisted, 'my only sun*shine*. You make me hap*py* when skies are *grey*.' It was as if for her the song contained a secret, confrontational meaning.

Kathleen avoided Nana. Her stomach reminded her that she'd not eaten any tea. She went into the pantry and scooped some cold boiled potato from a bowl, with her fingers. She hid some ginger snaps in the pocket of her skirt and filled a hot-water bottle. Trying not to alert Nana, she crept up to her little attic bedroom where she put on her pyjamas, wrapped herself in her eiderdown, and clasped the rubber bottle against the chill. She sighed deeply. She normally felt safe in her room, but today was different. Nothing, absolutely nothing, she realized, could alter the terrible reality of what had happened. It wasn't a dream, it wouldn't go away.

Kathleen's room had sloping ceilings and no window except a tiny roof-light. It was at the top of a steep staircase, away from the rest of the household. Neither Nana nor Joyce ever came up and she felt safe there, next to the sky, though often cold and lonely.

The tops of her chest of drawers and her desk were used to display her collections. When she was younger she'd made collections of bird's feathers, mounted moths, butterflies and unusual pebbles. She'd found them all and identified them herself. In a drawer, she also had a collection of picture post-cards in a bundle, held together by an elastic band. These she'd requested from her family, her godmother and her teacher and they were mostly colour renditions of Northern seaside resorts. Most precious were two from Spain and three from Africa.

Kathleen opened the drawer and took out her scrapbook. She turned the pages. Here were cut-out pictures of John Glenn and Yuri Gagarin in their space suits, as well as rocket launches, orbits and heroes' welcomes. The operating instructions of Da's Box Brownie were secured with Sellotape, in an envelope at the front. There were also birthday cards, with only their backs glued down so they could be opened. She studied one, which was a picture of a beautiful country girl, in a bonnet, holding flowers. Inside it said, 'Happy Birthday, love from Auntie Gloria.' The writing, as Kathleen had clearly remembered, was small, neat and cramped. It was nothing like the scrawled message on the mirror in the hairdressing salon.

Kathleen knew that Gloria was her real auntie, by marriage. She had lots of other aunties, some of whom were only neighbours. All female adults were auntie, if they were too close to the family just to be 'Missus'.

Gloria had been Da's daughter, this she knew. Auntie Joyce was Nana's daughter by her first husband. He'd been paid by the government to run away to Australia. Kathleen had heard this being discussed. She was also clear that Da was Nana's second husband, but not Auntie Joyce's dad. Finally, she knew that Nana was definitely her own grandmother. This was the extent of her understanding.

She looked through more cards. She hadn't kept any from Nana or Joyce. These she'd thrown away. And Da had never sent her a birthday greeting, although he always gave her a 'handful of silver' on special occasions. The preserved cards were from Gloria, Auntie Molly her godmother, Petra and a faceless auntie in Rhodesia who sent old-fashioned cards in envelopes with pretty coloured stamps.

Kathleen didn't know where her mother and father were living. She didn't even know who they were. She never enquired because she knew that Nana would just become angry and say, 'Ask me no questions, I'll tell you no lies.' Da had once said, mysteriously, that perhaps her daddy had gone away to sea. At first she thought he meant 'to see' and she imagined a shadowy faced man on top of a pit heap, holding binoculars, scanning the horizon beyond the colliery. Apart from this, there had been no clues.

Kathleen had one very distant recollection, perhaps her earliest memory, of sitting astride the shoulders of a man. They'd climbed a hill and she'd held on to his ears. At the top there was a lovely sweep of green, fanning out below, without any coal workings. This was dotted with other families, toiling upwards to the summit. The sun shone brightly and a lady, at their side, carried a red plastic shopping basket. Kathleen believed absolutely, without question, that this man and woman were her parents. Unfortunately, she could not, however hard she tried, bring their faces to mind.

She smoothed Gloria's card under her fingers and tried not to think about the body in the pond, but it was impossible. She shed a few more tears. Kathleen was used to feeling a sense of loss. She carried this around within herself, day to day. But this raw pain was new. It was the same as missing her parents, only much more acute. Gloria had been one of her four friends. Now Da, Billy Fishboy at the Essoldo and Petra were the only ones she could talk to. She thought about Inspector Glen. He was quite nice, she decided.

She put the scrapbook away and remembered the greasy stains, that morning, on the borrowed dressing gown. It had smelled awful. It was babyish and silly with embroidered bunnies on a chest pocket even though Petra was thirteen and had breasts. She looked at her alarm clock. Her friend probably wasn't in bed yet. She always boasted that as a teenager she was allowed to stay up every night, playing pop tunes on her Dansette record player until eleven o'clock.

Marek Koninsky was drunk. He stood in the bay window of his ugly Coal Board house, staring at the man-made mountains and the dull, watery glint of Jinny Hoolets. The sky had cleared and there was a sprinkling of stars.

Marek swayed. There was a small circle of colour, high on each of his pale, sculptured cheeks. He held a bottle in one hand and a priceless cut-glass goblet in the other. He drained the bottle and threw it hard against the wall. It didn't break, but bounced on to the faded oilcloth at the edge of the room. He tipped a slug of vodka down his throat. 'You two bitches!' he yelled. 'Where are you both hiding?'

Marek liked vodka. He ordered it from North Shields and it came in a crate, each bottle wrapped in straw and Polish newsprint. He drank a bottle nearly every day, although sometimes he went to the Causey Arms in the village and stood on his own at the bar, knocking back fast shots of neat gin in single gulps, insisting on a clean glass each time. But he preferred drinking at home, where he was able to weep and curse and grow angry – away from any suspicious, envious or desiring eyes.

Petra was in the cupboard under the stairs. It was dark, with mounds of coats, boots and shoes and it was half full of empty bottles and she was worried about spiders, but she knew her father wouldn't look for her there.

Marek stumbled into the hall. Petra held her breath. 'You bitches!' he shouted again. 'Come out from hiding!'

Her mother's voice floated down the stairs. 'Thy kingdom come, thy will be done, on earth, as it is in heaven . . .' Nadezhda leaned in the door of the bathroom, a filmy black mantilla over her head, a rosary clasped in her hands. She was dressed in a wide, net-skirted ballerina's dress, which was stained with mildew. On her feet were ragged ballet shoes and her skin was blue from the chill of the bare floorboards. Above her head a naked light bulb swayed in the draught from the open bathroom window. Around her, the landing walls were cracked and in need of paint. Cobwebs, the same colour as her dress, gathered in corners.

Marek threw the last of his drink at the lobby door and there was a crash and a cascade of glass as the pane broke into a thousand splinters. The heavy antique goblet lay unharmed, but the telephone table and the tiled floor glittered with shards. He walked through the debris, the sharp pieces cutting into his bare feet, but he seemed not to notice. He stood bleeding at the foot of the stairs. 'Drowned!' he shouted at the top of his voice. 'She is drowned. Dead, alone and drowned!'

Nadezhda carried on praying, her body bobbing to the ceaseless rhythm of her words.

'I drowned her!' Marek persisted. 'I drowned her and you drowned her, you filthy bitches, you whores!' He sobbed. 'I did it! Yes, I did it! We all did it!'

His daughter covered her ears with her hands. Her face was buried in her knees. She heard her father go upstairs and her mother retreat to a bedroom. There was a thump as a table overturned. Nadezhda screamed and there was a tussle. Antique fire irons jangled as they hit the unused hearth. China crashed and shattered. 'I will kill you now!' he threatened and his wife screamed again and called out to the mercy of Jesus.

Petra's heart was thumping. It was cold, but sweat had broken out on her palms. She pictured the thin body of Gloria under the sullied surface of the pond, her stylish haircut full of sludgy coal. 'I'm glad she's dead,' she whispered. 'This is all her fault, the two-timing liar.' She remembered her mother's exact words. 'That Christless jezebel.'


Kathleen looked through her skylight at the same heaven observed by Marek Koninsky minutes earlier. Since she'd returned home from the salon, the sky had miraculously cleared. She could see Cassiopeia and the Belt of Orion. The Pole Star shone high above the mine and the pit heaps whilst the grateful moon began to creep from behind last vestiges of cloud. She thought about satellites and rockets circling the earth with a kind of freedom that was denied to absolutely everyone she knew.

There was a gentle tap on her door and Da's face appeared in the crack. 'Get up,' he whispered, 'we may not see it like this again for months.' Kathleen heard him descending the stairs.

Her heart jigger-jiggered in her chest. Poor Da, she thought. A vision of Gloria's drowned face came into her mind. She closed her eyes and forced it away.

She put her school uniform on over her pyjamas and fastened her shoes. She tiptoed down. Nana's night light was on in her room and from behind Joyce's door there was the sound of dance music coming from her record player. The landing creaked. She borrowed Joyce's fur jacket from a hook in the damp passage and met Da outside in the back lane.

She grasped the pocket of his long raincoat instead of touching his hand. His gaze was directed upward. 'I'm sorry about Auntie Gloria,' Kathleen said immediately.

He didn't reply.

They set off towards the allotments. She took two steps for each of his strides. Kathleen felt short and dumpy in her pyjamas and layers of clothing.

Da's coat flapped against her. He was bathed and changed but, unusually, there was the scent of the pub on him. She knew he never drank more than a half of bitter but he liked his pipe. He occasionally went to the pub to get away from Nana and to smoke his pipe in peace. Or he went to his shed. This is where they were headed now. Kathleen looked up at his long nose, his best cap. He was fifty years old, five years younger than his wife, and whilst she was elderly with arthritis and never left the house, Da was still an active, healthy man. He said hewing black gold from rocks kept him fit. She squeezed his pocket but he didn't seem to notice. 'Da?' she said, tentatively. She felt horribly uncertain, but she wanted to communicate. The silence was unnerving.

'Yes, pet?'

'Have you heard about this Cuba thing?'

'Yes, I have.'

'Are you worried?'

'No.'

'Why not?'

'Kennedy's been asking for it. He was plotting to assassinate Castro. It serves him right.'

'Is there going to be a war?'

'No. The Soviets are too powerful. He'll back off.'

Da was once a stranger to County Durham. He had a soft, lazy accent, which he'd learned in Cornwall. He'd been a tin miner. Years before, he'd travelled North with his eleven-year-old daughter Gloria, anxious to transfer his skills to coal.

Kathleen decided her feet were cold without socks, but Joyce's beaver-lamb jacket was both weighty and snug. It reeked of mothballs and Jolie Madame.

As usual, Da lapsed back into silence. Kathleen could sense he was unaware that she'd been the one who'd found his daughter's body earlier that day. He was lost in his own thoughts and his sadness. She decided not to tell him, even though it would have been a relief to talk about it. She didn't want to make things worse for him than they already were.

They passed through the gate to the gardens and immediately beyond the neat vegetable plots they climbed a slope which was terraced with makeshift timber buildings. These were pigeon crees. Ahead of them now was a new landscape – a shallow valley to the south with graceful farmland. The ravages of industry were behind, as were the artificial glow of the village, the shunting all-night coal trains, the tramping miners headed for the late shift. The world here, on the edge of things, was peaceful, soothed by the subdued night-time cooing of the tame birds. It was bathed in silver starlight.

Da unlocked his shed and they both stepped inside. It smelled of creosote and it was very dark. Kathleen waited whilst he went around unfastening a series of bolts. They were oiled and slid smoothly, one after another. In a swift gesture he rolled back the roof on its special rails and the spangled sky was revealed. Unlike many men from the village, Da didn't keep pigeons. He had wider horizons. Instead of cages, in the centre of his wooden construction, he had a small reflector telescope, secure on an altazimuth mount. Next to it were two stools and a small table with notebooks, a torch, pencils and geometry equipment. 'Remember what I told you,' he said gruffly.

Da had always been interested in the heavens. In Cornwall, as a boy, in a clifftop cottage on the edge of the Atlantic Ocean, the sky had been immense, clean and fathomless. Night after night, he leaned in the window of the room he shared with his brothers, tracing constellations with his bare eyes. The firmament glittered and shone. Later, having followed his father underground, he emerged each evening from the mine by the sea, tired and stiff with bending, only to stretch his arms up to the sky, thrilled by the freedom of the open air, the ever-changing cloud and the mysterious spinning planets beyond. He bought his first hand-held eyeglass at fifteen. Now, at last, at fifty and with careful management of his bonuses, he had the equipment of his dreams.

Kathleen was calmer now. Her body, at least, had regained some self control. Da's company always soothed her. With dextrous fingers, Kathleen uncapped the flat then exposed the main mirror. Da had recently had them aluminized. She knew to treat them with the maximum of respect.

He opened the table drawer and took out a leather box. 'Which one d'you think?'

Inside were three eyepieces. Kathleen glanced nervously at the sky. It was luminously bright. 'Three hundred to three hundred and sixty,' she said, with more confidence than she felt. 'High magnification for good nights.'

Da picked up the eyepiece and attached it. 'I'll really show you the moon tonight,' he said enthusiastically, 'and that's a promise.' He swung the telescope into position in its cradle, pointing it at the glowing half disc, above their heads to the south. He manipulated the rod, which moved the instrument higher and turned a tiny wheel to make slow adjusting motions.

Kathleen understood patience. She tried to forget the horrible events of the morning. She removed her spectacles, putting them carefully into her pocket. It had been a long day. She thought about Gloria's feet in her new shoes, sticking out of the end of the stretcher. She remembered Petra's excitement and her lack of sorrow, Nana and Joyce's spite. She thought about Nosey biting the police inspector. She gazed upwards, locating the Plough. 'Alkaid, Mizar, Dubhe, Merak,' she recited automatically. ' The Pointers.' She sighed, knowledgeably. 'Ursa Major.'

After a while, Da murmured, 'Here you are, Kathleen. Have a squint at this.' He slid off his stool and they exchanged places. Kathleen looked through the telescope and gasped. The detail was astounding. Illuminated by an unseen sun, here were stark clusters of craters, bright uplands, peaks and waterless seas. It was a rugged landscape, ashen, colourless with deep rills and black shadows. In a curious way it mirrored the desolation of the mine below, but in place of dreary ugliness, it possessed unique beauty.

'Tell me what you see.'

'It's the eastern half of course,' answered Kathleen immediately. Her anxieties were forgotten. She paused. 'I can see Ptolemaeus, close to the terminator. Its floor's a dark mass but its edges are clear.'

'What else?'

'The Mare Nubium, the Mare Imbrium.'

'What about Copernicus?'

'Yes, I can see Copernicus.' She was excited. She sat on her shaking hands so as not to knock the instrument. She looked and looked and they were silent for a while. Kathleen was transfixed.

'That's enough now,' Da said gently. 'You'd best get home to bed.'

She sighed and moved aside. He had prepared his drawings and would continue his serious study. In conditions like this, the effectiveness of high power made delicate observations possible. It was a night to remember. They sat for a moment in silence, the telescope between them, gazing unassisted at the heavens. Kathleen suddenly thought of Gloria. She understood Da's inability to talk about his feelings, she knew he was cut off and remote, but she also knew that his unhappiness had to be somehow acknowledged. She was his daughter, she thought to herself, all that was left of his own family. Not only that, she'd been cheerful, elegant and wonderfully modern. She remembered the lipstick words on the salon mirror. She didn't believe her auntie had written them, but they contained a fundamental truth. 'She's up there,' she said suddenly, pointing to the immeasurable sky. 'She's up there, free and spinning. She's left all this behind.'

Da took out a handkerchief and blew his nose, noisily. 'Aye,' he agreed. 'And where do you think she's placed herself?'

Kathleen considered for a moment. 'Oh, the Pole Star,' she decided, 'or possibly Rigel. Gloria always liked to shine.'

# TUESDAY

The next day, the village came to life early as usual, with the shopkeepers pulling out their awnings before eight o'clock. The damp, greasy cobbles echoed to the sound of horses' hooves as loaded carts rumbled up and down. The routine never changed.

Housewives, dowdy in scarves, clutched their shopping, gossiped a little and prepared to queue for meat and bread. They glanced over at the salon, nervously, shaking their heads. Gloria had enjoyed the confidences of some as she'd titivated their hair, but she'd still been fully accepted. Because of this her death was viewed as shocking but not surprising.

'What a shame,' said a fat middle-aged woman, whose swollen feet spilled over the sides of her shoes. 'Mind, she was bonny. Bonny and a nice lass.'

'Aye, too bonny, maybe. She should have been at home with her family.'

The large woman lowered her voice. 'But what kind of a family is it? There's a question, mind. That lass thought she was better off living by herself. In spite of everything. A young girl like her, living all alone. She'd *moved out!* What does *that* tell you?'

Her friend stepped closer. She was a thin little person, with missing front teeth. She nodded in both wonderment and agreement, adjusting her headscarf over her rollers. 'Awful,' she whispered. 'But what can you expect? From that lot in First Street?' She dropped her voice even lower. 'I don't remember the last time I saw the mother. Is she still yelling and shouting at that man of hers?' She stepped back and spoke louder. 'Mind, she knew her job. That Gloria. She was from Cornwall, wasn't she?' She said this in a way that suggested it was as distant as Timbuktu.

'Mmm . . . somewhere down south. She certainly wasn't from *these* parts.' The fat woman edged away, having delivered her final verdict.

The air was chilled but stagnant with the smoke from three hundred hearths. The sky was overcast, threatening rain. An empty bus revved its engine then backed up on to the main road where a straggle of people had formed a listless queue. The pit buzzer sounded as the miner's cage was lowered and trains shunted endlessly, noisily, beyond the houses, manoeuvring loads of spoil across the black backdrop.

A newspaper vendor shouted and waved the local rag, which showed an old photograph of Gloria in a swimsuit. It had been taken when she'd won the Miss South Shields beauty competition a few years before. 'DROWNED' the headline shrieked, as if there was a connection between her scanty attire and her fate.

'It's terrible, man. Terrible.' Passers-by muttered to each other as their paths crossed. 'A terrible business.' Gloria's death had become conversational currency, taking the place of the usual subject, which was the weather. People were sombre. Suicide was not unknown but it was scandalous. Their faces were long and serious. They were united in their feeling. 'Terrible.'

A group of old men, retired miners, with caps jammed on their heads, sat on benches beside the war memorial, coughing and arguing. They too were exchanging opinions on the discovery at the pond the previous day. Huddled against the drizzle, they smoked, spat and speculated. All could remember the suicide of Geordie Jim, fifteen years earlier, who'd killed himself in a fit of despair after the death of his infant son, in mysterious, possibly criminal circumstances. He'd been a pork butcher. As well as this, some could recollect another, earlier death but only dimly and there was some dispute over the woman being a miner's wife or a miner's daughter, caught up in an incestuous love triangle. One octogenarian insisted a show-girl had taken her own life, decades before, after being raped by the son of a colliery owner in Dipton. All were agreed on one thing – Jinny Hoolets had claimed them and their endings had been solitary, cold and bleak as the polluted water dragged them down, filling their lungs with coal.

Kathleen turned uneasily in sleep, woke, blinked then remem-bered it was only the second day of the school holidays. She saw through her roof light that the sky was grey – as if its unclothed, shameless beauty of the night before had been no more than a dream. She rolled over and closed her eyes, trying to remember the sight, which Da had revealed to her through his telescope, but instead of picturing this new, glorious world, ready for examination, she slid back into slumber. Here, she saw instead an image of moonlight falling on the pond. Its reflection was distorted in the inky ripples and from the pale corroded disc there appeared the frightening sight of waving arms and bobbing heads. Frantic shouts rang out as a host of souls per-ished in the darkness.

Down in Stanley, Detective Inspector Glen sat on a small chair in a draughty corridor in the mortuary. He held his trilby and stared at his shoes. He looked at his watch. He was troubled. He was very close to retirement and hadn't expected to have to deal with a suspicious death. He'd imagined a straight, uneventful run up to the gold watch and handshakes. He sighed. It was unfortunate but he knew he couldn't let it go, cover it up. Other men in his position might do so, but he believed in doing his duty. He wasn't going to stop now.

A glass door swung back on its hinges and there was a whiff of formaldehyde. A young man in a white coat appeared, drying his hands. A splash of blood stained his hem. The Inspector glanced at this, then stood up and the two men entered an office. 'Well?' enquired the policeman.

'You were right,' said the pathologist, cheerfully. 'Bruising to the neck and abdomen, possible signs of attempted strangulation. Nothing conclusive there, I'm afraid. Death was definitely due to drowning.'

'You sure? She wasn't throttled first?'

'No.'

'Damn!' He swivelled on his heel, paced heavily across the room then returned. He looked into his companion's youthful face. 'This is a suspicious death, and I want a murder verdict from the coroner,' he said. 'I'm undermanned here. What I need is help. Serious resources.'

'I'm sorry,' replied the pathologist, 'but I'm afraid it's not cut and dried. If you'll excuse the pun.' He smiled, made an effort to straighten his face then sat on the desk and shrugged. 'She drowned.' He was very new to the job. 'When was our last suicide?'

'Oh, not long ago. We get lots of depression in these parts. Gas ovens. Hangings. That sort of thing. Not murders though.'

'When was our last murder?'

Detective Inspector Glen raised his eyebrows. His florid face had a purple tinge. 'I've no idea. I've never dealt with one. And I've been in this job thirty years.'

The young man whistled through his teeth. He'd trained in Newcastle where he'd processed the results of casual, violent crime every weekend. 'She was a looker,' he said, thoughtfully. 'Jealous boyfriend?'

The Inspector shrugged. 'She was different,' he mused. 'She used to do my daughter's hair. She was a bit of a go-getter by all accounts. She wanted a string of salons. She had her own car, her own mortgage. She wasn't typical of the females in these parts. She was one of these . . .' He hesitated. His expression became disapproving, his voice censorious. 'She was one of these new . . . dollybirds. You know. A modern sort of woman.'

'And not unhappy?'

'Not as far as I can tell. I need to find out. I need to ask a few questions.'

'There was one thing . . . it struck me.'

'What was that?'

The pathologist raked his fingers through his curly hair. 'As well as the bruising, there were scratches.'

'Scratches?'

'Yes. One or two, on her neck and breasts. Very superficial, but fresh. I'm told there's no vegetation at the scene so she'd been involved in some kind of fight before drowning. I'm pretty sure human fingernails scratched her but there's no evidence of serious assault on the body. No suggestion of rape.' He paused. 'She was bruised, strangled rather half-heartedly and scratched. Not long before her death. Someone with nails. But that doesn't mean the actual drowning wasn't suicide.'

'Someone with nails? A woman?'

'Possibly. Not necessarily. Oh! And something else.'

'Yes?'

'Thin. She was a little undernourished. A compulsive dieter?'

'I see.'

They looked at each other with respect. The Inspector firmed his hat on his head. 'Put it all in your PM report. All those little details.' He drew his mouth into a grim line. 'We've got a murder here. I know it. I can feel it in my bones. I'll find out who the boyfriend is. Chances are, our girl's gone and upset him. That's usually the way.' He turned and left the room. The young man watched him trudge down the shiny corridor in a way that was both slow and determined.

Da, uncomfortable in his best suit, and wearing a black cotton armband, stood in the outer office of the undertakers, which was next door to the Causey Arms. The reality of Gloria's death, the finality of it, was beginning to make itself felt. The pain was located somewhere in the middle of his chest. It was like an empty space, an odd, dull kind of hunger. He was close to tears but not very close. Crying would have been a relief, but it was a relief that was almost always denied him. Apart from those few private moments underground, he'd retained all dignity.

In vivid flashback he suddenly saw again his dead brothers and his father, their broken bodies carried on a line of stretchers from the mouth of the collapsed tin mine. It had been shocking, appalling. They'd been on shift together and they'd all been crushed and suffocated. One had died, trying to free the other four. He had stood stoically as they were brought up, his cap in his hand, unable to release his emotions. 'You're the lucky one,' people had said to him, but he doubted if this was true. Afterwards, in the breezy cemetery, high above the pounding sea, the grass had been spangled with wild flowers and the five graves were sorry gashes in the springy turf. He'd been unable to shed a single tear, he'd been unable to grieve, even though his heart ached with sadness.

It was the same when his first wife passed away. He had wanted to cry but remained impassive and closed off, even when alone. He'd loved her with a passion and she'd been taken from him the day before her thirty-fifth birthday. That final morning she'd opened her eyes, her poor face wasted and grey with pain, and she'd stared at him. 'Too soon,' she'd whispered and then she'd died.

Later he'd watched the earth fall on her casket; he'd cleared away her toothbrush, her reading glasses, her pretty clothes. He'd found a bundle of love letters, tied in red braid, which he'd written to her during the war. None of it, not even the letters had helped him to cry, helped him to let go. It was the same now.

'Jesus Christ,' he muttered with feeling. He wasn't swearing, even though he was an atheist. He stared at the purple folds of the velvet drapes, which hid the undertaker's interior from the street. 'Jesus, help me. Help me to bear it. Help me to bear this awful thing.' He fumbled in his inside pocket for his old wallet. He pulled it out and searched it for the photograph of his former wife and Gloria as a little girl. It wasn't there. He went through all his pockets, then patted the lining of his jacket, increasingly desperate. Where's that snap gone? he thought. It was the only one of her I had left. And I've been so angry with her lately. My very last words to her were angry and harsh.

He had a sudden vision of Gloria as a child. She'd been a little gawky, with big teeth and skinny legs. Her blonde hair had been curlier in those days and it was brushed back from her face like spun gold. He remembered her trying to learn to ride a bicycle. She had been determined but unsteady. She wobbled past and he'd grabbed her shoulders to stop her overbalancing. 'Leave me, Dad,' she'd shouted. 'Leave me be. I can do it!' He'd stood back, anxious as she swayed and finally toppled. He ran to her side, helped her up, worried she was hurt. She was laughing even though her knee was bloody. 'I'll get straight back on,' she'd said. 'That's what you have to do. You get straight back on and try again. Otherwise you lose your nerve.'

She was always brave, he thought. Nothing ever stopped her.

The undertaker appeared, grave and sober in black clothes,

his face etched with sadness. He talked about prices, respect, coffin styles, condolences, budget plans.

Da only half listened. 'There has to be an inquest,' he said. 'I haven't got a date for the funeral.'

The undertaker looked offended. He closed his catalogue of headstones. 'I see.'

'What I want to ask you is this. I don't want my daughter lying in that horrible place. I want you to bring her here and keep her in your Chapel of Rest.' He pulled a handkerchief from his pocket and blew his nose. 'I'm not religious,' he said hastily. 'Nor was she. We never had time for God or religion. But I don't want her in that place where they cut people up and make you sign forms. I want her in a peaceful place. A . . . ' He hesitated. 'A nice place, with – with—' He gestured with his hands. He struggled for words. 'With proper curtains.'

The undertaker nodded and stood up. He was brisk. 'Very well,' he said. 'I'll arrange it. Our only motto is service. Service and respect.'

'Good,' said Da, overwhelmed. He stepped quickly towards the door.

Outside, the street was filled with sheep. They were being driven by two dogs through the village, towards their winter field beyond the pit. Their fleeces looked grey with dust and they were panicked by the cobbles under their hooves. Da stopped and watched them. At that moment a figure appeared from around the corner. It was Koninsky. He was wearing his hat pulled low and a belted grey raincoat, unfastened, over his hand-stitched suit. He was elegant and sophisticated. In his hand he carried a briefcase. Sheep swarmed around his legs and he side-stepped them, gracefully. He stopped when he saw Da and seemed about to speak. There was a long moment when the two men regarded each other. Koninsky raised a hand, as if to detain Da. It was like slow motion. His lips parted, he pushed back his hat. Da gave him a long, searching look. There was contempt in his eyes. Don't you come near me, they seemed to say. Don't you even dare speak to me. You corrupted my daughter, you damned exploiter, you foreign devil. Marek Koninsky seemed bewildered, discomforted. Da turned on his heel and strode into the flock, which parted before his determined stride.

Kathleen sat up in bed, blinked then reached for her glasses. Her room was cold. She examined a poster on her wall. She had saved tokens from Sugar Pops breakfast cereal for several weeks in order to acquire it. A special Royal Mail van had delivered it in a long tube. It was an enlarged colour photograph of the MA-6 Friendship Seven launch, which sent the first American, John Glenn into orbit of the earth. Kathleen thought this was one of the most exciting pictures she'd ever seen in her life. The spacecraft was a silver elongated dart and its launch vehicle was filigree gold. The optimistic nose of the rocket was aimed upwards, pointing to a firmament which Kathleen assumed was the genuine turquoise of Cape Canaveral's heaven. It had an immediate backdrop of fluffy cloud, which might have been liquid oxygen and below, at the precise moment of lift-off, fuming from its tail, there was dazzling white-hot fire.

Kathleen was still saving tokens. There was another poster available which showed the recovery of the Mercury Sigma 7 from the Atlantic Ocean. This was the re-entry capsule, which splashed down confidently with John Glenn inside. It floated in a calm and luxuriant sea. She knew that he had circled the globe three times in under five hours and here, whilst he was buoyed up on these little waves, President Kennedy had been standing by, proud and patient, waiting to speak to him on the phone.

She tried to picture the President now. He would be in his office, she decided which was at the front of the White House and upstairs. There was a row of telephones on his desk, one of which was red. He was serious but calm, like a film actor. The red phone rang and he picked it up. 'Cut it out, Nikita,' he said in his glorious accent. He stood up and adopted a Humphrey Bogart pose, casual, one hand in his pocket. 'Get off my back, you hear me? Khrushchev? Just can it, will you? Cuba's for the birds.'

Kathleen got up, shivered and rummaged through her drawers. She had very few clothes. She found clean knickers and a jumper, which was darned and rather small. She found an old skirt, which was too short and a pair of mismatched socks. She got dressed and brushed her hair. She polished her spectacles on the hem of her bedsheet. She remembered Gloria's body in the pond, the sight of her poor feet sticking out from under the hospital blanket. She picked up her camera and stroked the case. There's nothing I can do to change what's happened, she thought sadly. It's happened and that's the end of it. She felt powerless, emotional and very alone.

She could hear Nana singing along to her wireless in the kitchen downstairs. This was Tuesday. Because she never went out, Nana spent a lot of time doing housework. She would be ironing today. She always ironed on Tuesdays. She liked ironing so she would be in a reasonable mood.

Kathleen sat on her bed remembering an occasion a few weeks before when she'd had the flu and been off school. Joyce had shouted up to her. 'Kathleen! What d'you think you're playing at? You're late!' She sounded angry.

She'd got out of bed, her head swimming and stood outside her bedroom door. 'I'm not well,' she'd called, her voice weak and tremulous.

Joyce had clumped up. She was in her uniform, ready for work. She went to the Essoldo three mornings a week for the newsreel and cartoons. She'd regarded Kathleen with suspicion. 'You staying off school then?'

Kathleen had nodded and climbed back into bed. She felt slightly sick and her body was clammy with sweat.

Joyce came over and placed her hand on her brow. 'You feel hot.'

'No, I'm cold. I'm shivering.'

Joyce bit her lip. 'You're very white.' She hesitated. 'Shall I send for the doctor?'

Kathleen recalled that the doctor was big, unconcerned and often drunk. 'No. I'll just lie here. I'll be all right.'

Joyce frowned. 'You sure?'

Kathleen nodded.

'I'm late for work.'

'You go.'

Joyce disappeared, but to Kathleen's surprise she returned five minutes later. She carried an electric bar, which she'd found in the cupboard under the stairs. She plugged this in and there was a smell of smouldering dust. 'You've got a temperature but you're supposed to sweat it out. Sweating's good. It flushes out the germs.'

'Thank you, Auntie Joyce.'

'And here. Take these.' She offered a glass of water and two white pills.

Kathleen struggled to sit up. 'What are these?'

'Anadin. They'll help your head. I've got to go now.'

Kathleen put the pills under her pillow, but drank the water, gratefully. She dozed a little, emerging into consciousness now and then, only to see her rocket poster slide across the wall in a mysterious, dissolving way. With the fire burning, the room was like an oven. Her pyjamas and sheets were wet.

Later, waking to find her mouth and throat parched, she went downstairs to the kitchen to fill her glass. She looked at the old clock on the wall. It said almost half past eleven. This day back then had been a Monday and Nana was washing. She could see and hear her, through the open door in the flat-roofed, windowless wash house, which was the old air-raid shelter, in the yard. Now this reinforced concrete building held the machine and also the gas boiler, used for bleaching whites. Nana sang and worked the agitator furiously, surrounded by a cloud of steam. The gas jets under the boiler roared and foam spilled over the sides of the washing as it was banged to and fro. 'Find a fallen *star*!' Nana sang angrily. 'Hide it in your *pocket*! Never let it fade *away*!' Her hair was tied in a turban and she had galoshes on her feet to protect them from the wet floor.

In the kitchen, Kathleen dragged a chair to the sink, climbed up and raised her glass to the cold tap. She slipped a little and the glass hit the tap and smashed.

Nana appeared in the door. She was very damp and hot. 'What are you doing here, madam?'

Kathleen tried to pick up the broken glass from the sink.

'Leave that, will you!'

'I'm off school. Auntie Joyce said I could stay off. I've got the flu.'

Nana advanced towards her. She climbed down and retreated to the other side of the table.

Nana picked up the pieces of glass and threw them in the bin. 'Go to school, madam,' she said, almost calmly.

'I can't go to school, I'm ill. Auntie Joyce said—'

'Go to school.' Her voice was louder.

'I've got a temperature. Auntie Joyce said—'

Nana roared. 'Go to school! Go to school! Go to school!'

Kathleen turned, left the room and climbed the stairs. She could hear Nana shouting and crashing about in the kitchen and in the yard. 'She's a damned nuisance!' she heard her exclaim. 'That's all she is! A damned nuisance!' After a while she heard her in the hall, talking to the dog. Her voice was soft, gentle. 'What is she, my pet? What is she, Nosey? She's a damned nuisance, isn't she?'

She sat on her bed, feeling weak and groggy. The room shifted uneasily. She put on her uniform and walked unsteadily to school. She spent the afternoon in the art room, watching some other children paint enormous paper cut-outs of trees which were needed for the end-of-term play. Fortunately, the teacher didn't notice that she failed to join in.

That evening, back in bed, she heard Nana and Joyce having a row in the passage below. 'You're a monster!' Joyce insisted. 'What's the matter with you? What difference would it have made to you?'

Nana's reply was the same as ever. 'As long as you all live in my house, madam, you'll all do as you're told. Right? ... Right?' There was the slam of the sideboard drawer, an angry rattle of cutlery. 'And you haven't given me your keep this week. You owe me two weeks' keep. What's this place supposed to be? A hotel?'

After eating a large quantity of Sugar Pops, Kathleen took Nosey into the village. A group of unwashed miners, just off shift, sat on their haunches outside the Causey Arms playing pitch and toss for money. Their concentration was total. They would have a drink or two at opening time and then go home for a bath. Their wives had long since disappeared, their daily shop completed. Their damp washing would still be steaming up their kitchens from yesterday, because they knew the heavy air would again be too coal-laden to risk stringing it across the lanes. They lived by routine and the pit buzzer and the strict work pattern of their men folk determined the shape of their joyless days. They never, Kathleen knew, let their thoughts stray beyond their hearth, their row, the village boundary. They would be busy now, preparing a hot meal.

Kathleen watched two huge dray horses, across the street, straining in their harness and she picked up Nosey to stop him barking. The postman passed by on a bicycle followed by a knife sharpener with his grinding wheel. She knew that soon he would be pursued by a gaggle of small children because he gave away balloons. A van belonging to a local builder chugged past, startling the horses. There were no cars. A man in white overalls, on a ladder, painted a window. She glanced up and down the street, which was as familiar to her as her own plain face in the mirror. She sighed. She knew in her heart that village life had barely changed in fifty years. Everyone here was looking backwards, clinging to a point in history when the mine had an immeasurable future, where both work and tradition were secure. The villagers' backs were turned on the modern world. They both feared and ignored the future. The feeling this gave her wasn't encouraging – she craved something brasher, something freer, a situation where people didn't just accept their fate – a different kind of world. So, of course, had her Auntie Gloria. And now Gloria was dead.

She put down the dog and he trotted along an alley. She followed and immediately saw Gloria's car in its normal place, parked off the road. It was a bright red Mini, almost new, with chrome trim. It shone in the gloom. It was as out of place as Gloria had been, as incongruous as her fashions and as much of a statement as her immaculately applied black eye pencil.

I suppose it'll just stand here, for ever, Kathleen pondered. Empty and unmoving. It's like part of her, left behind. She hesitated. Someone was next to the Mini – a man, crouched down, as if he were hiding. She decided it must be the police, with their 'inquiries continuing' and curious, wanting to record all the significant events surrounding her aunt's death, she stopped to unfasten the case of Da's Box Brownie. She deliberately centred the vehicle in the viewfinder. The light wasn't good. She stepped closer and pressed the exposure lever as far as it would go. She heard the click. The man hadn't noticed her but she saw at this instant that it wasn't an officer of the law. It was Marek Koninsky. His knees were bent and his body twisted as he struggled to see his reflection in the wing mirror. He was about to comb his hair.

Kathleen moved nearer the dark wall. Petra's attractive father smoothed his floppy locks backwards and teased the front into a half-quiff. He turned his head from side to side. His face was chiselled and pale with shadows in the hollows of his cheeks. His chin was firm with a small scar to one side. He had shaped symmetrical sideburns. He stood up, glanced into the car interior and, carrying his hat, he turned and walked away. His stylish coat swung and his leather-soled shoes rang out on the pavement. He was confident and urbane.

Kathleen watched him and decided that everything about him suggested that he came from distant parts. The faint scent of his cologne teased her nostrils. He's very good looking, she thought. She felt a strange sensation, which she barely recognized as desire. I wonder why he isn't at work? She put the camera away. As she walked past the car she noticed Gloria's big, round op-art earrings on top of the dashboard and a plastic shoulder bag on the back seat. She felt another wave of sadness and loss.

Petra was sitting in the window of Gallini's. Kathleen saw her straight away. They had arranged to meet there the previous day. 'Go home now! Go home to your Nana!' she said to Nosey and he stopped, wagged his tail and lay down in the doorway. 'Oh, all right, please yourself.'

Kathleen went into the coffee bar where a radio played

loudly. She knew the song – it was 'Love Me Do' by the Beatles. Her glasses immediately steamed up and she took them off to wipe them. She joined her friend.

Kathleen and Petra were in the same class, even though Petra was a year older. Kathleen had been moved up a year because she achieved one hundred per cent in all the tests. The two girls had little in common and had formed a relationship out of necessity. They were both unpopular; Kathleen because she was a 'swot' and had no parents and Petra because she was middle class and had a funny name. Kathleen was used to bullying, but Petra wouldn't stand for it. 'If anyone tries anything,' she often insisted, 'let me know. Those bitches can all get knotted. I'll smash their ugly Durham faces in.'

Kathleen slid into the seat opposite.

Petra was singing and moving her shoulders around, seductively, in time to the music. She held her mother's jewelled lighter in her hand and she was pretending to smoke a cigarette. It was burning, but she wasn't inhaling. 'Why are you wearing that old skirt?' she asked suddenly. 'Your school shoes?'

The smaller girl shrugged.

'You look like a refugee.'

Kathleen wasn't intimidated. 'You're the refugee,' she replied. 'You lot are from behind the Iron Curtain.'

Petra grinned. She liked Kathleen more than she admitted and this was because she was clever. They were both clever. She herself was wily and tough but her friend read books and knew the names of the planets.

'You're an ambassador from the Cold War,' added Kathleen, encouraged. 'Have you heard about this Cuba thing?'

Petra shook her head.

Kathleen squinted. 'You're wearing make-up. It looks a mess.'

Petra had backcombed her fair hair into a bird's nest and sprayed it with lacquer. Her lips were crimson and her eyelids were roughly smudged with blue. When she stirred her coffee cup her nails shone silver.

Kathleen fingered her own thin, girlish plaits and considered unfastening them. Then she changed her mind. She looked outside. 'There's your dad!' she said. She narrowed her eyes. 'He's walking along with our Joyce.' Joyce was wearing her violet usherette's uniform and her fur jacket was slung across her shoulders. They rounded a corner and disappeared.

Joyce is getting fat, Kathleen thought. She eats too much.

Petra deliberately turned her back to the window and pretended not to notice. She gestured to the old Italian behind the counter. 'Two coffees, please!' She took a ten-shilling note out of her purse. She always had money.

'Why's your dad not at work?'

The answer was a shrug. 'Why's your Auntie Joyce not at work?'

'The newsreel's finished by now,' said Kathleen, glancing at the clock. She sipped the unfamiliar drink and glanced around. Gallini's used to sell ice cream and cups of tea but recently they'd installed formica tables, orange plastic lampshades and a noisy contraption that added steamed milk to coffee. A new but second-hand juke box stood in a corner with a sign that said 'OUT OF ORDER'. The Italian family was struggling to be modern. They were copying a similar idea they'd seen in Gateshead. A few teenagers whiled away the evenings here but most villagers treated the enterprise with suspicion. Gloria had just smiled. 'I wouldn't be seen dead in there,' she told Kathleen.

'This coffee's strange,' said Kathleen. 'It's sort of nice and horrible at the same time.'

Tuned to the Light Programme, the radio continued to beat out tunes, some of which were real top-ten records. Mostly, though, the rest were old-fashioned live performances by Kathy

Kirby and Vince Hill, who'd been persuaded by the BBC to try to sound like real pop stars.

'We drink this night and day at home,' responded Petra proudly.

The two girls sat for half an hour. Both were reluctant to talk about the events of the previous morning. 'The police inquiries are continuing,' said Kathleen eventually. I've got to mention her, she thought. Auntie Gloria's dead. A familiar phrase came into her mind. Dead but not forgotten. I've got to speak of her. Otherwise, it's like she never happened. Like she never existed. She pointed at her friend's stiff helmet of hair. 'Gloria said that's a no-no. She said rollers are finished, as well as lacquer and backcombing. She said blow-drying is the new thing.' She paused. 'She said it's all in the cut. The skill of cutting is an art as well as a science. She talked about it all the time.'

'That Gloria was a whore!' exclaimed Petra, forcefully.

Kathleen jumped in surprise. She felt her cheeks redden and lowered her eyes to the table. She swallowed nervously.

'She nearly ended my parents' marriage!'

There was a silence. The radio played an unconvincing instrumental version of 'Devil Woman' then the real recording of 'Love Me Do' for the second time. Kathleen expected her friend to join in with the Beatles and pretend to play the guitar, like she usually did, but Petra was angry. She wasn't in the mood any longer for John, Paul, George and Ringo.

'What d'you mean?' enquired Kathleen, after a while, in a low voice.

Petra met her eye. Her face was serious, unhappy. 'That Gloria tried to take my dad away from us. They were having an affair.' At this moment the proprietor of the café turned off the music and tuned in quietly to the racing results. Petra's words hung menacingly in the air. 'She came to our house when my mam was at confession. She messed around with her things.'

'What things?'

'Clothes and things.'

Kathleen was shocked. 'Gloria was going out with Billy Fishboy from the cinema.'

'Maybe so, but she was still messing around with my dad.' She paused. 'And with my mam's things.'

'Are you sure?'

'My mam found the French Letters.'

'The what?' Kathleen was horrified.

'That's what you use, Dumbo, when you're having an affair,' said Petra, a bit too loudly.

The old Italian was listening.

'French Letters?' Kathleen blinked. She tried to picture Marek and Gloria, sitting together in a bedroom, composing lines of French.

'That's what they're called. They stop you from having a baby.'

Marek pushed open the door to the ruined barn at Jinny Hoolets, close to where the drowned body of Gloria had been found the day before. The area next to the water was still cordoned off with yellow tape and the ground was churned up from a hundred feet, but the Duty Constable had gone home for his dinner and the trampled edge, the trackside and the pit heaps beyond were deserted, black, indifferent. A single seagull wheeled overhead but discouraged by the opaque and dingy surface of the pond, merely circled higher then flew away.

Marek pulled Joyce across the threshold. 'Why here?' He smiled.

Joyce was clear. 'Because it's where you used to come with her.' I've got a man, she thought to herself. I've got Gloria's man.

The barn had holes for windows but ancient bales were piled up, killing the draught.

The earth floor was dusty and dry because although the walls leaned precariously, the roof of the building was sound. In a corner, surrounded by straw, was a heap of blankets and pillows. The Inspector had noticed them but not examined them when he'd sheltered from the wind. If he'd done so, he would have realized they were new, and not just abandoned rubbish, as he had assumed.

Marek spoke in careful English. 'Do you know why this is Jinny Hoolets?' He raised his perfect eyebrows and pointed to the rafters. 'It is because at one time Jinny Hoolets was the common name in these parts. For owls. They used to roost right here, in this barn. But they went away. Because of the coal.' He sat down on the floor, gracefully, like a dancer and pulled his knees up to his chin, in a foreign way. He gestured, palms upwards. 'Let me look at you then.'

Joyce was surprised. A little embarrassed, she removed her usherette's pillbox hat. 'What?'

He opened his palms wide. 'I want to see you.'

Joyce glanced at the gap in the door.

'No one will come.' He smiled again. His teeth were very straight, his dark eyes deep and heavily lashed.

Joyce reluctantly placed her fur jacket and her hat on the ground at her feet. She stepped out of her muddy stilettos, hesitantly.

'Take your clothes off.'

Joyce was uncertain. 'Is this what she did?'

He stared at her but didn't reply.

Joyce realized she would do anything. She unbuttoned her violet-coloured uniform and eased it over her wide hips. Her fleshy arms were covered in goose pimples. 'It's a bit cold, isn't it?'

He said nothing. His eyes travelled up and down.

She pulled her petticoat over her head and unfastened her suspenders. Joyce's voluptuous breasts were barely contained in a flimsy black lace brassiere. They almost spilled out as she bent down to remove her stockings.

'She wore tights,' he murmured, quietly.

Her face hidden in her long, shaggy red hair, Joyce unhooked her suspender belt, dropped it and pulled down her pants.

Marek rose to his feet in a single, athletic movement. He was a lot taller than she, and he enclosed her in his arms, bending to bite her neck. He groped for the fastening of her brassiere and pulled it aside.

'I'm freezing!' she cried out, laughing.

His hands moved swiftly, greedily over her body, then he guided her across to the heap of blankets. Almost roughly, he pushed her to the floor. 'Get down there!' he hissed, his voice urgent. He slid on top of her, forcing a pillow under her backside.


Kathleen, Petra and Nosey the Jack Russell walked down the track towards Jinny Hoolets pond. 'Do you have to bring that bastard dog with you, everywhere?' asked Petra.

Kathleen did not reply. Her legs felt wobbly and inside her chest, her heart felt as if cold fingers were strangling it. I'm afraid, she thought. This place makes me afraid.

There was no wind. The pit heaps loomed, blackly, the brittle fireweed was motionless and below them the water's surface was calm and soup-thick. Petra moved ahead. 'Are you sure it's here?' she asked crossly, over her shoulder.

'Yes, I dropped it when I saw . . .' Kathleen stopped. Her face was wet with tears.

'Come on then.'

'I don't think I want to . . . ' Kathleen looked at the pond and felt the shock again, the horror of finding Gloria. She wasn't just my auntie, she thought. She was my friend. She was so kind to me. Kathleen felt rooted to the spot. She couldn't walk any further. She remembered the waxy drowned face, the protruding teeth, the sodden jacket.

'There's nothing here now. The body's been taken away. Come on. D'you want to find that damned Chubby Checker LP or not?'

Kathleen remembered her Auntie Joyce's wrath. 'Yes, I do.'

'Well, stop being such a stupid cry baby.'

They left the track and picked their way over the soft, black mud towards the barn. In places, Petra's white, sling-backed shoes sank almost out of sight. There was a sharp, mineral smell that was both unnatural but familiar. It was a distillation of the atmosphere all around the village. It was the pure essence of coal.

'Hoy there! Where d'you think you're going?' It was the Duty Constable. He appeared from behind a pit heap and crossed in front of Petra's house. 'You two girls stay right there!'

They stopped. Nosey flew at the policeman and yapped furiously around his boots. He advanced towards them, ineffectually kicking at the Jack Russell. 'What are you up to?' He was tall and genial but was trying to sound stern.

Petra eyed him narrowly. 'I happen to live here,' she said, grandly, her hand indicating the devastated landscape.

'I'm looking for something,' declared Kathleen with more determination than she felt. 'I was here yesterday. I was the one who found . . .' She struggled for a word. 'I found . . . it.'

The officer was kind, replete and a little out of his depth. 'What've you lost and what've you found?' he asked, his tone suddenly gentle. Nosey stopped barking and jumped up to lick his hand.

'She found the dead body,' answered Petra, without emotion.

'And in doing so, she lost a long-playing recording by Chubby Checker. Have you seen it?'

Kathleen stepped across the scene-of-crime tape and looked about. There was nothing on the ground except the prints of official feet, a ghostly record of tragedy. Everyone's gone, she thought. Already. They've all gone. The tape, the footprints and the duty policeman seemed strangely inadequate. My Auntie Gloria *died* here, she thought.

'There's nothing,' the policeman confirmed. 'This pondside's been picked bare for clues.'

'Clues?' Petra sounded indignant. 'Clues of what?' She placed a hand on either hip. 'Have you seen a strange man hanging around here? A tall man with a long coat? Sunglasses?'

The policeman attempted a smile.

Kathleen glanced at the sky but still there was no sun. 'What man?' she asked. 'No one comes here, unless they have to.' Dark clouds were forming in the west. She sighed, stepped to one side and took Da's Box Brownie out of its case. 'Can I take your picture, mister?' she asked.

The officer smiled. Then he turned to Petra. 'My Inspector says this is a suspicious death.'

She snorted. 'Suspicious death? Like hell,' she replied, rudely.

Kathleen composed a picture of the policeman, her friend and the misaligned barn. Nosey waited patiently. The pale sky gleamed for a second and she released the shutter. At that precise moment Marek stepped out of the doorway, holding Joyce by the hand. He was shrugging on his coat. Joyce was smoothing her hair. Unwittingly, they intruded into the snapshot. Kathleen saw them, but the grinning policeman, the scowling girl and the panting dog were unaware of the couple as they then stumbled, arm in arm towards the railway and a towering mound of waste coal. Kathleen put her camera away and looked over at the house. Nadezhda Koninsky was standing at a bedroom window. She was dishevelled as usual. She wasn't watching her daughter, or the uniformed constable or the photographer. She was staring at the place where her husband and Auntie Joyce had disappeared, out of sight. Her face was drawn and sad. She fumbled under her shawl, then pushed open the casement with a flourish. She lit a cigarette, coughed and blew the smoke out into the still air.

I've got to get away from here, Kathleen thought. This is a terrible place.

Back at home, Kathleen sat in the unused parlour and shivered. The fire in this room had not been laid since Easter Sunday and the air was chilly and scented with lavender wax. Next door, in the warm kitchen, her Nana had a visitor. It was Auntie Molly, Kathleen's godmother. She always came to call on the third Tuesday of the month. However, although she brought Rolos, fruit gums and a copy of *Princess* magazine, she left them on the hall stand and never spoke to Kathleen.

Nosey peeped into the parlour, wagged his tail then disappeared to the comfort of the kitchen next door.

Kathleen tried to distract herself by looking at Da's books in the glass-fronted case above the bureau. She stood up and examined them more closely. She took out a book by Patrick Moore called *The Amateur Astronomer* and decided to read it. She recalled how only recently she'd discussed her reading with Auntie Gloria. 'You're a little bookworm,' Gloria had said.

'Why don't you read?' she'd asked. She knew her aunt was intelligent, but she only ever read magazines.

'I never got into the habit,' she replied. 'I was always playing outside when I was little, on the beach. I hardly ever went to school. Then we came up here and the lessons were so hard and different, I never managed to catch up. I think school put me off reading, to tell you the truth. It made reading a chore.'

'I like reading about the stars,' said Kathleen. 'The ones in the sky. And I like reading about foreign places.'

'I think you're going to do well. You should stay on at school.'

'Nobody ever does that. Not here.'

'Well, you should go to Durham, to the city. To a decent school. You could go from down Stanley on the train. It wouldn't be more than one change. You should stay on until you're eighteen and then go to University.'

Kathleen remembered how excited these words had made her feel. She considered them again now. University. No one in the village had ever gone to such a place. The Chemist's son had gone into the Tax Office and this had been viewed as a unique achievement. University. The word conjured up a vision of musty rooms, old men in gowns, elegant buildings with spires and towers. She saw herself walking across a windy quadrangle, holding a pile of books. In her mind she was undersized and childish amongst lanky youths and a striped scarf blew around her neck. University, she thought. Perhaps I'll have to go there if I'm going to be an astronaut. I might not have any choice. Or maybe I should join the Military like John Glenn or the Russian cosmonauts. I could join the RAF and train as a fighter pilot. She almost smiled. Both options seemed equally ridiculous, impossible, remote, bizarre.

She sat down with the book, perching on the edge of the cold leather sofa, listening to the conversation next door. She had done this every single time when Molly visited in recent months, ever since she'd found a photograph of her own christening behind Nana's bedroom commode. On the back of this snapshot it said, 'K's Christening, September 1950'. It showed Auntie Molly holding a tiny baby, Nana, Joyce, a very youthful Gloria and a blur of background figures. She believed that amongst these strangers lurked her unknown mother and father.

Da himself had taken the photograph with the Box Brownie, now entrusted to her possession. She was sure that if she listened regularly enough and closely enough to Molly's gossip, the secret of her parentage would eventually be disclosed. This had become a monthly Tuesday ritual. The doors to both rooms were slightly ajar.

'She must've been earning good money.' Molly's voice was high, compared to Nana's husky contralto. 'She'd put her prices up. Her perms were really dear. How many people do you know with a car and a flat that's not rented?'

Nana poked the fire aggressively in response.

'What was the matter with her?'

There was a silence. Kathleen could hear the grandfather clock ticking in the corner of her parlour.

'Did she have man trouble?' Molly persisted. 'Wasn't she supposed to be getting engaged? To that boy at the Essoldo?'

Kathleen heard Nana rattle teacups and distribute spoons.

'She wasn't' – Molly hesitated, her voice suddenly serious – 'in the family way?'

Nana sighed, lengthily. Eventually she said, 'No, I doubt it. Not her. She'd have taken care of all *that* side of things.'

'What then? What do you think?'

There was a gurgle of tea being poured. 'All I know is, this family's being blackened once more. As if things haven't been bad enough. Tongues wagging away.'

'But what d'you think happened? I mean *why?*'

'I don't know. She always did as she liked. When she moved out of here, I thought, well she's not *my* responsibility any more. And she was too thin. Our Joyce says that's a sign of some kind of disease these days. Maybe she wasn't doing as well as we thought. Joyce thinks she might have borrowed money—'

'Never!'

'From the bank.'

'Oh, from the bank.'

There was another silence. The concept of bank loans was a mystery to both of them.

'Your Joyce must be upset.'

'Hah!' Nana laughed harshly. 'Hah!'

'No?'

Kathleen heard Nana open a packet of shop biscuits and tip them on to a plate. She scrunched the wrapper and there was a flare of flame in the hearth.

'Our Joyce hated her. Don't tell me you didn't know.'

'Well—'

'Joyce hated her since she beat her in the Miss South Shields all those years ago. She said she *did it* with the main judge. He was a ballroom king.'

'Never!'

'Gloria always talked about us. She thought we were *funny*. She laughed at us. And she stopped our Joyce from getting married. You remember that nice Mr Dobbs who used to teach the Sunday school?'

'Yes.'

'Joyce went along there and took a class, just to try and get to know him. She was quite friendly with him, but our Miss Gloria put a stop to that!'

'I remember. Yes, wasn't that when . . .'

Their voices muttered on and on – scurrilous, incredulous, knowing, rising and falling in the age-old cadences of gossip. Kathleen heard a key turn in the front door. She slipped into the hall and hid behind Da's long raincoat, which was hanging on a peg. She didn't breathe.

Joyce came in and, unseeing, went to join the women in the kitchen.

Kathleen climbed up to the attic where she closed the door then wrapped herself in her quilt because the room was so very,

very cold. She removed the christening photo from a bundle of snapshots and examined it for the hundredth time. Joyce was slimmer, Gloria was childish and Nana, unusually, was outside the house, all the way over in the churchyard. Things *do* change, she decided. I think nothing changes here, ever, but they do. Everyone looks different. Everyone's changed. She sighed. Normally, her room felt like a safe place but today nothing was certain. Auntie Gloria's dead, she reminded herself. She stroked the unfamiliar image of Gloria in her hand. Nothing will ever be the same again. She felt frightened and insecure.

One of the background figures in the picture was a small woman in a tailored suit and neat hat with a veil. Her face was indistinguishable. Kathleen had decided a while ago that this must be her mother. She imagined her working in a department store in a place like Gateshead, selling cocktail dresses to ladies. She blinked, picturing her on her knees, pinning up hems, her hands deft and able. She was an expert on gowns, mantles, evening gloves and formal daywear. Her name was probably Audrey and she had a television set.

Kathleen brought to mind again her earliest happy memory. She remembered being high up on a man's shoulders and the rolling motion of his gait had made her feel giddy. She remembered the sensation of his neck between her legs, and her new, curious perspective on the world. He was wearing a white shirt, she decided and we were climbing a hill and there was a lady with a red plastic shopping bag. Everywhere was very green. But where was it? When was it? I was with my parents, so it was before they went away. She examined the photograph again. The woman's face in her mind was as blurred as the one in the photograph.

Everyone's changed, she thought again. I've changed too. Gloria going and getting herself drowned has changed me. I'm different inside and I'm going to get away from here before something happens to stop me. Poor Gloria never made it. That's not going to happen to me. She blinked again. When I'm a bit older I'll find my mother and father and I'll leave here and start a new life.

Detective Inspector Glen stood in the hallway in his police house, talking on the phone. He was polite but assertive. 'Yes, sir. I agree. But as you're aware, it's better to treat it as suspicious at this stage. True? Leave it a week and we'll be nowhere. They close ranks, the people in these villages.' He paused. 'That's right, sir. The shock wears off in places like this and then no one talks to you, no one wants to know. They close up like mousetraps.' He nodded. 'I need some men, sir. I need help here.' He listened for a moment. 'Righty-ho. Will do.' He swapped the phone to his other hand and began writing. 'The boyfriend, sir. I'll start with the boyfriend. Obviously. Fisher, his name is. Then the family. A bit of house-to-house, of course. The forensic boys have got the clothes.'

Billy Fishboy sat high in his projectionist's box tapping his teeth with his nails. He was half lit by his machine as the reels turned. He was ready to load the main feature and glanced at his watch. Five minutes, he thought, and Cliff Richard rolls again. He grimaced. The theme tune of the film was lodged in his brain but he was not a fan of mainstream British popular music. He liked the gospel sound of Ray Charles. He also liked rhythm and blues, particularly Sam and Dave. He bought their records from a special importer in Sunderland.

He stood, picked up the kettle and took it out to a small gas ring on the narrow landing outside his room. The flame flared blue in the darkness. He returned and spooned some tea into a pot. He sniffed a half-empty milk bottle. His movements were small, measured, as careful as a woman's. He smoothed his hair in his usual prissy way. He glanced around, his cod-like eyes staring, focusing on the framed prints on his walls. They were his own photographs of the Durham countryside in Teesdale, far away from the mines. They'd been developed in his own darkroom, which was a small cupboard, here, at the end of the corridor. He was restless. He looked at his watch again, retrieved the kettle, made his tea. He loved his job but tonight he wasn't in the mood. There'll be an inquest, his mother had said. An inquest? He might have to attend, even worse, speak to the court. 'God in Heaven,' he said again, aloud. He didn't want to talk about his relationship with Gloria. Especially not to some sort of a judge in a wig. He sipped from the scalding cup as the B-film drew to a close. He began concentrating on the job in hand, momentarily calmed by his own deft and swift manoeuvres.

Later, Kathleen lay on her bed reading *The Amateur Astronomer*. It was interesting but hard work. She rubbed her eyes and blinked, aware that her concentration was dispelling unsettling thoughts about Jinny Hoolets pond.

Petra was also in her bedroom. Her room was a lot bigger than Kathleen's and it was on the ground floor. Her wide bay window would have once given out on to a garden but now, instead, it overlooked only the lifeless pitheaps that had grown into mountains at the rear of the house. She checked her mirror. Her make-up was now livid and her hair was an even bigger bird's nest of backcombing. It was getting dark outside.

Petra removed all her clothes in the dim light and fingered a pile of soft coloured scarves stolen from her mother's closet. She tied the largest around her waist and another around her budding breasts. The rest she draped over her body in a random way. She glanced in the mirror. She thought she looked exotic, like a gypsy.

She stacked her record player with singles and pushed the

lever at the side of the turntable. As the arm descended on to the first disc she turned on all the lights. The room was very bright. The music started. It was Acker Bilk's 'Stranger on the Shore'. As the mournful and beautiful clarinet took up the melody she struck a formal ballet pose. She moved, without grace, to another and then another. After a while she began to dance. She jumped heavily and her limbs were unsteady but she knew by heart all the postures and steps. Slowly, trying to be seductive and knowing, she began to shed the scarves.

The record changed to the Everly Brothers singing 'Cryin' in the Rain'. She moved nearer the window and glanced outside. The sill was below her knees, the curtain pelmet a yard above her head. The window framed her, as if on a stage.

She continued dancing. One by one the draperies fluttered to the floor. Soon she was wearing only two. With her back to the outside world she removed the upper covering. She whirled around, flicking it above her head, briefly exposing her chest to the outside evening. Then for a second time she presented her rear to the window. Slowly, very slowly she removed the lower scarf. Completely naked and swaying her hips, she shimmied back and forth to one side of the bay and then to the other. She smiled in a way she believed to be sexy. After a minute or two she moved back into the room, put on her childish dressing gown and turned off the lights.

In anonymous darkness she returned to the window. She peered outside. To her surprise she could see nothing. She had half expected a gaggle of boys, who she knew would hang around almost silently, for hours, whispering and making lewd gestures. Recently, however, none of them had appeared and she'd performed for a single tall man, who always kept well into the shadows of the heaps and who was unrecognizable in a long raincoat and dark glasses.

*

At eight o'clock, well after dark, having read three chapters of *The Amateur Astronomer*, Kathleen thought about the Duty Constable's words and took her dictionary down from her bookcase. She looked up the words 'death' and 'suspicious'. She considered the definitions carefully. 'Cessation of life; state of being dead', and 'mistrustful; belief in the guilt of another, without proof'. Gloria's life had ceased. She was in a state of being dead. Inspector Glen had no proof. She herself was mistrustful and believed in the guilt of another. She lay flat on her bed, thinking. Mrs Koninsky did it, she decided. Nadezhda Koninsky drowned Gloria because of the French Letters. She blinked and rubbed her eyes. She felt afraid.

Harsh white tubes illuminated the upstairs Concert Room of the village Welfare Hall. Smoke curled beneath them from fifty cigarettes. There was a hubbub of conversation, the scraping of chairs, expectancy in the atmosphere. Precisely on time an elderly, retired miner with a white moustache, sitting at a trestle table at the front, called the meeting to order. He banged loudly with a hammer. 'Order, brothers!' he shouted. 'Order!'

The room became silent apart from muffled coughs, the rustle of papers. The chairman opened the lodge meeting by turning to Da, at the end of the top table. He expressed formal sympathy for his bereavement. There was a muttered 'hear, hear' from the assembly. Then, without further emotion, he called on the secretary to read the minutes of the previous meeting. These were quickly agreed and seconded, but an almost imperceptible impatience was generated in the room as 'matters arising' were methodically dealt with, then correspondence, then new business. One or two members yawned. Cigarettes were passed along the rows.

Eventually, the chairman turned to Da. 'Item number five,' he announced. 'Report from the District Delegate. Brother, would you like to address the meeting?' There was a murmur of antici-pation from the crowd.

Da got to his feet. He looked pale in his dark suit. He was wearing his black armband. He proceeded to report back from the District Committee, on which he'd served as lodge delegate for the last few years. After a few preliminaries he said, 'Clos-ures are possibly becoming a serious issue, here in north-west Durham.'

There was a restless shuffling amongst the men.

'It was the main item on the agenda, the last time we met. Other lodges in the area are instigating discussions with their colliery managers. I have to tell you, brothers, pits in this area are increasingly under threat. Officials are being briefed. They're worried. There were NUM full timers, from Redhills, present during our discussions at District level.'

A hum of muted conversation broke out.

'Order!' demanded the chairman.

'Spit it out!' shouted someone from the back.

'What the hell's going on?'

'Give it to us straight!'

Da put down his notes and walked around to the front of the table. He stared at the rows of pitmen, some dirty from their shift, some in work clothes ready to go down, others dressed in white shirts and ties. Da was a respected union member. Silence fell upon the room.

He took a deep breath. 'Medomsley pit is similar to ours in every respect,' he announced, before pausing. There was com-plete silence in the room. 'Medomsley's closing.'

There was an immediate uproar. Men jumped to their feet, others looked stunned. Even more waved their agendas and shouted. One young man ran out the door.

'Order!' yelled the chairman. 'I call this lodge to order!'

After a few moments, the noise subsided.

Da looked pained. There were deep furrows across his brow, down the sides of his cheeks. 'It's true. It's to be announced tomorrow.'

'What will happen?' asked the treasurer, from behind Da, sitting next to the chairman. He sounded scared.

Da half turned to him, but projected his voice forward. 'Some will be offered work on the coast. Those workings there – they're being described as longer life pits. Thicker seams. The Board's investing over there. Men will be bussed in.'

'If their faces fit!' called out an angry voice.

'The lucky few!' shouted another.

'One or two young lads, mebees. Not old-timers.'

Da paused. 'You're right. For the rest, it'll be the Employment Exchange.'

There was another welling up of noise and men exchanged anxious, almost panicked glances with their brothers, cousins, fathers. One or two got up, walked about, sat down again. A pall of smoke hung over them.

Da raised his voice. 'There's something else we need to think about here, brothers. There's something I'd like to raise. To discuss.'

Silence returned again.

'Carry on, Brother District Delegate,' prompted the chairman.

Da appeared nervous. He took a deep breath. 'I think we need to question the Board's use of special surveyors at the present moment.'

The room went completely quiet. For the first time the old clock above the door could be heard. It struck the half hour.

'There's a man here, a new man, as you all know, living down at Jinny Hoolets . . . ' At the mention of this name, the site of Gloria's drowning, Da winced. 'Living in Coal Board property and calling himself a surveyor.'

There was a buzz of agreement.

'However, he's not an ordinary surveyor. He's not one of the ones we know. Not a regular team member. He's not attached anywhere; he seems to move around, from place to place, from pit to pit.'

'Aye, he was in Yorkshire,' somebody commented.

'He's been seen at Sacriston, Tanfield, Marley Hill,' added another.

'Snooping around. Talking to management,' agreed his neighbour.

'He was at Medomsley,' Da said. 'Full time, for a limited period. He wrote a report. Only five weeks ago.'

He paused again as this information was absorbed.

'Shame!'

'Bosses' lackey!'

Da continued. 'I know what he's doing. He's looking for faults. He finds them and then assesses the seams beyond. He thinks the coal quality in these parts isn't high enough. He says the development costs to open new seams aren't feasible. He's intent on condemning these collieries. That's how it looks to me. And that, brothers, includes ours. This man, this Koninsky . . .' He flattened his hair, in a backward gesture, with both hands. 'He has a history of closing pits.'

'Foreign bastard!'

'String him up!'

'We're not afraid of him!'

Da held up an admonishing hand, demanding quiet. 'We should be afraid. We should be very afraid. I know about this man. I've been asking questions. Every pit he's been involved with for the last four years, not just here, but other parts too – they've been closed or threatened with closure. He's doing the Board's dirty work. *They're* trying to rationalize and *he's* coming up with the necessary recommendations. What can I say? It's obvious. He's their hatchet man. And now he's started here. We've all seen him recently. Measuring. Sampling. Assessing the lie of the land. *We've* got him now, brothers. He's here. He's amongst us. He's already started and he's controlling our future.'

This speech charged the Concert Room with anger. The chairman rose and banged his hammer five times. He shouted, 'What do you suggest, brother District Delegate?'

Another hush descended. 'I move,' said Da, his voice strong and full, 'I move that this lodge initiates discussions with the pit manager to determine Mr Koninsky's role. I move that we question his motives and his possible findings. I move that we request his removal from our mine and from our community!'

'Seconded!'

'Hear, hear!'

Da sat down. The fury, puzzlement and dissatisfaction of the men ebbed back and forth in waves. Marek Koninsky was the target of their abuse, their hatred. Eventually the chairman read out Da's motion. 'Those in favour?' he called out.

There was a sea of hands.

'Those against?' Not an arm was raised.

'I declare this motion passed. We've now reached standing orders. I call this meeting adjourned.'

Marek stood again in the front bay of his sitting room watching nothing except darkness. A train rattled somewhere close, there was a dull glint from the almost invisible pond, a few drops of rain pattered on the glass. He turned and sat down in a faded armchair. A table lamp glowed weakly in a corner. A cheerless fire burned in the grate. He leaned forward, and with the tongs dropped more coal on to the small blaze. As the flames were extinguished the room became almost dark.

Nadezhda appeared in the doorway. Her hair was down, she was wearing a silk kimono and in the poor light she looked sad, but almost young. She came into the room. 'I did not want her to die,' she said in English.

Marek stood up, went across to the dresser and poured himself a drink. He sat down again, glanced at his wife then stared into the hearth.

Nadezhda's voice was almost a whisper. 'It is not what I . . . intended. I prayed for her to die, yes, but I did not mean to—'

'I should never have brought her in here.' Marek spoke quickly.

'Into this house, no.' Nadezhda coughed into her sleeve.

'You know how it is with me. But not in the house. You are right.' He swallowed his drink in one gulp, throwing back his head. 'These people!' he exclaimed. 'These English do not understand! They fight me. They oppose me.' He paused and lowered his voice. 'Even the women.' He mused for a moment. 'Maybe her death can make it up to you. Yes?'

'No.' With a rustle and a sigh, Nadezhda turned. From the doorway she added, 'And our daughter is bringing a dog here. You know I do not care for dogs.' She disappeared.

Marek turned the empty tumbler in his long fingers. The fire flared and he added more coal. He stood up, poured himself another drink and went back to the window. The sky was black, the dense cloud faintly orange in the area above the mine. He was pale and forlorn. He drew the curtains together against the night.

Kathleen slept fitfully, her book open on the floor beside her. She dreamed she was circling the earth, way beyond the atmosphere, but without a craft or special suit. The universe was very beautiful and strange with a multitude of planets, stars and meteors and she was weightless, her progress possible without effort. However, after a few minutes she decided to go home. Nana was angry and she understood the need to return. 'I'm coming,' she tried to call out, but she was unable to control her movements. She flailed, helplessly. She was buoyed up; spinning in a current that was too strong to influence. She struggled and struggled. 'You get yourself inside, now!' Nana yelled.

Kathleen awoke. Without thinking, she got out of bed and made her way downstairs, almost sleep-walking. She hesitated outside the kitchen. Nana wasn't calling me, she thought, groggily. It was just a stupid dream.

The door was slightly ajar. Kathleen looked through the crack. The wireless was tuned to a gardening programme. The room was warm and peaceful. Nana continued her knitting, her bad eye shut and her short-sighted eye half closed as she struggled to focus, her attention devoted to complex casting off. She was shaping the shoulder of a cardigan with raglan sleeves. Nosey was asleep, wedged between her bony thigh and the arm of her chair.

Joyce also squinted in the inadequate light. She sat at her sewing machine, carefully gathering can-can petticoats into a ribbon waistband, which would eventually be attached under the top skirt of her new dress. It was difficult and fiddly because the gathers needed to be even. The hard netting made her fingers ache.

The radio programme was interrupted, as it had been the day before. A serious BBC voice suddenly broke into an item about carrot fly.

*President Kennedy has made a broadcast to the people of the United States, warning them of the grave situation. Since the discovery of Soviet medium-range missiles on the island of Cuba, only ninety miles off the US coast, he has mobilized his strategic air command's fleet of B-52 and B-57 bombers. The*

*American war machine awaits nothing but a 'go' signal from the White House.*

Nana was oblivious. She consulted her knitting pattern and measured her work against the ruler printed down one side.

Joyce unwrapped a boiled sweet and put it in her mouth. She spoke to Nana. 'It's this Sunday, you know, the Big Dance. D'you think Da might refuse to go because of Gloria?'

Nana didn't reply.

'He's got to take me,' Joyce continued. 'Even if bloody Gloria is bloody dead. I've been looking forward to this for a whole year.'

Anxious to hear the announcement, straining her ears, Kathleen moved almost into the room.

The newsreader continued. *The President's address to the nation was clear and unequivocal. This is what he said earlier today.*

Nana cast off three stitches, finished the row, turned, knitted a few more then cast off another three. Her slack lips worked against each other.

'Da's got to go with me, and that's all there is to it. It's not my fault I haven't got a husband to take me to the dance. It's not my fault I'm an old maid.'

Kathleen struggled to catch Kennedy's words.

*The nineteen thirties taught us a clear lesson. Aggressive conduct, if allowed to go unchecked and unchallenged, ultimately leads to war.*

Kathleen shivered in the draught from the front door.

The speech went on. *The cost of freedom is always high, but Americans have always paid it. And one path we shall never choose. That is the path of surrender and submission.*

Kathleen started to climb the stairs. Everything's changed, she thought again. And Da's mistaken. JFK's not backing off. He thinks those missiles shouldn't be there. He's going to check and challenge the Russians. He's not going to submit. He's going to start a war with Khrushchev and they'll bomb the living daylights out of each other. An idea occurred to her and she stopped in her tracks. We'll go in with them, she thought. We'll go in with the Americans, just like they came in with us, last time. Her heart skipped a beat. Fearfully, she imagined red fighter jets with painted hammers and sickles streaking over the eastern sky, breaking the sound barrier. They're coming, she decided. The Russians are coming to blow us all up.

# WEDNESDAY

Nadezhda sat under the low-watt, shade-less light bulb in her dingy scullery, wrapped in her kimono. Her faded hair and sallow skin were both the same unhealthy colour. Hunched over the table, she turned the pages of an old leather-bound photograph album. She coughed quietly. Used cups, crusts of toast and the uncleared dinner plates of the evening before surrounded her.

Marek, her husband, leaned in the doorway, freshly shaved and smelling of cologne. His attention was caught by the news on the wireless set. He walked over and turned up the volume. It was the voice of President Kennedy, broadcast again.

*Any missile launched from Cuba against any nation in this hemisphere will bring a full retaliatory response upon the Soviet Union.*

He frowned, listened to the rest of the report, poured himself an inch of vodka from a bottle on the draining board, swallowed it in one, then without speaking left for work. His wife stood up, turned off the news, went to the window and watched him approach the track between the sombre heaps of spoil. He looked elegant and out of place, his white collar gleaming, his briefcase in his hand. His Coal Board car was parked at the bottom of the hill. He disappeared inside and drove away, the small black vehicle bumping over the rough stones.

She glanced at the pond. It was a windless day, barely light, and the surface was still, but menacing. She raised her hands to her cheeks. She knew the smell of the water, the oily sludge of it, the way it appeared in all weathers. She tried to imagine herself sinking under its cold surface – a fantasy she'd allowed herself many times. 'Why her?' she whispered. 'Why always her? It should have been me.' She began weeping. She was quiet at first, her body shuddering, her hands covering her face, but after a minute or two her distress became loud, racking sobs.

Petra sat on the stairs in her childish dressing gown, looking at the lobby door, the heap of half-swept glass shards in the corner. She had her fingers in her ears and she was tunelessly singing the words of the Beatles 'Love Me Do'. Her mother's cries still reached her. Shut up, she thought, shut up, shut up.

Nadezhda often wept. She was so lonely and depressed she feared she might one day lose her mind. She also believed that her husband, in settling at Jinny Hoolets, had deliberately chosen to live in hell in order to torment her. She couldn't understand why he'd turned into a sadist, when all she'd ever tried to do was love him. She cried and cried and then eventually stopped. She heard Petra on the stairs. Her daughter was a disappointment too. She was ungainly and refused to carry on with her ballet lessons. She was copying unattractive fashions from papers such as *Mirabelle* and *Jackie*. She looked like a common English whore.

Nadezhda leaned against the dirty sink and rubbed her face with her sleeve. She began to calm herself in the only way she knew how. She brought to mind the opening of Te Deum Laudamus. 'We praise thee, O God: we acknowledge thee to be the Lord.' She rocked back and forth. 'All the earth doth worship thee: the Father everlasting.'

Kathleen woke up, blinked at her skylight, heard the start of pattering rain and pulled her eiderdown over her head. She slipped back into another disturbing dream. This time it was a dream of mothers. A parade of them trundled past, pushing invisible babies in old-fashioned perambulators. They were all dressed in shapeless coats and headscarves and their hands were raw from laundering nappies. She herself was wordless on the kerb as each mother ignored her. Then, a little behind the rest, separate but struggling to keep pace, was Nadezhda Koninsky. Unlike the others, she was dressed in a thin, unsuitable dress, which trailed on the cobbles. A cigarette burned between her lips. As the convoy headed off towards the Welfare, Nadezhda turned in the opposite direction. Kathleen followed and saw the baby struggle to an upright posture. It was Petra, but she wasn't a baby. She was thirteen years old, her fair hair was back-combed, she had make-up badly applied to her face and she was smiling in an unpleasant, know-it-all way. With difficulty, her mother pushed her onwards and suddenly they were all at Jinny Hoolets, at the edge of the pond. In one determined gesture, this unsuitable mother lifted up the handle of the pram, tipping the raised hood forwards. As it overbalanced into the water, Petra slid out like a fish, gaping, sinking beneath the surface with a surprised, indignant shriek. Kathleen watched but was unable to move. Slowly, the pram followed and became submerged. Nadezhda Koninsky clapped her hands once then turned and walked away towards her house.

When Kathleen awoke again she thought about Mrs Koninsky. The suspicion that her friend's mother may have drowned Gloria seemed ridiculous when she considered it afresh, but then the suicide idea was equally absurd. Even though this seemed to be accepted as the general view in the village, Kathleen didn't believe it. She thought about the possibility of an accident. Gloria didn't drink; she was sensible and practical in all things. It was inconceivable that she'd somehow fallen in the pond and died. In any case, the body had been quite near the edge where the water wasn't even very deep. Kathleen again remembered the corpse, its rigidity, its glassy-eyed stare – then pushed the thought aside. It was too terrible to dwell upon. Shivering in the cold, she groped for her spectacles and put them on. She felt both puzzled and dismayed.

She put on the same clothes she'd been wearing the previous day and went down to Nana's dim, warm kitchen, where there was a smell of baking scones. The clock ticked and chimed and the wireless was playing quietly. Nana was muttering to herself as she read *People's Friend* with Nosey the Jack Russell curled up asleep in her lap. Joyce leaned at her sewing machine as if she'd been there all night. She was surrounded now by yards of imitation lime green silk. She drew out a row of tacking stitches and began working the treadle, rhythmically. The fire glowed and the rain, which had become heavy, beat against the windowpane.

Kathleen took a deep breath. She rarely initiated conversations downstairs. 'Auntie Joyce?'

Joyce's mouth was a thin unlipsticked line, pins clasped between her teeth. 'Yes?'

'Why does everyone think Auntie Gloria killed herself?'

Joyce was startled. She removed the pins and stared at Kathleen.

Nana slowly lowered her paper and listened.

'Why do they?' Kathleen persisted. It was even more unusual for her to ask questions. 'Auntie Gloria wasn't unhappy. I know she wasn't. She was fine.'

Joyce gave her a searching look. 'You don't know that. You don't know that for certain, do you?'

Kathleen was aware that Joyce was struggling to balance her hatred of Gloria with the necessity to try and answer the question in a reasonable way.

'You don't know everything about her.'

'What don't I know?'

Joyce took a deep breath. 'You don't understand what problems she may have had. Just because she was nice to you doesn't mean that you really knew her.' She tried to smile. 'Does it?'

'What don't I understand? What problems? Tell me.'

'You don't understand that nothing's straightforward.'

'What's not straightforward? What exactly isn't straightforward about Gloria? What don't I know? What?'

Nana put down her *People's Friend*. 'Be quiet!'

Kathleen jumped. She looked at her grandmother, nervously. 'I was only asking—'

'Do as you're told! Be quiet!' Nosey woke up and hopped down on to the floor.

Kathleen paused. She moved towards the sewing machine and picked up a fold of green silk. She lowered her voice. 'You won't forget my dress, Auntie Joyce?'

Joyce was relieved. 'No, pet, I won't.' She went back to her stitches, working the treadle even faster.

Kathleen helped herself to Sugar Pops and sat at the table. Nana was glaring at her. She had an odd stare, one eye cloudy with cataracts. Kathleen tried to ignore her. She thought about the Isabella Miner's Supper in a few days time, at the Welfare Hall. She imagined a Glenn Miller dance band with trombone players with Brylcreemed hair and smart white suits, musical notes embroidered on their breast pockets. She pictured deft footwork around the floor, such as displayed in old films starring Fred Astaire.

There was always much excitement in the village around this event. It was held every four years to celebrate the sinking of the pit, dating back to 1892. It was commonly known as the Big Dance and a silver band was coming up from Stanley. Kathleen knew that women and girls were not allowed to attend unaccompanied. This was the tradition. Kathleen was now old enough to go. She secretly believed that her mystery mother might turn up, in a pumpkin coach like Cinderella and finally claim her.

She remembered Joyce's remarks from the previous evening. 'Da won't be going,' Kathleen said. 'Not now. But we could ask Billy Fishboy to take us.' She picked up the envelope from the dress pattern, which was beside her on the table. 'He can't take Gloria, can he?' She was aware, as she spoke, that her words sounded callous and she regretted them immediately.

She examined the envelope containing the paper pattern of Joyce's creation. It was shown as full skirted and nipped at the waist. Her shoulders, arms and chest would be bare and her large breasts supported on the rigid platform inside a boned bodice. Kathleen thought about the film star Marilyn Monroe who had recently died. She'd promoted this busty, feminine look in films at the Essoldo. She knew that Joyce was afraid of the cropped modern designs pursued by Gloria, but then so were all the women of the village – afraid, or in many cases, ignorant. Kathleen wondered if Joyce thought she was just too large for the new styles or if she thought that emphasizing her hourglass figure with fifties' silhouettes would help her get a man. Kathleen wished that Joyce would get a man – one who wasn't already married like Mr Koninsky, because then she would get her own house with its own furniture and she'd move away. She'd be happy and less desperate, Kathleen thought, and I could have her room.

Joyce didn't want to discuss the problem of an escort. 'You found my Chubby Checker record yet, fanny-ann?' Her tone was humorous, unlike it had been on Monday.

Kathleen put down the envelope and stepped towards the sink with her empty bowl. 'No.'

'Well, where's it got to?'

Kathleen was reminded of the ghastly discovery at the pond. All at once she felt desolate. 'You don't like Chubby Checker,' she retorted. 'You don't know how to do the Twist. You don't

84

like Neil Sedaka, either. You only buy their records to be in the fashion. Like Gloria.'

Joyce was rebuffed. She lowered her eyes to her sewing, rattling loudly down the length of another seam.

Kathleen's attention was suddenly drawn again to the words on Nana's wireless. As before, the announcer's voice seemed laden with doom. She went over and put her ear to the grille.

She discovered that weapons called nuclear warheads had been loaded on to fighter bombers in Spain and Morocco, as well as in England. This meant that England had got involved. The newsreader said that targets were the Soviet Union and Eastern Europe.

*These planes are on standby, but personnel are on full alert. Military leave has been cancelled. It is understood that Polaris submarines have left Scotland to patrol the North Atlantic.*

Kathleen bit her lip. The news bulletin continued. It was explained that twenty-five Soviet ships were steaming towards the Caribbean where the US navy and air force were ready for them. The American blockade intended to stop them, but the Russians were under orders not to halt or submit to a search.

Kathleen looked at Nana and Joyce. They seemed unconcerned. The newsreader went on.

*Interest in fall-out shelters has dramatically increased since the President's speech on Monday night. A spokesman has said that requests for survival information are coming in, ranging from 'above normal' to 'considerable' in some areas.*

Joyce's sewing machine muffled the words. Kathleen glanced back at Nana. She appeared to have fallen asleep. She wasn't reassured by their calm. The two women never left the village. Nana never even left the house, and hadn't done so for three years. Their perimeters were tiny.

Kathleen slipped out of the room. She stood in the passage, uncertainly. There's going to be a war, she thought. Those Russians are coming. We haven't got a fall-out shelter, only a useless wash house, which is the air-raid shelter left over from the last time. Those Russians are going to blow us all to bits. She remembered two words she'd read in a school book about Hiroshima. 'Nuclear Holocaust,' she muttered. She'd written an essay about this for her homework. The teacher had given her a grade 'A'. She suddenly imagined newspaper headlines with a photograph of a Russian aeroplane. 'Nuclear blast takes north-west Durham off the map. No survivors.' She felt sick.

She'd recently seen a newsreel at the Essoldo. Ranks of Soviet soldiers and heavy weaponry were paraded through the streets of Moscow. Billy Fishboy had shown it to her as a favour, when the cinema was closed, because a sequence showing Friendship Seven and John Glenn followed it. She'd watched the film and decided that the Russians were very angry and war-like people, led by old men in uniforms. And of course President Kennedy hated them because Yuri Gagarin had got into space first.

She'd mentioned all this to Billy but he'd just shrugged. He wasn't interested. 'You can come and watch that nice rocket any time you like,' he'd said, as if she was a little child. Kathleen knew he was being sweet to her because Gloria had asked him to. She'd told him her niece had practically no friends and no mother to care for her. This was embarrassing and she'd wished Gloria had kept quiet. But she'd enjoyed the film of Friendship Seven and John Glenn and she decided she liked Billy Fishboy. He was gentle, he had a kind face and he wore coloured shirts, with the collars buttoned down. In bed that night she'd imagined kissing him, but then felt guilty because he was Gloria's boyfriend and not hers.

She took off her glasses and cleaned them on her vest. She decided to go and see Petra because she probably had relations behind the Iron Curtain. She might know something.

*

Joyce sewed the wedge of petticoats she'd assembled the night before under the filmy silk top skirt, catching it in loose informal pleats. When dancing, she wanted the layers to bounce and the silk to float and ride up over the netting in a suggestive way. She stopped for a moment and considered Kathleen's words. Everybody, not just the girl, would be wondering why her stepsister had drowned herself. She thought again about how in the eyes of the village the suicide was a very unlikely thing. Perhaps the theory would fall apart. Perhaps the police would be asking a lot of questions. She decided to try not to worry. It would remain a mystery. They would get nowhere with their inquiries and people would lose interest, she decided.

She remembered Gloria arriving at the house, years before. Nana had advertised for a lodger and Da knocked at the door, holding the shoulder of a thin, blonde eleven-year old. They'd had strange accents and not much luggage. She remembered walking to school with the girl the following Monday. She herself was almost ready to leave education and she'd half abandoned her uniform, wearing nylon stockings and her blouse open at the neck, without a tie. Gloria had been properly dressed and nervous. She knew no tables, she admitted. She knew some of the Kings and Queens of England but she couldn't remember ever having studied grammar. She said she hadn't gone to school much although her dad was determined that this would change. 'He's a great one for books, my dad,' she said, proudly. Joyce had felt sorry for her.

After a while her sympathy turned to resentment. Joyce was used to being an only child, but now Gloria was sharing her room. Not only that, Gloria lost her gawkiness and soon became pretty and stylish. She borrowed Joyce's things and looked better in them than she did herself. This uneasiness reached a climax at the Miss South Shields beauty competition, five years later. Both girls entered, responding to an advertisement in the *Stanley News*. They travelled to the coast for separate heats and both got through to the final. Joyce could remember her dismay when Gloria opened her letter and proudly told the family of her intention to compete.

'But you can't be!' Joyce had spluttered. 'I'm in that! I'm the beauty contestant is this house! I always enter these shows!'

It was true. Joyce had been Miss Boldon Colliery, the Esh Winning Queen of the May then runner up in Miss Sunderland. She loved the attention she received. Her picture was in the paper and she enjoyed the sweaty kisses of Mayors and Councillors. She'd become a celebrity in the village on a par with local footballing heroes.

'We can go together,' Gloria had answered, sweetly.

Joyce knew, beyond doubt, that Gloria wanted to upstage her. She also suspected that Gloria believed beauty contests to be vulgar and in some private way she was having a joke at her expense. She often felt that Gloria was laughing at her.

When the day came, the dressing room was cramped and airless. Joyce unpacked her evening gown, which she'd made herself and new red swimsuit, with built-in busks. She struggled for a place at the mirror alongside girls she'd met before, at other, similar events. They eyed each other suspiciously and tried to force an atmosphere approaching camaraderie. They wound their hair in rollers and sprayed it heavily with lacquer. They spat into their mascara and built it up, layer by layer. They plucked their eyebrows and varnished their nails.

When Gloria ventured out on to the catwalk, the audience held its breath. Instead of heavy finery – ruched velvet, sequins, satin trains, diamante tiaras – her dress was a plain, black sheath which ended three inches above her thin ankles. She wore no jewellery and her hair was loose and clean.

In the bathing costume round, one by one the girls paraded themselves, their full figures gripped and moulded by whalebone, teetering on stilettos. Each was enthusiastically applauded. They had frozen smiles and awkward hands.

Gloria was a sensation. For the first time ever, in the north of England, a woman wore a bikini in public. She stepped out from behind the curtain and her feet were bare. People stood up, gasped and there was a clamour of astonishment. The members of the band blew appreciatively and discordantly into their instruments. The judges stared, open mouthed.

She walked quickly back and forth, her face serious. She refused to smile, thereby hiding her tombstone teeth. She stopped, directed a dismissive pout at the audience and turned on her heel. She looked European, arty, a little decadent, but because she was lithe, even gawky instead of voluptuous, and because she wore very little make-up, the swimsuit appeared fashionable rather than sleazy. After sixty seconds of shock there was wild clapping and stamping. Gloria was crowned and her photograph was printed in the *Daily Mirror*. She never entered another competition. She told everyone she had 'proved her point'.

Joyce refused to speak to her for almost a year. She lied to Nana and one or two others, saying that her stepsister had disappeared behind the bandstand prior to the event, only to emerge dishevelled twenty minutes later with the main judge, whose flies were undone. She never forgave Gloria and never recovered from her jealousy, her humiliation and her fury.

Sitting at her sewing machine, her mind wandering, Joyce felt again her anger, her sense of being not only usurped, but mocked. Bloody Gloria, she thought. *And* then later on she went and stopped me from getting married to that Mr Dobbs.

She returned to the recent past. She knew that Gloria had made a special trip in her car to Fenwicks in Newcastle to buy a swanky dress for the Big Dance. She'd listened to the details with horror. Billy Fishboy had been full of it, boasting and talking about it non-stop. He said it was a copy of some famous French designer and described it as having a Jackie Kennedy neckline, a tight bust and a tier of graduated organza ruffles descending from one hip over a narrow, ankle-length hobble skirt.

Joyce swallowed hard and bunched her own new dress together in her hands. It's all right now, she thought. It's going to be all right. She took two calming breaths, then managed to smile, suddenly remembering Marek's kisses, his urgent, insistent desire.

Inspector Glen stood in the foyer of the Essoldo, studying a poster. It was Cliff Richard swinging on the rail on the back of a double-decker bus. The film advertised was called *Summer Holiday.* He frowned in disapproval. He did not agree with young, unmarried people disporting themselves, unsupervised. And he hardly ever went to the cinema. The last film he'd seen was *The King and I* with Yul Brynner several years before and he'd been unimpressed. He considered modern films to be decadent and a waste of money; particularly those featuring pop songs. Inspector Glen disliked all popular music and was a fan of Ludwig van Beethoven and Johann Strauss.

He'd come to see Billy Fisher, his chief suspect, the dead woman's boyfriend. He was confident he was initiating a murder investigation.

Inspector Glen always insisted that the obvious line of inquiry was the best. In his experience, life threw up few surprises. He hadn't handled a murder before, but he'd had his fill of crime and he knew that motives were generally uncomplicated, violence always explicable. Robbers were poor and greedy. Rape victims generally knew their attackers who were bullies with a grudge. Assault was almost always domestic, unless it happened outside a pub. Stepfathers battered children.

Young lads battered each other. By the same token, murdered women angered their lovers. Inspector Glen didn't believe that good detective work was born of inspiration or intuition. He saw it as common sense combined with thorough spadework. He expected to clear up the matter in a few days.

A young man ran down the curved staircase. He was slightly flushed and nervous.

'Mr Fisher?'

'Yes, sir.'

'Detective Inspector Glen. I believe you're expecting me?'

'Yes, sir.'

They went through into the vast amphitheatre. Billy pulled a lever and a thousand bulbs illuminated the space. They both perched on the back of the rear row.

'Just a few questions.'

'Yes, sir.'

The policeman glanced around. Properly lit, the Essoldo was shabby and depressing. Its gold leaf was peeling, there were patches of damp and the seats were worn and threadbare. A smell of stale cigarettes tainted the air and the floor was littered with dog-ends and used ice-cream cartons. The enormous velvet curtains, which hid the screen were faded along their folds and stained at the hem. 'I believe you knew the recently deceased . . . ?'

'Yes, sir, yes.' He stroked his hair in a womanish gesture. 'We were engaged.'

The policeman examined him with his eyes.

Billy shivered. The temperature was low and he wasn't wearing a jacket or a sweater.

Inspector Glen noted Billy's dark-blue shirt with its white collar. It was a curious combination, without a tie, but buttoned at the neck and properly pressed.

Billy then primped his hair between his fingers. This was a

little long, in the Inspector's opinion, and combed forward in front of his ears and on to his forehead. Billy was clearly a fashionable young man, he reasoned; a little effeminate, but not spivvy. Definitely not spivvy in the style of Elvis Presley. This was a small blessing. He seemed very young and his eyes had a bulgy thyroid stare. 'How old are you, son?'

'I'm nineteen, sir.'

'And you say you were engaged?'

'That's right. Not officially. We hadn't announced it yet.'

'Where were you on the night of the drowning?' Inspector Glen noticed that despite the temperature perspiration had broken out on Billy's face. His hands were shaking. He was very frightened.

'I was here. I was working. Until eleven. Then I went home.'

'You live with your family?'

'That's right, sir. With my mam.'

The policeman made a note in his book. 'Which is . . . ?'

Billy recited his address.

'Your mother was in when you got home from work?'

'Yes, sir.'

'Awake?'

'Yes, sir.'

'You had a conversation?'

Billy thought for a moment. 'I made her a cup of cocoa, filled her hot-water bottle.'

'She's old, your mother?'

'She's retired. She retired early. She used to be a teacher—'

'You take care of her?'

He paused. 'Not really, no . . . I just like to—'

'You just like to what?'

'Do little things for her. You know. Tea in bed in the mornings, things like that—'

'She's not old?'

'She's forty-nine.'

'I see.' Inspector Glen gave Billy a hard look. He noticed the lad was trembling and his right leg was knocking uncontrollably against the seat. 'And you went out again, did you, after your mother went to bed?'

Billy started. 'No, sir.'

'Are you sure?'

'Why would I do that, sir? At half past eleven at night? It was raining.' He sounded panicked. He raised his hands, palms upward. '*Where is there to go?*'

'You are absolutely sure you were in all night?'

'Yes, I was.'

'Can your mother vouch for you?'

'Yes, sir. She can. She locks both doors before she goes to bed. She's done that ever since my dad died. She locks the doors, puts the keys in her handbag and takes the bag up to her room.'

'What about the windows?'

'The windows?' Billy looked nonplussed.

'Locks the windows, does she, lad? Does she lock you in? Eh? I doubt it.' Inspector Glen gave Billy a steely look. 'I intend seeing her later. I'll ask her. I'll see you later, too. At home.' As he got up to leave he could smell the sweat which was now soaking the armpits of Billy's clean shirt. 'Well, that will be all. For the moment.'

Billy was more than relieved. He'd lost his voice, his throat was so tight. He led the way to the foyer, pushed open the heavy glass door and wordlessly ushered the officer into the gloomy street. 'God in Heaven,' he whispered, after a moment.

Inspector Glen adjusted his hat against the rain. That boy's definitely got something to hide, he thought.

Wet from the weather and with Nosey at her heels, Kathleen walked up to the front door of Petra's house at Jinny Hoolets.

She was carrying Da's Box Brownie. She kept her eyes on the front door, away from the frowning mounds of spoil, away from the ruined landscape, away from the pond. The thought of the murky water made her sick and anxious. She could hear the little waves lapping in a sinister, mocking way and for a second she imagined a graveyard of undiscovered, drowned bodies, heaped up and naked, their limbs tangled, pale and forgotten in the evil, choking depths. Despite herself, she glanced behind.

There was no one about – the Duty Constable of the day before was nowhere to be seen. All was quiet except for the dull clank of a train, somewhere behind the heaps and the grating squeal of its breaks as it pulled its load of coal around a slow bend. The rain had become drizzle and Kathleen's skinny plaits were damp against her neck. She rapped on the door with her knuckles. Let me in, she thought. Let me in. She felt uneasy. She knocked harder.

Petra answered. Her hair was drawn back from her face with a plastic band revealing angry pimples on her forehead. She was dressed in black nylon trousers. They had elastic under each foot holding them in place like a pair of tight gloves. Above, she wore a black polo-neck sweater. Kathleen stared. She was sure these garments had belonged to Gloria. She said nothing but followed her friend inside. The little dog raised his ears quizzically on the threshold, looked at Petra then ran away around the side of the building.

In the scullery, Petra had tuned her transistor radio to the Light Programme and music blared loudly. The room was still untidy and the old photograph album was open as it had been earlier.

'Where's your mam?'

Petra turned the radio down. 'Gone out.'

Kathleen was relieved. 'Where to?'

'Don't know.' Petra adopted a grown-up tone. 'Would you like a cup of coffee?'

Kathleen was surprised. 'Yes, all right.' She moved over to the table. 'What are these pictures?' She glanced down and fingered the album. The pages were thick card and decorated with paintings of flowers and trailing vines. Each was separated from the next by a leaf of tissue paper. Sepia photographs were inserted into pockets, which had drawings around to look like frames. Kathleen stared.

Each was a posed portrait of a ballerina. She turned the pages. The dancers stood graceful and thin, their white arms extended or raised above their heads. One had a sad face and looked up at an ornate balcony. Her hair was smooth and held in a bun. Her calf-length dress was shaped like a flower petal. Another, raised on the very tips of her toes, wore a wide, stiff tutu and her flat body was as dainty as a snowflake. Each picture was a faded brown colour and very beautiful. 'What are these?'

Petra lit the gas under the kettle. 'They're my mother.'

Kathleen looked at her friend. Her voice was matter of fact, without the show-offy tone she adopted when she was lying.

'The famous Nadezhda Chekhanova. She danced her way across Europe.'

Kathleen held her breath. The theatre stages in the pictures seemed like places very far away. She turned another page. A dancer lifted a long, pale arm and leg in total symmetry, a ring of rose blossoms clutched to her bosom. The corps de ballet, arranged perfectly, like a fan, surrounded her. Underneath each photograph was gold writing in an unknown alphabet. 'I didn't know your mother—'

'Why should you? It's all over now.'

Kathleen swallowed. She forgot her suspicions about Mrs Koninsky. 'You're so lucky—' she began to say.

At that moment there was a noise outside the window. Nosey

was barking. This was followed by a sharp scream. The two girls looked outside. Nadezhda was backing away from the dog, who was standing quietly now, wagging his tail. She held her hands out as if she was about to be attacked. Between two yellow fingers burned a cigarette. Kathleen noticed, not for the first time, how mannered her gestures were, how self-consciously she placed her feet. She thought of the photographs. Petra's mother was old now and she looked peculiar. Her hair was hanging down in an uncombed tangle, her face was lined and her kimono hung open revealing an unattractive, skinny leg. She turned a half-pirouette and spoke to the dog in a foreign tongue. She saw she was being observed. Nosey barked again and sat down. Nadezhda held up her hands against him in a gesture that suggested mimed self-preservation and horror. Then she went off in the direction of the water, coughing, her movements exaggerated, as if she was trying to make good some kind of pretend, imaginary escape. She looks like a nutcase, Kathleen thought. She looks like a murdering nutcase.

Petra turned to the kettle and rattled the teacups on the draining board. She made the coffee. Kathleen sat down, saying nothing. She closed the album. She was embarrassed.

Petra banged the drink in front of her and pushed a milk bottle across the table. 'Everyone says your Nan's mad,' she said angrily. 'Your Nan's the maddest person around here.'

Kathleen met her eyes. 'Don't say that.'

'She talks to herself. She never goes out of that house on First Street.'

'She's not mad, exactly, she's . . . she's got bad nerves.'

'She cuts up your Da's best clothes with scissors and hides his keys and says he's got a fancy woman. She breaks things with her walking stick—'

'Who told you that?' Kathleen was appalled. It was all true, but she had supposed quite, quite secret.

'Gloria told my father. I heard him telling my mother, last night. Gloria thought it was funny.'

There was a silence. Kathleen sipped her scalding coffee. It tasted bitter. She remembered how furious Nana always became when she thought she was being discussed, gossiped about, in the village. She always accused Gloria of talking about her behind her back. It's true, Kathleen thought. Nana's right. Gloria was blabbing family secrets, and now, out in the world, they can't ever be recovered.

There was a scratching noise from under the window and a low whine.

'What's that nuisance of a bastard dog doing now?' asked Petra, irritably. She raised her fingers to her lips and exhaled, pretending to smoke. 'My mother told me she doesn't want that dog down here.'

Kathleen was at a loss for words. She wanted to leave. She thought how it was always the case that whenever she visited her friend she wanted to leave straight away. At that moment a loud bell began ringing in the hall.

'It's probably the bastard *police*,' said Petra.

Kathleen sighed. Speaking above the noise she said, 'I'll tell Nosey to go home.'

Petra got up to answer the phone.

Kathleen went outside. The drizzle persisted and it was cold. Nadezhda had disappeared. Thank goodness, she thought, but then she noticed that Nosey had something in his mouth, something he'd dragged along the ground. He looked at Kathleen proudly. She bent down and gently opened his jaws. She already knew what it was he carried – it was a shiny black plastic raincoat with outsize silver buttons. She held it up and examined it. It was muddy and the lining was torn, but there was no question about its ownership. There was only one such fashionable garment in the village and it had come from Binns in Newcastle. It was Gloria's.

'Go *home*, Nosey! Go home to your *Nana*!' Kathleen insisted. He looked at her reproachfully and trotted off in the direction of the track. Kathleen smoothed the coat and unsure what to do with it, spread it on a low wall next to Mr Koninsky's chopping block. She then eased the camera off her shoulder removed it from its case and took a photograph. She had no clear reason for doing this – she was unsure of her own motives, except that the coat belonged to her auntie, it was wet and somehow it reminded her of the body. She bent down and stroked it. Poor Gloria, she thought. She straightened up. There's something very funny going on here. She glanced about. The scene was lifeless, bleak and contaminated. She put away the camera and went back inside.

Petra was at the table, cradling her coffee cup in a way she'd noticed people doing in advertisements.

Kathleen looked at her friend. She had no real affection for her. Petra was a year older, her parents had money and she thought she was superior. She was a know-it-all. Kathleen didn't believe in her superiority, didn't accept it, but found it hard to deal with, all the same. She only persisted with the relationship because there was no one else. As hostile as their parents, the village children ignored her or called her names. They thought her lack of a mother and father was shameful and disgusting. When Petra arrived at the school she'd met up with similar antagonism. Her father was a professional, so this made her 'stuck up'. She had a foreign surname, which was considered both hilarious and suspect. Worst of all, those children who'd had occasional sight of a television set knew that there was a famous dog named Petra on a programme called *Blue Peter*. 'Woof, woof,' they shouted, following her around the playground. 'Woof, woof, woof.'

Kathleen sought her out with both sympathy and relief. They were united in adversity. Or they had been. Now the air between them was being poisoned by Kathleen's suspicion about Nadezhda.

'What do you think about this missile thing?' asked Kathleen, in a neutral voice. 'The missiles in Cuba.'

'What?'

'There might be a war with Russia.' She felt herself shiver with apprehension.

'I wouldn't know.'

Kathleen pointed to the album. 'Have you got family in Russia?'

'What?'

'You heard.'

'Russia?'

'Russia.'

Petra resumed her adult tone. 'I haven't the faintest idea.'

Kathleen sipped her coffee. The cup was cracked and it had no saucer but it was made of very delicate china. The drink tasted bitter and strong – not like the fragrant brew in Gallini's. 'Are you wearing Gloria's clothes?'

'Don't be stupid.' Petra had recovered her composure.

'There's a black shortie raincoat outside on the wall. That belonged to Gloria.'

Petra raised her badly pencilled eyebrows. 'No,' she said quickly, too quickly. 'That's mine. I just got it . . . er . . . the other day.'

'If it's new, then why's it been left outside, where the dog could find it?'

'I've no idea.' Petra's voice was cold. 'What are you suggesting?'

Kathleen shrugged. 'Gloria and your dad were having an affair. Maybe she left—'

Petra looked alarmed. 'Not now! She might hear you!' She glanced at the window. 'You'll set her off crying again!'

Kathleen persisted. 'My Auntie Gloria didn't kill herself.' Her words hung in the air.

'What are you saying?'

'Just that. I don't think she did. Why should she?' Kathleen swallowed some more coffee and grimaced. 'I think . . . ' she paused for effect, 'she was murdered.'

Petra leapt to her feet, overturning her chair. She paced over to the window, glanced outside, then returned. Kathleen stared at her. She'd gone white. The telephone rang again but she ignored it. She stood very still. The loud bell continued for five rings, then stopped and everything seemed quiet. There was a sense of the two of them being very alone. Petra removed the plastic hair band from her head and pulled it apart until it cracked.

Kathleen continued. 'That policeman, the old one in the overcoat, he doesn't think she killed herself.'

Petra tossed the broken hair band on to the table. Her overgrown fringe flopped forward covering her spots. She seemed as if she might burst into tears herself. 'I hated your Gloria,' she said. 'And I'm a bag of nerves.'

Kathleen got up to leave.

'I'll tell you something for nothing,' said Petra suddenly. 'I tried to tell you yesterday, but you weren't listening.' Her voice was rushed, anxious. 'A man's hanging around here. He wears this long coat. He's got dark glasses on, even though there's no sun, and . . . sometimes a cap. I've seen him looking in our windows. He's scary.' She sounded stressed. 'He was here the night Gloria drowned. I saw him with my own eyes.'

Kathleen looked at her friend levelly. 'Really?'

'Yes. He's always here. He's a Peeping Tom!'

Kathleen didn't believe this. She felt calm in the face of Petra's distress. She thought she was making up a story, like she often did. She was always inventing dramas, with herself at the centre of them. 'I don't think so,' she said, trying to sound indifferent.

Kathleen tried instead to picture the untidy, theatrical Nadezhda holding Gloria down under the water. There were bubbles coming from her poor drowning mouth, from her feeble struggle. She decided to tell Inspector Glen about this. He would know what to do.

Petra was grasping the edge of the table with both hands, her knuckles tense.

Kathleen walked towards the door. For once, she'd felt she'd got the upper hand. Her voice was assertive. 'You have got relations in Russia, haven't you? I know you have.' She thought again of the ballet company and an ornate theatre, with onion domes, surrounded by tanks.

Petra didn't reply.

'Those Soviets are bad men and your family is the enemy. There's going to be a war and your lot are on the wrong side.'

Kathleen walked back towards home. The rain was insistent and depressing. She'd decided to go and see Billy Fishboy and watch the Pathe Newsreel again, checking out the Russian Army as well as the American space mission.

She climbed the steep slope from Jinny Hoolets, the water behind her like a dark, full eye. Without intending to, she glanced back. The pond lay still and complacent, undisturbed by its own ugliness. For a second she thought she saw Petra's mother flitting around the barn, her kimono flapping – but her glasses were misted up and she couldn't be sure. She was shocked by her own suspicions about Mrs Koninsky, but she was unable to shake them off. Petra's mother's bizarre appearance made her seem like a person capable of anything, however extreme. She's really scary, she decided. This place scares me. Kathleen shivered. It gives me the creeps.

She considered Petra's embarrassment and her defensive attack on Nana. Petra had never met Nana, so she'd known nothing before. Gloria *must* have told. She felt angry with her Auntie Gloria for betraying family secrets. Nana was right, she told herself. And Gloria should have kept her mouth shut. I've never blabbed to anyone. It isn't anyone else's business. Anyway, Petra shouldn't have said that. Nana's not really mad. She's not mad like that . . . that barmy old ballet dancer down there. Sure, she never goes out, but she can hardly walk or see. And she gets annoyed with Da sometimes but she's not *mad*. She's not a *nutcase*. She trudged along, memories of Nana's outbursts forcing their way into her mind.

Instead, she deliberately tried to recall something pleasant. She returned to her earliest happy memory. The sun had been bright, the day she'd climbed a hill on a man's shoulders and she'd worn a white hat, the brim of which shaded her eyes. The grass, a long way below was speckled with flowers and the man held on to her legs, firmly. 'It won't be long now,' the lady had said at their side. A flock of birds flew overhead like a tossed handful of silver treasure and she'd pretended she was on the prow of a ship, holding her hand to her forehead, swaying and rolling, like a lookout in a pirate book.

Now Kathleen bent her head against the drizzle and trudged to the very top of the track. She turned again. She took off her glasses and polished them carefully on the hem of her skirt. She rubbed her eyes and replaced the spectacles, centring them on the bridge of her nose. She regarded the scene below. The Koninskys' house appeared to be nestling amongst the heaps. Suddenly, instead of looking incongruous, the dirty backdrop of man-made pollution was all at once appropriate. The heaps encircled and framed the dwelling as if this was how things were always meant to be. The deep tracks and ruts and passageways all led to the front door. The heavy sky, the black wink of the pond all created a picture, which if it had been natural and clean, would have been harmonious. It was a corrupted landscape, a negative of a picture postcard, monochrome, artificial, composed. It resembled a devilish travesty of rural England. This is what you chose, she thought, addressing the unhappy family who lived here. She removed Da's Box Brownie again from its case. You didn't have to come here. This is your place. You've found your true home. She captured the scene and released the shutter.

Approaching the village, Kathleen thought about Christmas Eve, the previous year. Everyone, including herself, had sat in the kitchen, holding a tiny tumbler of ginger wine. It tasted fiery and festive. A plate of Nana's mince pies was passed around. Joyce took three. 'I love your mince pies,' she'd said and Nana had smiled.

Carols played on the wireless and the ceiling was festooned with paper decorations, which swayed in the heat from below. Gloria had arrived with presents. As usual, they all sat in the kitchen and it was too hot, the range banked up against the frost outside. 'Phew!' Gloria had uttered. 'It's like an oven in here.' Nana, irritated by this presumption, gave her one of her long, strange stares.

Kathleen could remember, with perfect recall, a delicate brass ornament on the sideboard. It was the three kings bearing gifts, suspended above a small candle. As the flame burned the figures span around, chiming, circling their eternal central star. She'd never seen it before and she watched it, almost hypnotized.

Da got to his feet and removed a lidded bowl from the sideboard. He took it out to the cold, damp passage. There was a rustle from the hall-stand as he opened a paper bag full of nuts.

The bowl, Kathleen knew, was precious. Nana's uncle had

brought it back from China decades before when he'd been in the Merchant Navy. At one time it had contained something called jasmine tea and Kathleen sometimes sniffed it, imagining a delicate fragrance. It had a white background but was closely decorated with blue dragons, blue stylized trees and blue people in oriental clothes.

Suddenly there was a dreadful crash. Everyone in the room knew instantly – the bowl had hit the tiles and broken into a million pieces. Kathleen's stomach turned over. Joyce froze. Gloria's fists moved to either side of her face. All eyes were on Nana.

Slowly, Da entered the room. He looked shaken. His hands were still cupped in a bowl shape, as if he couldn't believe what had occurred. He met Nana's gaze and her face was full of hate. She stood up, grasping her stick and her shadow loomed huge in the light from the fire. At that moment the candle blew out below the three kings. Their pretty tinkling slowed in the silence and then stopped. The air was so hot from the fire it was almost unbreathable.

Nana roared. She stood tall despite her stiff joints and shouted and screamed. Kathleen covered her ears, Joyce buried her head in her hands, Gloria got up to leave. Da stood help-lessly for a moment then went to retrieve a dustpan. In the passage, he carefully swept up the shards.

Nana followed him, ranting about his fancy women and harlots. She insisted that Nadezhda Koninsky was signalling to him from the street, waving a long chiffon scarf at the windows. She accused him of sleeping with the greengrocer's wife and corrupting the daughter of the pit deputy. She moved effort-lessly into the parlour. Her anger made her movements supple and confident as she forgot her arthritis and poor eyesight. After a while she stopped shouting but she was panting. There was a sound of her stick thrashing. Kathleen got up and peered into the other room. Da was now gently restraining Nana and he'd removed her cane from her hand. He picked up Nosey the Jack Russell and placed him in her arms. The dog licked her face. It was clear she was calming down but she had wrecked the Christmas tree. The baubles were strewn around; many crushed. The tinsel was in a tangled mess on the sofa. The fairy was dislodged and many of the artificial branches were bent or out of place. The lights had, of course, fused. Kathleen felt tears spring to her eyes. It's ruined, she thought. It was so colourful and nice and now it's horrible, like this family. She heard the front door close as Gloria quit the scene.

Kathleen felt tears welling up as she walked along, rain soaking her head and face. She always tried not to think about Nana's obsessions and her accusations, but occasionally she couldn't shut them out. Sometimes she wished Da would shout back and deny them, but she knew this would probably be useless. Once Nana started there was no stopping her. Her rage had to run its course.

In the village, the sky was low and heavy with moisture and smoke from house-fires curled down and tainted the air. The drainpipes and gutters ran furiously and pools formed in the road. The dwellings seemed shut-up and dead. Kathleen noticed a drenched news sheet blown against a wall. Gloria was on the cover, smudged, soaked, stained. Kathleen forgot her auntie's gossiping and remembered her enthusiasm. She glanced at the mean dwellings. Everything here is so ugly, she thought. And the people here never appreciated Gloria or realized that she had a good brain. She kicked an empty cigarette packet. What would anyone here know about good brains?

A group of miners, haversacks slung over their shoulders, trudged in wordless single file towards the colliery gates. A small boy ran down a street with a whippet on a string and further on, a mother in a plastic rainhood dragged a pushchair across her threshold and closed her door firmly against the weather. Kathleen tried to imagine a Russian atomic bomb exploding in the area. She thought of it as a peculiar purple X-ray light, which was cold rather than burning. It revealed the skeletons of both people and buildings before they all immediately crumbled into dust.

She entered the main street and noticed that the bright window of Gallini's was steamy and running with condensation. There were no customers. Opposite, across the cobbles, the hair salon was dark and desolate and the price list, Sellotaped to the window, was curling at the edges. Litter had blown against the door, and lay in a soggy heap. The nylon curtains looked droopy and sad. It looks like it's been closed for ages, Kathleen thought.

She pushed open the door of the Essoldo and climbed the stairs to the projection room. Pictures of film stars were framed on the wall. Kathleen recognized Gregory Peck and Sophia Loren. She was expecting to find Billy on his own, with his feet up, reading *Amateur Photographer*. She felt an odd, unnameable excitement at the prospect of being alone with him again. She was surprised to hear voices. She crept to the open door and listened.

'Are you taking me or not?' It was Joyce. She's at work very early, Kathleen thought. The next performance of *Summer Holiday* wasn't due to begin for three hours.

'I don't know,' replied Billy. He sounded a little intimidated, as usual. He was not a confident person. 'It's not right to go enjoying myself after what's happened—'

'Look,' Joyce insisted. 'You don't have to stay. Just escort me, we'll go in together, have one dance then you can go home.' She paused. She was angry. 'Is it much to ask? I want to go. I *am* going to go.'

Oh dear, thought Kathleen. This is my fault. This was my idea. She knew that Billy was afraid of Joyce. She also knew that Joyce didn't care for Billy because he'd been Gloria's friend and because he wasn't interested in *her*. Gloria had told her this. Gloria had thought it was funny. 'She thought she was going to *take him off me*,' she'd laughed, one day. 'Do me a favour, will you? I mean, *honestly*!'

I should never have suggested this, Kathleen thought.

Billy continued with his excuses. 'I'm sorry but . . . my mother says—'

Joyce was exasperated. 'Bloody Gloria's ruined this for me! Again!'

'You can hardly blame—'

'Yes I can! She's ruined things ever since I can remember! For years and years and years!'

The silence was broken by a mechanical sound as one of Billy's reels rewound. His chair squeaked and he sighed, nervously. Kathleen could tell that he didn't know what to say.

'There's things I know, Billy Fisher.' Joyce's voice was ice. 'Things you wouldn't want to get out.' Kathleen strained to hear.

'You . . . you don't. What're you on about?' Billy sounded frightened.

'Yes I do. Your so-called fianceé was a tart and having it off with Marek Koninsky behind your back. She told him you can't get it up, not ever, not once. *And* you take photographs of boys.' She paused.

Billy said nothing.

'Gloria was playing you along. She never meant to marry you . . . Because you're a queer—'

The castors on Billy's chair ground against the floor as he suddenly stood up. 'Shut up, Joyce!'

Joyce continued. 'No I won't. I'll tell everyone what she said.

That you're a puff.' She paused for effect. 'You won't want that, will you?'

'Stop it!'

There was another pause. Joyce was breathing audibly. 'Are you taking me to that dance or not?'

'Yes, all right.'

'Is that definite?'

'Yes.'

'OK, then.'

Kathleen slipped along the dark corridor and concealed herself in the gloom.

Joyce bustled out of Billy's office, her nylons rasping, her little pillbox hat slightly askew as she dragged on her fur jacket. Her face was red. 'See you later,' she called out, as if she'd had a normal conversation.

Kathleen didn't move. It wasn't a good moment to ask Billy for a favour. She was sure Joyce had hurt him, telling him those things about Mr Koninsky. Poor Billy, she thought. Mr Koninsky might be very handsome, very suave, but Billy's much nicer. Billy's got a Vespa and he's interested in rhythm and blues. What on earth was Gloria doing? Mr Koninsky's married and old. *And* he might close the pit and throw everyone out of work. *And* no one likes him because he's a foreigner. Gloria made a big mistake. Poor Billy.

She felt tears spring to her eyes. She blinked rapidly. These Koninskys, she thought. Why did they ever come here? They could have gone anywhere – Paris, Rome, Sunderland . . . What reason had they for burying themselves alive in this tiny place and causing all this trouble? She blinked and adjusted her spectacles. She felt furious with them. They could have been free, she thought, and they chose here. This village. That awful house. They crossed Europe and decided to live *here*. It seemed beyond all reason.

Joyce left the Essoldo feeling triumphant. In the doorway, she took a chocolate bar out of her pocket and gobbled it down. She went over to the Causey Arms. She hesitated, feeling inhibited. She'd never before entered a public house on her own. She breathed the shameful smell of stale beer and smoke and felt a frisson of fear. She knew that a few older widows were encouraged to use the snug when they were with their friends. Nana's cousin Auntie Molly was a snug regular. And married or engaged women accompanied by their menfolk were welcome in the lounge. Women alone, women like her, were unheard of in here. Deliberately, thinking of Gloria's confidence under pressure and holding her head high, she entered the men-only public bar. To her relief, Marek was standing on his own staring into space. He looked worldly, sophisticated and clean. His hat was tipped back at a rakish angle instead of being courteously removed. One foot was on the rail in front of the bar and one hand was in a pocket. A group of men playing dominoes stared at Joyce. The room fell silent. She pretended to ignore them. 'Hello, Marek,' she said.

He glanced at her without smiling. He tossed back his neat gin and grimaced.

'I'm going to the dance,' she said happily. 'You've got to come, you know. You'll like it. I bet you're a good dancer.'

'My wife, she is the dancer. Me, I am the drinker.'

Joyce was embarrassed. She preferred the subject of Nadezhda to remain hidden, unacknowledged. 'I'm making my dress. I make all my own clothes.'

Marek raised his eyebrows, surprised. He seemed a little scornful.

Joyce was nervous. She continued prattling. 'It's green man-made silk with net can-cans. I got the pattern from Shepherds in Gateshead. It's a Butterick pattern, they're the nicest.'

Marek ordered another gin and a lemonade for Joyce. The

barman didn't meet their eyes. Marek swallowed the measure and said no more. Joyce drank half her glass, felt suddenly conscious of the many silent men in the bar and left. There was a low mutter of conversation from the tables as the door closed.

Nana was alone in the house. She stood at the sink, peeling vegetables. She'd already rolled out her pastry and put it in the larder to cool. Every few minutes she went to the range and gently stirred the bubbling steak and kidney on the hob. The room was scented by the rich stew. When she had an acceptable pile of potatoes and carrots she chopped an onion and fried it briskly on the hot plate. Then she lined her pie dish and heaped in the meat and onion. She sprinkled a little home-dried parsley on top and then wedged an upturned egg cup in the centre. Carefully she cut out the crust, laid it over and pressed the edges together. She glazed it with beaten egg and placed it on the draining board. She glanced at the clock. She was calm and absorbed. She loved cooking. She filled two pans with water and dropped in the vegetables. It was too soon to set them boiling. Finally she filled a dish with milk, sugar, nutmeg and pudding rice and placed this in the top of the hot oven at the side of the fire.

Later, the small black Ford stopped at the bottom of the track at Jinny Hoolets a few yards from the Koninskys' dwelling. It was Marek's Coal Board car. The horn sounded but no one inside the building stirred. After a few moments two men emerged from the vehicle. One was dressed in a dark suit and a broad-brimmed hat, the other was a workman in soiled blue overalls. They were from the mine. They began pulling something from the back seat. It was another man. They dragged him out then each hoisted one of his arms across their shoulders. His feet touched the ground and he attempted to walk a little, but he was barely conscious. They half-carried him to the entrance, pushed open the door and took him inside. They laid him clumsily at the bottom of the stairs, then left. They went back to the car and one of them hooted the horn again. They set off walking up the slope. After a minute, the workman turned. He saw two dim faces in an upstairs window. They were partially obscured by the curtain, but they seemed afraid. Marek's wife and daughter were hiding in a bedroom. 'They're there,' he told his companion. 'Look. You were right. They're both there, the kid as well.'

There was a sudden burst of angry rain which slanted into the surface of the pond like a thousand knives. 'Who'd live here?' asked the man in the suit gesturing towards the mountainous pit heaps and the ugly, threatening sky. 'What a place! It's no wonder the bastard hits the bottle.'

Marek had been brought home drunk on previous occasions, but the regular surveyors and technical staff at the mine closed ranks and covered for him. This was the accepted code – it was not because they liked the man. They found him arrogant and opinionated and distrusted his foreign ways, his clothes, his pedantic methods, which were diligent, thorough, but so different from their own. They also distrusted his motives. If the mine closed their futures were threatened. As well as this, they thought their wives were in love with him.

On one occasion he'd been carried off a train at Tantobie. On another he'd been seen with drink down the mine, which for anyone else would have meant dismissal. He was frequently in the Causey Arms but he didn't socialize or play darts or show interest in the terrier racing. His colleagues understood he was a lone drinker, single minded, surly, resentful. If spoken to when drunk he muttered terse rebuttals, veiled insults. They knew his appointment was temporary and he was to move from pit to pit. They collectively held their breath and waited for him to go.

*

Much later, as the day gave up the unequal struggle and succumbed to darkness Kathleen tapped on the door of Da's shed. She went in and found him sitting at his table with his torch, making calculations alongside a drawing of the Mare Crisium and the moon crater Cleomedes. He was using a protractor and a slide rule and his writing was neat and precise. She noticed his black armband. He smiled at her but said nothing. Kathleen leaned against him and kissed the air above the top of his head. 'I've been reading your book,' she said. '*The Amateur Astronomer.*' She studied his work on the table below. It was complex and ordered. 'You're so clever,' she murmured.

He sighed and laid down his tools. He smoothed the sheet under his calloused hand.

'Da,' she said timidly, 'can I ask you something?'

'Yes, pet?'

Kathleen's voice was trapped in her throat. Without meaning to she merely said, 'Can I have my pocket money?'

He felt in his pocket and handed her some coins.

She decided to try again, but it was almost impossible to speak to Da of personal things – he was so distant, so closed off, so unapproachable. She took a deep breath. We both loved her, she thought. 'Did you know that Auntie Gloria was . . .' She hesitated.

'What's that now?' He was as absent as ever, his pencil again in his hand, drawing an isosceles triangle.

'Did you know that—' Kathleen forced out the words in a rush. 'Having an affair?'

There was a silence. Da wrote a few figures as if he hadn't heard. He said, 'Your auntie was going out with Billy Fisher from the Essoldo. I saw him earlier. He's a nice lad. He's got a beautiful camera. He's very upset.'

'No, I don't mean him.'

'What do you mean, Kathleen? Exactly?'

Kathleen swallowed. 'Marek Koninsky.'

Da dropped his pencil. He straightened his back, forcing Kathleen to move away. He pushed his papers to one side and stared straight ahead, his face like stone. 'So it's out!' he exclaimed, quietly. In a louder voice he asked, 'Who told you that? What are people saying?'

Kathleen suddenly felt very nervous. Her conversations with Da were usually about abstract, unemotional things. They were close, but not as a result of words passing between them. 'Petra,' she replied. There was a silence. 'Petra Koninsky. His daughter.'

Da sighed. 'Your little friend is a very mischievous girl.'

Kathleen decided to get her worries off her chest. 'I'm scared that Auntie Gloria was murdered, by somebody on purpose. I don't think she drowned herself. Why would she do that? She had plans for the salon and . . . everything. She was happy. I'm scared that somebody killed her because she was having an . . . affair.'

Da turned towards her. His face was grave, his words measured. 'I don't know what happened to—' His voice broke a fraction. 'My Gloria. I wish I knew. But the police will decide. It's not our business to speculate. The proper authorities will look at the situation and we'll be informed. I don't think you should be talking this way with your friend.' His face looked older than usual, as lined and furrowed as a field.

Kathleen felt reprimanded. Da hates Mr Koninsky, she thought. Maybe that's why he was so angry with Gloria recently. Maybe he knew about the affair and was furious with her. He's very old-fashioned, she reasoned, and Mr Koninsky is, after all, a married man.

Dissatisfied but at a loss, she changed the subject. 'Do you think there's going to be a war?'

Da relaxed slightly but remained serious. 'Don't believe what they tell you on the BBC.'

'Why not?'

'Premier Khrushchev is a friend of the Cuban people. He's defending them against the Americans. President Kennedy's been threatening their socialist revolution. America never wants anything to happen over there which it doesn't control. Absolutely control.'

Kathleen let these statements sink in. 'Yes,' she said, 'but is there going to be a war?'

Da spoke quickly. He sounded very sure. 'No, there won't be a war. The Soviets are too powerful. Kennedy will back off.'

'Good,' said Kathleen. She wasn't convinced but she wanted to get on to familiar ground. 'Can I look at the sky? It's stopped raining. It's not so bad now.'

Relieved, Da unfastened the bolts and rolled back the roof. Kathleen was right. The rain had ceased. 'It's a pretty cloudy old night,' he said. He watched as Kathleen prepared and adjusted the telescope. Then he went back to his calculations.

'I'm cold,' she said.

He stood up and draped his long raincoat around her shoulders. 'That better?'

'Yes.' She swung the telescope almost randomly.

Da resumed concentrating on his geometry.

Kathleen saw the village made enormous and the sidings and railway lines eerie in the illumination from the headstock at the mine. 'Which way's Cuba?' she asked.

Da pointed. 'West.'

She turned the telescope west, then south over open countryside. It was very dark. I wonder where those two are living, exactly, she thought to herself. She trained her vision on the indistinct trees, fences and fields. My mother and father. I wonder where they're hiding themselves. She pulled Da's coat around herself and shivered. She felt some things rattle in the pocket and she groped them expecting to feel his pipe. She fished them out. She was surprised. As well as his penknife, which he always carried, there were a pair of prescription sunglasses, given to Nana by the eye hospital several years before. Kathleen recognized them. Up until recently they'd been in the drawer of the sideboard, wrapped in an old duster. 'Have you been wearing these?' she asked.

Da looked over, frowned in a puzzled way, then shrugged.

Kathleen thought about Petra's words earlier that day. She shivered and swallowed hard. She's trying to upset me, she thought. She's a mischievous little girl. She's seen Da in these sunglasses and she's deliberately trying to make me scared. She felt dismayed. I want to go home, she decided.

For once the shed was not a haven of quiet and meditation. It's peace was sullied and disturbed. Kathleen left Da to his mathematics and left to walk home on her own in the dark.

The moon gleamed dully behind thinning cloud and one or two stars were bright enough to shine. The pit buzzer sounded and two laden trains clanked past one another, hooting, spilling dirty light from their cabs on to the tracks. She crossed the coal-strewn rails, listened to the winding wheel and thought about her socks turning black as she took a short cut through the sidings. This pit is everything, she thought. And it makes the place so dirty. I wonder if there'll ever be a day when there are no mines in Durham and no miners and we don't use coal on our fires and we get energy from . . . outer space. She raised her face upwards, turning her attention to beautiful Telstar spinning and spinning invisibly above her head, accompanied for ever by a tune from The Tornados. The sky was calming. 'Infinite nothingness,' she said, contemplating the universe. 'Intergalactic spaces. Light years.' She called to mind the names of all the astronauts who, unfettered by day-to-day concerns, had made this thrilling, weightless journey. Yuri Gagarin, she remembered, once said that from Space, the Earth is blue. She ran through the familiar litany. Gherman Titov and John Glenn, of course, Scott Carpenter, Andrian Nicolayev, Pavel Popovitch, Walter M. Schirra Junior. They're ambassadors from the future, she thought, remembering this phrase from an article in her scrap book. She sighed happily, released for the moment from terrestrial worries, but almost immediately her anxiety returned. She thought of President Kennedy who had seemed so young and so nice but who was now on the brink of blowing up the whole world. Da doesn't like him, she thought. I used to like him a lot. Now I'm not so sure. Everything's changing. Gloria's gone, there's probably going to be a war. I'm changing. I'm changing every day. She adopted a deep American accent. 'Before this decade is out,' she quoted aloud, to the deserted streets on the grimy outskirts of the village, 'we'll land a man on the moon and return him safely to Earth.'

As she approached the shops, Nosey rushed out from a back lane. He jumped and wagged his tail, excitedly. Kathleen stopped and made a fuss of him and he began yapping. She picked him up and cuddled him. 'Good boy,' she said. 'Good dog. Be quiet.' Suddenly he began struggling and leapt from her arms. He ran off in the direction of Gloria's salon. Kathleen followed him.

The dog began barking in a different way. It was his aggressive bark. He growled and there was a low male cry. 'Get away! Get lost!'

Kathleen ran towards the voice, then stopped, pleased. 'Hello!' she said. It was Billy Fishboy.

'Kathleen, get this dog away from me!'

'Go home, Nosey! Nosey go home to Nana now!' Kathleen remembered that Billy hated dogs.

Nosey growled, eyed Billy's trouser leg with interest, walked to a corner, cocked his leg then disappeared.

Billy was standing at the side of the salon, outside the entrance to Gloria's flat. He was relieved. He pulled the door closed.

'What are you doing?' asked Kathleen.

'Nothing.'

'You've been upstairs.'

Billy seemed sheepish. 'That's right.'

'How come?'

'I've got a key.' He was trying to conceal something in his arms.

'What you got there?'

'Nothing.'

'I'd like to go up. Will you let me in?'

'Not tonight.'

'When?'

He shrugged. He tried to edge away. He walked a few steps into the street. It had begun drizzling again but only lightly. He was wearing a long raincoat over his tieless shirt.

Kathleen accompanied him, staring at his bundle. 'That's our Gloria's op-art dress. What are you doing with our Gloria's op-art dress, Billy?'

He hesitated for a while but Kathleen maintained an expectant silence.

'It's . . . it's a keepsake. I loved her in this dress. She looked like a model in a fashion magazine, wearing this. She wore it with her white kinky boots.'

Kathleen regarded him keenly. It seemed like a reasonable answer, but poor Gloria's clothes were being scattered to the four winds. Gloria won't have any left soon, she thought, irrationally.

There was a silence. 'Do you want me to walk you home?' Billy enquired.

Kathleen was surprised and pleased. 'But you're not my boy-friend,' she said.

'Do you want me to or not?'

'All right.'

'Don't let that dog come near me, that's all.'

They crossed the square towards First Street. 'I don't think Gloria killed herself,' said Kathleen. She'd said this so many times in one day her voice was flat and unemotional.

'Neither does that policeman,' Billy replied. He stroked his hair. 'He thinks I did it.'

# THURSDAY

Kathleen woke early, remembered again it was the school holidays and tried to doze. She felt sad and tried unsuccessfully to chase thoughts of Gloria from her mind. Eventually she got up and looked through her scrapbook. Near the back, after the birthday cards, she'd pasted an invitation to a Trip, which had taken place in the summer. It was only a few months before, but felt like much longer. It felt like years ago. She saw herself as a younger person then – more like an innocent child.

The invitation explained in some detail how the village chapel and church were historically linked to a charity in Elswick in Newcastle upon Tyne. The organization was called the Fresh Air Fund. Rich ladies ran it and they'd arranged a special omnibus for the poor slum children, to bring them out to the country so that they could have the opportunity to breathe properly. Kathleen read this and thought about the black dust that settled everywhere around the village and frowned. They came to the wrong place she decided, ruefully. In June her Sunday School had been invited to meet up with these underprivileged city dwellers – for a picnic at Causey Arch.

On the agreed afternoon, Mr Dobbs, the Superintendent, had arrived at the Welfare Hall, red faced, flustered and wearing a heavy tweed suit. The members of the Sunday School were assembled and excited. Kathleen looked for Petra, but to her dismay, she failed to appear. Petra's stopped coming, she decided. She thinks it's babyish.

'As you know, children, these dreadful slums are in Elswick, on Tyneside,' he boomed, 'but you pronounce it El-sick. You must be nice and friendly to these unfortunate youngsters,' he continued, 'and set them a good example. Good behaviour is essential. You must be generous of spirit. Some of them' – and to Kathleen's horror, he turned and placed a hand on her shoulder – 'are like our friend here – fatherless and born of sin. The rest have been plucked from the feckless poor.'

Kathleen's cheeks burned. She retreated to a corner of the Hall, embarrassed, until eventually, in single file, they all marched a mile down the road to the deep wooded valley beneath the ruined stone arch, which over two hundred years ago had been built for dragging coal. It was a green place now and overgrown. Rediscovering it, the council had put up signs explaining that the bridge was very, very old and because of this, famous. They'd also provided litter bins.

The Sunday School waited a long time for the special bus to appear. Kathleen had stood on her own, holding her bread wrapper full of egg sandwiches, which she'd made herself. She listened to two village boys as they giggled and pretended to push each other into the stream. 'Courting couples come here,' one of them sniggered. 'I've seen them necking in the bushes.' At the time, Kathleen thought about Auntie Gloria and Billy Fishboy, wondering how exactly they 'necked' and whether or not they bothered to conceal themselves effectively from view.

Now, sitting on her bed, she smoothed the old invitation under her fingers and supposed that Gloria had in fact 'necked' in that place with Mr Koninsky instead. She might have had an affair with him there, right under the ancient, famous stones. It was hard to picture this, but she could remember the blistering hot day, the smell of rotting vegetation from the swampy water below, the canopy of trees. She'd worn an old cotton dress which was pretty, but faded and which Joyce had agreed to iron.

The bus had roared in, like a big beast, churning up the newly laid gravel and the town children tumbled out, using a lot of swear words. Some of them didn't have socks, two didn't have shoes and one or two had shaved heads, probably as a result of creepy-crawlies. The boys ran off and peed in the bushes. Some had forgotten their food, but Mr Dobbs said it didn't matter because there was plenty of spare bread and butter to go around.

Everyone had been given a number and told to find their partner. Kathleen's town friend turned out to be a small, younger girl. She was very friendly and immediately caught hold of Kathleen's hand. 'I'm Alison,' she said. Despite the heat, she was wearing a holey jumper, a kilt and wellingtons. She had glasses similar to Kathleen's but the frames were pink plastic instead of wire and one lens was covered over. 'I've got a lazy eye,' she said confidentially when she saw Kathleen notice it. They all set off down a track in a crocodile.

'How do you do,' said Kathleen politely, remembering her manners after a minute. 'My name's Kathleen.'

Alison swung their arms in a jolly way. 'Your dress is a bonny colour. I'm dead jealous, me.'

They entered a wide clearing and Mr Dobbs told them to sit on the grass. He said a prayer and then began handing out packets to the children who'd arrived without a picnic. Two other Sunday School teachers poured pop into paper cups and distributed fairy cakes baked by the Labour Women's Guild.

'Do you like the country?' Kathleen asked her new friend. She was now glad that Petra wasn't here, because she would have said something rude about Alison's wellingtons. She would have been insulting.

'Nah,' laughed Alison. 'Sheep shit? Fields? Do me a favour!' She paused. 'Why? Do you?'

Kathleen bit into a sandwich and offered one to her partner. She was surprised to see how quickly it disappeared. 'The village is boring,' she agreed. 'There's only the pit and a few shops. I'm going to get away.' She looked up at the clear blue sky. 'I'm going to be an astronaut.'

Alison devoured a cake from the circulating tray. She ate her bread and butter and helped herself to two more egg sandwiches. 'These are lovely,' she said. She stared at Kathleen's Clarke's sandals. 'You're lovely too.'

Kathleen remembered removing Da's Box Brownie from its case and taking two pictures of Alison. She took another of the whole group and one of Causey Arch and a landscape shot of the steeply wooded valley. Some town boys stood on their hands but collapsed as the shutter clicked for the sixth time. Kathleen laughed. 'Do another one, do another one!' they begged. She obliged.

Alison had revealed that she had nine brothers and sisters. She knew all the words of 'Bobby's Girl' and went through it twice, pretending to hold a microphone and making appropriate hand gestures. Kathleen took a photo of her, whilst she was singing. She had a big, inviting, Susan Maughan-type smile on her face. Everyone crowded round. Kathleen was proud that her very own partner on this Trip was so talented and popular.

'That's really, really good,' enthused Kathleen.

Alison had just sunk into a deep curtsy. 'I once met the Beverley Sisters,' she said, but she didn't sound boastful, like Petra. She was matter of fact. 'They were on at The Majestic. My mam used to work there, in the foyer. She's met all the stars. Frank Ifield. Helen Shapiro. Acker Bilk.'

'Chubby Checker?' asked Kathleen.

'Nah. Not him. He's a yank, isn't he?'

'Yes. I think he's a darkie.'

On the way back to the bus, Kathleen told Alison that she had no brothers or sisters.

'That must be heaven.'

'It's a bit lonely sometimes. I haven't got a mother or father either.'

Alison said she was sorry. She looked sympathetic. 'I think you should come up to Elswick and visit us,' she said. 'You can share my family.'

Just as she was about to leave, Alison fished in the pocket of her kilt and pulled out a square of cardboard. It had a red sun in the middle and underneath it said 'Flags of the World'. 'Do you collect these?'

Kathleen took the card and shook her head.

'You get them out of bubble gum machines. That one's a swap. You can have it if you like. It's the flag of Japan.'

'All aboard!' shouted Mr Dobbs. He was in a good mood.

'I've had a great time!' Alison climbed on to the bus and grinned through the window. She had gaps in her teeth, which proved she was quite young. As the vehicle pulled away with a huge roar, she waved frantically. All the town children were waving. Some of the boys pulled their mouths wide with their fingers or pressed their faces against the glass. They're more fun than the village children and not nearly so spiteful, Kathleen decided. Maybe El-sick isn't so bad after all. She stood there, smiling happily. 'I want to be Bobby's girl,' she'd hummed. 'I wish I was Bobby's girl.'

Kathleen read through the Trip invitation again. It always gave her a warm feeling, despite the cold in her room. She got up and rummaged in her drawer, trying to find something to wear. First of all she found the photograph of her christening. She stared at Gloria who was nothing like her recent self. She would have been about my age then, she calculated. She would have been the same age as I am now. The young Gloria was wearing a floral dress with a wide collar and her grin revealed large teeth. Kathleen raised the image to her lips as if to kiss her Auntie

Gloria then realized she didn't feel connected to it at all. She put the snapshot to one side. She looked for the photographs she had taken herself, that more recent, hot, sunny summer's day. They were together with the flag card of Japan. They'd come out fairly well. There were two of Alison sitting on the grass eating Kathleen's sandwiches and holding her cup of pop. In one, she was squinting at the camera, her lazy eye obscured by its patch, giving her a piratical glare. In the other she was in profile and looked very small and sweet. Another showed her singing, holding a pretend microphone in one hand and making an expansive gesture with the other. Kathleen smiled and examined the other shots. The bridge was high and elegant but the one of the valley was just a blur of grey trees. There was a picture of laughing boys collapsed in a heap and another of them standing on their hands. There was also a shot of the whole group of children sitting in an untidy semicircle around the Sunday School teachers. Kathleen looked at this closely, trying to identify Alison. For the first time she noticed that in the background, outside the group, there was an indistinct figure, also holding a camera. It wasn't a Box Brownie – he held it up to his eyes, in the modern way. Kathleen was surprised because she'd looked at these pictures many times. The man was very tiny, but he too was taking a picture of the children at exactly the same moment as Kathleen. There was no doubt. It was Billy Fishboy.

Well, thought Kathleen, at least it's not Marek Koninsky. Maybe Gloria was necking there in the bushes, with her proper fiancé, after all. She examined all the shadows and grainy blobs. She blinked. Unfortunately, there was no sign of Gloria. I haven't got a nice picture of Auntie Gloria, she thought sadly, except the christening, and I didn't know her then. I wonder why I never took one of her. She was my friend. She remembered the photographs still in her camera. Some of them were of

Gloria dead. I suppose they're better than nothing, she reasoned. She blinked again, trying not to cry.

Downstairs, Nana was black-leading the range, her bad eye shut, gauging the shine. As she polished she sang quietly to the Jack Russell, 'How much is that doggie in the window? The one with the wag-gel-y tail.' Nosey was asleep and unaware in the chair, dreaming of policemen. The old wall clock ticked steadily and chimed the hour.

Joyce was eating a piece of cake and examining an old curtain. It was faded in places and a little stained with damp, but it was a pretty royal blue and made of cotton velvet. This'll do for *her* dress, she thought. She held it up to the light. She'd forgotten Kathleen was on holiday from school, so didn't call her down. She spread the curtain on the table, dusted off the cake crumbs and placed on top of it an old faded summer dress, belonging to the girl. Then with great confidence and allowing a little for growth, she set to work with her scissors. She cut out the bodice, front and back, and estimated a considerable width for the skirt, which she imagined as full, gathered and short – like a puffball. She also cut out two little sleeves. Joyce didn't know that Kathleen was on the verge of puberty. She pictured a dainty dress with a satin cummerbund, such as she'd seen on chocolate boxes. She intended telling Kathleen to twist her poor hair around rollers in order to create ringlets. A matching ribbon would complete the outfit. She sighed. I hope the little blighter's grateful, she thought. It's more than she deserves.

She sat at her machine. Her own, uncompleted dress was bundled in a corner of the room. There wasn't much more sewing needed to finish it, except work on the bodice, hooks and eyes and some final decorative flourishes. She fished around in the drawer and pulled out some lace trim and blue buttons.

She selected a blue cotton, threaded up and began pounding down the main seams.

As she worked, Joyce thought about Marek. With a thrill of pleasure she remembered his lovemaking and his passion. She wished he was more talkative, friendlier, but she excused his silences on the basis that he wasn't English. He's not that familiar with the language, she reasoned, or with our Durham ways. She allowed her imagination full rein. She pictured herself in a gorgeous wedding dress, similar to that worn by Princess Margaret two years before. It had a train, a high modest neckline and it was embroidered all over with pearl droplets. Her hair was wound in a topknot and around it was secured a pearl coronet. From this cascaded a spectacular veil. Her shoes were white and dainty and she carried a bouquet of lilies and white roses. She saw herself emerging from the church, blushing and happy. Everyone was throwing confetti and Marek was at her side, dapper, deferential and proud. He was as handsome as Anthony Armstrong-Jones, but in a foreign kind of way. They climbed together into a big black car.

The whole village, including Gloria, had turned out for her big day. Joyce needed Gloria in her fantasy, to show off her triumph. She pictured her diminished in a doorway, looking jealous and surprised. There was only one person absent from the scene. As the car drove away, Joyce imagined, in the periphery of her vision, a dank shuttered building. It might have been a prison, or possibly a convent. Nadezhda peeped out from behind bars looking woebegone and haggard.

At that moment there was a noise on the stairs. Kathleen appeared. Joyce jumped with surprise. 'Why aren't you at school?'

'School? It's the holidays.'

'I'm doing your dress.'

Kathleen stared at the material. She was horrified. 'That's a curtain.'

'That's best quality velvet, at least ten bob a yard. So don't complain.'

'What's it going to be like? I wanted a tartan pinafore with a black polo neck.'

Joyce snorted. 'Don't be stupid. Who d'you think you are? Bloody Gloria?'

'I don't want to look babyish.'

'It's going to be an alice blue gown. Like in the picture. You'll be Princess Anne. As long as you do something about these rat's tails.' She grabbed one of Kathleen's little plaits and pulled her roughly towards her.

'Ow!' exclaimed the girl.

Joyce picked up her tape measure and wrapped it around Kathleen's chest. 'Hmm,' she murmured. She measured her waist and the distance between her collarbone and knee. 'You've grown.'

'I'll be a teenager soon. I'm in my thirteenth year.'

Joyce pursed her lips. 'Don't say that. You make me feel old.'

Billy Fishboy was at Jinny Hoolets. Despite the rain, a group of his young friends from the Cub Scouts were careering down one of the pitheaps on sledges and tin trays. They shrieked and yelled and flung up damp dust, which made their faces black. 'Watch me Bagheera!' shouted the smallest lad to Billy as he tried to stand on his head, his tray sliding crazily from side to side on its descent.

Below him, Billy smiled and crouched down on one knee, holding his camera up to his eyes. Although the light was poor and the sky thick with cloud, he wore a pair of heavy, square-tinted glasses, which were for show rather than to correct his eyesight. Billy had bought these after seeing someone wearing them in a French film, at the Essoldo. His hair was stuck to his head with the drizzle and his fashionable cheap raincoat was soaked. He took out a cap from his pocket and put it on. It was a different shape to the caps worn by other men in the village and it was blue denim. His winkle-picker shoes with their long, pointed toes and side zips were caked in coal. He took his shot and wound on the film.

'Take one of me, Bagheera,' entreated another boy, pulling his sledge up the groove that had been worn into the heap. He grinned and his teeth were very white against his dirty face.

'All right, Geordie!' called out Billy and prepared to shoot another frame. 'This one's of you!'

Sometimes Billy joined in with the children's games, but on this occasion he didn't want to spoil his new trousers. He was popular with the village boys because he was a good sport, because he was generous with his loose change and because parents universally supported the Cub Scouts. Billy had been Bagheera for three years and everyone said he was first rate. He had plans to take the pack to camp, but had to convince Akela that this was feasible. Akela adhered to tradition and the young Cubs had never been away before. Billy argued that there had to be a first time for everything. He knew that the older Boy Scout Troup had tents and equipment, which the youngsters would be able to borrow, so no expense would be involved. He hoped to persuade his senior and get the trip organized for the Easter holidays. He fancied going to Barnard Castle or possibly Corbridge – neither place was very far.

The trays and sledges whooshed past, churning and spraying the spoil as if it was black snow. Billy stumbled a little as he tried to climb high enough to get a picture of all the boys together. At the summit he could see over to the Koninskys' house. It crouched next to the grimy, morbid pond. God in Heaven, he thought. He deliberately turned his back on its dim lights, the thin plume of smoke from its chimney. He took off his cap and stroked his hair, trying to arrange it satisfactorily. He hummed along to the theme tune from the current feature at the cinema; *Summer Holiday*. The jaunty, carefree rhythm was stuck in his mind. For these few minutes of fun with his pals, he didn't want to think about Marek, about Marek and Gloria, about Gloria's death. He thought about this all the rest of the time. He needed a break.

In the early afternoon, Kathleen took her pocket money and caught a bus to Quaking Houses. Rain hammered on the windscreen and the big wipers churned rhythmically. She was the only passenger, so the bus bounced and rattled along the half-flooded road, creating great waves through the puddles. She sat at the back and rubbed the window with her sleeve. The pit headstock disappeared with the village, and the railway lines, the heaps of spoil, the loaded wagons grinding east towards the coast. The landscape turned from black to green, as open countryside appeared, then after a while it went black again, as the road crossed the border of another, neighbouring mine. Black-green-black-green, thought Kathleen, as the engine throbbed and the driver crunched the gears. Mines, houses, fields, farms, fields, houses, mines. She sighed. Rain. Black-green.

After a while a motor scooter caught up with the bus and travelled between, but untouched by the twin arcs of spray. The rider was a woman. Kathleen stared at her through the back window. She's on Billy Fishboy's Vespa, she thought, surprised. I'm surprised he's allowed her to borrow it. She squinted through the spattered glass at the unknown, impassive face. The stranger had wet cheeks, which were streaked with rouge. Black artificial-looking hair poked out from under her helmet. Her face is the image of Billy, decided Kathleen. At that moment the

Vespa groaned and overtook the bus in a burst of speed. Kathleen stood up and stared through the windscreen at the back of the departing figure. She was wearing a narrow grey skirt in a fashionable cut below a pretend leather jacket. It was puzzling. He must have a sister in another village. Or maybe a cousin. She's exactly like Billy Fishboy, dressed up in women's clothes.

Kathleen alighted and at the end of the road there was a house, which had a sign saying 'Durham Constabulary'. She stood outside hesitantly. Water ran down her face and down her legs and into her shoes. She had been expecting a proper office with a counter, 'wanted' posters on the wall and maybe, at the back, cells. Instead, this looked like an ordinary dwelling, except it was very new and stood alone. It had a normal front door and curtains at the windows. Bedraggled chrysanthemums and dahlias collapsed in the front garden. She took a deep breath and rang the bell.

Inspector Glen answered. He was in his shirt sleeves and his trousers were hoisted above his belly with red braces. His tie was loosened and he had a napkin tucked into the collar of his shirt. He raised his eyebrows. There was a smell of frying bacon.

'Mission control,' said Kathleen, trying to be humorous. She'd planned to say this. 'Reading you loud and clear.'

The policeman stepped aside and gestured her indoors. 'Roger. This is Friendship Seven. Standing by.'

Kathleen handed him her coat and wiped her feet. She entered a prim but modern sitting room.

'I'll just finish my lunch,' he called out, 'I won't be a minute.'

She sat on the edge of a floral sofa. There was a big bay window, streaked with rain, an electric fire with fake coals and a carpet, which went right up to the walls. On the mantelpiece were brass ornaments and a colour photograph of two small children. This is nice, but I wonder where the criminals are kept she pondered. There was a rectangular cabinet in one corner, with sliding doors. It's a television set she decided. She picked up a copy of *Reader's Digest* and glanced through it. She felt as if she was at the dentist's.

Inspector Glen reappeared with a drink of lemonade. He'd removed his napkin. 'Here you are,' he muttered, gruffly. He sat down heavily, in an armchair.

She took the glass. 'Roger, Friendship Seven. Over.'

His face was a deeper purple than ever. 'Go ahead, Cape. I am receiving you. Over. Where's your camera today?'

Kathleen drank some of the sweet liquid, then put the glass carefully on a coffee table. She paused. 'I've come about my Auntie Gloria.'

There was a silence. Kathleen looked at a clock on the wall. Unlike the one in First Street, it was electric, with a plastic rim and the pointer moved in soundless, even jerks.

'I see.'

Kathleen steadied her breath, then continued. 'I don't think she killed herself.'

There was another long pause. This is awful, she thought to herself.

'I see.'

'She . . . had no reason.'

Inspector Glen fastened his tie. 'I don't think she killed herself either.'

Encouraged, Kathleen continued. She'd been right. The policeman was on her side. 'She had big plans. She was a modern girl. She wanted to expand the hairdressing. I told you. She was a stylist.'

The policeman gave her a steady look. 'I'm treating the death as suspicious. That's no secret.'

Kathleen remembered that the Duty Constable had said this, by the pond. 'Suspicious?'

'We've got the post-mortem results. Do you know what that means?'

'Yes.'

'Gloria drowned but I'm not happy. There may have been foul play.'

'Foul play,' repeated Kathleen, considering the words. Without meaning to, she saw a line of dancing chickens. She tried not to smile.

The policeman looked at her steadily. 'There was, of course, the question of the message on the mirror. Forensic tests for fingerprints have shown hers, as well as . . . others.'

'What others?'

'I'm not at liberty to say. But your auntie's fingerprints were on the mirror. Next to the message.'

Kathleen was impatient. 'Well, they would be, wouldn't they? She worked there, right next to it, five and a half days a week.'

The policeman nodded.

Kathleen's mind slipped back quickly into another gear. 'Anyway, Gloria didn't use dark lipstick. She used very pale, chalky lipstick like the models in the fashion magazines. And that wasn't her writing. Her writing was small and neat. She was never messy. Never.'

Inspector Glen seemed very interested. He leaned forward, towards her, his fingertips together. 'That's very helpful, my dear.'

'She was going to open another salon.'

'That's correct. She'd signed the lease for premises in Gateshead.'

Kathleen gasped again. 'See! I was right! I knew it!'

'Is there anything else you want to tell me?'

Kathleen paused. She remembered Da's anger at her interference. She decided she had nothing to lose. Not here, with this man. He was doing his job, after all. He didn't know Gloria. He was uninvolved. 'My Auntie Gloria was having an affair.'

He coughed, as if he was offended. 'She had a boyfriend. Mr Fisher. At the cinema. I've talked to him.'

'No, not him.' She paused. 'Well yes, she did ride around on the back of his Vespa and go to a blues club in Sunderland sometimes, but I've heard–' She swallowed. 'I've heard that they weren't, they weren't actually–' Kathleen's voice trailed away.

The policeman interrupted. 'I understand. Go on.'

'Gloria was having an affair with Marek Koninsky. He lives at Jinny Hoolets. Down by the pond. Where . . . where the body was found.'

Inspector Glen stood up, took a notebook from the pocket of his jacket, which was on the back of a chair, then sat down again. He took a pencil from inside a little fold in the notebook and licked it. 'Go on.'

'I don't know what she thought she was doing. I mean . . . Billy Fishboy's nice.' Kathleen was suddenly on the verge of tears. 'Mr Koninsky is a horrible man. He might be going to close down the pit and throw everybody out of work. That's what he's here for. To check the seams for coal.'

Inspector Glen wrote slowly. 'How do you know about this . . . relationship?'

'I'd rather not say.'

'You won't be mentioned. As the source of this information.'

'My Auntie Joyce knows about it, but you mustn't tell her I've spoken to you. And my friend Petra. That's Petra Koninsky. She told me. But she wouldn't want her parents to know she's been talking about it.'

'And do you think it's important? This affair?'

'I think . . . I think—' Kathleen felt the enormity of what she was saying. Her heart pitter-pattered and to her horror, tears began to run down her face. She licked them and then wiped them with her hands. She hated crying in front of people. She took a short drink of lemonade. 'I think Mrs Koninsky might have tried to hurt Gloria. I don't know. Maybe she held her under the water, or something, in the dark. She knows all the paths around there, all the muddy bits, the dry bits, the pond itself. And she's mad. I'm really scared of her. Have you seen her? She's off her head. She's stark raving bonkers.'

The policeman paused and frowned. 'This is a very serious allegation, Kathleen. A very serious allegation indeed.'

At that moment the phone rang. Inspector Glen got up with difficulty, and went out to the hall. After a few brief monosyllables, he returned. He sat down and raised his eyebrows.

Kathleen felt reprimanded again, but not so seriously as she had when she'd tried to talk to Da. Her tears had dried. 'Yes, well,' she said sullenly. 'That's what I think, anyway.' She dropped her voice to a mutter. She used a modern phrase favoured by Petra. 'Take it or leave it.'

'Tell me what you know about Mr Fisher.'

Kathleen's voice came out in a rush. 'Oh, he didn't do it. He wouldn't hurt a fly.' She remembered Billy's kindness when he'd shown her the Pathe News. She remembered wanting to kiss him.

'Do you know him well?'

'No. Not well.'

'Tell me about him.'

'He helps out at the Cub Scouts. He's got a great camera. It's German. He does his own developing and printing upstairs at the cinema. He's got a dark room. He does mine.' She swallowed the rest of her drink. 'He likes American darkie music, lives with his mother. She used to be a teacher in our school. He was never going to go down the pit.'

'And your auntie spent a lot of time with him?'

'Oh, yes. But he was younger than she was. And not as . . . not as—'

'Go on.'

Kathleen hesitated. 'Brainy. Gloria was a brain-box, like me. She made things happen. She wouldn't have stayed in the village. She was too go-ahead for the village. Billy Fishboy's a bit of a stick in the mud. He's boring. Gloria was . . . well you know . . . She wouldn't have married Billy. I don't think so. She was using him really, waiting for someone better to come along.' She paused. 'Gloria told me he talked about the engagement just to please his mother. They weren't really engaged.'

'I see.'

'Can I go home now?'

The policeman glanced outside. It was still raining. 'I'll give you a lift.'

Kathleen perked up. 'In a car? A police car? Does it have lights going on and off?'

He smiled. 'Next time you want to talk to me I think your mother and father ought to be present.'

There was a silence.

'I haven't got a mother or a father.'

He stood up and put on his jacket. 'I'm sorry. I didn't realize you were an orphan. Who looks after you then?'

Kathleen followed him into the hall and put on her wet coat. 'I'm not an orphan. I live with . . . with my Da. Gloria's father. He's an astronomer. I look after myself.'

He opened the front door and pulled on his overcoat.

'Inspector Glen?' Kathleen ducked her head against the rain.

'Yes?' He adjusted his hat.

'Do you think there's going to be a war?'

Later, Kathleen took Nosey, the Jack Russell, for a walk around the rows. The rain had almost stopped but the sky remained hazy and overcast. Why did they build all these houses exactly the same? Kathleen wondered. Dominated by the high metal headstock, they looked mean and small. Prim at the front, with scrubbed steps and matching front doors, their rear sides had walled yards. Beyond these, across the back lanes there were still a few outdoor netties, shared between families, and vegetables and chickens struggled with the thin dirt and piles of disconsolate rubbish such as rusted oil drums, ash, broken down remains of sheds and abandoned furniture. No wonder my mother and father went away, she thought. Inspector Glen had a nice new house. It's the only one, for miles around. It must have been specially built by the Police Force. No one else will ever bother to build new houses here. What would be the point? Nothing else is new in this place. Even the words that come out of people's mouths have all been said a thousand times before. There's no future here, just past. No one with any sense lives here unless it's for the work and everyone knows that miners put up with cramped houses without bathrooms.

A cart rumbled past, the horses' hooves slow and weary. It was laden with free coal and the housewives were out, counting the bags in. They didn't trust the coal man and they were making sure they weren't being cheated of their ration. Kathleen looked at their pinched faces, prematurely aged by hard work. Some of them had rollers in their hair, under scarves. They wore aprons or housecoats and down-at-heel slippers. They were dowdy and narrow minded. None of them spoke to Kathleen, but she was used to this. They turned their faces away from her, as if in shame. You think you're better than me, Kathleen thought, savagely, just because my mam and dad have gone away, but I bet every single one of you has something to hide. Behind those net curtains I bet there's affairs and French Letters and all sorts of suspicious foul play. And I bet you don't even enjoy it.

She stuck out her tongue at a middle-aged matron who closed her back gate with a crash.

She passed by the Welfare Hall. This was the day the midwife and the nurse came up from Stanley to weigh the babies and check the toddlers. There was a strange purple glow coming from inside. Kathleen thought again of a nuclear attack, and an X-ray blast, which would blow away the whole village, reduce it to dust and rubble and bones – but she knew that really it was just the sun-ray treatment given to the under-fives. They sat naked under the lamps wearing special goggles on elastic. The peculiar light made them stronger, apparently. It worked alongside concentrated orange juice and cod liver oil. It went with immunization, regular bathing and warm vests with liberty bodices. Kathleen avoided the National Health Service and its practitioners. This was because as far as she knew, no one had ever taken her to the clinic when she was little and she considered it a waste of time.

Kathleen waited as Nosey sniffed around some dustbins. A group of mothers came out of the Hall, busy with pushchair hoods and umbrellas. Some of them had big, commodious prams. Others had distended bellies. They glanced at her then exchanged wordless looks with each other. They think I'm bad luck, Kathleen thought. They think I'll give their ratty little babies the evil eye. She frowned. Maybe I will.

Using the remainder of her pocket money, Kathleen bought a red lollipop and a newspaper from the corner shop. She sat on a wall, reading and sucking the sweet. The paper had a small picture of Gloria at the bottom of the front page – the same one that had been enlarged on the Tuesday edition. A few words said that police inquiries were continuing.

Kathleen didn't like to see her auntie wearing something as brief as a bikini. It seemed improper to reveal herself in this way, especially now that she was dead. She tried not to think about

Marek Koninsky reading this paper, staring at her naked stomach, her small breasts, the fold of thin material, which disappeared between her legs. He'll see this and remember her naked, she thought. His appraising, lascivious eyes came into her mind and this gave her a strange feeling which she tried to dismiss. Gloria's body is cold and in the morgue, Kathleen reminded herself. She remembered the waxy stiffness of the corpse and shuddered.

She unfolded the paper and sat on a wall. 'Medomsley to Close,' read the headlines. 'NCB Betrayal Says Union Boss'. She skipped over the main story. Underneath it said 'Mac Backs Kennedy' and detailed how Mr Macmillan and Lord Home, who was called the Foreign Secretary, were backing President Kennedy to the hilt over Cuba. It said that the moment of crisis – the first meeting between a Russian ship and an American warship – was near. It showed a picture of 'a medium range ballistic missile base in Cuba,' and said that the Americans had turned down a truce proposed by the United Nations. Her heart raced. This war might happen in Europe, she decided. Western Europe versus Eastern Europe. She remembered her history lessons. The Americans will send boat loads of GIs like the last time. She had a mental image of gum-chewing, lazy American soldiers in Germany, confronting wild men such as Cossacks with fur hats and daggers between their teeth. These were using medieval ladders to scale the heights of the Berlin Wall. Her mind wandered. Is the Berlin Wall the same thing as the Iron Curtain? she wondered. She pictured a high metal barrier, with folds. She considered taking the newspaper home for Da, but uncomfortable about events in the Atlantic, and with a sense of profligacy and daring, she dropped it in a litter bin. She set off for First Street.

As she closed the front door softly, intending to creep upstairs, she heard a raised voice in the kitchen. She froze. Oh, no, she thought, frightened. Nana's off again. And she'd been so quiet, recently.

'I never thought I'd live to see the day,' Nana shouted, emphasizing each syllable. *'I-nev-er-thought-I'd-live-to-see-the-day!'*

Kathleen hesitated in the hall. She peeped through a crack in the doorway. Nana was banging her bread tins and turning out her loaves. She did this furiously, as if engaged in an act of revenge. Her face was angry and her big shoulders squared.

Da was standing silently by the fire, leaning against the mantelpiece, in his pit clothes and ready for work. His face was hidden by his sleeve.

There was a silence. The news was playing quietly on Nana's wireless. Kathleen heard the words, coming from the sideboard, despite herself. She was unable to ignore them, they seemed connected with Nana's wrath. *A Soviet-chartered ship reached the American blockade this afternoon. It was stopped and boarded* . . . Kathleen stared at the golden bread with its perfect crusts. *Congressman John McFall said that America is prepared to act with immediate force should Cuba attempt to arm its ballistic missiles.*

Nana drew breath and recommenced. 'What does he mean? Suspicious death? Coming round here, standing on my doorstep! In broad daylight! Making remarks! We're the talk of the neighbourhood. What has that brazen hussy done now? Your damned Gloria? As if this family hasn't been dragged through the dirt enough! *Suspicious* death! Just who and what are suspicious? Exactly?'

Nana's temper was alarming. Da raised a single hand, then dropped it, knowing the gesture to be futile. He hung his head.

Nana leaned across the table her breathing suddenly laboured. 'Wasn't her *gossiping* bad enough? Wasn't it enough that she stopped my Joyce from *getting married?*' She beat on the chenille cloth with one fist. 'Now this! I won't have it!' she yelled. '*I-won't-have-it!*' She lurched towards the fireplace and grabbed her walking stick. 'And I won't have you deceiving me behind my back with loose strumpets like that *foreign* woman from Jinny Hoolets!' She raised the stick above her head, moving towards her husband.

Kathleen watched, paralysed, trying to force herself away and trying not to hear.

Da stepped back, holding up his arms against the expected blow.

Nana suddenly reeled round and slashed her walking stick along the top of the fireplace. Her china ornaments crashed to the hearth and shattered. Her photographs in their frames tumbled down. There was a flutter of playing cards, the tinkle of falling coins. She beat ineffectually against the heavy broken mantel clock, sobbing and gasping. Then she let out one long, protracted scream.

Kathleen slunk upstairs and closed her door. The shouting continued for a while, but up in the attic it was distant and muffled, and seemed no more threatening than the perpetual uneasiness, which formed the everyday backdrop of her life.

Inspector Glen's been here already, she thought. Oh dear, what have I started? What have I done? Then she remembered his phrase 'suspicious death'. The Duty Constable by the pond had used the same words. She remembered the dictionary definitions. Someone would have come anyway, she reasoned. It was only a matter of time. She looked up in her dictionary again the words 'suspicious' and 'death'. Inspector Glen needs to be down at Jinny Hoolets, she thought, not wasting his time here. That's where he needs to be asking questions. Jinny Hoolets is the key to this. She turned to the word 'foul' in the dictionary. She blinked. It said 'very dirty, filthy, disgusting'. That's Jinny Hoolets, she thought. That pond is foul. That whole place is foul. Its dirty, filthy and disgusting. Mrs Koninsky is foul too. Jinny Hoolets is where the foul play happened and that's where he'll solve the mystery. She traced the words with a finger. Underneath it said 'f. *play* – murder, treacherous violence; (sport) breach of rules'.

She closed the volume, closed her eyes, and grasped it tight in both hands. The icy fingers that had recently taken up residence around her heart closed in cruel spasm.

My Auntie Gloria was treacherously and violently murdered she thought. She felt her whole body shake with fear.

Marek Koninsky sat in the same place occupied by Kathleen earlier, in the living room of the police house at Quaking Houses. Inspector Glen had telephoned him at home and he had chosen to be interviewed here.

The officer showed him in with deference, clearly conscious of his suit, his collar and tie, his middle-class status. Marek wasn't afraid of him. He'd heard him say he was a Detective Inspector and he didn't wear a uniform, but he was old. He was probably used to nothing more than the humdrum routine of village crime, which required only basic policing. Marek sipped surreptitiously from his flask then hid it away. He listened. The policeman was now speaking in monosyllables on the phone in the hall.

Inspector Glen leant against the banister. He was overseeing one of his Detective Constables who was conducting house-to-house inquiries. 'Just get on with it,' he muttered to his subordinate. 'Don't take no for an answer. This is a murder investigation . . . Not a picnic.' He listened for a moment. 'Yes, I know. He's here. I've got him here now.' He put down the phone and faced the doorway of the living room. This Koninsky's wearing scent, he thought. What a pong.

'Thank you for coming, sir,' he said politely, sitting opposite

Marek in the armchair next to the electric fire. The room was light and airy. It was warm but not too warm.

'What can I do for you, Detective Inspector?'

The policeman made a steeple of his fingers. He could smell something above the cologne. It was spirits. He frowned and looked down. He's a bit of a dago he thought. A drinker and a dago. Handmade shoes and all. But he's a cool customer. 'I'm investigating the occurrence of a body in the pond next to your house. Not to beat about the bush, sir, I believe you were . . . intimate with the deceased.'

Marek coughed. He pulled himself upright, examined his clean nails. 'Ah. I knew her, yes.'

Inspector Glen breathed out, heavily. His tone changed. 'I've not got time for games, sonny. You were having an affair with her. She's dead. What happened?'

Marek was a little startled. He resisted the idea of having another drink. 'I . . . er . . . I . . . she was my mistress for a time. That is correct.'

Inspector Glen wrote in his notebook. 'Go on.'

'I do not want to upset my wife.'

'Your wife's no concern of mine at the moment. But you tell me the truth, straight and simple, we get this sorted out, then maybe we won't have to involve her.'

Marek hesitated. He looked at the fire, the wall clock, the closed-off cabinet that might have been a television set. 'I ended my association with Gloria over two weeks ago.'

'You finished with her?'

'Well, not exactly.'

'What exactly?'

'She finished with me, to tell you the truth.'

'As I said, the truth is what I'm interested in, Mr Koninsky.' Inspector Glen met his eye. He's a good-looking devil, he thought. Suave. He's used to having things his own way.

'Her father did not approve.'

'I see.'

'I am married man. She was an unmarried girl. Her father did not approve.'

'Go on.'

'Her father does not like me. He is a Union man. He sees me as ... as a capitalist conspirator. A hyena. He is opposing my work for the Coal Board. He told her to stop seeing me. She obeyed.'

Inspector Glen wrote for a moment. He pretended to resume his deferential manner. 'And how did you feel about this? Sir?'

'I felt ... I felt—'

'Yes?'

'I felt resigned.'

'You felt resigned?'

'That is what I said. I felt resigned.'

'You weren't upset?'

'Upset? Yes, I was quite upset. She was a fine girl. Intelligent, actually. More intelligent than most. She was attractive. She was ... what is it you say? With it? With it. Yes, I was upset.' He paused. 'But I did not kill her. She killed herself, no?'

'No.'

'I see.'

'She didn't kill herself. I think not, Mr Koninsky. No.'

Marek felt in his pocket for his flask but resisted getting it out. 'What are you suggesting?'

'I'm suggesting that she was murdered.'

Marek exhaled loudly. He slid down slightly on the settee. He closed his eyes. He seemed weary and defeated. 'Oh.'

'Have you any comments to make, sir?'

'Comments?'

Inspector Glen felt suddenly impatient. 'Where were you on

Sunday evening? Sunday night? After eleven o'clock? Where were you when it happened?'

Marek became suddenly more alert. He moved upright and sat on the edge of his seat. 'I was at home. I was at home in bed with my wife.'

'You're sure about that?'

'Absolutely.'

'And when was the last time you saw the deceased?'

'I had not seen her since the final discussion. Two weeks ago. She ended our relationship and I did not see her again. I did not try to see her again. I thought—'

'You thought?'

'I thought, there are plenty more fish in the sea.'

Inspector Glen inhaled sharply. He was offended. 'And your wife? Your wife didn't know about this affair? Is that right?'

'Oh, yes, she knew. She always knows. My wife and I . . . My wife and I, we have an understanding. She understands. She turns a blind eye, as long as—'

'As long as what?'

'As long as I don't rub her nose in it.'

Inspector Glen wrote some more and was silent. He's a cad, he thought. A dago cad. He scratched his head. 'We may need to interview your wife.'

'To establish, how you say? An alibi?'

'That is correct.'

'Will you need to discuss with her my . . . my relationship with Gloria?'

'Not necessarily.'

Marek stood up. He was taller than the policeman. 'I would appreciate it, Detective Inspector, if you would be tactful. As one man to another—'

'Don't rub her nose in it? Yes, yes, yes. I want to know who killed this young woman. That's all. I'm not interested in your sordid assignations.'

Marek looked hurt. He walked out to the front door. 'Will that be all?' he said abruptly.

'Yes.'

He left, pulling the door behind him.

The policeman heard him get into his car and drive off. He's definitely a cool customer, he thought. He thinks he can smooth-talk his way out of this, but he's not out of trouble yet. He mused over Marek's accent, his appearance, his manner. He thinks he's so clever but really all he's interested in is spirits and women ... Inspector Glen sat down heavily. Spirits and women ... He pondered and scratched his head. There's a motive somewhere. Drink and sex. The main causes of violent crime. He nodded to himself. Fisher and Koninsky. They're not out of trouble yet. Neither of them. Not in my book they're not.

There was a tap on Kathleen's door. It was Da. He entered. 'It's all right,' he said. 'She's calm. She's gone to bed.' He paused. 'You know this house gets her down. It's damp and dark and she never gets across the doors ...'

Kathleen regarded him. He always says this, she thought, every time. He has to make an excuse. He looks tired and worried. He must be late for work. He was wearing a black cotton armband over the sleeve of his work-shirt. She noticed for the first time the extent to which his hair had receded. He looks older than usual, Kathleen decided. It's all aged him, this foul play, this treacherous and filthy breach of rules. His face was pale, his eyes sad.

'What d'you think is going on?' she said, knowing he wouldn't want to talk, but anxious to communicate with him. 'The police coming here, and everything.'

'I don't know.' He came over and sat on the bed, pushing Kathleen's scrapbook to one side.

'They think that Gloria was murdered.' Kathleen tried to keep her voice level.

'There'll be an inquest.' He spoke slowly. 'That's a special court to decide what's happened.'

'I know that.'

'Until then, I don't think we should jump to conclusions.'

He's playing for time, thought Kathleen. He doesn't want to face it. He's putting off facing it. 'She wouldn't have killed herself, Da. She was going to open another salon. In Gateshead.'

Da looked at her sharply. 'How do you know that?'

'She told me,' Kathleen lied.

Da picked up the bedspread and rubbed it between his fingers. 'I hate all this,' he said. 'It's bad enough that she's dead, without all of this.'

You don't like fuss, Kathleen thought. You don't like your life disturbed. You hate emotions and feelings. You can barely manage Nana. You don't want more trouble.

'You know what you were saying, the other night?' He was hesitant.

'About the affair?'

Da looked pained. 'I think it might be better . . .' he paused. 'I think it would be better, if you didn't repeat all that, outside this house.'

Kathleen nodded.

'Marek Koninsky is a—'

'Is a what?'

'He's a womanizer and a drunk. Do you know what that means, pet?'

'Of course I do.'

'Marek Koninsky has been brought in by the Coal Board to

close down the mine. He's a traitor. A self-server. He's a man without principles, without ideals—'

'He's a bad man,' Kathleen interrupted, knowing that Da could begin one of his speeches.

'That's right. He's a bad man. I want you to stay away from him and his daughter.'

'All right.'

Da rubbed his face with his hands. He muttered to himself 'to think that a daughter of mine could have lowered herself—' He stared at her and changed tack. He said more clearly, 'Gloria wasn't involved with him. I want you to believe that. I don't want it said. I don't want to hear gossip and slander about my daughter. Is that clear, Kathleen? She was never involved with him. Yes?'

'Yes.'

They sat for a few moments in silence. Kathleen was dismayed. She decided then that she preferred the casual intimacy of their silent vigils, their love of the heavens, the way they walked along together, at night time, without speech. This embarrassing dissimulation was unbearable. To her relief, Da got up to go. Without intending to, she said something she'd never said before. 'Da?'

'Yes, pet?'

'I love you.'

He seemed close to breaking point. He ruffled her fringe. His work-worn hand felt dry and callous on her brow. He normally never touched her, but to her surprise she didn't mind. 'I know,' he replied.

She heard him blow his nose, vigorously, as he went down the stairs.

Later, after the rain stopped, Marek Koninsky stood on the brow of a low hill his hat pushed back, his hand raised, shielding his eyes from the dull glare, which hid the shape of the sun. There were low, scrubby gorse bushes behind him and an open pasture sloping below. A couple of retired pit ponies looked up at him, startled, then went back to grazing. Across the valley was the black mine and the jumble of scruffy roofs that was the village. He tried to see his own house and the pond but these were in a depression in the landscape, hidden from view. He glanced down. His trousers were a little muddy and he was wearing overshoes, which were caked in clay. He dropped his theodolite and ranging rods, sighed, took out his flask and swallowed a restorative mouthful of vodka. He glanced again at the sky.

Marek was a disappointed man but his soul was once suffused with poetry. The softened light and the gentle formation of the illuminated cloud reminded him of his spot-lit sweetheart lightly drifting across a distant stage, in a far land, years ago. In an instant he was transported to his past and could hear the romantic strains of a hundred violins, see the delicate patter of her toes, the beautiful arched curve of her back, the sophisticated, effortless symmetry of her posed, slender limbs. He was leaning in a box at the side of the stage planning to marry her. He remembered how the theatre goers had held their breath, marvelled at her grace, her poise. Her dress had been as delicate as a dove's feather, or a puff of smoke, or a cloud, he thought, watching the cirrostratus shift slightly and change, in the distant sky above the valley, above the cold field, above the relentless mine, above the grimy English settlement beyond. He returned to himself, helplessly, to the ugly prison of the present day and his wife's sadness. He wiped a tear from his eye. He pulled out his measuring tape and notebook and pencil and set off down the slope, startling the ponies, which cantered away.

*

Towards evening, Kathleen went below to eat some Sugar Pops. As she descended she checked that Nana was lying down in her room with the curtains drawn. There was a strong smell of eau de cologne and snoring. This was the normal routine after an outburst. Having cleared away, Kathleen stood in the window of the chilly parlour, staring out into the front street. The grandfather clock ticked steadily, its pendulum swinging to and fro.

Shocked by her own suspicions and discomforted by her conversation with Da, she tried to think of something pleasant. She was immediately back on the top of the sunny hill when she was a very small child, sitting astride a man's shoulders. She remembered him lifting her down in an effortless gesture into grass, which was bright and spangled with daisies. A bee settled into a purple flower, which, Kathleen decided, had probably been a clover. The lady who was with them spread out a tartan rug which was warm and soft on top of the springy grass. The air had smelt clean and the bee buzzed, contentedly.

Kathleen's mind cleared and she returned sharply to the present. A figure appeared round the corner of First Street. She was horrified. Quickly she rushed out to the passage, retrieved Da's Box Brownie from the hallstand and then repositioned herself, just behind the curtain. Nadezhda Koninsky was approaching. It was unusual for her to be seen in the village. She was wearing a man's overcoat over a trailing cotton dress, torn at the hem and white lacy gloves. Her hair was tidier than usual. Combed back from her brow, there were streaks stained yellow with nicotine. In one arm she carried a large bouquet of dead fireweed. She handled it tenderly, as if the flowers had life and beauty, whereas in reality, they were dry and brown, ugly, with even their cotton wool seeds long-shed. In her other hand she held a cigarette. She walked in a deliberate straight line, as if to do so took all her concentration. She placed her feet self-consciously, as if she knew she was watched. As she passed, she stopped and coughed delicately but lengthily into her sleeve. Her thin face was lined and drawn. Foul play, Kathleen thought and captured her on film. 'Got you,' she said aloud. She remembered her conversation in Quaking Houses, in the tidy police house. That's a very serious allegation, Kathleen, she thought to herself. A very serious allegation indeed.

She slipped outdoors and forcing herself to be brave, tailed Mrs Koninsky at a distance. Nosey ran behind. She's going to church, Kathleen decided. That's the only place up here she ever visits. She's going to speak to the priest about her sins, confess to the filthy foul play.

A Methodist chapel came into view but this she knew was not their destination. It had recently become a bingo hall and there was a garish board painted with pound signs nailed to the front portico. This was surrounded by yellow light bulbs. Despite the initial head shaking and contempt that had swept through the village, Kathleen was sure there'd be a long queue waiting for it to open at seven o'clock. Joyce had been once or twice. 'Legs eleven,' she'd joked mysteriously, on her return. 'Two fat ladies.'

Kathleen pursued Mrs Koninsky past the reconditioned chapel to the gate of the Catholic church. 'Stay,' she ordered Nosey. 'Stay!' She knew that Mrs Koninsky didn't like the Jack Russell. She didn't want him alerting her to the fact she'd been followed.

The Catholic building was still used for worship, but regarded with suspicion by most villagers. '*Stay!*' she told the dog again. She then dodged behind graves, advancing stealthily, nervously, towards the inner leather door. Her quarry pulled a flimsy scarf from her pocket and tied it around her head. She started praying aloud and disappeared into the gloom. Kathleen hesitated then followed. She was very afraid of Nadezhda Koninsky, afraid of her stained fingers, her drowning hands, but her suspicion and curiosity overcame her nerves.

There was a peculiar sweet smell just inside, which halted her progress. She took a deep, tentative breath. It was an unknown, forbidden scent. It made her think of plaster saints, sacred hearts, unlikely genuflections and the man in Rome with the high white hat, whom Nana always called the Tarry Rope. It was foreign, a little exotic. She took two steps forward. Here there were tiered banks of guttering candles, ornate carvings, darkness. In the distance there was a glitter of gold, a fold of tapestries, a suspended, painted figure on a cross, a dull suggestion of apostles in stained glass. She took off her spectacles, polished and replaced them. She was scared. Everyone in her family sneered at Catholics as if they were a crazed but dangerous sect. 'Cats', they called them, knowing they were referred to in return as 'Proddy Dogs'.

She saw Mrs Koninsky enter a wooden box with a carved roof. That's where she's going to confess her crime, Kathleen decided. That's what Catholics do. They tell Father Connor about their sins and then actually believe that his stupid prayers make everything all right. She experienced a wave of anger as she contemplated this procedure. You can't do filthy foul play and drown someone in a pond and then make it better with a bit of old Latin, she reasoned. Determined, she walked over to the confessional and pressed her ear hard against the side. She could hear only a dull rush, like water in a cistern.

At that moment she saw a group of five nuns advancing towards her down the aisle. They looked Papist and threatening in their headgear and habits. They rustled, their footsteps echoed and one of them wore a black eye patch. Another stared hard at Kathleen and raised what appeared to be a withered hand.

Her heart pounding, Kathleen dodged to the door, then

outside, through the headstones and back into normality. The smoke-laden air of Station Road tasted familiar and almost clean. Nosey cocked his leg contemptuously against the Catholic wall. Phew, she thought, hurrying away. A band of Cats, coming right for me. Nuns! *What* a lucky escape.

Kathleen shivered. She wasn't wearing a coat. She glanced over her shoulder but there was no sign of the mad Mrs Koninsky. Approaching home she saw a team of uniformed policemen knocking on doors. They were working in pairs. One or two were women and Kathleen reflected that she had never seen most of them before. Inspector Glen was leaning against his car, his hat pushed back, writing again in his notebook. She felt a rush of warmth. There's no reason why he can't be my friend, she reasoned, even if he is a man and quite old. She approached him and issued a low warning to Nosey, who dropped his tail and crossed the road, disappointed.

Despite everything, she tried to speak jauntily. 'Friendship Seven? This is Cape, are you receiving me? Over.'

The Inspector looked up and smiled. He had a red stain on his tie that was probably tomato ketchup. 'Roger, Cape,' he responded. 'Reading you loud and clear.' He closed his notebook and glanced at his officers, slowly working their way along the terrace.

Kathleen followed his gaze. 'Inquiries are continuing, affirmative? Over.'

He sighed. 'This is Friendship Seven. Standing by. We have undermanning, but inquiries continuing. Affirmative.' Then he chuckled. 'It's a little bumpy along about here.' He tapped her on the head with his pen. 'Zero-g and I feel fine.'

Kathleen was impressed. He's listened to recordings of the space mission as carefully as I have, Kathleen decided. But I must tell him. Suddenly nervous, she stood on one leg like a stork holding her foot against her bottom, raising herself on to one toe. To her relief, she didn't wobble. 'I've got perfect balance,' she said, as a preamble. 'Not only that, I have an IQ of one five nine. The highest in my school.' There was a brief silence. Kathleen took a deep breath. 'Friendship Seven, you're wasting your time here, doing this door-to-door stuff. Right at this very minute, Mrs Koninsky is with the priest confessing to the foul play. You should all go over to that Left Footer's church with tape recorders and microphones. You'd hear it all pouring out of her mouth. I've told you, she's a raving lunatic. She used to be a ballerina in Leningrad or somewhere, and now she's an ugly old housewife, stuck here at the far end of nowhere with a horrible husband and it's made her go *right* off her rocker.'

At that moment the car radio crackled loudly.

The Inspector turned and with difficulty eased his bulk into the vehicle.

'I'm telling you,' Kathleen raised her voice, 'the answer's down at Jinny Hoolets.'

'Over and out,' he said coldly, pursing his lips and meeting Kathleen's eye. He shook his head sadly, closing the door and picking up a handset.

'That's a very serious allegation, Kathleen,' she mimicked, 'a very serious allegation, indeed.' She continued on her way.

Half a mile underground, in complete darkness, Da sat at the extent of a quiet disused tunnel, finishing his bait, which was a jam sandwich, an apple and tap water in an old lemonade bottle. He was with his mate, Jonty Dickinson, both sitting on stone-dust sacks. A couple of transport boys ate alongside them, squatting on their haunches, swapping lurid stories about Saturday night's beer and accompanying darts, tarts and legovers, each trying to outdo the other. Da suddenly switched on the lamp on his helmet, rummaging in his haversack for a chocolate biscuit. One of the younger men noticed his armband. 'I'm sorry for your trouble,' he said suddenly serious and ashamed.

'Yes,' coughed the other. 'We're forgetting.' They were in awe of the older miners who were face workers, and therefore senior. They recognized Da as a union man. 'We didn't mean nothing. No disrespect.'

'Thank you for your sympathy,' said Da, with dignity.

The two youngsters self-consciously stood and moved down the tunnel towards the noise and the thick dust of the conveyor belt, which roared and rattled ceaselessly on its rollers, carrying its load of coal.

'When's the inquest?' said Jonty Dickinson.

Da tilted his head so that the beam of his lamp fell just to the side of his marra's face. Illuminated, he seemed concerned more than curious.

'A week's time. Too long for her to lie unburied.'

His friend hesitated. 'What d'you think went on?'

Da turned off his lamp. Plunged again into blackness he said, 'She killed herself in a fit of despair. We get them, don't we? She had these moods as a child, after her mother died. I thought they'd gone but they hadn't. She might have waited for it to pass but she didn't. She ended it all.' Da fastened his haversack. He leaned back against the shiny dark surface of the redundant coal wall and rubbed his eyes with the black backs of his hands. He was uncomfortable with lies and he knew this wasn't true.

'I've heard otherwise,' said Jonty, gently.

'Aye,' said Da. 'I daresay.'

'In the manset on the way out, yesterday and today, I heard her name linked with Koninsky—'

'No!' replied Da, vehemently, standing up, shouldering his bag. It was airless in the tunnel and he could feel sweat breaking on his brow. 'No! Not him! It's not so!' He strode away and Jonty heard him splashing through a stream of underground water. 'I'm going inbye,' he called which meant he was returning to work, even though he was only halfway through his break.

Later, alone in the kitchen with Joyce, Kathleen sat on her cracket, almost out of sight, turning over the pages of Nana's *People's Friend*. I should have stayed, she thought. I shouldn't have run away from those stupid old nuns. If I'd stayed I'd have heard it all and Inpector Glen would have listened. He'd have listened if I'd been able to tell him exactly. If I'd been able to say the words of her *confession*.

She read a short article on the Soviet build up of nuclear weapons, which was referred to as a stockpile. Nowhere's safe, she thought. This kitchen isn't safe, my room isn't safe, Da's shed isn't safe. She had a momentary vision of the telescope, mangled, burnt and half melted, overturned amidst a heap of rubble. One wall of the shed remained, with Da's raincoat, charred but still hanging on its hook.

Kathleen swallowed hard. Da was still at work and Nana was still in bed. Her snores resonated gently from above. Joyce sat at her sewing machine wearing only her slip. Her plump, naked shoulders glowed in the firelight. She'd put Kathleen's dress to one side and was working on her own, constructing a compli-cated series of seams, which secured the stiffeners inside the bodice of her dance dress. The machine rattled in short, sharp bursts and her mouth was a thin line of pins. Kathleen put the magazine aside and watched.

Joyce, she reflected, had no true hobbies or interests. Her sewing was merely a routine means to an end. Joyce was not a happy person and she tried to relieve her misery by going out. She attached huge importance to social events and of course the Isabella Miner's Supper, 'The Big Dance', was the most important in the village calendar by far. She was determined to be the belle of the ball. Kathleen watched as she held up the bodice. It was well crafted, with clean lines.

'Don't think I can't see you sitting there, fanny-ann,' she said to Kathleen through clenched teeth. 'Get over here and help me.' She spat out her pins, then eased the strapless corset-like structure around her bosoms.

Kathleen stepped over and gently joined the edges together at the rear. The bodice was shaped at the front like a cupid's bow. The back was low. 'It's lovely,' she murmured, trying to be agreeable. 'It fits.'

'Put some pins in, will you? Hold it together so I can see it on.'

Kathleen inserted a line of four safety pins, pulling the waist tight. This was a struggle but it was necessary to achieve a nipped in effect.

Joyce sniffed, pleased, and admired herself in the mirror of the sideboard. 'Not bad,' she agreed, smiling for an instant, turning this way and that. She looked like an hour-glass, her raised half-naked breasts as rounded as footballs, her middle a narrow bridge between their unlikely fullness and the swell of her generous hips.

Kathleen glanced at the voluminous lime-green skirts lying in a heap on the floor. Joyce caught her gaze. 'There's more can-can netting to go in underneath,' she mused, 'I thought I'd finished, then I decided, what the hell, let's have more.'

'What about sequins?'

'Do me a favour. Sequins? What d'you think I am, a Christmas bloody fairy?' but she laughed. 'Unfasten me. There's a good girl.'

Kathleen obliged, warmed by her aunt's good humour. Then she returned to her stool. She decided not to spoil the atmosphere by asking about her own dress. At least it was started. It was under way. It could wait until another time.

She leaned back against the wall. It was too warm in the room and the continuing noise of the sewing machine was soporific. She closed her eyes, drifting a little. Her mind strayed to another distant memory. It had been the prelude to the Big Dance, not the last time, but the time before that. She was sitting on the fireside rug in this kitchen, playing with cut out paper dolls, listening to Joyce asking Da to show her how to foxtrot. Joyce said she was ashamed because she'd never learned. She insisted that Gloria could manage several different dances, even though she was just a kid. 'It's a showing up,' she'd exclaimed. 'There might be nice young men from down Stanley and suchlike. Some of them work in offices! I bet they can all foxtrot. I bet they foxtrot every night of their lives.'

It had been dusk. The weather was quite warm for October and Joyce opened the window. She moved the wireless to the sill, so that it was facing outside.

'Be careful with Nan's wireless,' said Da, jovially.

She turned up the volume. The radio was tuned to the Light Programme, which played recorded dance music. The sound echoed clearly in the open air.

Kathleen climbed up on a chair, then sat on the windowsill next to the music. Because of the noise, several lights went on across the lane.

'Come on,' said Joyce, grabbing Da's hand. She was thinner then, with a ponytail. 'I've got to learn before the Big Dance.' She pulled him out into the yard.

Kathleen watched. Da's dress shirt was undone, showing the hair on his chest. He wasn't wearing a collar, and his hair, bushier then, wasn't Brylcreemed. He looked young and amused. He took hold of Joyce, outside the coal house and began guiding her through the steps. His back was straight and his head high.

Joyce wasn't sure at first. She stumbled a little and giggled but after a minute she seemed to put her trust in Da, taking her chances with the footwork and the rhythm. The music changed to what Kathleen would discover in later years to be 'Chattanooga Choo Choo'. At this point Joyce became bold. They danced faster and faster, reeling around the small space, like moths in the growing dark. Their feet flashed, but curiously, they seemed to be floating above the ground. Joyce leaned back in Da's arms as he spun her on the dizzying turns. Suddenly she called out, 'Better have your ham and eggs in Carolina!' His gold teeth gleamed as he grinned.

At that moment, there was a cold draught, the sound of a door slamming at the front of the house and the sensation of a dark figure entering the room. Kathleen slipped down under the table. Da and Joyce were oblivious. She heard Da shout, 'All aboard! Get aboard!' and glimpsed her grandmother's long thigh, her extended arm, as she leaned across to extinguish the music. Finally, she remembered covering her childish eyes with both hands and her ears with her knees.

Kathleen roused herself gratefully from this daydream and slipped off to bed, leaving Joyce to her immaculate darts and tucks.

Upstairs, she opened the camera case and turned Da's Box Brownie around and over in her hands. She checked how many exposures she'd made. Eight, it said in the little red window. The film was finished. This one didn't last long, she thought. She switched off the bedroom light and as an extra precaution crawled under her bed. She felt for the winding knob and pulled it out, then gently prised up the small button on the top of the camera. She began turning the last portion on to the take up spool. When she felt it give, she slid down the front of the camera and removed the film. Working in complete darkness, she pulled it tighter and licked the gummed tab, securing it into a roll ready for developing. She pulled herself out from under the bed and wrapped her photographs in the black rag, given to her by Da for the purpose, when he'd told her she could borrow the camera.

She switched on her bedside lamp, undressed and got under the covers, but her mind was not still, however, or peaceful. She picked up her astronomy book and read Chapter Eight which was entitled 'Aurorae and the Zodiacal Light'. It said that the aurorae's ghostly beauty is best observed with the naked eye to the north or north-west but that they are impossible to spot anywhere above street lamps or other forms of artificial light. Similarly, zodiacal light is a feeble radiance like a cone extending upwards from the hidden sun after dusk or just before dawn, but is obscured by dusty air.

I'm not going to see much of anything here, in this place, with my naked eyes, Kathleen reasoned. Not beside this twenty-four-hour mine with its lights and dust. This hard-to-see, glimmery stuff is definitely for the future.

At the dead of midnight Kathleen's imagination filled with disquieting images. She dreamed that Billy Fishboy was wearing Joyce's new dress. It was very bouffant on him, too tight around the waist and very green. The bust was nothing but two empty caves. His mouth was a garish carmine streak. 'Who are you?' Kathleen asked, blinking and realizing that she herself was completely unclothed. She tried ineffectually to cover herself. He smiled horribly. 'Who am I? What a question! Don't you even know that, fanny-ann? Don't you know anything? I'm only your mother.'

Petra was still awake at twelve o'clock, even though her mother and father were asleep upstairs. They never checked if she'd cleaned her teeth or climbed into bed or turned out her light. She roamed about, as usual, eating cream crackers, reading her father's mail, pretending to smoke.

At twelve thirty she stood in the front bay window staring out at the pond. It was dark, deserted and bleak and rain appeared to be falling. I hated you, she thought. She dragged on an unlit cigarette. You had no right to come here. She remembered Gloria's light voice tinkling from her parents' bedroom. Horrified, she'd peeped around the door. Her father was lounging on the unmade double bed, still wearing his suit, his hat and his shoes, although his tie was pulled down and his collar was undone. He was drunk and a little out of control. Gloria was laughing and going through her mother's wardrobe.

Petra remembered freezing on the spot. She knew that her father was having an affair, she'd heard arguments about it, but she never expected to see his mistress inside the house. And she knew how important the clothes in this wardrobe were to her mother. He's too drunk to stop her, she realized. He's too drunk even to care.

Gloria pulled out a silver beaded cocktail dress, then a feather-trimmed cloak. 'Oh, God,' she'd exclaimed. 'Oh, my God, look at these!' She picked a pair of crocodile shoes with long fronts and low shaped heels. 'I don't believe these!'

Marek yawned and swung his legs over to the floor.

Gloria continued her rummaging and her giggling, finding hats, shawls, a tiara, a dainty silk parasol. She loved everything she said, but she was laughing in a way that Petra knew was mocking. She's making fun of my mother she thought. It's because her things are so old. She watched Gloria replace everything, but in an untidy, haphazard way. She left tissue paper strewn around, the hats weren't returned to their boxes.

Petra retreated to her room, dismayed. Soon, she heard the careless female voice on the stairs, in the hall, then finally outside. She heard the car engine revving, its cough and splutter as her father drove Gloria home. She'd thought about going to her mother's wardrobe, tidying it, removing the evidence,

because she would come home from church and spot the interference – but she didn't. He deserves to get it in the neck, she
decided.

In the dark, in the silent house, Petra now wandered through
to her own bedroom. She placed a record on the turntable,
turned the volume down low and switched it on. It was Acker
Bilk's 'Stranger on the Shore'. The mournful notes made her
want to cry. She sat on the low sill of the bay, struggled to
push open the casement, then lit her cigarette with her mother's
stolen lighter. She tried to inhale but coughed. She threw the
cigarette outside and closed the window, quietly. She remembered the boys who had been sliding down the heaps earlier in
the day. They had probably seen her dancing in the window at
times in the past. None of them came any more. They'd been
frightened away by the stranger whose face was hidden by
sunglasses and a cap and whose body was concealed in a long
raincoat. He came at odd times, but usually every other day. He
kept well back when she was dancing but then did scary things,
like coming right up to the house, looking in the windows or
emerging unexpectedly from behind the heaps, sometimes even
in daylight. He wasn't like the old audience. He didn't obey the
rules. I'm afraid of him, she thought. I don't know who or what
he wants. Kathleen didn't believe me and she thinks I'm a know-
it-all but I don't know what to do about this. It's my own fault,
she thought. It's my own fault but I can't help it. I can't stop.
She turned on her main light and began dancing to the music,
began clumsily undressing, even though she was frightened,
even though there was nothing or no one outside, except the
grim night, the sky, the desolate pitheaps and the rain.

# FRIDAY

Kathleen sat in the window of the cold parlour, watching the rain. All morning it had squalled and eddied up and down the terrace. Housewives, laden with shopping, fought with umbrellas, their coats flapping in the gale. A horse clopped past, dragging a cart, the water bouncing off its steaming flanks.

Kathleen sighed and turned to stare at the steady, clunking pendulum of the grandfather clock. She was thinking about Gloria's teeth. They had been large, protuberant and very, very white. They were the whitest teeth in the village, the cleanest Kathleen had ever seen. She wondered if they'd been the best kept teeth in the whole world. Gloria's smile had been dazzling; it lit up everything, like gleaming stars. Her own, Kathleen reflected sadly, were naturally cream. Nana's were false, Da's were chipped with at least two made of gold and Joyce's were neglected. She thought about mad Mrs Koninsky's teeth. She couldn't remember ever having seen them because Nadezhda Koninsky never smiled but they were almost certainly fouled by her cigarettes, discoloured yellow, like her hair.

I'm going to have to do something about her, Kathleen determined. She's mental. She drowned poor Gloria by leading her like a lost sheep into the pond in the dark. And all because of Mr Koninsky and the affair. She pressed her forehead on to the glass and considered for a minute. Now Auntie Joyce has started hanging around with him. It's because he's so handsome. Maybe she'll have an affair with him as well, and Mrs Koninsky will kill her too. Somehow, I'm going to have to make Inspector Glen see the truth. He'll realize he's been on the wrong track and he'll arrest her. She felt a rush of excitement. It's up to me, she decided. I'll sort it out for Gloria's sake, because she had a beautiful smile and she was my friend.

Kathleen let her mind wander and imagined Nadezhda in an underground dungeon, chained to a wall. She was drooping and dressed in filthy rags. Father Connor appeared in his robes, holding aloft a jewelled cross and intoning in Latin. Behind him were two of the scary nuns from the church. They unfastened the weeping woman and led her down a gloomy corridor. At the end was a blank-faced statue of the Virgin Mary together with a scaffold and a rope. 'Hanged by the neck until you are dead,' Kathleen said aloud, even though she knew the death penalty was probably going to be abolished. She pictured Nadezhda Koninsky swinging like James Hanratty, only her feet were dirty and bare and her tongue poked grotesquely from between her bad teeth. It'll serve you right, she thought. You'll be dead, then Petra won't have a mother, either. She'll be exactly the same as me.

Kathleen could hear Nana in the kitchen, banking up the fire. She was heating water, preparing to scrub the house. She always did this after one of her turns. It was as if rigorous cleaning could exorcise her own personal demons in a cloud of steam and Domestos. Da was at work and Joyce had disappeared early, wearing too much dark-red lipstick and a dress and shoes entirely unsuitable for the weather.

Kathleen unfastened her hair and stood on tiptoe to see into the mirror above the fireplace. She attempted to re-braid the thin strands into a single plait but couldn't do it because there were too many short ends. Her hair was wispy and flyaway and a very unsatisfactory colour. I wish I was pretty she thought. She examined her face. It was round and small and ordinary.

Her glasses were unbecoming and her nose was broad and freckled. She gathered her hair into a rat-like pony tail and sighed. I wish I had more clothes to wear. Gloria would have helped me, she decided. Gloria was my friend and she could have helped modernize me and made me more lovely. I'm going to be a teenager next year and I'll just have to stay ugly because I don't know what else to do. She thought about Petra's unattractive make-up and teased, knotted hair. That wasn't the answer. I wish my mother would come home, she thought for the umpteenth time. It would be her job to get me some clothes and sort me out.

For some reason, the image of Marek Koninsky came into her mind. He thinks I'm plain, she decided, that is, if he's even seen me at all. Without knowing why, this notion was disturbing, humiliating. She considered it for a moment, then realized that because of his extraordinary good looks, his ability to make girls tremble at the knees, Mr Koninsky was the local arbiter, the judge, the examiner of female sex-appeal. His roving eye passed over the women of the village, selected and condoned the attractive ones and rejected the rest. At that moment, Kathleen knew suddenly and with absolute certainty that she herself would always be one of the rest – now and for ever. Not everything about the future is something to look forward to, she decided. Marek Koninsky is the future too, with his measurement of women's value, his assessing eye, his surveys, his reports and his fancy suits. 'Marek Koninsky is the future,' she whispered. 'Nuclear bombs are the future.' She felt discouraged.

She moved over to the bureau and folded down the lid. There was a smell of ink inside. She took a piece of blue notepaper and an envelope from a compartment at the rear. She uncapped Da's fountain pen. She thought for a moment, listening to the steady beat of the grandfather clock, aware without looking now, of its relentless swinging pendulum. Carefully, she inscribed her address, adding for good measure, England, Great Britain, The Commonwealth. Then, in her best writing she continued.

*Dear Major Glenn,*

*I am a twelve-year-old girl from England. I am very interested in orbital flight, space exploration and the solar system, especially the circumpolar constellations. I have many pictures of Friendship Seven, the Atlas Rocket and the Mercury Capsule. I thought your journey in February was magnificent. I have myself made serious lunar observations. I intend one day to be an astronaut like you. I hope you don't mind my saying this but I always used to think that it might be better if you worked alongside Major Gagarin and Captain Titov, instead of being in a Space Race with the Russians. However, I can see now that this is impossible. Do you think there's going to be a war?*

*Yours sincerely . . .*

She signed her name with a flourish, then printed it neatly. She folded the sheet and placed it in the envelope, licking it, then sealing it. She addressed it to *Major John Glenn, Astronaut, Cape Canaveral, United States of America.* She remembered President Kennedy's words on the wireless and added *The Western Hemisphere.*

In a tiny drawer at the side of the desk there was a sheet of postage stamps. She tore off five and stuck them on the envelope, carefully writing below *Par Avion.* She regarded the letter for a moment, trying to imagine this row of Queens' heads in her hero's well-nourished, republican hands. She felt calmer. 'Well, I'll be darned,' she imagined him saying. 'All the way from liddle old England!'

*

Joyce lay naked with Marek in the corner of the barn at Jinny Hoolets. The straw and rough blankets were scratchy on her back and thighs but she was laughing. He was unclothed except for his shirt and he held her close in one arm and whispered in her ear. He took a swig from a silver flask and offered it to her but she grimaced and shook her head. He put this to one side and stroked her stomach and breasts, murmuring some more words before biting her gently on the neck. His hand wandered to her pubic hair, which he pulled gently. Pretending to be modest, she pulled the covers up to her chin but this exposed her feet and calves. She giggled again into his chest. Her hair was tousled and half hid her face. Marek pushed the blankets partially aside and nuzzled her breasts, sucking each nipple in turn. 'I don't want to,' she said, with fake reluctance. He raised his head and grasped her hand, pulling it towards his body and placing it between his legs. 'You have a lot to learn,' he said loudly then sighed as she obliged. She fumbled a little and grasped him more firmly. He whispered in her ear again. 'No!' she protested. 'In her mouth? Never! I don't believe she did that either.' She laughed again. 'You're a liar, Marek Koninsky!'

The barn was dim and scented by vodka and Marek's cologne but despite the inclement autumn weather it was dry. Ancient bird droppings stained both walls and beams from the days before the owls flew away to look for a habitat free from coal. It was a cool, mysterious place which had been entirely ignored by everyone until Marek decided to make use of it. It hadn't stored hay for more than sixty years.

Joyce contemplated this man's perfect features, his red cupid's bow upper lip, his arched, poetic eyebrows. She concentrated on pleasing him. Even though he was married and a Catholic, she could hardly believe her luck. He was known as the best looking man for miles around. He was better than Omar Sharif, President Kennedy or even Billy Fury. He was secretly admired, desired even by the miners' wives who feared his occupation. Not only that, he'd first been Gloria's lover. Now he was hers. 'D'you like that?' she whispered, rubbing him harder. 'Am I doing it right?'

Outside, in the storm, Nadezhda leaned against the barn wall, coughing quietly, looking through the open hole that was the window. She was wearing a soaked cotton dress and her shoulders were wrapped in a musty shawl. Her hopeless hair hung in strands and her legs were bare. She had been standing there for some time. On her feet were muddy ballet shoes. She could see her husband and Joyce in the corner but she was sure she was out of their line of vision. She strained to hear their words but only a few were audible. Her face was drawn and her mouth was a thin line. Water ran down her cheeks and dripped from her nose and chin. It was a mixture of rain and tears. Her expression was one of pain rather than anger.

Marek groaned. 'Do that some more,' he said. 'I am almost ready for you again.'

Joyce rolled on to her side and continued for a moment then Marek sought her mouth with his, bruising her lips, grazing her face with the dark shadow on his chin, pushing her roughly on to her back. Breathing heavily, he eased himself on top, kicking the blankets entirely away. He quickly entered her. At the same moment he shouted some aggressive words in a language that Joyce didn't understand.

From outside, Nadezhda watched his off-white rear moving up and down excitedly below the stark brightness of his best shirt, which she had ironed the previous day. He was fervent, hasty. She could see little of the woman now, except both her unmoving legs, open wide to receive him. After a moment Joyce began uttering small cries. Nadezhda stood very still in the rain until she knew her husband's passion was satisfied for the second time. Then she turned and picked her sodden way along the pond's edge, back to the house.

Marek exhaled loudly then slid off Joyce and lay on his back, staring at the wooden roof supports above. They were riddled with worm but still solid. He rubbed his eyes.

She hesitated for a minute, maybe two. 'Do you care about me?' she asked, pulling the covers over them both, trying to nestle low into his side. She was warm but she wanted to be held close again. 'Do you, Marek?'

He didn't answer. He stretched his arms then pillowed his head in his hands. His handsome cheeks were a little flushed, his nostrils were dilated and his black eyes were unreadable. After a minute he sat up and drained his flask.

The colliery undermanager sat in his poky office, waiting for a tap on his door. He was expecting a visit from a prominent member of the Lodge, the District Secretary, and he wasn't looking forward to it. He knew the man was persistent and well informed and that he had the respect of the members. He knew he'd refused promotion, saying it would be class betrayal. Despite everything, he actually liked the fellow. He sighed. There was a gentle rap. Let's get this over with, he thought to himself.

Da entered. The undermanager saw his black armband first, then the hollowed out bruises under his eyes, the tight lips. He remembered. 'I'm deeply sorry about your sad loss,' he said. 'I'd like to extend the sympathy of all the management.'

Da nodded.

'Sit down, sit down. What can I do for you?' He bustled about, shifting files and other paperwork. He knew very well what the man wanted. He moved uneasily behind his desk and perched on the arm of his chair.

Da remained standing and got straight to the point. 'Sir, this is unofficial but we want a meeting with you and the manager. I'm here now to put you in the picture. It's about Koninsky.'

'Ah. Yes. Of course.'

'We don't want him here.'

The undermanager looked nonplussed.

'We want him out of here, somewhere else, not on the Durham coalfield.'

'Mr Koninsky is merely carrying out essential surveys—'

'I know what he's doing, sir. I'm not daft.' Da paused. 'He's measuring, taking samples and drilling. He's ahead with the explosives long before the hewers. He's closed down Medomsley and he's looking for an excuse to shut us. He's ringing the death knell for this colliery.'

The undermanager stared at Da's armband and coughed into his hand. There was a silence. 'That's not my understanding of his role.'

Da responded quietly but angrily. 'He's got a record, man! Look at his history. I've checked him out, done my homework. He's bad news. We want him gone, on a fast train to nowhere. We're not co-operating with him, we're not working with him below ground or anywhere else around this pit.' His expression remained mild but there was no mistaking the menace in his attitude. 'We've got district support. You know what that means.' His hands were on his hips. He dropped them in a placatory gesture and raised his palms. 'Look, neither of us wants a strike. You don't and we don't. You can't afford it and the men can't afford it. I'm just laying it on the line. You know what our demand is and we don't want deadlock when we meet officially. That would do neither party any good.'

The undermanager stared at his desk. 'I can't help you on this one. It's way above my head.'

'Well talk to someone who can. I mean it, sir. It's serious. We want rid of Koninsky. And that's the beginning and end of it.'

Da turned and left the room. He went down the wooden stairs and across to the pithead. The onsetter opened the cage and gave him his token. As he plummeted into the depths of the earth he thought about Koninsky and his daughter. Still angry from his discussion in the office, he felt bitter. This was a rare emotion for Da, usually only brought about by a sense of injustice, but once aroused it was difficult to quell. He tried but failed to dispel an image of his enemy fondling Gloria's lovely short blonde hair, kissing her on the mouth. His wrath welled even higher. What did she think she was doing, he asked himself for the hundredth time. She wasted herself, she just threw herself away on him. He pushed the door to the bottom of the shaft and switched on his lamp. 'That Koninsky. I'll see him in hell,' he muttered. 'I'll see him in hell before he does any more harm.' He kicked a stone, sending it skimming down the tunnel.

Da set off towards the coal face, two miles away. He was alone, behind his marras on the morning shift and he'd have to walk. His resentment had now become free floating, indiscriminate and at that moment he thought of his second wife.

Da had married his landlady within three months of coming north. He didn't love her but she'd seemed an honest woman and a good housekeeper and his daughter needed a mother. The other young girl in the home had appeared as a bonus. He thought she'd be a friend for Gloria. He'd imagined he was doing the best possible thing for everyone concerned. Then, within weeks of the wedding, Nana started accusing him. She followed him, searched his pockets, his shed, examined his clothes with a reading glass, spied on him in meetings, around the door of the pub, questioned him ceaselessly about his movements. She was convinced that he was having affairs with half the women in the village. He became a figure of fun amongst the men, then he was pitied, but eventually he gained the respect of most of those around him through his hard work, his intelligence and his dedication to the union.

Over the years, his wife hadn't let up; in fact she'd got worse. Now she was saying he was seeing Koninsky's wife. The fact that Nana never ventured outside spared him humiliation in the street, and this was a small blessing, but her venom indoors had become unpredictable and wild. He thought about the recent scene, provoked by the police inquiry about his daughter. He'd been angry with Gloria, but then he'd had a reason. His wife's response had been callous and groundless. The injustice of it, the complete lack of sympathy, the accusations flung at the dead girl, the unmitigated selfishness of her words suddenly made his blood boil. I've had about just as much as I can stand, he decided.

He recalled his wife's tantrum. She insisted that Gloria gossiped about the family and laughed about them all behind their backs. He doubted if this was true. She said she'd spoiled Joyce's chances of getting married. He was sure this had just been a silly girlish spat, years before. He never normally retaliated against his wife's taunting, but now he made a fist and punched hard the palm of his other hand. He ducked under a low prop, brushed against the side of the tunnel, swivelled to avoid a trickle of water from above. His boots sounded metallic on the uneven stone. You evil old bitch, he thought. He was shocked by this phrase, which had entered his mind unbidden and sounded like a curse. You evil old bitch. You berated me and yelled at me and accused me of made-up crimes, even in the depths of my grief. You've no respect. He rubbed his eyes with the back of his hand. He let out his breath in a gasp. I'll pay you back for this.

That afternoon, Nana was still on her hands and knees, despite the pain in her joints. With long, rhythmic strokes, she washed the uncarpeted floor of the passage, singing furiously. Her body moved back and forth as she grasped the scrubbing brush in both hands. 'My old man said follow the van and don't dilly-dally on the way!' The normal smell of damp in the hallway was overpowered. Her eyes were poor, but working instinctively she'd already washed down the walls, the stair rails, even the ceiling. The staircarpet had been freed from its rods and it was hanging outside, sorry in the rain, where it had been punished earlier with a cane beater.

Kathleen edged past, nervous, holding her shoes. The foaming floor soaked her socks. 'I'm away out,' she said. 'D'you need a message?'

Nana stopped and straightened her back, easing it with one hand. Her thin face glowed with exertion. Her hair was rolled in metal curlers. She stared at her granddaughter in a hostile way, then shook her head. Kathleen opened the front door and escaped.

She was wearing her school raincoat and she raised the hood against the driving weather. On the corner, she dropped her letter into a post box. There was no one about except for a teenage boy delivering tea, door to door, from a large wicker basket. He was wearing a cap and a white overall, which was several sizes too big and he was attempting to keep his tea dry with his sleeve. He winked at Kathleen as she passed and she felt her cheeks burn. 'I like the hood,' he said, contemptuously.

Kathleen felt a wave of bitterness towards both him and his lowly occupation. She remembered a phrase of Gloria's. There's no beauty in his life, she thought. And I'll show him. I'll show everybody here, when I finally circumnavigate the planet.

Kathleen was headed for the prefabs at the edge of the village. She knocked on the door of number seven Memorial Avenue, which was named after the statue of the dead soldier who stood grimly, leaning on his rifle, above the corner. Auntie Molly opened up cautiously. Immediately Kathleen noticed that her hair was blue. She'd used something on it – something which Gloria called a blue rinse. 'Hello,' said Kathleen, shyly. 'Can I come in?'

Auntie Molly clucked anxiously, beckoning her goddaughter inside, out of the unceasing rain. 'Yes, yes, yes,' she said, 'wipe your feet, give me your coat, sit yourself next to the fire. My goodness, what weather! Blinking cats and dogs!' She looked Kathleen up and down. 'What a surprise!' She was wearing a nylon housecoat and lots of make-up.

Kathleen entered the small front room. It was like a doll's house. Auntie Molly didn't save it for 'best' like most people did with their parlours, because apart from her bedroom, it was the only room she had. Instead of a cosy back kitchen with a range she had something called a kitchenette, which was very modern but was merely a cupboard with a sink and a gas cooker.

Kathleen sat next to the roaring fire and sighed. She hardly ever spoke to Auntie Molly but she liked it here. She'd visited several times before, as a matter of duty, accompanied by Joyce. She heard the kettle being filled and a rattle of crockery. She looked around. The wall above the fireplace gleamed with polished horse brasses. The mantelpiece, sideboard and china cabinet were crammed with small glass animals. There were hundreds of them in an assortment of colours. Kathleen knew they were dusted every day. The sofa was piled with hand-embroidered cushions, the net curtains were gathered and trimmed like old-fashioned underwear. It was a very feminine place. Auntie Molly lived alone. Her husband, a miner had been crushed below ground, years before, when they were newly married. She was a cousin of Nana, but not a close cousin. They were both related to the woman in Rhodesia who sent Kathleen birthday cards and boxes of exotic candied fruits. Auntie Molly was herself very feminine and used lavender bath cubes, Pond's Cold Cream. She always wore fluffy gold-trimmed mules indoors, which struck Kathleen as decadent and frivolous. Auntie Molly was Nana's only friend, but Nana still criticized her. She said she had more money than sense.

The rain spattered the window. It was becoming dark, although the day had never managed to lighten. Kathleen picked up a copy of the local weekly newspaper. Molly bought it because of the crossword and was mocked by Nana who said, of course, that it was a waste of sixpence. When Molly finished with it, she rolled it in a special wrapper and sent it off to Rhodesia. Kathleen often wondered if all those black people, under a yellow sky, who could barely read the words finally passed around Auntie Molly's old papers when they were weeks out of date. Stanley United must amaze them, she thought. I bet they can't believe the Problem Page.

The headline said '*Stalemate Turns to Fear*'. Kathleen glanced through the report, which mentioned that Soviet troops in Cuba were working around the clock to assemble their ballistic missiles, even though Khrushchev said a peaceful solution to the crisis needed to be found. She read that Americans were discussing food reserves and were calling for an all-out invasion of Cuba. The article ended by saying that America is bristling and ready for war.

Molly reappeared with a tray. She'd removed her housecoat. She carried part of her china tea set and a plate of chocolate biscuits. 'Well! What a surprise!' she said again. 'You're just in time.' She fussed with the cups and milk jug, as if Kathleen was a proper guest.

'I hope you don't mind,' muttered Kathleen. It was the first time she had called here alone.

'No school today?'

'Holidays.'

'I see.' Molly sat on a velvet pouffe and poured the tea.

She squinted at her tiny watch. 'It's on in a few minutes.' She gestured to a wooden cabinet in the corner.

Kathleen realized she meant the television set. Auntie Molly was the only person she knew who owned one, except perhaps Inspector Glen.

'It's a film about Uganda getting its independence.'

Kathleen frowned, puzzled. 'Uganda?' Auntie Molly was not normally interested in world news.

'The Duke and Duchess of Kent. They took the place of Her Majesty two weeks ago.' She moved to the set, opened its sliding wooden doors and switched it on. A bright dot appeared in the centre of the screen and classical music began playing. 'The film is on today. You've timed it just right, Kathleen.'

Kathleen was surprised that Auntie Molly hadn't mentioned the drowning. 'Don't you think it's sad, about Auntie Gloria?'

Molly nodded. She didn't reply. They both watched the screen as the set warmed up.

*Auntie Molly doesn't want to talk about it*, she thought. *She's embarrassed.*

Kathleen knew that Molly was preoccupied with the Royal Family. She kept several scrapbooks; one devoted to Her Majesty, one for each of the Royal children, one for the Queen Mother and another for subsidiary Royals. She combed newspapers and magazines for articles and pictures and was very knowledgeable about their genealogy, their interests and their official engagements.

She continued, 'Mind you, I don't know what Her Majesty thinks she's doing, giving all these countries away. She's given away most of the world, it seems to me. She won't have hardly any countries left soon and then where will she be? She'll be Queen of nothing.'

'Well, there *is* the Commonwealth,' ventured Kathleen, who was never short of an opinion. 'She's still head of that.'

Molly looked offended. She wasn't used to being contradicted. 'It's not the same,' she insisted, a note of petulance in her voice.

Kathleen picked up her cup and a chocolate biscuit, aware of the need to be polite. The National Anthem began playing and a picture flickered then took shape on the screen. It was a big white building with a flagpole. The Union Jack hung limply in the inappropriate African heat.

'That must be the governor's mansion,' said Molly sadly. 'He'll be on his way home now.'

A small black man with a very long name appeared in an embroidered robe. He was carrying a cane with a fat feather attached. This was the new head of state, informed the announcer, in tones of disbelief. The black man smiled broadly and happily as the Duke and Duchess of Kent emerged from a car. Auntie Molly gasped. 'She's so radiant!' Kathleen stared. The Duchess was wearing a matching chiffon floral dress and coat, a string of pearls and an onion hat. Her husband was covered in medals. Everyone wore white gloves. The scene changed to the Scots Guards marching and blowing bagpipes and then it was night, with the Duchess on the Duke's arm, sheathed in silk, diamonds in her hair. 'A fairytale!' enthused Molly.

Kathleen's eyes were glued to the screen. I wish we had a television, she thought. The announcer explained that at exactly midnight that night, Uganda had become a new young state. The British flag was lowered and its replacement was raised. This was described as red, black and gold and it fluttered for a second, heroically. There was a lot of cheering and the 4th battalion rifles fired their guns into the air. The Duke and Duchess looked very pale and rather small amongst the excited crowds of Africans.

Kathleen sipped her scalding tea. She remembered being

taken to see the Queen Mother when she was small. Auntie Molly had worn her own best costume and hat and they'd travelled on a bus to Durham. They'd stood at the side of a road with their Union Jacks and it had snowed. They waited a long time. Eventually a long black car swept past and Kathleen caught a glimpse of a pale lemon glove and a yellow shoulder. She'd waved her flag furiously but the car was gone in an instant. 'Damn and blast!' Auntie Molly had exclaimed. 'Damn and blast it!'

Kathleen remembered looking up at her godmother, puzzled.

'That was the Lady in Waiting,' Molly said, absolutely furious. 'We're on the wrong side of the damn and blasted street!'

They waited another long time for a bus back. 'Why is she called the Queen Mother?' Kathleen asked on the way home. This had been bothering her for some time. 'Why isn't she called the Queen's mother? That's what she is, isn't she? The Queen's mother?'

Auntie Molly always answered questions seriously. 'It's because she's more than just Her Majesty's mother, as important as that is. It's because she's also a Queen herself.'

'How come?'

'Because she was married to the Queen's father. And he was our former King. God bless him.'

Kathleen remembered being very pleased with Molly's explanation. The *Queen* mother, she said quietly, to herself. The *Queen* wife. The *Queen* auntie. The *Queen* nana. This new understanding seemed the most significant thing that had happened all day.

After the programme finished Molly sighed with satisfaction, turned off the set and closed its doors. Then she cleared away the tray. She disappeared for a while and there was a sound of washing up in the kitchenette. Kathleen noticed that it had become completely dark outside. She felt more relaxed than she had for days. I could fall asleep she thought. She suddenly realized that she felt much more at home here than she ever did in the house in First Street, in the kitchen with Nana and Joyce or even in her own cold room. Molly reappeared, emptied the coal scuttle into the hearth and drew the curtains. She looked at Kathleen as if she expected her to leave.

Kathleen took a deep breath. She remembered why she had come – and the fact that Auntie Molly was a truthful person. 'Can I ask you two things?'

Molly looked a little uncomfortable. 'Of course you can. Is it to do with your religious education?'

'No.'

She appeared relieved. 'Well, what is it then?'

'Do you think there's going to be a war?'

Molly crossed her legs and her nylons rasped. Her face assumed a serious expression. Her painted lips puckered into a creased circle as she considered her reply. 'There might be. But I don't think it will matter to us.'

'But we're America's allies.'

'Mr Macmillan is too sensible to drag us into it. What's it got to do with us? Nothing. Where is this place anyway?'

'It's south of the United States.'

'That's what I mean. It's miles away, on the other side of the world. I didn't vote for Mr Macmillan, of course, but he's a good man. He knows what he's doing.'

Kathleen was not reassured. She looked at Molly's stiff blue hair, her doughy powdered cheeks and her disappointed coral-pink mouth. She had a sudden vision of them melting in a flare of flame – like a plastic doll, thrown on the fire. Her face dissolved, then her hair, then her entire body. Those Russians have very big bombs, she thought. The familiar fear gripped her heart. She felt her pulse race. They're big and atomic and they can reach a long way. Maybe they can reach right across the Atlantic Ocean.

'What's the other thing?'

Kathleen hesitated then plunged ahead. 'Do you know where my mother is?'

Molly was clearly startled. She gave Kathleen an astonished glance then focused her eyes on the fireside rug. There was a long silence.

Kathleen's voice became small. She produced the christening photograph from the pocket of her skirt and held it out. 'Is she in this picture?'

Auntie Molly looked at the snapshot but didn't take it. After a while Kathleen put it away.

Molly squared her shoulders as if trying to gather her wits. She breathed in. 'Who . . . where . . . do you think she is?'

'I don't know. I've been told she's gone away. I don't know where, or why.' She paused. 'Is it because she didn't want me?' Without intending to, she sounded plaintive.

Molly answered this immediately. 'Oh, no! Not that. No!'

'Where is she then? Where's she gone?'

Auntie Molly swallowed audibly. 'Your mother wasn't—'

'Wasn't what?'

'She wasn't married.'

Kathleen let this sink in. 'You mean I haven't got a father?'

'Well, yes, you have a father. Obviously. But he wasn't married to your mother.'

'Well where are they both then?'

Molly paused again. She was still looking at the floor.

Kathleen noticed that she held the corner of her cardigan, tightly. She's nervous, she thought.

'Your mother was very young. She'd only just left school. She'd started in service, working at the vicarage over on Marley Hill.'

'She was a servant?'

'Yes. A housekeeper. I think that's the modern word.'

'She worked for a vicar?'

'Yes. The Reverend Taylor. He was a good man. He's retired now. Moved back to Northumberland. Warkworth I think it was. That's where he was from.'

'What happened?'

'Well, he kept your mother on for as long as he could. He was a kind man. A Christian. In the end the work got too much for her and she had to leave. She went into a special home for unmarried mothers.'

Kathleen had an immediate vision of a Victorian building – grey and forbidding with a heavy bolted door. 'Did she stay there? Was it like a prison?'

'I . . . I don't know.'

Kathleen thought for a moment. She bit the back of her hand. 'This Reverend Taylor. Was he my dad?'

Auntie Molly gasped. 'Oh, no! Of course not. He was a gentleman, a man of the Church. In any case, he was old.'

Kathleen pictured a girl in a maid's uniform with a frilly cap, languishing in a cell with barred windows and an empty cot.

Auntie Molly stood up and moved towards the door. She retrieved Kathleen's coat and handed it to her. 'I really don't want to discuss this, pet.' She paused. 'It's not my business. I've told you all I know. Why don't you talk to your Nana or your Auntie Joyce?'

Kathleen put on her damp coat. She followed Molly to the front door. 'Thanks for the tea,' she said, automatically. 'Thank you for having me.' Her godmother looked upset. She cares about me, Kathleen thought. She's sorry for me because I'm practically an orphan. Without thinking she said, 'Auntie Molly? There's one other thing.'

'Yes?'

Kathleen blurted out some more words. 'Did you know I was the one who found Auntie Gloria's body?'

'No!'

'Yes. In the pond. I was going to see my friend Petra Koninsky. She lives at Jinny Hoolets. I found Gloria dead and drowned. I phoned the police. It was awful.' She paused. 'I was scared. Actually . . . I'm still scared.'

Molly took two steps forward and unexpectedly encircled Kathleen in her arms. She smelled of cosmetics and something stale. Kathleen tried to step away but she was pinioned. She felt the small mound of Molly's bosom, the softness of her cheek, her lips, the dry mesh of her overtreated hair. After a few seconds she was released.

Kathleen opened the door. She noticed a tear on Molly's cheek. 'Goodbye,' she said, stepping outside into the darkness and the rain.

'Goodbye dear. You can come here you know . . . whenever you want.' She held out her hand. She was offering a pound note.

Kathleen accepted the money then turned her back on the lighted doorway and hurried away. She realized she'd wanted sympathy. However, when it was given she'd been horrified. I don't like being touched, she thought to herself. She remembered the smell of her Aunt's breath and her skin and shuddered.

She walked back through the village. She knew that having a baby without being married was a very shameful thing. I was an illegitimate baby, she thought. I'm a bastard child. She'd read these words in books. That's what Mr Dobbs meant at the Sunday School Trip when he said I was fatherless and born of sin. She thought about the neighbours and mothers in the village who never spoke to her. She remembered how her classmates never invited her to play. My mother must have been a tart, she decided. No wonder Nana hates me. I've brought shame on the family just by being born and she thinks everybody's still talking about it to this very day. She's right. They most certainly are. And my mother went and ran away and left me to carry the guilt. She had sex before marriage, like a common tart, when she was just a girl. Kathleen stopped walking for a minute and looked at the black rain-filled sky. This idea was too painful and shocking, so she tried to put it away.

Think a happy thought, she told herself. She brought to mind the hill with the green grass and the tartan rug and the bumble bee sipping from a clover and the man and the woman who she knew were her parents. This faraway lady had unpacked a picnic from her red plastic shopping bag. She'd given Kathleen a special mug with a rabbit painted on the side. Kathleen looked down the slope and watched other people climbing up and there was an expectant feeling in the air. The sun warmed her limbs and the faraway man firmed the white hat on her head. 'We don't want you to burn,' he said. 'Keep your hat on, pet.'

Kathleen smiled. She suddenly remembered her letter to John Glenn. It was in a Royal Mail van. She saw it in a sack, being loaded on to a train to London airport and then into the hold of an aeroplane. It crossed the Ocean, like Mr Krushchev's ships, landing eventually in New York. She wasn't sure what would happen next. She pictured a wagon train with cowboys and heard in her mind a song, called 'Last Train to San Fernando'. In the end, the letter approached the shining edifice of Cape Canaveral, which was surrounded in an aura of celestial light. Inside, in a huge hall, full of winking equipment, dials and telephones, it was pulled from a bundle, by a secretary who looked a little like Gloria, only she was chewing gum. Major Glenn himself approached in his military uniform, tanned, attractive, easy mannered and jovial. 'A letter for you, sir,' she said, flirting with him. He smiled his beautiful, leisurely American smile and answered, 'Why thankee kindly, ma'am.'

As Kathleen approached her house on First Street, she saw Petra. In the light from a lamp post she was hesitating and shivering outside Kathleen's front door. She had a transistor radio held up to her ear. She was wearing Gloria's plastic raincoat and her hair was covered by a disposable, polythene hat, which tied under her chin.

'What're you doing here?' she said. Petra never called at her house. She knew Kathleen was not allowed to invite anyone indoors.

Petra turned off her radio. She appeared anxious and distracted but tried to muster her usual hostility. 'You're wearing your school gabardine.'

'You're wearing a dead woman's coat and a plastic bag on your head.'

'You always look like a little kid.'

Kathleen swallowed her response to this. She didn't really want to talk to Petra, because doing so was reminding her of the evil Nadezhda. And she had just found out this terrible thing about her own mother and needed time to decide what to think about it. 'What d'you want?'

Petra was unusually nervous. 'You coming to Gallini's?'

'I've no money on me.' Kathleen felt the pound note in her pocket. She needed this to get her pictures developed, to buy another film.

'That's OK.'

Kathleen relented. They walked into the centre of the village, which was deserted and unwelcoming. The public benches were empty, the pavements and rooftops glistened, the gutters surged with water. Kathleen noticed a police car, parked down a side street. There were two men inside. As she approached she realized they were Billy Fishboy and Inspector Glen. The policeman was talking and Billy was shaking his head.

Gallini's was lit up like a refuge in a sea of darkness, its windows running with condensation. They went inside. The only customers were two teenage boys who regarded Petra with interest. Unusually for her, she failed to acknowledge this. She sat at a table with her back to them. She placed her small radio on the table between them. A middle-aged Italian woman approached silently. 'Two coffees please,' said Petra with authority.

Kathleen took off her wet coat and leant on the formica-topped table. She realized she wasn't pleased to see her friend. She wished she hadn't come. She wanted to go home and sit in her room and think about her mother. She thought of the scary Mrs Koninsky again and her desire to see her punished. 'I saw your mother yesterday,' she said. 'She was on her way to church. Was she going to confess her sins?'

Petra ignored this. The drinks arrived. Petra stirred hers with her little finger extended. Kathleen supposed she'd seen someone do this in a film. She was unusually quiet.

'What's the matter?'

'Nothing.'

'Something's the matter.'

Petra hesitated. 'I'm frightened.' She took a cigarette out of a packet and lit it with her mother's gold and diamond lighter.

Kathleen hesitated. 'Frightened of what?' She decided that Petra must be scared of her mother. She thought to herself, she's discovered her mother's a murdering fiend.

'There's someone hanging around our place. I told you. Today, he was right up at my bedroom window, looking in.' She tried to inhale and coughed and spluttered for a minute.

Kathleen stared at her friend. There was none of her usual bravado, or know-it-all, show-offy tone. She was white under her make-up and her hand trembled slightly. She seemed close to tears. It must be true, she thought. 'Did you get a good look at him?'

'No. I got such a shock, I pulled the curtains and ran upstairs.'

'Have you ever got a look at him?'

'No. He's usually back amongst the heaps. He . . . sort of . . . blends in. Once he was near the woodpile. Another time he was on the track. Sometimes I think I see him in the dark but it might be just shadows or rain. Sometimes he's over by the pond. I can't explain . . . but when he's a long way off, in the dark, it's like he belongs there—'

'Like a ghost?'

'Yes. Yes, that's right. He's been like a ghost for weeks. But recently he's started coming in daylight and coming much closer. I think—'

'What?'

'I think he's going to rape me.'

'Rape you?' Kathleen was dismayed. 'Why rape you?'

Petra seemed about to explain; she appeared to be on the verge of some great and important confidence, when she was interrupted.

'How's the dancing, Petra?' sniggered one of the teenage boys, as they got up to leave. He deliberately collided with Petra's arm.

'Get knotted.'

'How's the striptease show?' asked the other. He picked up the radio, examined it in an insolent way, replaced it, winked lasciviously, then followed his mate out the door.

'What do they mean?' enquired Kathleen, after they had disappeared. 'What are they on about?'

'Nothing,' muttered Petra. She was sullen. Her head was bowed and she stared into her coffee. She switched on her radio and it played Del Shannon's 'Runaway' in a thin, tinny, unsatisfactory way.

'They must have meant something.'

'They meant nothing, right? I've never seen those lads before in my life.' She sounded angry. She puffed furiously on her cigarette. She hummed along to the song.

Kathleen waited a while. She drank her coffee in silence. The peculiar cold fingers circled her heart again in their icy grip. Something very strange is happening, she thought. There's something really bad going on at Jinny Hoolets. It's a bad place. 'Have you told your mam and dad about this man?'

'No.'

'Why not?'

'They wouldn't be interested.' She extinguished her butt aggressively.

'They might be. They might—'

'They wouldn't be interested, right?' Petra's voice was raised. The old Italian woman looked over, surprised.

'Ssshh!' said Kathleen, embarrassed.

'Just forget it. Forget I mentioned it.' Petra leaned back in her chair and fluffed up her backcombed hair with both hands.

Kathleen finished her drink. She didn't know what to do or say.

Petra stood, pulled on Gloria's raincoat and went over to pay for the coffees. 'Where's that bastard dog of yours?' she asked on her return. She took out her rainhat and carefully eased it over her haystack hair.

'Dog?' Kathleen felt awkward. She got up, ready to leave.

'Yes dog, deaf-lugs. *Dog*. Where is it?'

'You mean Nosey? I don't know.' She thought for a minute. 'I don't think I've seen him today. Why?'

'I wondered. He's normally waiting outside of here, being a bastard nuisance.'

Kathleen let this pass. She decided she wasn't up to sparring and arguing with Petra this evening. She wanted to go home. 'I'm going home.'

Petra looked upset again. Without saying goodbye she dashed

to the door. She turned and Kathleen could see that she was crying. 'And another thing. Don't think I didn't hate your Gloria! Because I did!' With this, she ran out into the night.

Kathleen was astonished. She looked at the old Italian woman who was turning the pages of a magazine, licking her fingers each time. She suddenly felt she had failed Petra in some important, but unknown way. She blinked, feeling close to tears herself and walked towards the exit.

'Don't forget your music,' said the woman.

Kathleen went back and rescued Petra's transistor. She turned it off. 'It's my friend's,' she said. 'I'll give it to her.'

Billy Fishboy sat in a cold, semi-dark room in the police station down in Stanley, observing his profile in the shadow cast from a desk lamp. It was distorted on the wall and his nose appeared rather long. He turned his head from side to side. He took out his tinted heavy-framed pretend eyeglasses, put them on, then took them off again. He was uncomfortable, bored and dismayed. Detective Inspector Glen had brought him here in his police car after asking a lot of questions and now he'd left him in this room on his own and locked the door. There was nothing to read except a poster saying KEEP DEATH OFF THE ROADS and another about becoming a Blood Donor. His chair was hard and fastened to the floor. The window was above head-height and barred. I've been arrested, he thought. God in Heaven. I might be here all night. He was worried about his mother. The irritating tune from the film at the Essoldo repeated and repeated in his mind.

After a long delay, the Inspector returned. He was in his shirt sleeves, despite the chill and his braces hoisted his trousers high above his belly. His face was purple. He was carrying a cup of tea, but there was none for Billy.

Billy stood up. 'I need to tell my mother where I am,' Billy said. 'She'll be concerned.'

'Sit down, son. We've told her.'

Billy sat. He was tense and anxious. 'I should be at work.' He looked at his watch. 'I should have been at work ten minutes ago.'

The Inspector regarded him steadily. Fishboy, he thought. He does look like a fish. 'I've already telephoned the cinema.'

'And told them what?'

'Told them you can't come to work because you've been arrested.'

Billy flinched. 'I'll lose pay. I . . . I might lose my job.' He rested his head in his hands, his elbows propped on the desk. 'I'm very hungry.'

Inspector Glen sat down, stirred then slurped his tea and pulled a pencil from behind his ear. 'Well, I feel sorry for you, son. I really do. But it's the chef's night off tonight. No duck à l'orange. No chicken supreme with rice.'

The Detective Sergeant came in and shut the door. He stood behind his senior officer, hands behind his back.

Billy Fishboy looked from one to the other. 'You've got no right to keep me here. I haven't done anything. I don't want to talk to you. When can I go home?' He suddenly sounded very young. He smoothed his hair in his habitual, effeminate way.

The Sergeant's voice was kind. 'You help us, Mr Fisher, and we'll see what we can do.'

'Help you with what, sir? I've already told you everything. I went to work, I went home, I went to bed. I never saw her on Sunday night. I hadn't seen her since Saturday lunchtime when I went into the salon and told her I'd got tickets for Long John Baldry. I've said it a hundred times. What else can I say?'

Inspector Glen eyed him seriously. He felt inside his jacket, pulled out a big envelope, extracted the contents and fanned them out in his hands. It was a sheaf of black and white photo-graphs. He spread them on the desk in front of Billy, then leaned back as if to disassociate himself. He was suddenly like an injured and disappointed father.

Billy glanced at them then looked away.

'Well?' said Inspector Glen. His voice was cold and carried the ancient threat of a thousand hidings, stopped pocket money, cancelled treats.

Billy said nothing.

'What have you got to say about . . .' He gestured towards the desk, 'these?'

Billy shrugged. There was a long silence.

The Sergeant stared at the wall above Billy's head.

'You must have some comment,' the Inspector persisted.

Billy shook his head.

'We found *these* in your bedroom.' He sounded disgusted.

Billy swallowed. 'You've searched my bedroom?'

Inspector Glen gave a short, harsh laugh. 'Not as thoroughly as we intend to, sonny-Jim.'

'What did my mother say?'

'About what?'

'About you searching the house?'

The Sergeant replied. He was gentle, reassuring. 'She under-stood the necessity—'

Inspector Glen broke in. 'This is turning into a murder inquiry and with murder inquiries we never mess about. Right? You're in big trouble, son, and you know it.'

Billy turned and met his eye. His face was open and im-ploring. 'I haven't done anything, sir. Honest, I haven't. I've done nothing and you can't keep me here. It's not a crime to take photographs.'

The Inspector got to his feet abruptly, gathered the photos in an impatient gesture, drained his tea and made for the door. 'Lock him up!' he barked.

Joyce sat in the booth in the foyer of the Essoldo, selling tickets and giving change. A long queue snaked out into the rain. She was wearing her violet uniform with a cardigan over her shoulders, but without her hat. Her breasts and hips strained against the nylon material. She was a little slow at the arithmetic because she wasn't used to it. This was the manager's job. He appeared behind her, harassed and flustered. 'It's going to be a full house,' he muttered. 'Don't forget, when you get to seven-three-nothing-five on that green ticket roll, we're full.'

'Righty-ho.'

'I can't believe Billy's not here on Friday night. I mean . . . it's Friday night! He's never, ever let me down before!' He adjusted his bow tie, which was on a piece of elastic. His bald head was damp with perspiration.

Joyce counted out change from a ten shilling note. 'You said it. He's been arrested.' She smiled at the consternation these words created in the queue. The phrase passed down the line. Within minutes, she knew, most of the village would be informed.

'Why couldn't they arrest him on Sunday, when we're quiet? It's Friday night!' He turned towards the stairs. He was about to act as projectionist. He'd already told Joyce to get inside the auditorium as soon as possible because the ticket holders were finding their own way to their seats, stumbling and cursing in the total darkness without the aid of her torch.

'Joyce, pet!' he called out as he disappeared, his old-fashioned dinner suit flapping. 'Don't forget to put the takings in the safe.' His head reappeared over the banister. 'Joyce! I've locked the firedoors. Without you in there we'll have tearaways coming in without paying. Leave them both locked.'

'Arrested?' said a woman friend of Joyce as she handed over her money. 'Never in a million years!'

'Oh, yes,' said Joyce loftily. She was enjoying her privileged information. 'He's down in Stanley now.' She smirked. 'In handcuffs.'

People crowded into the lobby, shaking their umbrellas and hats. It was steamy inside, out of the cold. 'Arrested!' people muttered to each other. 'Billy Fisher's been arrested! The bobbies've got him in handcuffs!' The shock of this passed back and forth in waves. 'I can't believe it!' someone said. 'Not here.' They shook their heads. 'Nothing like this ever happens here!' One or two women tittered, out of nervousness rather than amusement. 'What's the world coming to?'

'I always thought he was odd,' confided Joyce's friend as she counted copper coins into her purse. 'He's always been a nancy boy.'

'Stand back!' Joyce shouted with authority from behind her glass screen. She was imitating the manager's Friday night manner. 'Stand back! An *orderly* queue for *Summer Holiday*, ladies and gents. Please!' She tore off some tickets, whispering as her friend prepared to move away, 'Bloody Gloria probably asked for it. She was far too easy with her favours.' She unwrapped a Mars Bar and took a big bite.

Nadezhda Koninsky was in her unheated bedroom sorting out her wardrobe. She never tidied anything else and her house was dirty and messy but she found it necessary to ensure that the clothes from her past life were neat, straight and categorized. This enabled her to stay calm. Since the Christless jezebel's interference almost three weeks earlier, she'd done this nine times. She still couldn't believe Gloria's impudence. 'She was curious,' Marek had said, a little desperately, trying to excuse his own failings. 'She was impressed by your fame.'

Nadezhda rattled the hangers. She counted the evening dresses and arranged them in colours. She smoothed the mink collar of a coat, opened a box and unwrapped the tissue paper from a pair of beaded, lilac ballroom pumps. She examined then replaced them carefully. She pulled out a flesh-coloured tea dress and held it to her face. It still smelled of gardenias, even after all these years. She breathed deeply. Was she imagining it? No, there was a faint trace, a hint of perfume, a memory of happiness. This was the dress she'd worn when she'd first stepped out with her husband. She held it up to the light. It was weightless, almost opaque, exquisitely cut and hand-embroidered by Hungarian peasant girls who'd worked in the dim light of the couturier's garret, ruining their eyes. 'Moscow,' she murmured, dramatically. 'Oh . . . oh . . . oh. Moscow!' She allowed the memories of her youth to flood her mind as she closed her eyes. She'd lost none of her theatrical manner. She placed the back of one hand against her brow, bending both knees, as if about to faint.

Nadezhda had danced for Stalin, Mussolini, Roosevelt and more than half the displaced aristocrats of war-torn Eastern Europe. She'd performed for Charlie Chaplin, William Randolph Hearst, and the Duke and Duchess of Windsor. At one time, at the Bolshoi, she'd been amongst the most celebrated prima ballerinas in Russia. She'd been a star. Her feet were insured for a hundred thousand roubles, she travelled Europe in her own railway carriage, she ate oysters and caviar whilst millions starved, she slept in silk sheets and wore a rare French perfume made from wild musk and hot-house gardenias. This honeyed life lasted for five years until she met Marek, until she fell from a stallion and broke her back, until she had three miscarriages and one stillbirth, until Marek drank away her money, until they had to hide from the Communists, until her looks were gone and her bones ached and she lost all hope of anything good ever happening at all.

Nadezhda couldn't remember why they'd come to England after the war. Displaced and penniless like so many, they'd been heading for America, where she knew she had friends, but somehow, instead, they'd arrived in England and got entirely stuck. Nothing had worked out. She remembered teaching in an undistinguished ballet school in Guildford until the owner was arrested for interfering with the girls. She recalled her struggle with the language, the late-night lessons in bleak classrooms with gaslights. She'd even tried translating work and piano accompanying and chorus lines in seedy backstreet theatres. Then, what seemed both a long and a short time ago she'd managed to have a healthy child. The recent years were more of a blur, the last two a nightmare, but she didn't expect to leave Jinny Hoolets. In a strange way, she was certain that Jinny Hoolets had always been her destiny. It was a place where she had to search very, very hard to find God.

Nadezhda unfastened her kimono and threw it to one side. Her underwear was ragged and baggy, her stomach was protruding, her arms and legs were like sticks. She pulled the dress over her head and smoothed it down. 'Oh . . . Moscow!'

In the dank, cobwebby room she turned a half pirouette. 'Thank you kindly sir,' she said in her accented English, pretending to take the arm of her imagined soon-to-be lover, her soon-to-be husband, Marek Koninsky. He was so handsome, so charming. She was exquisite in a cashmere wrap. 'The weather is very fine, yes, but warm? The boulevards are very beautiful, are they not? The blossoms? And have you travelled far?' She pulled a boa from the recesses of the wardrobe and it shed a drift of ancient feathers as she wrapped it round her chest. She sat on the bed and began to pull on a fine nylon stocking. 'And have you yet seen our Alexandrovsky Gardens? Our famous Virgin of Tikhvin?'

At that moment an arc of headlamps shone on the wall and a car sounded on the track outside. She glanced out of the window, immediately pulled off her finery and tied her stained kimono over her ruined body. She opened the casement and fished in her pocket for her cigarettes. She lit up gratefully, breathing the smoke out into the rain. At least that dog is not here any more, she thought. Her husband parked and she heard him enter the scullery. She finished her cigarette, closed the window, pulled the curtains shut and returned to the wardrobe, where she continued arranging, rearranging, straightening and stroking her beautiful old clothes.

Kathleen walked through the village but passed right by the entrance to First Street. She moved quickly. In the dark, in the wet, she followed the footsteps of her friend, down to Jinny Hoolets. She was holding Petra's radio, which she turned on and off, nervously, only half-hearing the merry crackle of Radio Luxembourg as it disturbed the silent lanes. She didn't want to go but she felt there was something unfinished with Petra tonight. And she was worried about her. She's living with a *madwoman*, she reasoned. No wonder she's seeing things and imagining funny men. Down at Jinny Hoolets. Down at Jinny Hoolets pond. The place made her feel afraid. It wasn't safe. A picture of Mrs Koninsky came to mind, wandering through the heaps as restless as a crazy ghost, a scrawny, tattered tangle of hair and rags and smoke. A disturbed and murderous deceived wife.

Kathleen approached the top of the track, stopped and looked around. The sky and pitheaps and distant fields blended together in a wall of night. Cloud obscured the moon and stars. She pushed the radio inside her coat and fastened it to the neck.

The rain fell, hush-hushing on the stones, on the grim slope, on the inky hole of the pond below. The Koninsky's house was in darkness, with the curtains drawn, except for a glimmer, which may have been the dying glow from a downstairs hearth.

She had never before been to Jinny Hoolets at night. She hesitated. It was very quiet. Even the trains were still. She looked around. A faint breeze blew the raindrops sideways and there was a movement, just on the edge of her vision, to the left, down below. She was startled. She wheeled around. She could see nothing. She took off her glasses, rubbed them on her sleeve then replaced them. Her heart started to beat perceptibly. She was afraid. Maybe there really *is* a funny man, she thought. Maybe Petra's not making him up. She looked from right to left. Well I hope there's no funny man hanging around here now. I hope he's not watching me or planning anything dirty.

Mentally, and to reassure herself, she ran through the names of the invisible constellations. Pegasus, she thought, Perseus. Gemini. Hercules. I know you're all up there. I know you're there. I just can't see you. You're like tulip bulbs in the ground, in the winter, waiting to come out and show yourselves.

She set off on the track, taking care on the loose lumps of coal. She sniffed the familiar black smell. Halfway down, the wind lifted with a cold rush and made an eerie moan. Again she thought she saw movement in the corner of her eye. She stopped and stared. It was a clump of dead fireweed blowing along in a tumbling motion. The rain hit her face and spattered her glasses. I can't really see, she decided. These shadows could well be a long raincoat, or trousers or a funny man's sleeve. He might be hiding from me or he might not. Or maybe it's the madwoman. Her heart clenched again with cold fear. Mrs Koninsky might be out, wandering about and laughing to herself. She had a sudden vision of Nadezhda, standing in the filthy shallows of the pond, kicking at the water with a bare foot, as distracted as a child at the seaside.

She considered going home. Don't be stupid, she told herself. There's no one here. It's only weather. At the bottom of the path, she looked over to the pond. She hesitated. There *was* something in the water. Her chest started thumping again. It's like the last time, she thought. What on earth is that? I'll take no notice. I'll just go straight to the house, give Petra her radio, then get myself away home. She stopped. It was no good. As before, she knew she had to go over to the water's edge and have a closer look. She spoke aloud to divert herself from her own terror. 'I wish there was a film in my camera. If there was, I would've brought that Box Brownie.'

Ahead, the house looked dead and uninviting. The gusty breeze was gaining strength and it whistled around the building, stirring the pathetic clumps of poisoned grass. Mr Koninsky's car was black and silent. The door of the abandoned outside netty banged feebly, the pile of dog-ends in the porch glowed like a drift of snow. Kathleen turned, left the track and felt her feet sink into the soft black mud of the pond's edge.

The wind moaned and the water lapped. There was no other sound. Kathleen saw a ripple and a flutter and the splash of a tiny wave. She swallowed hard and shivered. There's no one here, she told herself firmly. No one. She took off her glasses for a second time and smeared away the rain. She put them back on and squinted at the odd shape in the shallows. It could be a shopping bag, she decided, or a sack of cement, or . . . and she had an unnerving sense of déjà vu . . . It could be something blown off Petra's mam's washing line.

She entered the water in her shoes. I'm already soaked, I can't get much wetter, she reasoned. Her feet gurgled and squelched as she raised them one after the other. The cold, polluted water inched above her ankles, approached her knees. The light-coloured, waterlogged shape was just then beside her, yet she was still uncertain. Tentatively, she reached out and touched it. It sank, turned a little and resurfaced. She gasped and then cried out. 'Oh, no!'

# SATURDAY

Nana sat by the fire, in the kitchen, rocking and sobbing. She'd been there all night. The embers shifted and sank low in the grate and Kathleen gently tipped some coal on top to keep the flames burning. 'I'm so sorry, Nana,' she murmured again, but there was no indication that her grandmother had heard. She made a high, keening sound in between sobs, wringing her handkerchief in her fingers, tipping her chair to and fro, to and fro. It sounded pitiful and strange.

Kathleen made a pot of tea and handed her a cup, but she appeared not to notice. The girl placed it on the hearth. She was conscious of standing in the space on the proggy mat, next to the fender, normally occupied by Nosey. 'Drink your tea,' she whispered. 'Drink it, you'll feel better.'

'He was all I had,' cried Nana suddenly. 'That little dog was all I had.'

'I know,' said Kathleen, understanding that in an odd way this was true. 'I know.'

Nana continued, desperately. 'He was all I had and he's been taken away from me.' She started sobbing again and straightened her handkerchief and placed it over her face. Her shoulders shook in an uncontrolled way.

Kathleen stood watching her, completely at a loss. Because she'd been the one to find the dead Jack Russell, carry him home, break the news to Nana, she felt responsible for her distress. 'Can I get you anything?' she asked again. 'What can I do?'

Nana carried on crying. Kathleen retreated to her cracket in the corner and clenched her fingers into fists. The wireless was playing music very quietly and the mournful rise and fall of 'Stranger on the Shore' brought tears to her eyes too. What a terrible thing to do to Nosey, she thought, imagining the mad Nadezhda Koninsky forcing him under the water, laughing like a crazy fiend. He was only a little dog. He never meant anyone any harm. She felt close to tears herself. Last night, after finding him in the pond, she'd struggled home with her sodden burden and sobs like coughs had come from her own throat. Jonty Dickinson, her Da's marra from the pit, had seen her at the end of First Street, taken the dog from her aching arms and carried him to the back gate. 'It must have fallen in,' he said, helplessly. 'I don't know how, mind.'

'Lay him down,' Kathleen had gasped, 'put him here. I'll go in and tell Nana. You go home.'

Now Kathleen watched Nana as she sank back in her seat, the handkerchief still over her face like a shroud. Eventually, she became quiet. First Gloria, now Nosey, she thought. What's going on? It's like a war. It's crazy and pointless and horrible. She thought of Gloria's big white smile, Nosey's cheeky bark. They were both cheerful and kind, she remembered. They were both my friends. They've died for nothing, for no good reason at all. They've been murdered.

Da came into the room. He was wearing a clean shirt and tie, his black armband and the trousers from his suit. This meant he wasn't going to work today. He looked stern and tall. His wife pulled the handkerchief from her face and regarded him steadily. Her weak eyes were puffy and she looked old and ill. Kathleen gazed from one to the other as seconds went by. Nothing was said. Da looks so much younger than Nana, Kathleen decided, as she'd done many times before. He's so tall and strong. The old clock on the wall struck the hour in what sounded like a meaningful way.

'I'll bury the dog,' Da muttered eventually.

'Yes,' replied Nana. She sounded broken and pathetic.

'I'll bury him out the back.'

'That's right. Bury him out the back.'

Da nodded to Kathleen. 'Get the spade.'

Kathleen moved towards the door.

'Let me tell you this,' said Da slowly, speaking to his wife. His words were measured and distinct. 'I will not, I repeat not have another bad word, not one more bad word said about my daughter in this house. Is that clear?'

Nana met his eye then looked away. She didn't reply.

Why is he choosing to say this now? Kathleen wondered.

Da dug a deep hole in the patch of ground across the lane from the yard. He tossed aside some slug-eaten cabbages and sprouts and unearthed a number of stones. Kathleen wrapped the stiff body of Nosey in an old cot blanket she'd taken from the airing cupboard.

'He doesn't look like himself,' she said, sadly, covering his face. 'He looks like nothing. Like a toy dog that's been thrown away.'

'Aye,' agreed Da, panting from the digging. 'Gloria looked like nothing too. Like a shell of a person with all the life gone.' He sounded sad but resigned.

Kathleen crouched down and placed the bundle in the hole. 'Goodbye,' she said aloud. I loved you, she thought. I loved Gloria too.

Da began shovelling the earth and the stones on top of the body. They made a thudding sound. The blanket disappeared. He's gone, Kathleen thought. She stood up and felt tears spring to her eyes. She poked behind her glasses to wipe them away. She took a deep breath, trying to force herself not to cry. Da's refusal to succumb to grief made her feel that she should act the same.

The rain had stopped but a thin mist hung in the air, mingled with the smoke from all the chimneys in the row. Kathleen stood watching the grave fill. She felt a weight of grief and loss in her heart. The pit buzzer sounded, imperative and long. In the distance she thought she could hear the tramp-tramp of boots as miners left together to go on shift.

Da leaned on his spade, breathless. 'Poor little beggar,' he said.

Kathleen looked up, blinked and realized that he wasn't speaking about Nosey. He was referring to her.

Down at Jinny Hoolets, Nadezhda was reciting the hundred and second psalm. She was wearing another old, torn net ballet dress with faded silk rosebuds around the neck and, over the top of this, a man's tweed overcoat. Her feet were bare and blue. 'For I have eaten ashes as it were bread and mingled my drink with weeping . . . My days are gone like a shadow and I am withered like grass . . .' She raised the back of one hand to her forehead, like an actress in a tragedy.

She went into Petra's bedroom on the rear of the ground floor and looked around, puzzled, as if she'd never been in there before. She went over to the window, opened it with difficulty and lit a cigarette. She blew the smoke outside. After a few puffs she began coughing, stubbed it out and threw it away. Wandering around, she picked up some record covers, then dropped them contemptuously on the bed. She retrieved clothes that had been scattered across the floor, folded them and stuffed them randomly in a drawer. She examined a tiny pair of black lace panties, which she had never seen before. The room was untidy and cold. She stood in the bay window and stared outside at the encroaching heaps that surrounded the house like mountains of the moon. Thin fog drifted about in wraiths. It was Saturday today, but her daughter hadn't been at school all week. What did this mean? Perhaps she was no longer attending. She pressed her forehead against the glass and closed her eyes. She feared what was to become of Petra. Her daughter seemed no good at her lessons. She was lazy. She couldn't sing, she couldn't dance, she had no head for cartography like her father. Nadezhda was worried that she would soon be working in a shop in the village, slicing bacon and weighing sugar into blue paper bags. She would wear a cotton overall and a hairnet, talk with a local accent. She would hate her work, quickly marry a stocky miner, secure a substandard dwelling, fall pregnant and end up despising both him and her own narrow fate.

Nadezhda sighed. She looked down and stroked the rough surface of her discolouring ballet skirts. She pulled the coat together against the chill. She wandered a little aimlessly around her daughter's bedroom, picking up then discarding a tube of orange lipstick, a five pound note, a packet of sanitary towels, a garish pop music magazine. As she was about to leave she noticed a brightly coloured pile behind the door. She bent and examined this, then picked it up. It was a tangle of thin scarves, printed chiffon and spun silk which she knew immediately had been collected from all ends of the continent. She frowned. These are mine, she thought, my old things, from before. She divided them then bundled them inside her coat pockets, impatiently. The girl shouldn't have taken them. These are mine. She's been interfering with my things.

Later, as Nadezhda sat in the gloomy scullery next to the potbellied stove, which emitted only a suggestion of warmth, her husband came in and perched on the edge of the table. He smelled of cologne and he was wearing a baggy, white shirt with silver link armbands gathering the sleeves, a dark waistcoat with a silk back and narrow trousers. He was tie-less and a little dishevelled and he smelled of both cologne and vodka.

'The police have been back,' she said, impassively.

'I know.'

'Is there no end to it?'

'They will give up eventually.' Marek picked up the coffee pot, felt it and poured himself a luke-warm cup. He cradled it in his fingers.

'The dog, it is drowned too.'

'Yes.'

Nadezhda spoke in a measured way. 'You should not have let your mistress come into this house. You know I do not like my things being touched by others. They are fragile. They are all I have to remember my home.' She wasn't accusatory. Her words sounded as if they'd been repeated and repeated, like a tired, expressionless litany.

'Yes, I am sorry. I have told you many times I am sorry.'

'I do not . . . I do not—'

'I know. Do not rub your nose in it.'

There was a silence. She appeared to be considering this odd English expression. After a while Nadezhda continued. 'The girl has been touching my things, also. It never stops.' She looked around at her husband and he raised his eyebrows.

'She has been going through my things and taking them. Hiding them in her room. I found some in there today.'

'Why would she do that?'

Nadezhda shrugged. 'Why does she do any of the things she does?'

Marek put his coffee down and went to the draining board where he found a bottle amongst the dirty dishes. He rinsed a glass and poured himself three clear inches and drank them in a gulp. He closed his eyes as the spirits burned his throat. He put the empty glass in the sink.

Nadezhda stared at the floor. 'I am worried about the girl. She is not going to school.'

Marek thought for a moment. 'I believe it is the holidays.'

Nadezhda let out a long breath. She leaned towards the inadequate heater, her hands outstretched, as if she were miming. She shuddered, dramatically. She picked up a cold foot, now encased in a ragged ballet shoe and rubbed it with both hands.

Marek watched her and the gesture reminded him of long ago. Nadezhda had massaged her feet in this way before a performance. He pictured her then, a Degas danseuse, as light and fresh as an apple blossom. He went over and stood behind her. She leaned back and raised one thin expectant hand. He took it and pressed it against his mouth in the old way, then he bent down and with a mixture of courtesy, tenderness and passion placed his lips underneath her matted hair and kissed her, lengthily, on her neck. He whispered something in his foreign tongue and his wife almost smiled. Then quickly, suddenly anxious to leave, he went to the hall, gathered up his jacket and stepped outside.

Marek Koninsky was the illegitimate child of the youngest son of a Count and his mother was a trainee, assistant milliner. His boyhood near Krakow had been harsh and short but in early adolescence he perceived something extraordinary – a secret usually discovered and exploited by a few lucky members of the female sex. That is, he realized the power, the inviolability, the complete irresistibility of his own beauty. His ambitions soon became as huge as his vanity and within a few short years he was a professional, a dandy and a gigolo to aristocratic women. His looks and good manners never once failed him in these years as he tirelessly pursued both status and pleasure.

Marek met Nadezhda Chekanova in Warsaw when he was still only twenty-three. She was twenty-eight and a prima ballerina touring with the Bolshoi at the height of her stardom and fame. He fell in love for the first and only time in his life because at heart he was neither mercenary nor calculating but susceptible to grace and artistry. He'd become tired of work and tired of selling himself and tired of society. He was sick of mind games and chatter. He craved private passion and security.

Now, trapped at Jinny Hoolets, he saw clearly and hopelessly that his love for this snowflake bride had been his single big mistake. Their personalities were too similar. As a couple they'd been elegant and exquisite but neither had the strength to support the other in the face of accident, disaster, alcoholism and war. They couldn't manage and they were weak. They couldn't cope with crises, big or small. Happiness escaped them both, even in the early days and quite quickly they ceased to expect it – they forgot the very word. They became lost. They made one bad decision after another. And now they were middle aged and at the end of a long bleak cul de sac, without the energy or courage or resourcefulness to turn around. All they could do was distract themselves.

Marek walked into the village intending to wait outside the cinema. He hated the boredom and insularity of the place and the way everyone here clung on to the mine, looking only ever backwards to a past where they saw a fanciful, mythical prosperity. He swaggered a little. He was drunk enough not to care who saw him. He no longer even asked himself why he constantly pursued women, but it was true that most of the time he didn't find it enjoyable. Gloria had seemed modern and fresh at first, but she'd turned out all wrong with her ambitions, her teetotalism, her outspoken ideas and her hostile father. The sister, Joyce, was both stupid and fat but she'd thrown herself at him, time and again, even before Gloria had ended their affair.

He hated them both absolutely and he also hated himself. If he thought about them seriously for more than a single minute he found himself imagining the water of the evil stinking pond closing over his own head, bringing a choking dread followed by pure oblivion and relief.

Kathleen retreated upstairs after the burial of Nosey and tried to comfort herself by listening to the Light Programme on Petra's radio. Edmundo Ross and his orchestra were playing a selection of tunes from stage musicals. She fiddled with the dial, searching for the Beatles or Helen Shapiro, but there was no proper pop music anywhere to be found.

She searched in her drawer for a black and white photograph of the little dog, which she had taken herself. She propped this up against her clock and regarded it, steadily.

The news was announced and she began listening. She picked up the radio and held it close to her ear in the way she'd seen Petra do.

*Mr Krushchev is willing to remove Russian missile bases in Cuba if America will do the same in Turkey,* the newsreader declared. *He gave this pledge in a message to President Kennedy today.*

The report went on to suggest that the Soviets felt threatened by nuclear weapons in Turkey, close to their borders, in the same way as the citizens of the United States felt uneasy about a nuclear capability in the Caribbean. It said that Krushchev's tone was aggressive and uncompromising and revealed that the United Nations were to be involved in the forthcoming discussions.

Kathleen switched off the radio, worried about using up Petra's batteries. This Cuba thing's not getting any better, she thought. They're just playing games, waiting for an excuse to start a big war and blow us all sky high. She thought about fallout shelters again and Nana's washhouse in the yard that had been the family's air-raid protection in the blitz of the last big conflict. She knew it was built of special strong concrete. She tried to picture herself, Da, Joyce and Nana sitting in there, with the boiler, the mangle and the packet of Fairy Snow, trying to hide from the Russians. It seemed ludicrous. That puny shelter won't be any use now, she decided again, not with these modern bombs that blast away whole cities. She clenched and unclenched her hands.

Feeling the need to divert herself she picked up the copy of *Princess* magazine which Auntie Molly had brought earlier in the week. She read a picture story about Angela who was a District Nurse with a bicycle. She was brave and rather glamorous in her fitted coat and brim hat. She removed these garments in order to descend bravely on a rope down a pothole where she rescued an injured man without, apparently, laddering her nylons. Distracted for a moment, Kathleen smiled. She turned the pages. There were recipes for biscuits, articles on ponies, hats from around the world and a poem about a lost dog, which she couldn't bear to read. The girls in the stories lived in big houses with sunny gardens and said 'Oh golly!' or went to boarding schools where they wore blazers and ties and said, 'Jolly good show!' Kathleen blinked and read on.

Detective Inspector Glen sat on the edge of his sergeant's desk in the police station down in Stanley, thumbing through Gloria's post-mortem report. He re-read the neatly typed paragraphs, almost randomly. The pathologist's estimate of the time of death was wide open. He'd said it was at any point between nine p.m. on Sunday night and five a.m. on Monday morning. The dead woman had eaten a small meal at teatime on Sunday. There was no alcohol in her bloodstream. She had blisters on her heels, suggesting that her shoes were new. There were abrasions to the body possibly indicating a struggle. She had perfect teeth with no dental work. She was underweight for her height but not malnourished. Despite her hair being naturally blonde it was artificially lightened. She was nulliparous. Nulliparous? wondered the policeman. What's that? Then he remembered. This meant the victim had never been pregnant. Although not a virgin, there was no evidence of recent intercourse. He frowned, disapprovingly.

The Sergeant was simultaneously leafing through another folder. He read that the young girl had found the deceased in the pond at approximately eight fifteen a.m. 'I wonder what that youngster was doing out so early in the school holidays,' he mused, 'the one who found the body.'

Inspector Glen tossed the report to one side. 'I asked her that. She said she woke up at the usual time and got up without thinking. She said she never looked at the clock. She's a funny one, mind you. Very bright. Head in the clouds.'

The Sergeant sighed. He noted his superior officer's high colour. This case is going to give him a heart attack, he decided. 'Well, sir, we've been through it all with a fine tooth comb. The fact remains, that bugger in the cells has an alibi. He was at work from five until eleven fifteen at night. Confirmed by several witnesses. Three separate individuals saw him and said good night to him on his way home. His mother insists he came in at the normal time and she secured all the locks before they both retired. She keeps the house keys in her handbag at the side of her bed and she's a very light sleeper. She's absolutely sure he didn't leave the house during the night. The doors weren't tampered with and none of those windows have been opened for years. She says she went into his room at seven the following morning and he was sleeping like a baby.'

'She might be lying.'

'You've met her, sir. She might be, but I doubt it.'

Inspector Glen was impatient. 'Respectable little old ladies lie, Sergeant. Like the best of them. Sometimes.' He took out a handkerchief and blew his nose. 'The fact remains, this lad was being made a fool of. His girlfriend was seeing that dago from Jinny Hoolets and making no secret of it. If that's not a clear-cut motive, then I don't know what is.' He examined the contents of his handkerchief. '*And* his fingerprints were on the mirror in the salon.'

The Sergeant shook his head and sucked the top of his biro. He picked up the sheaf of photographs and flicked them through his fingers, dismissively. He looked at some of them again, holding them at a distance from his eyes, squinting in the harsh, overhead fluorescent light. They were all photographs of young boys. They were playing happily in the street, on the football pitch and in trees at the edge of the village. A few were in Cub uniform. Some of them were in close up, and these had possibly been taken inside a building. All the boys were cheerful and they were all fully clothed. 'He came down for breakfast as usual and told his mother he'd got tickets to take the victim to a blues concert. He was pleased about it. He'd put them under a vase on the mantelpiece. They're still there.' He paused and whistled through his teeth. 'Don't you think we ought to let him go?'

The Inspector scowled, picked up his hat and jammed it on his head. 'What's a blues concert?'

The Sergeant smiled 'It's music. Rhythm and blues.' His face became immediately serious again. 'I mean it, sir. Shall I let the lad out?'

Inspector Glen moved heavily towards the door. 'No, keep him locked up. Let him sweat. Take his house apart.'

Although it was lunchtime Kathleen sat at the kitchen table eating Sugar Pops. Joyce was at the Essoldo for the cartoon matinee, Da had disappeared and Nana sat very still by the fire, staring straight ahead, her fingers pulling anxiously on an elastic band she had found down the arm of her chair. Kathleen was conscious of the silence and tried to be as quiet as possible. She noticed that Joyce's dress was hanging on the back of the door. It looked very green, big and frothy. Her own curtain dress was still in sections on a chair next to the sewing machine. She chased the last pieces of cereal around the bowl with her spoon trying to imagine what the dance tomorrow would be like. Remembering Pathe News films of American Big Bands, she pictured sophisticated lighting, which made invisible the more utilitarian aspects of the Welfare Hall. The musicians were arranged in smart tiers. They wore white jackets and bow ties and above them, suspended from the ceiling were giant silver revolving quavers and semibreves. Instead of worn linoleum, the floor had been magically transformed into glowing parquet.

In her mind's eye, caressed by a spotlight, Gloria and Marek glided into the centre of the space. He was wearing a white shirt and black tie, a tailed evening jacket and trousers with discreet piping. His hair was slicked back, close to his head with Brylcreem and his shoes were patent leather. He was elegant, tall and sure of himself. Gloria was wearing Joyce's dress, except it had a sleek, narrow bodice over her slim frame and the skirts were filmy rather than stiff. On her, it was contemporary and chic rather than tarty. Their feet pitter-pattered through the quickstep and as the music changed rhythm they broke into an erotic tango. Gloria kicked her legs, leaning back in his arms, revealing green knickers above her shiny nylons.

'Don't worry, pet, she'll get it finished,' said Nana, unexpectedly.

Kathleen was startled. She realized she'd been sitting, head in hand, staring at the sewing machine. She sat up straight.

Nana continued: 'I know you haven't anything to wear. She

promised me she'd do it tonight. You'll have your dress all right. Don't you worry.'

Kathleen regarded her grandmother. She seemed calm and mellow. This was a rare mood, brought on by the catharsis of crying. 'I hope it's going to be nice,' she offered. 'Not babyish.'

Nana rubbed her one short-sighted eye. 'It'll be lovely. Your Auntie Joyce is the best dressmaker in the village. You're a very lucky little girl.'

'Yes.'

'What are you?'

'I'm a very lucky girl.'

Marek leaned against an upright beam in the barn and poured the remains of his flask down his throat. He was unsteady, unshaven, his tie and collar were undone and his hat was pushed back. Joyce noticed his dishevelment and the fact that his shoes were muddy. He burped.

'Marek, I do believe you've had too much.'

He shook his head, then closed his eyes briefly. He seemed unwell.

'Are you listening to me?'

He nodded.

'As I was saying. We could leave here, start a new life. There's nothing for either of us here. We could go to Newcastle or Sunderland. You could get a good job, with your qualifications. I'd start up as a dress designer, I could even have my own shop with a bit of money behind me.' Her voice had a pleading edge to it. She hesitated. 'Bloody Gloria wasn't the only one with ideas,' she added coldly.

Marek rubbed his face with one hand. 'I have a daughter,' he said, almost in a whisper.

Joyce considered. 'Well, I suppose she could come too. We could all go. Kathleen as well. When they're older they could both leave school and help me in the shop. It could be a great new start for—'

Marek lunged towards her and grasped her in both arms. She giggled nervously. 'I was just saying . . . I think we should—'

He fastened his mouth on hers and silenced her. They swayed together for a few moments, Joyce stiff with surprise. He pushed her towards a jutting stone in the wall, pulled up her violet uniform to waist height then dragged down her underwear. Grunting slightly, he lifted her off her feet and sat her on the stone shelf. She was a heavy woman. He panted with the effort.

Joyce laughed again. 'What on earth are . . .?'

He forced her legs apart with his thighs and kissed her again, pushing his tongue into her mouth.

Joyce realized then what was required of her and she did not protest.

She encircled her arms about his back, tentatively, as he rested his head on her shoulder, unzipped his trousers and entered her. She was surprised and a little shocked. She stared impassively at the empty space that was the window opposite. He grimaced and groaned loudly and uttered a foreign curse. Joyce thought he's taking his time today. As he finished, she saw a head appear. She froze. There was no mistake. Someone was watching them. It was Nadezhda.

Kathleen decided that despite her dread of Jinny Hoolets, she must return Petra's radio. I can't keep it, she reasoned. It's not mine. She stood in the damp passage in First Street, clutching the transistor to her chest. She noticed Da's long raincoat resting on a hook, over the top of her school gabardine. She lifted it down. The sunglasses were still in a pocket, with his penknife and his cap. She hung it back up and put on her own coat, buttoning the radio inside. First, however, before going to Jinny

Hoolets, she would take her film to be developed. Billy Fishboy would do this for her. He charged only three shillings to cover the cost of the special silvered paper. Once he'd let her come into his darkroom, upstairs at the cinema and she'd watched, enthralled, her elbow touching his, as the images appeared like magic in the watery trays. She'd tried not to breathe the acrid smell, behind the locked door, under Billy's red light.

Kathleen approached the cinema, as a crowd of matinee children disgorged through the doors in a hubbub, some of them making rude faces at her. 'Hi there, knacky-knees!' said a boy from her class at school.

She ignored him. 'Where's our Joyce?' she asked the manager, who was holding open one of the heavy glass doors.

He looked tired and emotional. 'She's just gone off with lover-boy,' he said trying to speak above the noise. Three girls, arm in arm, chanted the lyrics to 'Summer Holiday'.

She raised her voice. 'What?'

The manager ducked as two boys wrestled, fists flailing. He had deep circles under his eyes.

'What did you say? What did you just say?'

He shouted. 'I said she's just . . . walked away with . . . a friend.'

'What friend?' Kathleen yelled.

The excited voices moved out of the lobby and into the street. The manager was a little discomposed. 'Your auntie has just met Mr Koninsky.'

'Where've they gone?'

'I really have no idea.' The very last of the children milled outside and he tried to close the door in her face.

Kathleen shoved her shoe in the crack. It was quiet now. 'I want to see Billy Fishboy.'

The manager was very impatient. He pushed the door, squashing her foot. 'He's not here. Go away.'

Kathleen shouldered the door, unsuccessfully.

'He's gone and got himself arrested.' The glass shut and he turned the key.

Now, half an hour later, Kathleen stood outside the chemist's shop waiting for the pharmacist to open up after lunch. A yellow grey fog hung in the air. Everything was still and muffled and there were only two people passing by; an old lady with a shopping basket on wheels and a young woman in a headscarf with rollers underneath, who was pushing a pram. They both glanced at her then looked away. Kathleen frowned at their departing backs as they disappeared into the gloom. You're staying here, she thought, you're stuck. There's no beauty in your lives. She stepped on and off the curb. Unlucky old you. But I'm getting out of here. Lucky me. Lucky, lucky me. She moved her feet quicker and quicker. Lucky me, lucky me. She stopped suddenly. She was breathless. I might not get away. Not if the Russians fly in those ballistic missiles and blow us all to kingdom come. She imagined a flattened landscape, smouldering, with half-buildings and stumps of blackened trees.

She waited. It was cold and the fog tasted strange. She could hardly believe Inspector Glen's stupidity. It's not as if I haven't tried telling him, she thought to herself. And that madwoman Mrs Koninsky is on the loose, drowning people's dogs and their aunties, whilst Billy, who wouldn't hurt a fly, has been locked up in a prison somewhere. She pictured a gloomy room with a metal door similar to those she'd seen in American westerns. Billy was handcuffed and his legs were fastened together with a chain. He had a dusty cowboy hat on his head.

She kicked a stone, suddenly angry. No one ever listens to me, she thought. But I know that madwoman ought to be in a straitjacket. She wasn't sure what this might be, except that it was a garment used for subduing lunatics. She pictured a tight white overall with sleeves sewn up at the cuffs. A straitjacket.

She saw Petra's mother wriggling and flailing helplessly as she was taken away in a van, a doctor standing over her with a horse syringe. She rubbed her eyes behind her glasses. And now our Joyce is getting too friendly with that awful man. Da had called him a womanizer and a drunk. That means he's always having affairs. She remembered his slim waist and the narrow leather belt he sometimes wore, attractively low on his hips but then pushed this thought aside. Maybe *he* killed Gloria, she thought. She froze. She balanced on the edge of the pavement. Maybe it wasn't his barmy wife after all. Maybe he did it because he wanted to have an affair with Joyce instead of Gloria. Perhaps he'd quarrelled with poor Gloria. Maybe Joyce caused the death of her step-sister without even realizing it. Kathleen thought about this. Joyce didn't like Gloria but she would never have wanted her dead. Would she? Kathleen took a deep breath. She felt confused.

At that moment there was the sound of a car engine and a pair of headlamps penetrated the fog. A vehicle stopped nearby. Kathleen realized it was the police car. She walked over as the Inspector was getting out. He slammed the door and immediately the uniformed officer at the wheel drove away.

Despite everything she was pleased to see him. 'Friendship Seven? Do you read? Over.'

Inspector Glen didn't smile. He was in a bad mood, Kathleen decided. 'Roger,' he muttered.

Kathleen persisted. '*Seven* this is Cape. I repeat Cape. Receiving you loud and clear.' She looked up at him a little plaintively. 'Our dog's been drowned,' she said.

'What's that?'

'Our dog's been drowned. The one that tried to bite you. I found him in the pond last night just like I found my Auntie Gloria.'

The policeman squatted down so his face was just below Kathleen's. 'Your *dog*'s been drowned?'

'Roger, Friendship Seven. Affirmative.'

'Your *dog*?'

Kathleen nodded. Tears sprang to her eyes making her unable to see. She poked them away with her index fingers. 'Poor little Nosey.'

The Inspector sounded baffled. 'Couldn't he swim? Dogs can swim, can't they?'

Kathleen stamped her foot, impatiently. 'Listen to me, will you! Will you listen? He didn't just *drown*. Of course he could swim. He was a great swimmer. You should have seen him at Marsden Rock on the Trip two years ago. He was an Olympic swimmer. What I'm saying is, somebody went and deliberately *drowned* him.'

'But why would anyone—'

Kathleen shuddered involuntarily. She was worried she was going to cry properly and make a fool of herself. She felt words pour out of her mouth. 'Why does anyone do anything? Why did someone kill our Gloria? Why did my mam and dad run away? Why does everyone hate me at school? Why is our Joyce meeting Mr Koninsky after work? Why does my Nana have bad nerves? Why are the Americans and the Russians going to blow up the whole world? Why *everything*, Friendship Seven?' The tears ran unchecked down her face. 'Why everything? What are you doing about it all? Nothing I bet. All you're doing is arresting the wrong person. You're completely useless.'

Inspector Glen stood up extended his arms then leant forwards, holding Kathleen gently. 'Ssshh!' he said, kindly.

Kathleen felt Petra's radio press into her chest, then the rough wool of his overcoat, the brim of his hat, then to her horror, the soft warmth of his cheek. She stepped backwards out of his loose embrace. She sniffed heartily and rubbed her nose with her fist. 'I've told you and I'm sick of telling you. You should listen to me because my teacher thinks I'm a brain-box and tells everybody to listen to me, especially when we're doing sums.' She enunciated very clearly. 'The answer to everything's down at Jinny Hoolets.'

Humiliated by her tears she turned and walked away into the fog, heading for the Chemist's shop, which was now lit up, its large coloured flasks gleaming like jewels in the window. She pushed open the door and a bell tinkled. There was a smell of ointments and a dryness in the air which made her think of bandages.

The pharmacist appeared in his white coat. He was a thin elderly man who reminded Kathleen of a goat. When he wasn't dispensing medicines he preached at a Methodist chapel in a nearby village. She had seen him on Sundays, with his knobbly body and wispy grey hair, accompanied by his fat wife, setting off to make the five-mile round trip on foot, carrying his bible.

Kathleen handed him her film. He took it and passed the black cloth wrapping back to her. He put the roll of film in a brown envelope and licked the flap. Kathleen knew that he had an enlarger in a darkroom out the back. 'When can you do them for?'

He looked at her steadily. 'Have you been crying, my dear?'

'Crying? Me?' She rubbed her cheeks with her sleeve. 'No, mister, I have not.'

'Are you sure? Are you all right?'

Kathleen nodded wordlessly.

'They'll be ready Monday.'

She handed him her pound note.

'Pay when you come to collect them.'

'I want another film.' She pocketed the new box with her change and turned away to leave. Outside, the fog was thicker. The policeman had vanished and it was so dark it was almost like night. She walked over to Gallini's and looked inside. Petra was sitting on her own, pretending to smoke, stirring a cup of coffee. Kathleen went in and joined her. She slid along the slippery bench seat.

Petra didn't smile. She glanced away and then back as if Kathleen's presence was an irritation, something to be endured. Kathleen noticed she was wearing a school blouse but instead of her usual tie, the top three buttons were undone revealing her brassiere.

Kathleen pulled the transistor radio from out of the breast of her coat. She placed it on the table.

Petra was haughty. She looked at it as if she'd never seen it before. 'Your nose is all red. Have you been crying?'

'My Nana's dog's dead.'

Petra picked up her cup, sipped some coffee and grimaced. 'That little brown and white one?'

Kathleen stared at her. 'He drowned near your house. In the pond. Like Gloria did.'

Petra stared at the ashtray. She stubbed out her cigarette. She said nothing.

She knows something, Kathleen thought. I bet she knows her barmy old mother did it. 'Did you see anyone? Was that funny man there?'

On reflection, Kathleen had decided that she definitely didn't believe in Petra's 'funny man'. She thought it was just an attention-seeking device, to counteract the drama surrounding the death of her auntie. Petra never liked to be upstaged. She'd invented the 'funny man' to exaggerate her own problems. Not that she hasn't got problems, Kathleen reasoned. Her mother's a murdering nutcase and her father's a womanizer and a drunk.

Petra hesitated.

Kathleen persisted. 'Have you seen your "funny man"?'

'When?'

'Yesterday.'

'Don't know. He might have been. He's sometimes there, sometimes not.'

Kathleen crossed her fingers. 'I'm going to tell the police about him. He might have drowned poor Nosey.'

'Don't be stupid. No one drowned him. He probably just . . . fell in or something.'

Kathleen was suddenly emotional. 'He could swim! And he couldn't have fallen in. He was at the edge, where it was quite shallow, just like our Gloria was. Anyway, he never went into Jinny Hoolets. He wasn't daft. Not even if you threw a stick. He wouldn't go in there. It stinks.'

Petra pursed her lips, thoughtfully. 'Maybe he had a dog heart attack. Or a dog stroke. Maybe he lost his way. Maybe he was chasing a girl dog and got all excited and—'

Kathleen's anger welled up. 'Shut up, Petra! Shut up, will you?'

The Italian proprietor glanced over and rustled his newspaper, disapprovingly.

Petra's mouth dropped open. 'Well so*reee*!' She sniffed. 'Sorry I spoke.'

Kathleen swallowed hard. 'I don't want to talk about it, right?'

'Well you brought it up.'

Kathleen said nothing. She knew from long experience that it was often best to let her friend have the last word. They both stood and Petra pulled on her coat, dropped her radio into her oval wicker shopping basket that she'd started carrying because she thought it was in the fashion. She paid for her coffee and they stepped outside.

Petra coughed. The air was a dense, opaque yellowish-grey. Lights glimmered indistinctly from the shops opposite. Kathleen noticed that her friend was wearing Gloria's raincoat, black fish-net stockings which might have been Gloria's and a pair of pink satin shoes which seemed too small and which looked expensive.

'Are those our Gloria's shoes?'

Petra answered immediately. 'They are, as it happens.'

Kathleen was surprised by the ready admission. It had been a long time coming, she decided. 'How's it you've got them on then?'

She looks guilty, Kathleen thought, but she's made up her mind to tell the truth. She waited as her friend rummaged in her basket and produced a key on a key ring, which was a miniature Eiffel Tower. 'This is the key to her flat,' she said.

Kathleen gasped. 'Where'd you get that from!'

Petra said nothing for a moment. She shivered.

Kathleen noticed, in the light from the plate glass window, that Petra's make-up was caked around her eyes as if she'd applied more on top of yesterday's efforts. Her lips were orange pearl.

'She got it cut for my dad. I told you why. I took it out of his pocket when my mam got upset. I was going to throw it in the pond. I think he stopped seeing her around then anyway. The time when my mam first cried. It was about three weeks ago. I was going to throw it in the pond to stop him going there, but then I decided he'd stopped anyway, so I kept it.'

'You've been in our Gloria's flat?'

'Yes.'

'When?'

'Not recently.'

'You mean, you went in there when she was alive?'

Petra stared at the damp pavement. She was embarrassed. 'Yes.'

'Have you been in there since she died?'

'No. I didn't . . . I didn't . . . There's police there all the time.'

Kathleen turned in the direction of the salon. 'Come on.'

Petra followed, reluctantly. They crossed the foggy square. The salon was in darkness but the door to the flat upstairs was open. Kathleen looked inside. She could see Inspector Glen at the top of the stairs. The landing light was on and he was writing in his notebook. Petra grabbed Kathleen's arm and pulled. 'Let's go!' she hissed, urgently. She was frightened. 'Let's get away from here.'

The two girls set off in the direction of Petra's house. There was a silence for a while. 'You've been stealing my auntie's clothes,' said Kathleen eventually, in an accusatory tone.

'No,' replied Petra, miserably. 'Not stealing. Just borrowing. I wore them, in my room, usually. Not outside. Like, I tried them on. That's all. Then I took them back.'

'You were going in there like a thief. Like a burglar. When she was at work.'

Petra was ashamed. 'Only two or three times.'

'You went through her cupboards and drawers.'

'Well she did that to my mam! She went into my mam's things and—'

'Two wrongs don't make a right!'

There was another silence. The fog muffled all sounds. Even their footsteps were inaudible.

'So you took them back, did you? Like heck you did. What about that coat, that black polo neck and those stretchy pants? Those pink shoes? Those net stockings?'

Petra seemed close to tears. 'I was going to take it all back. Honest. Then she drowned. Then the police were always there. And I was scared. I was scared to go into a dead person's house. I wanted to tell you, but . . . I just didn't.'

'You weren't too scared to wear her things though, were you?'

Petra hesitated then spoke softly. 'Well, that's because they're

221

so lovely. And I don't know where she got them from.' She paused. 'I hated her for having such lovely stuff when I've hardly got anything nice. You can't get things like hers round here. She must've got them from down London.'

'London? Don't be daft. She got them in Newcastle. She went up to Fenwicks and Binns and shops like that. Specially. In her car. On her days off.'

'I suppose so.'

'Of course she did, stupid. You don't know anything. You don't know a single thing even though you think you know everything.' She took a deep breath of the contaminated air. 'I don't like you any more!'

Petra said nothing. She hobbled painfully in the too-small pink shoes that were getting stained from the wet. Kathleen noticed beads of moisture in her stiff, lacquered hair. What a state, she thought. Her last words hung in the clouded air and wouldn't go away.

They passed the entrance to First Street. For reasons Kathleen couldn't explain, she didn't turn off and go home. She kept on walking alongside Petra, in the direction of Jinny Hoolets. She was angry and disturbed, but more important than this, she knew she was right. She wanted to savour this rare power.

They trudged in silence to the track, which led down to the pond. Kathleen felt churned up inside. She was excited. What's happening to me? she thought. I'm not usually like this. Inexplicably, she accompanied Petra towards her lonely house, over the rough stones and lumps of coal, down the gloomy slope. Everything seemed dim and muffled. It was very, very silent. The heaps glowered behind the thick fog. A whitish mist hovered above the pond like a shroud. Kathleen glanced at the water and then looked away. She was too angry with Petra to think about the madwoman in the soiled kimono, her drunken husband or the 'funny man' who probably wasn't hanging about, who probably wasn't a pervert, who probably wasn't a ghost. A faint unwelcoming light shone up from the dwelling.

I wonder what the real John Glenn is doing, Kathleen thought, trying to calm herself. It's either earlier or later in America. He might be having his breakfast. She imagined a ranch-style house with gingham curtains like the one in *Seven Brides for Seven Brothers*. I expect it's sunny over there and warm and his plate will be all heaped up high with corn, grits, beans, eggs and ham and he'll have a slice of his momma's apple pie. And Coca-Cola, with ice of course. And maybe a shot of bourbon, whatever that is. She sighed. There's always plenty to eat and drink in America.

The girls entered the dingy scullery and Petra threw some coals into the sulking stove. 'Hello!' she shouted. There was no reply. 'There's no one here,' she said, pointlessly.

'They're out,' said Kathleen, in agreement. She was at once relieved. She sat down. I know why it is I come here all the time, she thought to herself. It's because I don't like being at home. She considered this. I don't like being here, either.

Petra was still chastened. 'What d'you want to do then?'

Kathleen considered. She tried to imagine Petra in Gloria's flat but failed. 'I want to see inside your mam's bedroom,' she said decisively. 'Like Gloria did.'

Petra frowned. She was very pale, even with her thick application of Pan Stick. She took off Gloria's coat and hung it behind the door. She eased off the shoes and kicked them under the table. 'They're killing,' she muttered.

Kathleen stood up. 'Right?' She wanted to get even with Petra. She also wanted to find out something about her mother, understand the madwoman's secrets. She wanted to find something, anything that would enable her to go back to Inspector Glen and say, 'See? I told you so. I told you she's the one.'

Petra seemed unhappy. 'You know my mam doesn't like people touching her—'

'I won't touch anything.'

Reluctantly, Petra moved into the hall. Kathleen followed her up the stairs, noticing the broken glass of the lobby door, the cobwebs, the bare boards of the landing, its shadeless light bulb. Petra tentatively shoved open a door and switched on a table lamp. 'This is it,' she said, without emotion.

Kathleen entered. The room smelled sweet, like the Catholic Church she'd visited, following behind Mrs Koninsky earlier in the week. She stared. On the wall opposite hung a huge picture of the Virgin Mary with her heart all red and exposed as if she'd been cut open. She didn't appear to be in pain, but pointed at the glowing organ, within her chest, smiling peacefully. Behind her halo, a couple of dumb-looking angels circled. Kathleen turned her head away. That's really yuck, she thought. She noticed that the double bed was unmade and the heavy damask curtains were drawn, sealing off the room from the world outside. There was an undersized altar in the bay. A hassock was positioned in front of this, for praying. A rosary was lying next to a gold, diminutive cross and candlesticks.

'This is her wardrobe,' said Petra, resignedly.

Kathleen took her time. She looked around, absorbing everything. She crossed the room. On the mantelpiece and on tables there were several plaster models of saints in bright colours, which cast distorted shadows up the walls. Above the bed hung a smaller painting made of wood, which was hinged, like open doors. It was mainly gold with other faded colours in the background. It was very beautiful and showed Mary again, holding the baby Jesus.

Petra opened the wardrobe and Kathleen saw a neat rail of what looked like party clothes. They seemed rather ordinary. 'Where are her ballet dresses?' she asked.

Petra was relieved. 'Oh. They're in the spare room.' She closed the doors and moved back towards the landing. 'Come with me.'

Kathleen followed her into a box room, which was unfurnished, uncurtained and smelled of mice. Petra closed the door, switched on the light and pointed to an old trunk. 'You can look in here. She's not bothered about this old stuff. She's only funny about the clothes she used to wear to parties in Moscow. She's sort of preserving them.' She threw open the lid. 'These old rags she sometimes even wears. She looks stupid in them now, but she says nobody ever sees her, so it doesn't matter.'

Kathleen knelt down. She pulled out a cream-coloured tutu with its stiff short pelmet. It had a boned bust and hook and eye fastenings which were partly torn away. She slipped it over her head and struck a pose similar to one she'd seen in *Princess* magazine.

'That's not right,' said Petra, her old confidence returning. She demonstrated some movements. 'First position. Second position. Arabesque.'

Kathleen ignored her and continued to rummage.

Petra suddenly dropped the ballet position and started dancing like Elvis Presley, turning her hips in an erotic swivelling motion.

Kathleen pretended not to notice. She pulled out a delicate camisole and a white embroidered dress with a long flowing transparent skirt. The trunk smelled musty. There were, she noticed, a lot of fabric shoes, most badly worn.

Petra peered inside too. 'She used to practise in this stuff. Her proper costumes belonged to the company.'

Kathleen pulled out a woollen wig, a tap shoe, a peasant blouse, a blue petticoat with hoops. It's all true, she thought. These people lived in Moscow and Leningrad and Warsaw. She tried to remember where these cities were on the map. 'Why did she come here?' she said. 'I mean, isn't it a bit strange, her coming *here*?'

Petra sniffed, then sneezed. 'I don't like the smell in here,' she said. She met Kathleen's eye. 'Search me, why. They emigrated to England. It was something to do with the war.'

At that moment, a door slammed below. Petra grabbed Kathleen's arm. 'Oh, no,' she breathed.

Kathleen tore off the tutu and shoved everything back in the trunk, closing the lid. Petra switched off the light and tiptoed on to the landing. Suddenly a voice rang out from below. It was Marek and he was shouting. There was a crash and the sound of crockery breaking. Kathleen couldn't understand his words. He shouted again. He cursed in a foreign tongue. He was banging around the scullery and seemed to be overturning things.

Petra pulled Kathleen towards her. 'In here!' she whispered urgently. Her heart pounding, Kathleen ducked down into darkness and Petra closed a door behind them. They were in the airing cupboard. Kathleen moved from her haunches to her bottom. Her head was on her knees and she could smell the wet leather of her shoes. It was cramped and dusty, but warmer than the bedrooms. Kathleen was afraid, but as it became obvious they would remain undiscovered, she slowly grew calmer. She tried to see her friend and after a while, in the chink of light from under the bottom of the door, she could see her terrified profile.

'What's the matter?' Kathleen whispered.

'He's drunk again,' Petra replied.

'Why are we hiding?'

'He's looking for a bottle.'

'But why are we hiding?'

'Because I'm scared of him when he's like this, that's why.'

Kathleen began to get cramp. She said nothing for a while. The disturbance continued downstairs. The shouting got louder then subsided. This is even worse than my house she thought, even worse than Nana having one of her turns. She tried to get comfortable. Her mind wandered and she remembered the time, one of the most terrible memories she had, when Mr Dobbs from the Sunday School came to tea.

Joyce had started working as a Sunday School teacher in order to meet Mr Dobbs, the Superintendent. Kathleen knew this because she'd heard Joyce tell Nana about her plans.

'He's not from this village and he's got a good job,' she said. 'He's a rent collector for the council. He wears a collar and tie to work.'

Nana nodded. 'I knew his mother, back in the days when I went outside the house.'

'I think he likes me. We had a good long talk. He's putting me in with the infants.'

'They're religious, mind. But they're a nice family. Very clean. His father was a seaman, I believe. Dead now. Killed in the war.'

'He's not as old as he looks. He might be baldy headed but he's only twenty-nine.'

Kathleen remembered that Joyce had worn no make-up for the Sunday School classes, she'd tied her hair back and worn a plain, demure worsted dress. The groups sat in corners of the Welfare Hall. She herself was in the juniors. Mr Dobbs took the seniors and Joyce was in charge of one of the two groups of infants. She gave them pictures of Jesus to colour in with crayons and read them bible stories from a book. At the bottom of every page she held up the book to show the infants the illustration. 'Now look here, children.'

Towards the end of the second meeting, as Mr Dobbs led the entire Sunday School in prayer, a gust of wind blew open one of the high windows. Joyce quietly left her position, found the window pole and stood on a chair to ease it shut again. Kathleen furtively opened her eyes. Mr Dobbs began the concluding

Lord's Prayer in his usual melancholy and holy-sounding way, speaking very slowly, but his eyes were glued on Joyce and his cheeks were more pink than usual. He ran his fingers around the inside of his collar as if it was too stiff against his neck. Kathleen turned round and saw that as her auntie strained upwards with the window pole, her dress was creeping over her hips, revealing an inch or two of petticoat. He likes her, she remembered thinking. Joyce is right about that. Mr Dobbs looking at her in *that* kind of way. His mind's not on Our Father Who Art in Heaven. He's definitely interested.

A couple of weeks later, Kathleen had waited a while for Joyce outside the Welfare Hall at the end of a meeting. It was cold and feeling impatient she went back inside to see if her auntie was ready. There was no one there so she crossed the alley and went into the back of the Anglican Church. Inside, she froze in surprise. Joyce was standing stiffly beside the font, eating a chocolate bar. Mr Dobbs was leaning against her. His chin was on the top of her head, the folds of his neck creasing above his tight collar. His hands were moving, feeling her wide bottom. At their feet was the collection plate, full of children's pennies.

Quickly, Kathleen had withdrawn. I wonder what they're doing, she'd thought at the time. They aren't kissing. She tried to imagine what it must be like being touched by Mr Dobbs. Pretty horrible, she decided, but then Auntie Joyce is desperate.

After a month, Joyce invited Mr Dobbs to tea. Nana spent the morning baking scones and jam tarts and Joyce made special cold tongue sandwiches with the crusts cut off. There was shop-bought fruitcake and tinned oranges with evaporated milk. Nana took the best china from out of the sideboard and told Kathleen more than once to wash her hands and face. The drop leaf table was pulled out in the parlour and the fire was lit. Da wore his suit and Joyce got Gloria to do her hair in the upswept style, favoured by Grace Kelly, which made her appear older.

'He can take us as he finds us,' said Da.

'He's her last chance,' replied Nana. '*And* he's from a good family.'

Mr Dobbs arrived early and was very hearty in the passage as he took off his dripping overcoat, hat and galoshes. Everyone was nervous and squeezed around the parlour table, which was too big for the room. Kathleen was sitting so near the fire she was practically in the hearth. She felt the back of her legs burning and there was a smell of hot varnish from the wood of her chair.

There were a few awkward silences as Nana rushed in and out with the teapot. Da said nothing as usual. Joyce chattered intermittently about the weather and about the latest film showing at the cinema. She waved her hands around in a strange new way. Kathleen noticed that she'd removed her nail varnish but that tiny half moons of scarlet were still showing. Gloria passed heaped plates of food towards Mr Dobbs.

Kathleen examined him closely for the first time. His pink face was hairless and smooth and he had pimples on his chin. His scant hair was parted firmly on one side and he had a little gold cross in the lapel of his tweed suit. He caught her eye and too late she stared down at her plate.

'And what year were you born, exactly, Kathleen?' he asked.

Kathleen raised her eyes, took off her glasses, polished them briefly then put them back on.

He waited.

He must be thinking of moving me up to the seniors, she thought. It's because I'm a brain-box. 'I was born,' she said clearly, 'in August, nineteen fifty.' She met his gaze again. 'Anno domini.'

Nana came in and sat down.

Mr Dobbs smiled in a cold way. 'You really are *a lot* younger than both your sisters.'

Da coughed.

'Sister? I haven't got a sister,' replied Kathleen.

Joyce rattled her cup against her saucer, unsteadily, spilling some tea on the tablecloth.

'Have another sandwich, Mr Dobbs,' said Gloria in a near whisper.

'I see,' he said to Kathleen, holding up his palm against the proffered plate. 'You have no sisters. I see.'

'Kathleen really likes Sunday School, don't you, pet?' said Joyce hurriedly.

Kathleen transferred her gaze to her aunt. 'Yes, of course,' she lied. She tried, but couldn't think of anything complimentary to say about it.

Nana spooned up her tiny oranges, trying to eat quietly. 'I hear you are a rent collector,' she said in a strained voice, trying to minimize her local accent. 'That must be very interesting. We don't pay rent here of course. This is a colliery house.'

'It's a pity Kathleen hasn't got such pretty hair as the other two,' said Mr Dobbs glancing from Joyce to Gloria. He transferred his attention to Nana. 'But then Kathleen isn't your daughter, is she?'

'No. Joyce is my only daughter,' said Nana stiffly. 'We're not . . . we're not a regular family.'

'So I've heard.' Mr Dobbs dabbed at his lips with his paper serviette. Seeing this Joyce automatically did the same.

Kathleen was so hot by the fire she could feel sweat running down her back.

'Mother's been asking questions,' he said directly to Joyce. 'That's all.' He'd adopted a slightly accusatory tone, suggesting Joyce had somehow been trying to dupe him. 'She's discovered one or two things.' He turned to Gloria. 'Hasn't she, Gloria?' He gave Gloria a long look. Then Kathleen saw him make the same gesture he'd made in the church hall when he'd watched

Joyce struggle with the window pole. He ran his fingers around the back of his tight, stiff collar. Gloria stared at her plate.

'She does a lot of good work, your mother,' said Nana, hastily.

There was another long silence. This is awful, Kathleen decided. Joyce stood up suddenly, jerking the table and rattling the crockery. She seemed close to tears. She ran out the door. In the shocked quiet that followed, Gloria rose up and followed her. Mr Dobbs finished his tea without speaking. He seemed at ease, even satisfied. After a few minutes he got up and followed Nana into the hall, put on his hat, coat and galoshes, thanked her politely and left.

I wonder why he's so pleased with himself, Kathleen thought.

The scene that followed was the worst Kathleen had ever witnessed. Nana waited for Mr Dobbs to get to the end of the row, then she screamed and screamed. 'This family's being dragged back and forth through the mud!' she kept repeating. For some reason, she blamed Gloria. 'She can't keep her mouth shut! She just cannot keep it shut! Does she know what she's done this time?' Da tried to restrain her as she pulled the table-cloth from under the best china scattering food and breaking several cups. 'You leave me alone, you devil! Get back to your dirty whores and harlots!' Kathleen ducked under the table as she threw the teapot at the wall, then hurled a plate of sand-wiches into the fire.

Later, after Da had gone on shift, Joyce sat at the kitchen table crying quietly. No one knew where Gloria had gone. Nana held a bundle of photographs, which belonged to Da. Some of them were of his brothers but most were of his first wife and Gloria. One by one she fed them into the flames of the fire.

Back at home, Kathleen sat on her bed in her attic room, running over the final conversation she'd had with Petra in the airing cupboard, in the dismal, untidy house at Jinny Hoolets. She tried to remember exactly what had been said and why, because it was all too unreal.

'Is he like this a lot?' she'd ventured to ask about Petra's father. Her voice was low. 'I mean, do you always hide in here?'

She could tell her friend was trying to decide whether or not to share her fears. Kathleen was half expecting her to become defensive or to shrug off the situation or to insist that Kathleen's Nana's behaviour was much, much worse.

It had become quiet downstairs. Petra took the plunge. 'Yes,' she whispered, 'in here. Yes I do hide a lot.'

'What are you frightened of?'

'He hits my mam when he's drunk.'

Kathleen was shocked. She remembered wondering if Marek had killed Gloria. Maybe he had hit Gloria too, and then things had got even more out of control. 'Does he . . . does he hit you?'

'No.'

'Do you think he might?'

'I don't know.'

Kathleen wasn't sure what to say. She knew the truth was much, much worse. Murders had happened here, in this place. Marek's drunken rages were nothing compared to her awful discoveries in the pond. Gently, she squeezed the other girl's arm. After a moment she realized Petra was crying. 'At least you've got a mam and dad,' she murmured, trying to be consoling. This sounded inadequate. 'I mean, they might not like each other, but at least they're . . . here.'

Petra sniffed and rubbed her nose. 'That's another thing I've wanted to tell you,' she said miserably.

'What?'

'As well as the stuff about borrowing Gloria's clothes . . . I would've told you everything, but I wasn't able to . . . say it.'

'What's everything?'

232

'Gloria told my dad something. Then he told it to my mam on Tuesday night. I was listening at the door.'

'What? What was it?'

Petra took a deep breath. 'Your Auntie Joyce isn't your auntie. She's your mam.'

In an instant Kathleen's mouth went very dry and her heart started to pound. 'No,' she breathed. 'That's not true.'

'It's what Gloria said. She told my dad. She said your Joyce got into trouble just after she'd left school. She got a job working for a vicar somewhere but she had to leave because of . . . you. So she went to a home for unmarried mothers. Everybody knows but no one talks about it. Except Gloria, that is.'

Kathleen had lunged awkwardly forwards, pushing open the door of the airing cupboard. The electric light on the landing blinded her. Unable to see, she ran downstairs through the scullery and out the door.

Now, sitting in her cold bedroom, dismayed and shocked, she examined her christening photograph yet again. Auntie Molly stood in the centre, looking young with rather a lot of dark lipstick and costume jewellery. She was holding a white bundle like a doll that Kathleen knew was herself. Nana was at her side in an old-fashioned utility suit and no-nonsense hat. At the edges of the frames were Joyce and Gloria. Despite a smart coat with layered lapels, which she'd probably made herself, Joyce appeared frightened, Kathleen decided, and her eyes were half closed. Gloria was a toothy child; gawky in her cotton dress and cardigan, a ribbon tying back her short hair. Da had taken the photograph on the Box Brownie, which in those days had been his. Kathleen stared and stared. The dim figures in the background, in the churchyard, were no more than shadows. Why had she assumed one of them was her mother? They weren't posed in the family group. They were practically strangers. Passers-by. They weren't important at all.

She tried to imagine herself as a baby, bound in a white shawl, looking not at the camera, but beyond Auntie Molly's face to the shivering autumn trees in the churchyard and the cloudy sky. Instead she remembered instantly the high, bright hill and the tartan blanket and grass with a buzzing bee. How old could I have been? she wondered. I was carried up that bank on a man's shoulders. He was wearing a white shirt. I sat on the rug and opened a paper bag full of nuts and raisins. 'Chew them, don't swallow them,' the man said to me. The sun was hot on my arms and legs. I made a line of peanuts on the tartan, then a line of raisins. The lady with the red plastic shopping bag gave me a green square in a white cardboard frame. 'That's for looking through, later,' she told me.

Kathleen crawled under the bed with Da's Box Brownie and groped at the rectangular package she'd bought at the chemists. She opened it, broke the foil seal, slid open the camera and placed the metal spool in the top position, turning it so the flanges slipped into place. She then drew out the paper backing, which protected the start of the film and wrapped it around and under the bottom of the Brownie, inserting the tab into the empty take-up spool. She closed the camera and pushed in the winding knob. She crawled out from under the bed and circled the winder until a red number one appeared in the little window. She lay on her bed cradling the camera on her stomach. It was loaded again, ready for use. For some reason this was strangely comforting. Taking pictures was close to, if not quite the same as taking control.

Kathleen dozed for a while. When she opened her eyes the poor shadow of a day had disappeared completely and it was dark and she could see nothing. She remembered Petra's words. Your Auntie Joyce isn't your auntie. She's your mam. She considered this statement from different angles. Maybe Petra had made the whole thing up. Maybe Mr Koninsky had made the whole thing up. Maybe Gloria had made the whole thing up. This last possibility wasn't unlikely. Gloria might have thought Joyce was interested in Mr Koninsky. She might have been jealous and so tried to blacken her character. Auntie Gloria was always contemptuous of Auntie Joyce, Kathleen remembered.

She sighed. She had a headache. As she lay staring at the dim ceiling a bizarre vision took shape in the cold, dead air. She saw Joyce in her underwear, voluptuous but serious, holding hands with Gloria who was drowned and ghastly but strangely resurrected. In turn, Gloria was holding hands with Marek Koninsky whose fingers linked Joyce's in a revolving circle of ghosts. They turned and turned, pale, luminous and tragic. 'Ringa-ringa-roses,' Mr Koninsky, intoned quietly. 'Ringa-ringa roses, a pocket full of posies.' He sounded mournful but resigned.

In the middle of the circle, Nadezhda Koninsky appeared. She didn't move, but merely stood as the spectral, repetitive game enclosed her. Kathleen stared for a while at the feet, legs and trailing hem, which were muddy from the pond, but when she raised her eyes upwards, her heart was once more gripped in the icy clasp of fear. The vision of Mrs Koninsky's face was distorted with madness and fury. Her eyes popped and her mouth was open in a snarl. Her tangled hair hung down. Worst of all her hands were raised as if she was about to break out from the mysterious circle and throttle Kathleen. Her nicotine stained nails were more than six inches long.

Much later, uneasy in her room, uneasy in the house, Kathleen decided to go to Da's shed. She still couldn't decide if Petra's revelation was true. She couldn't take it in. It was too much of a shock. She *was* sure, however, that Gloria had said these things to Marek Koninsky. Gloria had gossiped in a disloyal way. Nana often accused Gloria of spreading rumours about the family around the village. In fact, Nana's sporadic anger about this very thing was the reason Gloria had moved out of the house in First Street into the flat above the salon. Her doing so had made Nana even more furious. 'There's no telling what that *hairdresser* might be doing or saying *now*,' she'd declared.

The fog hadn't lifted. Kathleen was carrying Da's Box Brownie. There wasn't a breath of wind and it tainted the air like smoke. The village was as eerie as a ghost story. Buildings loomed and retreated in unnatural ways. Kathleen could see the blurred outlines of the mine and hear the noise of the machinery but the pithead gear was lost in the darkness. There was no sky. The immediate distance, the far distance and the heavens were merged together in a blur. She decided to take a photograph, because everything was so odd. She took it straight into the lights from the pit hoping to capture the peculiar refraction, framed by grim houses on either side.

She went into the phone booth on the corner of Second Street. It was lit by a dirty electric bulb. She read the instructions carefully, lifted up the receiver, pushed some coins into the box and dialled the number that was displayed on a notice above. When she heard a voice she pressed the button marked 'A'. 'Hello,' she heard Inspector Glen repeat. 'Who's there?'

'Friendship Seven?' she enquired nervously. She'd never used a public telephone before in her life. 'It's Cape. Are you receiving me? Over.'

The policeman sounded distant but concerned. She remembered the last time she'd spoken to him she'd been crying.

'Please listen,' she said a little desperately. 'You've got to listen to me. You're my only hope. Mrs Koninsky killed our Gloria. She killed Nana's Nosey. The thing is, she used to be beautiful with lovely clothes and stuff, and now she's ugly. She's jealous. She was jealous of Auntie Gloria. And I don't think she's stopped. I think she might kill my Auntie Joyce.' Her voice came out in a choked sob. 'I mean my—'

The line crackled.

'My mother,' Kathleen gasped, inaudibly.

Inspector Glen said something she couldn't understand.

'Listen. Friendship Seven, you must listen. This is terrible. I think she might kill my Auntie Joyce. I keep telling you. You must go there with your officers. The answer's at Jinny Hoolets and you have to go there and sort it all out.' Carefully, and swallowing down her emotions, she hung the telephone back on the hook.

Kathleen reached the edge of the village and made her way through the pigeon crees, amongst which was the unlikely lunar observatory. The captive birds were silent, still and bemused by the fog. More bad things are going to happen here, she thought. I can feel it. It's not over. None of this is over yet.

A glimmer of light came from under the door of Da's secret world. She opened it and stepped inside. The roof was closed and it was stuffy from the paraffin heater. Kathleen's glasses steamed up. She took them off and rubbed them. Da immediately became nothing more than a hazy blob in the light at his elbow. She heard him turn towards her and she replaced her spectacles. 'Hello,' she said, noncommittally, as he came into focus.

'A thick old night,' he replied.

'What you doing?'

He gestured towards a sheaf of calculations and drawings. 'Moon work,' he said.

Kathleen stood at his side and watched as he continued.

'What exactly *is* fog?' she asked.

'Fog is water vapour. It happens when moist air cools.'

'Why is it yellow?'

'It mixes with the smoke from the fires.'

'You can't see a thing, out there.'

'I know.' Da wrote out a complicated equation.

'It's very strange not being able to see where things begin and end. It's like not wearing your glasses.' She thought about Gloria and Nosey. It's also like being sure what happened to them, she decided. Knowing but not knowing. Seeing but not seeing.

Da was examining a cross section of the lunar crater Eratosthenes. His representations of it were neat and methodical, his figures tiny and obsessive. Kathleen read the words across the top of the diagram – outer country – rampart – central elevation and then in reverse – central elevation – rampart – outer country.

'Outer country,' she murmured, liking the sound of these two words. 'Outer country.' They made her think of the hidden fields outside the shed, sloping away towards foggy thickets, valleys, hills where she'd never ever been. This led as usual to her missing mother and father, lost in an unknown wilderness. She licked her lips, on the verge of telling Da what Petra had said about Auntie Joyce and to inform him that the comment had originated with Gloria. She stopped herself. There was no point. Da would just get agitated and say something about Petra being mischievous. Or he would be angry with Gloria. He wouldn't be prepared to shed any light on the matter. He wouldn't look at it. He wouldn't willingly discuss anything personal or even be able to move it easily around his mind.

'Da?' she said tentatively. She hesitated. If I can't ask Da, she thought, then I can't ask anyone. That means I'll never know. I must ask him.

'Yes, pet?'

She swallowed and the words got stuck in her throat. It was impossible. 'You know you said President Kennedy would back off over this Cuba business?'

'That's right.'

'Well, he's not, is he? I mean, he's sticking to his guns.'

Da leant back and sighed. He seemed exhausted. He tipped his head and stared at the wooden roof. 'It's worrying you, isn't it?'

'Yes.' Kathleen gulped, audibly. 'Isn't it worrying you?'

Da turned and faced her. He looks tired, she thought. He looks ill. He seemed so strong this morning, but really, he's changed in the last few days. It's all been too much for him.

'It's worrying me, pet, but it has to take its place in the queue. I'm worried about my daughter lying unburied whilst the authorities try to decide what to do. I've been at the police station nearly all day and I can't get any answers. They just keep asking me the same things over and over again.' He rubbed his face with both hands then shoved his fists into the sockets of his eyes. 'I'm worried about your Nana's bad nerves. They're getting worse. I'm worried about Koninsky, the future of the pit and the jobs of almost all the men in this village.'

Kathleen reached out and nearly touched his shoulder, but then withdrew her hand. She still felt unable to discuss anything personal, even with this encouragement. 'If we go in with the Americans there might be a war in Europe.'

'Kennedy doesn't want a real war. It's more a war of nerves. He's trying to prove a point.'

'I keep thinking about a big bomb being dropped on the village and everything crumbling into dust. The pit, the shops, the rows, the Welfare, the bingo, the railway lines . . .'

Da reached out and pulled her towards him. She leant against his chest feeling suddenly more secure. She could smell his pipe and the ink from his fountain pen below on the table. She didn't want to move away. I wish I could stay here like this, she thought. It's nice in here, with Da, with the heater on. It's like a little island in the sea of fog.

# SUNDAY

Nadezhda Koninsky lay in bed staring at the painting of the Virgin's Sacred Heart. It seemed to glow, as if alive. Through her mind, a familiar prayer ran almost unacknowledged. She glanced towards the window and noticed a chink of sunlight slanting into the room. It penetrated under the curtain and fell in a bright pool on her small altar. God's goodness is shining into my life, she thought irrationally. It has driven away the fog. It is the Lord's day, today. I will arise and go to Mass.

Nadezhda was depressed, but occasionally, very rarely, her spirit soared. This morning she felt her pulse race, her energy rise. She turned and examined the sleeping face of her husband. He looked young and carefree for a change, lost in slumber. His hair was tangled like a boy's and his long eyelashes cast shadows on his cheeks. Gently she stroked his naked arm. Poor Marek, she thought. His life is such a disappointment to him and he has no faith. She watched as he lazily opened his eyes. Still dazed from sleep he smiled and, seeing this, Nadezhda rolled towards him.

'I am going to Mass,' she said, happily. 'The sun is shining today.'

Sensing her change of mood, he lifted his arm and drew her into his side. She nestled on his shoulder.

From downstairs there came the sound of Petra's record player.

Nadezhda coughed. 'That awful music.'

They listened together for a moment. There was the clash of electric guitars.

'Everything will be all right,' Marek said, hopelessly. 'Trust me.'

'You always say the same thing.' She rubbed her face on his neck. 'My husband.'

'You are my little sparrow. And I keep you in this awful cage.' He turned on to his side and kissed her on the mouth, his hands groping for the hem of her night dress, pulling it up. 'I need you.'

Back home from Sunday School, Kathleen stood on the top stairs, outside Joyce's bedroom. She rubbed her eyes, tempted to go back to bed for a while. She had slept very badly, restless, dreaming of arguments and empty buildings.

Confident that the coast was clear she crept soundlessly into Joyce's room. She opened the bedside cabinet and took out a flat wicker basket with a lid tied on with string. Carrying this, she tiptoed back up to her cold attic and closed her door.

Joyce kept all her personal documents in this basket. Kathleen had occasionally observed her examining her wage slips or her post office savings book. Now, unsure of what she was looking for, she felt compelled to search through any secrets which her aunt might be hiding. She opened the basket on the bed. Carefully, methodically she went through all the documents it contained. I should have done this before, she thought, wide awake, her heart thudding with anticipation.

At first the scraps of paper and correspondence seemed boring. It was a mixture of guarantees, bills, communications from the National Insurance scheme, receipts for shoe repairs, an old school report. Kathleen opened them, inspected them and stacked them into a neat pile. There were no personal letters or postcards, no birthday or Christmas cards. The papers all seemed unsentimental, pedestrian, run of the mill. Joyce had kept everything official and everything useful. Kathleen persevered. Finally, and having almost given up hope, towards the bottom of the basket she found an old package. From this she pulled two letters written in a florid hand. The stamps indicated that they were not recent. Kathleen took the folded sheets from their stiff envelopes. She read them quickly, then feeling dizzy and a little sick, she went through them again. One was dated July 1950 and the other September 1950. They were both from the Reverend Taylor in the Vicarage on Marley Hill. It was clear that Joyce had worked for him as a housekeeper. It was the exact situation described by Auntie Molly. In the earlier of the two letters he enquired after Joyce's health, hoped her spirits were high and told her to pray for guidance and strength. He said he missed her cheerful presence, her hard work and her mince and dumplings. He said the Lord moves in mysterious ways His wonders to perform. He mentioned the weather, his own plans to retire, a broken window in the summerhouse. Kathleen checked the envelope. It had been sent to Joyce 'care of' The Society for the Unmarried Mother and Her Child. Across the front someone had scrawled 'Ashgrove Court' and it had been forwarded.

The second letter said the Reverend Taylor was delighted to learn that Joyce was being so brave and so sensible. He insisted upon rejoicing in this new life because every baby was a child of the Lord and a blessed member of His Flock, whatever the unfortunate circumstances. He said his arthritis was playing up and he'd made arrangements to move to Warkworth in May. He wished Joyce luck and told her that we all live under the succour and protection of a forgiving, beneficent God. He said he very much liked the name 'Kathleen' which was both serviceable and feminine. He said he enclosed ten pounds. This second letter had been sent directly to the house in First Street.

Her hands shaking, Kathleen emptied the package. Her heart almost stopped. There was a pair of tiny bootees, knitted in white wool with pink ribbons. There was a lock of fine brown baby hair tied in red string. There was a studio portrait of 'Kathleen 1950' lying in a nappy on a sheepskin rug. There was a yellowing card with infant weights and measurements, charted by a nurse at the village Welfare. Her own and Joyce's name were filled in boldly across the top. It's true, she breathed. Our Joyce is not my auntie, she's my mam. She searched and searched, but there was no birth certificate. She returned the basket to Joyce's cupboard. She felt light headed, nauseous and dismayed.

Later, trembling a little, Kathleen went downstairs. Joyce was alone in the kitchen, at her sewing machine. 'Come here,' she said brusquely, her mouth full of pins, 'let's try this for size.'

'Where's Nana?'

'In her room.' She slipped the bodice of the alice blue gown over Kathleen's head. It was trimmed with lace and buttons and it was tight.

Kathleen took a deep breath. 'It's too small,' she said, surprised that her voice was so steady. She regarded the short sleeves with suspicion. 'It's babyish.'

Joyce spat out the pins. 'It'll be fine with nothing underneath. If you don't wear a vest it'll fit perfectly. It's supposed to be tight. It's nice.' She deftly measured Kathleen from waist to knee and picked up the skirt, which was almost complete. 'There was going to be a cummerbund but I haven't got the satin.'

'I don't want a cummerbund.'

'Then that's all right then.' She smiled. 'Don't disappear. You'll need to try it on when I've sewn it all together.'

Kathleen said nothing.

'Well. What do you say?'

She eased off the bodice and laid it on the machine. She was dumb.

'How about thank you Auntie Joyce?'

'Thank you.'

Joyce pushed the hem of the skirt under the needle and rattled away. She hummed violently.

Kathleen suddenly didn't want to go to the dance tonight, but couldn't admit this. 'How will we get in if Billy Fishboy's still in gaol? Da won't go. We can't go on our own.' She moved towards the door.

Joyce paused. 'Billy? He'll be out by tonight. They'll let him go. It's not as if he did it. Is it?'

'No.'

'Billy Fishboy's too big a coward to go down Jinny Hoolets on his own after dark, let alone push bloody Gloria in the pond.' Joyce was unnaturally cheerful. Her excitement about the dance that evening was almost electric. She hummed again, racing along the hem.

'Is it all right if I go out just for a bit?' She escaped towards the door, relieved to be getting away.

'Don't be long.'


Kathleen left for Jinny Hoolets. Her dread of the pond, her fear and distrust of the Koninskys were overcome for the moment by new warm feelings towards her friend. She felt she could risk going down there in order to tell Petra she was right about Joyce being her mam and to apologize for rushing off the previous day. It was the least she could do. I might never have known, she realized, if it wasn't for Petra Koninsky. I might have gone on and on, not knowing.

The fog had miraculously cleared and the sky was white with small patches of blue. A thin, half-hearted sun came and went but the air was cold and sharp. Kathleen shivered and chewed the end of one of her plaits, which today had finally become long enough to reach her mouth. I don't want our Joyce to be my mam, she thought. She doesn't love me.

As she was going down the slope towards the lonely house a cloud moved in from the village covering the sun. The pit heaps straight away took on their normal dismal, life-denying appearance. A ragged plume of smoke trailed from the chimney of the dwelling and the sulky water frowned a warning. There's no 'funny man' Kathleen reminded herself, firmly. Jinny Hoolets is foul, but so are lots of ruined places around here. This *is* the Durham coalfield and it's foul, black and dirty. Petra was either inventing or imagining things with her 'funny man'.

The sky seemed to mass with cloud and the day turned dark. An invisible train clanked and rattled without energy. Kathleen's feet disturbed loose lumps of coal which skittered down the steep slope. There's no ghosts, no peeping toms, she repeated. Mr Koninsky is a bad man and his wife... She stopped and considered. His wife is a murdering nutcase and the police are coming to arrest her. I hope I don't bump into either of *them*, this morning she thought. She continued on her way. 'That's a very serious allegation,' she said aloud. 'A very serious allegation indeed.' She deliberately avoided looking at the water. A Russian bomb would flatten all this, she decided. The pond would turn to steam.

At the bottom of the hill, behind the area normally occupied by Mr Koninsky's car, Kathleen saw a red rectangle. She went over to have a look, passing along the side of the building. I wonder if that's Auntie Joyce's Chubby Checker LP, she thought, the one I accidentally lost. She drew close to the object but discovered it was an old tin tray, advertising beer. It had come from the pub and Kathleen knew that boys, sliding down the heaps, had probably used it as a sledge. Disappointed she approached the rear of the dwelling. I'll never find that LP now, she decided. Suddenly she caught sight of Petra and stopped.

Her friend was standing in the ground floor bay window of her bedroom, holding her body in a stiff ballet position. Her face was distorted with concentration. Kathleen stepped to one side, out of view and watched. Petra was wearing the same short, ragged tutu that she herself had tried on in the spare bedroom, yesterday. The window framed her, almost as far down as her feet, as if she were on a stage. A light in the corner of the room illuminated her from the side. She moved awkwardly, holding one stylized pose after another. She's hardly a ballerina, thought Kathleen. She's a bit of a cart horse, actually. I bet her mam's disappointed.

After a while, Petra's movements became freer and she began dancing. Abandoning formal movements she threw herself around with enthusiasm but no grace. She's got her record player going, Kathleen decided. She's listening to Bobby Vee or maybe Helen Shapiro. She smiled. She looks funny in that ballet costume. It's all torn at the back and baggy between the legs.

After a while Petra approached the glass. She was red cheeked and clearly breathless. Her mouth made a bleary circle on the pane, which partly hid her face.

Kathleen raised Da's Box Brownie and positioned her in the viewfinder.

Petra, facing straight ahead, pulled down the shoulders of her mother's tutu, at exactly the same moment as Kathleen released the shutter. She'd exposed her adolescent breasts. Her stance was defiant.

Kathleen stared through the camera, horrified. She glanced about. To her relief, there was no one else around. What does Petra think she's doing? Boys come to these heaps to play. People walk along here quite often. It's a footpath. Why's she taking her stupid clothes off? She was both shocked and embarrassed.

Petra slid the tutu over her hips, standing briefly naked, facing the outside world, before yanking the curtains closed.

Kathleen moved slowly towards the front door. She adjusted her glasses. Maybe there really are funny men hanging around here, she decided. The sort of men who look at dirty pictures and wear raincoats and expose themselves in alleys. If Petra's been doing *that* sort of thing in her window with the light on, I'm surprised there aren't hundreds of them. She's mad. The whole family's mad.

Marek was miles away, driving in his car. He had no particular destination in mind. He had set off because the weather was pleasant, for a change. Now, he noticed, after a few exhausted sunbeams had played around briefly then gone in, clouds rolled across the high moors above Consett. The sky was a panorama of angry colour. The fells were dotted with sheep. They sloped away for miles above and below this narrow, unlikely road in their steep curves of rock and dead heather.

The little black Ford struggled with the gradients. I could drive off here, Marek thought, tumble down, over and over and burst into flames. No one would ever find me. He regarded the vast landscape, the inhospitable summits, the negligible impression made by man. Would anyone bother to look? He changed gear as the engine ached. He watched a bird wheel overhead then plummet. I could stop the car, start walking and never be seen again. I could lose myself breathing fresh clean air. I could melt into this English earth.

He thought about Nadezhda and her high spirits that morning as she prepared herself to go to mass. She'd had a bath for the first time in months. He knew her mood wouldn't last. Now the sun had gone in she would be wretched again and downcast. She was lonely and depressed and had no control over her life.

Just then, a blinding flash bisected the windscreen and there was the dull roar of far-away thunder. Huge raindrops splashed on the bonnet and glass. So much for the sunshine Marek thought. He wanted to laugh. I have got to do something about this awful girl Joyce, he decided. I cannot stand her prattling any longer. I have got to rid myself of her.


Later, in the house in First Street, Nana came down to prepare the Sunday lunch. She was quiet, still sad about Nosey, but absorbed. She said nothing to Joyce.

'I'm hand-stitching this lining,' said Joyce, sitting behind her sewing machine, quite lost herself in concentration. She was attaching the skirt lining to the alice blue gown. 'I've only got the thinnest of seams to work with,' she reported. 'She's grown so much, there wasn't enough material.'

The air was scented with the smell of roasting beef. Nana silently removed the joint from the oven to pour off a little sizzling juice into a flat dish. She arranged potatoes around the meat and basted them, before floating her hour-old batter in the separated fat, putting it in the top oven for Yorkshire pudding. She returned the roasting tin to the range. She mopped her face with a teatowel. She prepared cabbage and carrots and a pan of early Brussels sprouts. She laid the table with her second best china, which was used on ordinary Sundays. Polishing the glass tumblers, she held them up to the window, squinting with her short-sighted eye. She brought out a pitcher of home-made ginger beer from the pantry. She looked at the clock, which ticked steadily, its face glowing orange in the reflection from the banked-up fire.

The wireless played familiar hymns. 'I wonder if that dirty hussy from Jinny Hoolets makes a proper dinner,' Nana said.

'She'll be too busy praying,' commented Joyce. 'Or spying on people.'

Detective Inspector Glen stood opposite Billy Fishboy in the interview room at the police station. His hands were on his hips and he was scowling. The Sergeant lounged by the door, impassive. Billy was slumped in the uncomfortable chair by the desk, one hand shielding his eyes from the light. He was unshaven and sweaty, despite the chill. He was tired. He looked ill.

'I won't say it again,' threatened the Inspector. 'What have you got to say for yourself?'

'Come on son,' murmured the gentler policeman, from the sidelines. 'Spit it out.'

Billy was immobile, silent for a full two minutes.

'We've got nothing but time,' said the senior officer.

The Sergeant sighed. 'Today, tonight, tomorrow, tomorrow night . . .'

Billy shifted and sat upright. He primped his hair. He looked at a single large black and white photograph on the desk. It was glossy in the lamp glare. He placed one hand on top and smoothed it with his palm. This was a gesture of ownership. 'God in Heaven,' he whispered to himself.

'Well?'

'Gloria took this, sir,' Billy admitted at last.

'In the salon,' agreed the Sergeant.

'In the salon.'

There was another pause. Billy shook a little, as if crying, and he closed his eyes but there were no tears. 'I'm sorry,' he whispered.

'There's no need to be sorry, son,' said the Sergeant kindly. 'There's nothing to be sorry about.'

'It's not easy,' Billy agreed, 'being like me.'

'Of course it isn't.'

The Inspector moved heavily to the desk, picked up the photo, snorted, then threw it down again.

'It must be very hard,' added the Sergeant for good measure. 'Very, very hard.'

Billy placed one index finger on the picture drawing it towards him. He stared. 'This is how I like to be seen, sometimes,' he said. 'Like *this*. This is how I like to see myself sometimes. As Mina.'

'Mina?'

'That's right.'

'I see. Mina.'

The picture showed Billy in a pink evening dress. He was sitting in one of Gloria's hairdressing chairs and his legs were awkwardly crossed within a long, tight skirt, his toes pointed, in a parody of femininity. His face was heavily made up and he was wearing a black wig, which was elaborately styled. He didn't really resemble a woman. He looked instead exactly like himself, in fancy dress.

'This is Gloria's new gown. The one she got for the dance tonight.' For a moment he was animated. 'It's pink moiré with organza ruffles – a little bit tight, I admit. We were trying a new hairstyle.'

Inspector Glen was speechless.

The Sergeant struggled for words. 'Go on, Billy,' he stuttered.

'Gloria loved dressing me up. She said it was a challenge. Making me presentable.'

Still wordless, the Inspector placed his own fat finger on the image.

'Yes,' said Billy as if answering a question. 'I wrote that on the mirror with lipstick. *I was trapped, now I'm free.* That's how I felt, sir. That's how I feel when I . . . transform myself.'

'When was this?' said Inspector Glen, curtly.

'The Sunday she died. In the afternoon. The salon was closed of course. I got dressed upstairs then we went down for the hairdo. Later on, I changed back into Billy and went to work.' He swallowed hard. 'I never saw her again.'

Inspector Glen sat down. He coughed. 'What exactly *was* your relationship with . . . with the dead woman?'

'Well, it wasn't the usual kind of thing.'

The Inspector snorted again. He was horrified, angry and out of his depth. 'You said it, son.'

'We were friends, that's all.'

'Friends?'

'Friends.'

'She dressed you up?'

'Yes. She did my make-up, everything. I think she thought it was a laugh.' Billy considered. 'Gloria thought lots of things were a laugh, sir. Me, her family, Koninsky's wife. Gloria was cynical. She took the mickey out of everything.' He paused. 'Except her own future. She was very serious about that.'

There was a silence.

'You're a puff, are you?' asked the Inspector.

Billy was surprised. 'Pardon?'

'You're a puff. A shirtlifter. A homo.'

'No, I'm not.'

The Inspector laughed, harshly. 'Don't pull my leg.'

'I'm not pulling your leg. I'm not homosexual.'

'You like little boys.'

'Not in the way *you* mean, sir.'

'You take photographs of little boys.'

'So?'

'You're a homo.'

'No, I'm not.' Billy sounded desperate, frustrated.

The Sergeant walked towards them both.

Billy looked at him appealingly. 'The photos of the boys . . They're nothing. They mean nothing. It's just that . . . it's just—'

'What, son?' asked the Sergeant.

Billy paused, collected his thoughts. 'They remind me of time in my life when I was happy.'

'What?'

'I was happy when I was nine, ten. Everything was all righ then. Since then . . . I've been . . . unhappy. I take the photo help out at the Cubs, spend time with boys . . . to remind mysel of those days, to relive them. When I was ten. That's all. It nothing sinister. I—'

'But you're a puff,' Inspector Glen interrupted.

'I am not.'

'Only a puff would carry on . . . ' The Inspector gesture contemptuously towards the photograph. 'This way.'

'No you don't understand, it's not *like that*—'

'You're a pervert, a nancy boy, a five bob note.'

Billy let out a long sigh. He leaned back in his chair and stare at the ceiling, his arms dangling. 'You don't understand.'

'You're right. I do not. Understand, that is. I do not under stand, *thank goodness*.'

No one said anything for a while.

Billy tried again. 'There *are* one or two homosexuals in thes parts—'

'Oh yes? More of you, are there? And who may they be You've got a homo club started round here, have you? A puffs coven?'

Billy continued, levelly. 'There are homosexuals living i these parts, going about their business, harming no one, gettin on with their lives. But I'm not like them. I'm different. I jus like dressing up, that's all. It's perfectly simple—'

'Simple?' The Inspector was deep purple. He looked ready t explode. 'Hah!'

Billy leant towards him and met his eye, directly. 'Inspector?'

'What?'

He spoke very slowly. 'You – know – nothing.'

The Inspector laughed hollowly, yet again.

'You know nothing. You understand nothing. You've experienced nothing. You're an ignorant man.'

The Inspector stood up, glowered, adjusted his trousers, shoved his chair aggressively under the desk, turned on his heel and left the room.

'You've really upset him now, Billy,' said the Sergeant.

Da sat in a corner of the Causey Arms smoking his pipe. He nursed a half of bitter whilst his marra, Jonty Dickinson, went to the bar to get himself another pint. Da never drank much. He disliked being drunk. He wasn't interested in getting out of control.

'I don't see how,' said Jonty, returning and sitting down, 'if all this is true, I don't see how getting rid of Koninsky's going to help. In the long run.'

'No. You're right. If their agenda is to close us then they'll close us. It's just a question of when. But I want to drag it out. That's our only hope. Not for months, though. For years.'

'What's your plan?'

Da sucked on the stem of his pipe for a few seconds in silence. A haze of fragrant smoke surrounded him. Then he took it from his mouth and examined it carefully. In another booth there was a rattle of dominoes and a group of young miners played darts on the other side of the bar.

'Like I said. Time. We've got to play for time. If we can get rid of Koninsky we'll get a reprieve. A reprieve may mean a chance for more negotiation at district, even national level. We'll string it out. I'll buy time. But as long as he's writing that damned report, we haven't time. He's the Angel of Death.'

Jonty nodded. 'They're putting all their resources in at those pits on the coast.'

'That's right. We're under-mechanized here. We've got no facilities. We're a small pit with a limited life. The thing is, there's plenty of coal still down there. We could go on for a lot more years.' He frowned.

'Why do they want to close us?'

'Economics, strategy, business planning. As you say, they want these modern pits with big outputs which go for miles under the sea.'

'What about our communities? Villages?'

Da smiled, ruefully.

'This village was made for coal. There wasn't a village here before the pit.'

'This village *is* coal. That's the beginning and end of the story.' Da gestured around the room. 'And these people are coal. The houses, shops, and school are coal. The chapel and churches are coal. The streets are coal. Everything's coal. There's nothing else.' He put his pipe back in his mouth, struck a match and pulled in the flame. He breathed in the smoke, exhaled then pointed with the pipe. 'If coal goes, the whole village goes. End of story.'

Jonty stared into the foam on the top of his glass. 'What are you going to do?'

'Threaten and argue and plead. I'm going to rid us of that damned foreigner with his fancy suits and silk neckties. He'll be sent packing.' He sounded sure. 'Very soon.'

Jonty swallowed half the beer in his glass. His adam's apple jiggled up and down. He sighed.

Da turned his own glass around thoughtfully. 'I could kill him,' he said. 'I could ring his blasted Polish neck.'

*

Petra opened the front door wrapped in her stained dressing gown. She was still slightly red-faced and breathless.

Kathleen followed her inside without indicating she'd seen the performance in the bedroom window. 'Are you by yourself?'

Petra nodded. She picked up the kettle. 'Coffee?'

Kathleen was relieved. 'No thanks.'

There was an awkward silence. They stood in the dirty scullery, each of them wary. 'I'm sorry about yesterday,' said Kathleen eventually. She noticed that Petra's feet were bare and grimy.

'Sorry for what?'

'Running off like that.'

Petra shrugged. 'Come through to my room,' she suggested. 'It's warmer in there.'

It was hot and dark in Petra's bedroom with the curtains closed. There was a smell of sweat mixed with cosmetics. A small lamp lit one corner and an ancient looking electric fire with frayed wires was plugged in next to the record player. It glowed orange in a friendly way.

Kathleen sat in the gloom, on the unmade bed and Petra switched on the music. She placed the needle on a Cliff Richard long player.

'You were right about my Auntie Joyce,' said Kathleen, her voice breaking slightly.

'Have you talked to her?' Surprisingly, Petra lay down next to where she was sitting, on the bed.

'No.'

'Aren't you pleased?' Petra raised two empty fingers to her lips, pretending to smoke.

'Pleased?'

'Pleased you've got a mam?'

Kathleen considered this. 'I suppose so.'

'I thought you would be, but I was scared to tell you. Gloria gossiped and my dad talked about it and I knew I should tell you straight away. But then I thought you might not believe me. I thought you might and go and tell your nan.'

'I don't talk to Nana.'

'You were illegitimate.' She said these words in her usual know-it-all manner.

'I suppose so.'

'It's better than being an orphan.'

'Yes.' Kathleen thought for a moment. 'I'd rather Gloria had been my mam.'

Petra hesitated. 'I'm sorry about your dog.' Her voice was softer.

They listened to a song called 'The Next Time'. It was slow and sentimental. Petra reached over to her bedside table. 'D'you want a fruit gum?'

'Yes.'

There was a rustle of paper. 'D'you think Cliff's good looking?'

'He's all right.'

Petra stared at the ceiling, jiggling one foot in time to the music. 'D'you know what I think?'

'What?'

'I think Cliff'll stay up at the top with Elvis. I don't think the Beatles will last. They're good, mind, I'm not saying they aren't. That 'Love Me Do' is great. But they won't last. They're a flash in the pan.'

'Gloria said the opposite, when she bought the record,' replied Kathleen, regretting this immediately.

Petra didn't get angry. She didn't rise to the challenge.

She's in a very agreeable mood thought Kathleen. It's because she's trying to make it up with me. She's still ashamed about borrowing Gloria's things. 'Are you coming to the dance tonight?'

'Are you going?'

'Yes. Well, maybe. If Billy Fishboy from the cinema takes us, I'm going with Auntie Joyce.'

'Your mam.'

'My mam.'

'If you're going I might go.' Petra sounded keen.

'You have to be partnered. Your dad or someone will have to take you. D'you think he will?'

'He might.' Petra rolled over on to her side, closer to Kathleen. 'Have you got anything to wear? D'you want to borrow something?'

'It's OK.' Kathleen could smell her soiled dressing gown and the fruit gum on her breath. She moved back against the wall.

'I'm sorry about Gloria,' said Petra. She reached out and took hold of Kathleen's hand. 'I know I said I hated her and everything, but I'm sorry about wearing her clothes. It was wrong. Unfair. It was . . . shocking. Cross my heart and hope to die – I wish I hadn't done it.'

Kathleen swallowed. She was embarrassed. She didn't like Petra touching her. I want to go home, she thought. 'It's all right,' she muttered.

'Are you still my friend?'

'Yes.' Kathleen blinked.

Petra sighed with relief. She squeezed Kathleen's hand. 'That's good.' She sounded happy for a change. 'You're the only friend I've got in the whole wide world.'

Joyce sat at her sewing machine as the vegetables bubbled on the hob and Nana clattered back and forth with cutlery, a dish of horseradish, the second best cruet set. She watched as her mother banged the pan lids and poured out cooking water for gravy, stirring violently and humming along to 'Dear Lord and Father of Mankind' on the wireless. The meal's nearly ready, she thought.

The smell of roast beef always reminded her of a sailor she'd known when she was young. He came to the house in First Street several times when he was on leave and once he brought her a bunch of fabric roses, which she'd later sewn on to a straw hat. He'd had a good appetite. She'd been sure he was going to propose. She'd loved him, in a way, or maybe she'd just loved his uniform. It was too long ago now to be sure. He was called Ken, she remembered, as she stitched and tucked, neatly. Ken, yes. Ken. She sighed. Ken what? She couldn't recall his surname. One night, in the light from her torch, she'd seen him in the back row of the Essoldo, his arm around Gloria, who was only fifteen. Joyce had been furious about them coming to the cinema, when they could have gone on a date anywhere. At home, after work, she'd slapped Gloria's face. She'd confronted *him* some time later. 'I'm too young to be a father,' he'd sneered.

Joyce broke off her thread and held up the finished skirt of Kathleen's alice blue gown. Bloody Gloria, she thought. And *then* she sold me down the river with Mr Dobbs from the Sunday School.

Later, after lunch was cleared away, Kathleen stood in her knickers in front of a roaring fire in Nana's kitchen. The flames were too hot but also comforting on her bare skin and were reflected in her spectacles. She stepped away, into cooler air, then back again. The light from the blaze lit up the centre of the room whilst the corners stayed in shadow. Kathleen flopped into the big chair, conscious of the empty space at her feet where Nosey used to lie. She pushed Nana's knitting down the side of the cushion, to stop the needles jabbing her bare flesh. 'Where's Nana?' she asked Joyce.

'Asleep I expect.'

'Where's Da?'

'Gone out.' Joyce's voice rose against the noise of her sewing machine as she trundled up the edge of a zip fastening. She neatly finished off the ends, then tore at the threads with her teeth. She picked up a needle and began hand-finishing the top and bottom of the zip. 'Nearly there,' she commented. She was even more excited than she had been earlier.

There was the sound of Big Ben striking on the wireless and the news began. Kathleen listened. The broadcaster said the situation was still serious, still unresolved and there was a sense of time running out. A Soviet surface-to-air missile had shot down an American U-2 spy plane whilst it was gathering intelligence over Cuba. Mr Krushchev had issued a second ultimatum about US troops withdrawing from Turkey. American politicians were calling for an all-out invasion of the island.

Kathleen lay back in the chair, experiencing her usual rush of fear. She imagined Kennedy and Khrushchev, both sitting at huge desks surrounded by telephones. The Russian was stony faced, wearing a fur hat and coat. It was snowing outside his window and somewhere in the background there was the sound of balalaika music and energetic Slavic shouts. The American was warmer and more relaxed in a modern suit and haircut. He had an uneaten hamburger on a plate. His wife Jackie flitted around the room wafting a feather duster along the picture rail, a frilly apron protecting her slim, impeccable outfit. Each man held a fat thumb over a red button. They're going to press them, Kathleen thought. They're going to press them and blow up the whole stupid, bastard world. She considered this phrase. It was the kind of thing Petra would say. She liked the sound of it. She whispered it to herself. 'The whole stupid, bastard world.'

Joyce turned irritably towards the wireless and switched it off. 'There's a good turn out expected tonight,' she offered, cheerfully. 'The Co-op have had an order for over a hundred pie and pea suppers.' She stood and proudly held up Kathleen's dress. 'Here you are. All done.'

Kathleen stared. It *was* babyish. It had a short gathered skirt, puffed sleeves and a peter pan collar. The bodice was trimmed with parallel lines of lace and fabric-covered imitation buttons. She stood up and Joyce slipped it over her head, pulling up the zip triumphantly. 'An alice blue gown. You couldn't have got nicer in a shop,' she asserted, 'even if I do say so myself.'

'Thank you,' said Kathleen miserably. The dress was tight but the fabric soft and luxurious.

'Have you got any decent socks?'

'No. And I haven't any shoes. Only my school shoes and one welly.'

'I've got some flatties you can borrow.'

'But you've got size six and a half feet.'

'We'll stuff paper in the toes.'

Kathleen sighed.

'Cheer up, misery! You'll be Princess Anne!'

Kathleen attempted a smile.

'You stay here. I'll go and try mine on. Don't move.' She took the dress on its hanger from behind the door and disappeared.

Auntie Joyce is my mam, Kathleen thought for the hundreth time. She smoothed her skirt and considered. At least she takes the trouble to make dresses and doesn't run about the pitheaps like a crazy woman in rags. At least she's not a mad, scary murdering nutcase. At least she's not going to get arrested and hanged by the neck until she's dead like bastard Ruth Ellis. She stood on her toes then lifted up one leg, holding it against her bottom. She counted the seconds she was able to hold her balance. She toppled then turned two pirouettes. I look about seven years old in this, she thought. I wish I hadn't told Petra to come. She'll never get over it.

Joyce returned wearing her dress. It was very green. She turned on the main overhead light. Kathleen took off her glasses, polished them on her hem and replaced them. Joyce was flushed and happy. 'What do you think?'

Kathleen looked her up and down. Her skirts were standing out at almost ninety degrees from her body, buoyed on a raft of can-can petticoats. There's too much net, Kathleen thought. The lime, imitation silk bodice was boned throughout, shaped in a deep heart. It clenched her waist and thrust her breasts upwards and out. Her arms, shoulders, chest and back were uncovered. Most of her breasts were bare although the nipples were hidden. It's tarty, Kathleen decided. 'It's lovely,' she lied. Auntie Joyce is my mother, she suddenly thought and she thinks by wearing this, she'll get a man.

From behind her back, Joyce produced two pairs of shoes. The green stilettos she dropped on the floor, then climbed into them, increasing her height by five inches. The white flatties with cut out shapes she offered to Kathleen. 'Here.'

Kathleen slipped them on. They were enormous but rather grown up. 'Nice,' she muttered, grudgingly.

Grinning, Joyce tottered to the sideboard and took Nana's hairbrush from a drawer. She pulled it through her own thick locks. 'For once, I wish bloody Gloria was here,' she said. 'I'm going to have to put this haystack up on my own.' Kathleen noticed she was wearing nylons with seams up the back. Gloria hated those, she recalled. She said they're not modern.

Joyce turned. Her cheeks were flushed and her gestures quick with anticipation. 'I can't wait,' she said. 'Come here.' She unfastened each of Kathleen's plaits. She placed her in front of the mirror and stood behind. Gently, she ran the brush through the girl's thin hair. She coaxed it back, then made a parting and took it over to the side. 'We're going to have to sort this out,' she said. 'You want ringlets?'

'Ringlets?' Kathleen was horrified.

'Maybe not.' Joyce considered. 'You'll have to wear it up, like mine.'

Kathleen was pleased. 'I don't know how we'll manage,' she replied.

Joyce experimented. She gathered Kathleen's hair into a pony tail, then two bunches. She brushed it more vigorously.

Kathleen enjoyed the sensation.

Joyce wound it into a french pleat, then tried a top bun. She was enthusiastic. 'It'll go up,' she insisted. 'It'll take a lot of clips to hold these ends in. We'll need to lacquer it.'

Kathleen didn't want her to stop. 'I like you brushing my hair,' she said.

'I'll do it properly later.' She put the brush away and switched the wireless back on. The BBC orchestra was playing the tune of 'Speedy Gonzales', but slowly, as if it was an old-fashioned melody. Joyce crossed the room and turned off the main light. Kathleen smiled. She felt a lot better. Joyce's happiness was catching. We're going to have a good time, she decided. I'll look all right. It'll be a great lark at the dance, all dressed up with hair lacquer and everything.

Joyce grabbed her arm and waist pulling her against the bouncy net underskirts. She whirled her round. They pretended to waltz for a minute in the illuminated small space between the table and the hearth. 'Mind yourself!' Kathleen shouted joyfully. 'Mind you don't catch yourself in the fire!'

'I can't wait for tonight,' exclaimed Joyce. 'I can't wait another minute!' She glanced at the clock. 'But first I have to go to bloody work.'

Upstairs in her room, Kathleen hung her dress carefully over the back of a chair. She stuffed paper into the toes of Joyce's shoes. She looked at the black and white photo of Nosey propped up on her chest of drawers. I'll go bare legged, she decided, then people might think I'm wearing stockings.

She climbed under her bedclothes because it was cold, away from the fire downstairs. She picked up, but then immediately discarded her copy of *Princess* magazine. Instead, she began reading another chapter of *The Amateur Astronomer*. At first she couldn't concentrate. Her mind was racing and images of Nosey, Inspector Glen, Gloria, Petra and Nadezhda jostled through her consciousness. In the background was the repeating phrase 'Joyce is your mam, Joyce is your mam'. Her excited anticipation from downstairs now changed to a feeling of dread. The Russians are coming, she thought, illogically. She tore back the paper from the packet of fruit gums, given to her by Petra earlier, and chose an orange one.

Kathleen dozed a little. When she awoke she realized she'd been dreaming about the high grassy hill which she'd ascended on the shoulders of the man she believed to be her father. This gave her a warm feeling and she snuggled under the covers. However hard she tried, she could not bring to mind his face. 'It won't be long now,' the lady had said, looking at the sky. She remembered making lines on the blanket with nuts and raisins. She was wearing a white hat with a brim to stop her face from burning. The man's shoulders had been wide and strong and as he carried her, as she rolled from side to side, high above the world, she'd pretended she was on a ship.

She sat up and turning to the appendices in her book, she forced herself to understand the words and numbers. After a while she found them calming. She studied the Important Periodic Comets and the Important Annual Meteor Showers. She skipped through The Constellations and Proper Names of Stars as she knew them already, but paused with astonishment when she came upon the Greek Alphabet. How does anyone ever remember *this* gobbledegook, she wondered. She examined a table called the Stella Spectra. It was divided into columns headed 'Type', 'Surface Temp.', 'Colour', 'Typical Example' and 'Remarks'. She studied each category with interest and then began memorizing it. This seems very useful, she decided. Da will be pleased if I know all this.


Billy Fishboy knocked on the door of the house in First Street at exactly the time specified by Joyce. He had bathed and shaved and his hair was styled. He was wearing a shiny narrow suit in the Italian style, and winkle-picker shoes. He rubbed his eyes when Joyce appeared, her hair in a high tower, held in place by a sequin-spattered net, her shoulders covered by a Persian lamb stole.

'So you're out of clink,' Joyce said in greeting, as he stepped into the passage.

It smells of damp again in here, Kathleen noticed. Nana's cleaning can't change that.

Hiding his astonishment at Joyce's appearance, Billy nodded, in a resigned way.

'I knew you'd be out. They wouldn't make you miss the Big Dance. They're not sadists.'

'I'm not so sure.'

She took his arm. 'Come on, Kathleen.' She then stopped in the doorway. 'You're not taking that camera.'

'Yes I am.'

'No you're not.'

'Yes I am.'

Da appeared in the kitchen doorway. 'They won't come out,' he said to Kathleen. 'You'll just be wasting your film.'

She put his Box Brownie on the hall-stand

'Are you sure you're not coming?' Joyce said to Da. She was so excited her voice was squeaky.

Da followed them into the street and looked at the sky. It was clear but in the far distance there was a rumble, which may have been thunder. 'No. I'm away to the shed,' he said. He was remote, disconnected from Joyce's mood.

'Where's Nana?' asked Kathleen. No one replied.

She walked behind Joyce and Billy. In her high heels and with her piled-up hair, Joyce seemed taller than her escort. Kathleen could hear her humming the theme tune from *Summer Holiday*.

Kathleen was careful on the cobbles, picking her way gingerly. Her legs were cold and her too-big shoes flapped up and down. She felt her own hair. It was pinned tightly in an uncomfortable topknot, the sides cemented with spray. She wore her school gabardine over her new dress. She was nervous. I wonder if there'll be boys there, she thought, from my class at school. I hope not. She imagined being asked to dance. Fat chance, she concluded.

Inside the entrance of the Welfare Hall, everything looked the same as usual. Kathleen felt a wave of disappointment. Two matrons from the Labour Women's Guild were sitting at a trestle table, taking money and issuing tickets on the door. They were very slow at giving change. The lobby smelt of disinfectant just like it always did. There were a few remnants of paper streamers still attached to the ceiling, left over from last Christmas. Details concerning the Leek Club and the Baby Clinic were pinned on the wall. Some men stood around in their caps and mufflers, holding pints of beer they'd brought down from upstairs. They stared at Joyce. A woman in a turban and overall pushed a bucket and mop into a bulging cupboard and tried to close the door.

'We're early,' remarked Billy.

'Let's go up,' said Joyce haughtily, ignoring everyone.

'It's the Queen of Sheba,' Kathleen heard someone say.

Upstairs in the Concert Room, the fluorescent lights glared brightly revealing the cracks in the walls and the shabby linoleum. There was a smell of old beer and ashtrays, and from the stage, the echo of a thousand stale jokes. The musicians were setting up their instruments but they weren't like Glenn Miller. They were elderly and resembled the band that played in the park on Sundays. They wore navy uniforms instead of tuxedoes.

Billy unstacked three chairs from a pile and Joyce sat down, on the edge of the floor, her nose slightly in the air. She's got goose pimples, Kathleen noticed. Her arms look fat. Billy went to the bar and bought some drinks. The steward glowered at them all as if they were intruders, as he tried to organize the float. The three of them waited, glumly, not speaking. Kathleen was worried. She pleated and unpleated the velvet of her skirt. It's going to be awful, she decided. Poor Auntie Joyce.

After a while the strong overhead lights were turned off and Kathleen noticed a spangly silver ball hanging from a rafter. Coloured spotlights from the corners of the room were directed at this and as it turned it shed a myriad of motes, everywhere, like summer petals. Above this, she saw for the first time, a net holding up a hundred balloons. People started to arrive. The stage lights went on and the band began playing Helen Shapiro's 'Walking Back To Happiness'. They were confident. Their instruments gleamed and the trumpeter got to his feet in the proper way. There was a buzz of conversation and laughter and a few couples began to foxtrot. The hired barmen, both strangers in white jackets, moved like lightning but the crush at the bar became three deep. This is better, Kathleen decided. She sipped her warm lemonade, feeling relieved.

Jonty Dickinson came over, nodded to Kathleen and asked Joyce to dance. He was wearing his medals. She accepted graciously and the two whirled away. No one else here has dressed up like Joyce, Kathleen decided. Other women were wearing ordinary summer dresses and cardigans although one or two had put on gold sandals.

'Your Auntie Joyce looks very glamorous,' said Billy approvingly.

Kathleen was at once proud. 'She made that dress herself.'

'Come on, kid.' He pulled her to her feet.

'Me?'

He laughed. 'Yes, you.'

Kathleen kicked off Joyce's too-big shoes.

The music changed to Roy Orbison's 'Dream Baby' and Billy guided her out into the centre of the floor. With one hand, Kathleen felt the softness of his palm, with the other, the hard flesh of his waist above the top of his trousers, underneath his jacket. I'm touching him, she thought. This seemed for some reason, like a miracle. I hope my hands aren't sweating. 'I don't really know the steps,' she admitted.

'You're doing fine.'

They circled the room, steadily. Kathleen tried to be graceful and light, remembering to let him lead. She noticed that Jonty's wife was sitting tight-lipped as her husband moved stiffly, Joyce cradled politely in his arms.

When they all returned to their chairs, Billy asked Joyce for a dance and happy and giggling, she agreed.

Kathleen realized there was no one here from her class at school, which was a blessing. She looked around for Petra. She wished her friend had seen her dancing in such a grown-up way, with a proper partner. Billy's so nice, she thought. He's quite handsome really, but, of course, he's too old for me.

She watched the spinning couples caught in the shimmer from the silver ball. She finished her lemonade and picked up Joyce's drink. It was lager and lime and it tasted very bitter. She put it back on the table. For a moment the people in the room seemed magically transformed by the music and the raindrops of colour and the happy mood. Their lives aren't all grey and mean, she decided. There *is* a bit of beauty and happiness in this place.

After a while Billy disappeared. Joyce danced a couple of energetic numbers with the new man from the Co-op Butcher's. Kathleen could tell he was a teddy boy by his long jacket, bootlace tie and Elvis Presley hair style. She saw him speak to the band leader and make a drumming gesture with both hands. The music changed to rock 'n' roll. He began a different kind of dancing with Joyce and a space cleared for the two of them in the centre of the floor. Joyce was a little hesitant but the butcher really knew how to jive. His footwork was spectacular in his peculiar buckled crêpe-soled shoes. He span Joyce like a top and Kathleen noticed the upper silk layer of her skirts sliding about on its netting in the way it was designed to do. At the end everyone clapped and cheered and Joyce returned to her seat, giddy and perspiring, her hair partly tumbling down in an attractive way.

'He's a good dancer,' said Kathleen admiringly.

'He's engaged to a telephonist,' replied Joyce, but her spirits were high.

Kathleen noticed her Auntie Molly and waved. Molly was wearing a sleeveless blouse made entirely from black beads and she sipped from a little glass containing dark liquid. That's the same as she drinks at Christmas and at funerals, Kathleen thought. She always has that. Auntie Molly suddenly laughed so loudly at a joke her voice could be heard above the music. In the odd scattered light from the silver globe above, her hair looked very blue.

Fortified by port and lemon, Molly got to her feet with a woman friend. She signalled to the band and a trombone player called out, 'Take your partners for the Gay Gordons!' The music changed to a jolly reel and with whoops and flourishes, Auntie Molly skipped like a girl.

The band stopped for a short break, mopping their brows. Suddenly a hush descended upon the room. Kathleen turned and to her surprise she saw Mr Koninsky. Everyone stared at him briefly, then turned away. No one greeted him. The hubbub in the room immediately built up again. There was a squeal of laughter from a group of women sitting together at a table, as one of them stood up and tried to demonstrate how to do the Twist.

Joyce became very still and quiet. She didn't wave to her lover, but it was clear to Kathleen when she began tidying her hair that she expected him to join her.

Instead, Marek Koninsky ignored Joyce and went up to the bar where the crowd parted to let him through. He stood alone for a moment before ordering a glass of spirits. His face was shadowed as if he needed a shave. He wore a foreign-looking wing collar with a floppy, loose bow tie. His suit was dark and immaculate as usual. Kathleen's heart quickened and she looked away. She could see that several women in the room were pretending to be unaware of his presence. Their eyes flicked towards him, surreptitiously. They patted their hair, self-conscious and anxious. He downed his drink in one, then went back to the entrance where he extended a hand to his wife. He drew her across the threshold. She seemed afraid. The two of them sat in a corner, their heads close together, talking. Nadezhda smoked a cigarette in a long holder. She was wearing elbow length gloves. Kathleen was transfixed. Inspector Glen's not arrested her yet, she thought. What's he playing at? She was suddenly anxious again. I'm going to have to telephone him *again*.

Even in the poor light it was possible to see that Joyce had gone white. Kathleen thought she might cry. Petra can't be coming, she thought. She leant towards Joyce. 'He *had* to bring *her* along,' she said assertively.

'Sshh!' said Joyce. She sipped her drink. She glanced about furtively and whispered 'What did you say?'

Kathleen spoke quietly. 'Mrs Koninsky. He had to bring her.'

'How do you know that?'

'Petra told me. She said her mam kicked up a stink. She used to be a dancer and she never gets taken to a dance.'

'Are you sure?'

'Oh, yes,' Kathleen lied.

Joyce sniffed. 'It's nothing to me,' she insisted, 'whatever he does.'

The music began again. For the benefit of the older people, they played a string of wartime favourites. They *can* do Glenn Miller after all, Kathleen realized. They're quite good, actually.

By now the room was very crowded. People queued at a hatch for pie and pea suppers and the throng at the bar was unrelenting. Shiny-faced but dextrous, the barmen pulled pint after pint and decapitated bottles of brown ale. Some of the young pitmen were tipsy. They stood together in a swaying huddle and began singing. Kathleen waved to Jonty Dickinson as he tucked into his food, a paper napkin in the neck of his shirt, protecting his tie.

When the band struck up 'The Blue Danube', Marek led Nadezhda on to the floor. Joyce turned her back to them. Unable to help herself, Kathleen stared appreciatively at Petra's mam. She was wearing an old white gown whose ankle length skirt was a waterfall of alternating layers. They were of embroidered silk and gathered lace. The high-fronted bodice was stiff with pearls and the low back was trimmed at the waist with a bow. That's probably her wedding dress, decided Kathleen. Nadezhda was thin, her face ravaged, but she was exquisite. Her usually wayward hair was rolled in a ballerina's bun. Her lips were painted red and she carried a satin clutch bag in her gloved hand. Kathleen was reminded of celebrities on Pathe News at the Essoldo. Nadezhda Koninsky looked like an ageing film star on a visit to the London Palladium or a Hollywood premiere, or the Oscars. She looked *important*. By comparison, the rest of the women in the room were dowdy and poor. Molly was at once ridiculous. Joyce's outfit was garish and home made.

The Koninskys danced in a sweeping professional motion, demonstrating the true limits of the waltz. They swirled and wheeled like airborne birds. The other dancers seemed merely to shuffle around them, hopelessly, as stiff as puppets. Finally, as the lengthy Strauss medley ended, they glided back to their seats and something brilliant seemed lost.

Kathleen followed Joyce into the ladies cloakroom. Oblivious to the women passing by on their way to and from the lavatories, she stood examining herself in a full length mirror. She turned from side to side then bent forwards. She looks fat, Kathleen decided.

'I thought my bosoms might fall out, doing that jive,' Joyce confessed miserably. She unfastened her collapsing hair and combed it down with her fingers, before reassembling it with a lot of pins. She reapplied her lipstick. 'Are you having a nice time?' she asked Kathleen.

Kathleen looked in the mirror. This hairdo makes me look like a hamster, she decided. 'Yes, thanks.'

Joyce moved forwards, stared at herself in close up in the mirror. The light was unflattering.

She's disappointed, thought Kathleen. She's jealous of that raving nutcase, Mrs Koninsky. 'Your dress is the best,' she said. 'It's the best by miles and miles.'

Joyce turned, and drew Kathleen gently towards her. She smiled down into her face. 'No, pet,' she said. 'Yours is. Your lovely alice blue gown.'

At the end of the evening, after the balloons had been released and burst, as the crowd began to thin and the bandsmen packed away, Joyce sat with the cinema manager and his wife. 'I wonder where Mr Fisher went,' the wife asked.

'Billy?' replied Joyce. 'Oh, I think he's here somewhere. He escorted me.'

'I haven't seen him for hours.'

Kathleen was tired. She stared at the Koninskys who chatted with the pit manager and his married daughter. Nadezhda Koninsky seems a lot less mad than usual, Kathleen thought. She watched her nodding to the conversation in a perfectly normal way. Marek seemed animated. He was waving his hands in the air and making cutting gestures that seemed to indicate the end of something.

The steward was clearing away. He called out loudly, 'Can I have your glasses, *please*!' He began putting the chairs on top of tables. 'Have you lot not got *homes* to go to?'

Kathleen was glad she'd come. At least I know what it's like now, she thought. The Big Dance. I quite liked it. Of course, it was old-fashioned because everyone here wants things always to be the same. I knew they wouldn't play 'Love Me Do' or anything modern. But it was still good. I liked dancing with Billy.

She was aware, as they descended the stairs to the lobby that Petra's parents were immediately behind. Nearly everyone had gone home. A group of people collected in the entrance and she realized that a torrential downpour had just begun. One or two ventured into the night with umbrellas, but most were waiting for the rain to ease. At that moment, thunder crashed overhead and there was a flash of lightning.

'It has arrived,' she heard Marek say. 'There was a storm above Consett earlier today.'

Kathleen was conscious, as Joyce wrapped herself in her fur stole, that her auntie was resolutely ignoring Marek, as he had been doing to her, all evening. She stayed close to her side.

Where's Billy? she thought. Joyce exchanged remarks with an elderly couple about the weather. Kathleen could tell she was embarrassed by Marek's proximity. She found herself doing something she'd never done before. She held Auntie Joyce's hand.

The thunder crashed again, even more loudly. A woman shrieked.

'Oh, no!' someone shouted.

'My Goodness!'

'Make way, make way!' yelled one of the barmen, rushing inside then herding people backwards, away from the lashing rain in the street.

At that moment a man stumbled into view. He was coatless and soaked from head to foot and his hair was plastered to his head. He was struggling heroically with something in his arms. He staggered towards the door, breathless. He half fell through the entrance and sank to his knees. His chest heaved. He was almost sobbing. His burden slid away from him on to the floor.

Kathleen saw his black armband. It's Da, she realized.

Another woman screamed and there was a burst of confused conversation. The barman bent down with a hand on Da's shoulder. In front of him, someone grappled with a heap of muddy clothing and Kathleen realized with horror that Da had been carrying another person in his arms. She gasped. She pushed her way forward through the confusion. On the ground, in front of Da, lay Petra. She too was wet from head to foot and dirty. Her face was grey, her eyes were closed and water ran from her lips.

Da stood up. He was shaking. His eyes suddenly became focused, fixed. Kathleen turned. He was staring at Mr Koninsky but his expression was unreadable. The thunder exploded overhead, the lights went off and on and the whole building seemed to rock. Joyce was suddenly on the floor with Petra and she gathered her up in her arms, almost lovingly, before arranging her on her back. The cinema manager knelt alongside. 'Stand back, stand back, stand back!' he shouted, like he did when there was a pressing queue at the cinema, waiting for a film. Between them, in turn, they fastened their lips to Petra's and began breathing air into her mouth. Joyce blew rhythmically several times, then the cinema manager took a turn, then Joyce again. Both became smeared on their legs and hands and chest with black sludge from Petra's hair. It stank of Jinny Hoolets.

'What's happening?' Kathleen said, several times. She was almost frozen with fear. 'What's happening?' She could hear someone telephoning for help.

Marek suddenly crouched next to Joyce. 'It's no good,' he said helplessly. Kathleen could smell his cologne.

The cinema manager pounded Petra's chest. He bent to blow into her mouth once more.

'Keep trying,' said Joyce. She was desperate. 'Keep trying.'

Kathleen turned. Mrs Koninsky had fainted and two women were trying to bring her round.

The cinema manager straightened up.

Joyce bent again, exhaling sharply into Petra, then punching her very hard.

'It's no good,' the manager agreed. He was in tears. 'She's gone.'

They kept on trying to revive Petra until the ambulance arrived.

Petra was placed on a stretcher and she was accompanied to the hospital by Marek, silent and pale, a hysterical Nadezhda and by Da, who was shaking uncontrollably.

'He's in shock,' someone said.

The doors of the vehicle closed with a dreadful finality. As it drove away the siren and lights were extinguished. They're no longer in a hurry, Kathleen reasoned. There's no point in breaking the speed limit. Making a racket. Not when she's already dead.

The cinema manager cried some more and blew his nose. People stood around not sure what to do. Someone volunteered to wait for the police, who were on their way. Joyce was handed a towel and she unsuccessfully rubbed at the mud on her hands, legs and dress. There was a lot of muttering, embarrassed fare-wells and gradually, everyone began to drift away.

'I need a pee,' said Joyce.

Kathleen stepped outside. She looked at the sky, which was impenetrable and black. The pithead light was just visible and it hung like a hazy imitation moon. The rain still fell but the thunder had moved into the distance where it continued to bang and rumble. A sheet of lightning winked, momentarily illuminating the street. Kathleen was startled. She rubbed her eyes with her index fingers. Sheltering in the doorway, opposite, a lady stood on her own. She was beckoning to Kathleen fran-tically.

'Who is it?' asked Kathleen shakily, as she crossed the road. She was puzzled. This wasn't anyone she'd ever seen before. The woman was wearing a bright pink ruffled evening dress, which was too tight. The outfit seemed familiar to Kathleen but she wasn't sure why. She looked closely, took off her glasses, rubbed the rain off them, then put them back on. The stranger had black stiff hair and false eyelashes. She was dressed and made up for the dance, but Kathleen couldn't remember seeing her inside. 'Yes?' she asked.

'Kathleen, it's Billy.'

'Billy?'

'Yes, it's me. What's going on?'

Kathleen joined him in the doorway. 'Why are you wearing—'

'Ssshh!' said Billy. He indicated Joyce who had come out of

the building opposite, and was looking up and down the road for Kathleen. She set off in the direction of First Street.

Kathleen suddenly remembered. 'Why are you wearing our Gloria's frock?' Despite everything she suddenly wanted to laugh.

'I was going to come into the dance ... like this. I wanted everyone to see me. But then, in the end, I couldn't. I lost my nerve.'

Kathleen felt giddy. She placed a hand on the wall to steady herself. It's not funny, she reminded herself. None of this is funny.

'Kathleen, why was there an ambulance here?'

Kathleen ignored this. Tears suddenly spilled unbidden down her cheeks. She was disappointed in Billy. 'You shouldn't have done it,' she said quietly. 'Dressing up as Gloria is wrong. It was wrong when Petra did it too. It's unfair. It's shocking. Cross my heart and hope to die, I wish you hadn't done it.'

# MONDAY

Kathleen couldn't remember going to bed, but she awoke troubled by dreams of explosions. She stared at her small skylight, then reached out blindly for her glasses. She remembered a blast of red flame bursting outwards, shattered rock, a hurricane wind, destruction, smoke, uncontainable energy. Was I dreaming about the start of the universe, she wondered, or the end of the world?

She got up and felt a stickiness between her legs. Tentatively she pulled down her pyjama trousers and touched it with her fingers. With horror she saw that it was blood. Oh, no, she thought. The Curse! I've started. Not this as well as everything else!

Despite the cold of her room, she was sweating. She sat on the bed, protecting the sheet with her folded pyjama bottoms. She was shaken. Not this too. Not today. She breathed deeply and steadily for a minute until the shock subsided. She rummaged in her bottom drawer trying to find something to wear. In the end, she pulled on the same underwear, the alice blue gown, a pair of grey socks and her school shoes. She rolled up a handkerchief and pushed this into her knickers. She hid her pyjamas under the bed. I'm not going to school, she decided. I don't care what anybody says, I'm not going today, and that's it. She took the clips from her hair and brushed it. Dried lacquer fell out like dandruff. She dragged it back into her usual ratty pigtails.

Petra, she thought. Petra Koninsky. She was a sad, unhappy

277

girl. Even if she was a know-it-all, she was still sad. Kathleen's eyes filled with tears, remembering her words. Just yesterday she'd said, 'You're the only friend I've got in the whole wide world.'

Kathleen took off her glasses, wiped her eyes then put them on again. An uneasy feeling lurked inside her throat and it was something to do with letting Petra down. No, she decided firmly. It wasn't my fault she went and drowned herself. It's because her mother's a raving nutcase and her father's a womanizer and a drunk. Her life must have been awful down there in that disgusting place with all its foul play and filthy breaches of rules. Kathleen swallowed hard. She knew that to think otherwise, or to blame herself at this moment would be more, much more than she could possibly bear.

She fastened the ends of her hair with elastic bands and sucked each of them in turn. These plaits are getting longer and longer, she decided, but not prettier. She remembered the way Petra used to backcomb her hair. She had a vision of her pretending to smoke. Attention was all she ever wanted, Kathleen thought. Attention and love. Poor Petra. She's drowned. Like Nosey and Gloria. And now I've got the Curse. She blew her nose on another handkerchief and stuffed it under her pillow.

She checked her Auntie Joyce's room on her way downstairs, but she'd gone out. In Nana's kitchen she poured herself a bowl of Sugar Pops. She could hear her grandmother in the wash house. She was singing loudly and, as usual on a Monday, billows of steam and foam escaped through the open door. There was a blue flare from the gas jets under the boiler, illuminating the dense, hellish interior as Nana's big, limping frame could be discerned, threshing the agitator of the machine vigorously, punishing the shirts and the sheets. Kathleen kept an eye out for Nana as she crunched her breakfast. She'll try and make me go to school, she decided, and I'm absolutely, definitely not going.

She washed up her bowl, checked the time on the kitchen clock. In the damp passage, she pulled on her school gabardine. She picked up Da's Box Brownie. She didn't want to meet any of her classmates. It's all right, she decided, they'll all be at their desks by now. Except for Petra, of course. She's in the hospital morgue, or maybe at the undertakers. With our Gloria.

Kathleen stepped outside. The storm had passed away and become nothing but a memory. The rain had changed to fine misty drizzle. The sky was pale grey with darker cloud on the horizon and it was chilly. Two housewives passed by with shopping bags, ignoring her. A police car drove by the end of the street with two uniformed officers inside. Kathleen followed it on foot, in the direction of Jinny Hoolets.

At the top of the bank, above the Koninskys' house, she paused. There was a lot of activity down below. It's like the day after a night when a bomb's dropped, she thought. She remembered Pathe Newsreels shot during the Blitz. She deliberately pushed away all thoughts about Cuba and the Russians.

A large van was parked awkwardly near the bottom of the track and men appeared to be carrying furniture from the house and packing it inside. The police car was stationary behind. One of the officers disappeared into the building and the other leaned on the vehicle. Kathleen approached. Another man she recognized as the doctor from the village came out the front door and trudged towards the waiting policeman. Kathleen drew close.

'She's sedated,' she heard the doctor say. He seemed as big and unconcerned as she remembered, but he was sober. He put his bag on the rough stones and began fastening his overcoat. 'She's quiet now. She's stopped all that crazy praying.'

'What's going on?' asked the Constable, gesturing towards the removal van.

'It's his idea. They're leaving today. They're going to a colliery house in Leadgate. He's taking his missus across there this afternoon.'

Kathleen stepped nearer. The doctor saw her but merely nodded slightly.

The policeman continued. 'He says he doesn't want his wife here, near the pond. He says he's worried she might do the same.'

'The same?'

'The same as the girl. Throw herself in.'

'So that's what happened, is it?' The doctor indicated Kathleen's presence with a movement of his head. 'I think the mother's all right now. But she's very highly strung. Was she ever on the stage?'

The policeman turned. He frowned at Kathleen. 'Run along now!' he said, brusquely.

Kathleen passed by them without speaking. She walked slowly towards the side of the house. She carried on listening.

'So you think it was suicide?' the doctor asked again.

'Aye,' confided the Constable, sighing. 'We reckon. Two suicides in a week.'

'I thought there was a question mark over the first one.'

'The DI thinks so but he's got no backing. We're waiting for the inquest. Me, I think it was suicide both times. That's only my gut reaction, mind.'

'No sign of foul play last night?'

'None.'

'They should pull this place down,' called out the doctor, walking away, back up towards the top of the track. 'They should fence it off. It's not safe. Children come here to play and it's dangerous.'

'You're right there,' ventured the policeman.

Kathleen passed Mr Koninsky's Ford and went round to the back of the dwelling. She looked in Petra's window. Nothing had been disturbed. The bed was still unmade, record covers were scattered across the floor, the surfaces were littered with make-up, tissues, miscellaneous bits of underwear. It was exactly as she had left it yesterday. Only Petra herself was missing. Her stained dressing gown hung on a hook behind the door. This is awful, she decided. I can't believe this has happened. She swallowed hard but tears still came to her eyes.

She walked away towards the heaps then began climbing up the slide, worn into one of the mounds of spoil by the playing boys. Inspector Glen's not going to arrest Nadezhda Koninsky, she decided. He can't see the truth. He's useless and he's got no backing. She stopped and considered. Maybe it doesn't matter, she thought, resignedly. Petra's suicide is her loony old mother's true punishment. Maybe it's enough.

She climbed to the top of the mound. From here she could see the roof of the house, the little black Ford, the van with men toiling back and forth, loading the furniture, and the top of the police car. Beyond all this, gaping and bleak, was the pond. Its dimpled surface was emotionless and too dark to reflect the mild grey of the morning sky. But Kathleen understood completely that trapped and contained within its depths was the black chaos of yesterday's storm – death, fury, despair and all the other unspeakable secrets of the night. She shuddered. She took off her glasses, blinked and rubbed her eyes. She raised the Box Brownie and took a photograph.

At the Essoldo, Joyce sat in the cinema manager's office her hands circling a cup of tea. Detective Inspector Glen perched on the desk, writing in his notebook. 'And where was Mr Fisher at this point?' he asked.

Joyce was sulky. 'I've told you, I don't know.'

'You don't know? I thought you were together, at this . . . shindig.'

'I keep telling you. Are you listening or what? We went together. He was there. We danced one dance. He bought me a couple of drinks. Then he disappeared.'

'Disappeared?'

'Yes. He went home, I suppose. I don't know. You better ask *him*.' Joyce drained her cup. She was wearing her tight uniform and her little pillbox hat had become lopsided. Her eyes were blackened from last night's mascara, which she'd forgotten to remove. She unwrapped a chocolate biscuit.

'What time was this?'

'I've told you already. I don't know. Ask the ladies on the door.'

'I have. He didn't leave by the front exit.'

'Well ask him. *Ask him.*'

Inspector Glen stood up and moved heavily. He nodded to the manager as he passed into the foyer. 'I will,' he called out, 'just as soon as I find him.'

The manager came into the office and half-smiled at Joyce. 'We did our best for the poor child,' he offered.

Joyce bit into her biscuit. 'What's going on?' she said, her mouth full. 'First my bloody step-sister. Now this girl. What's the matter with everybody?' Her hand trembled, proving she was more affected by events than she was willing to show.

The manager sighed. 'Take the day off, Joyce. I'm not going to open today.' He closed a drawer of his filing cabinet in a frustrated, dismissive way. '*Summer Holiday*'s finished its run, anyway. Let's go home. To hell with it.'

Joyce was relieved. 'Where's that Billy?'

'Good question.'

*

Marek stood in the window of the dingy scullery at Jinny Hoolets, watching the police car disappear up the track. It backed slowly, unable to turn around. At the top it squealed out on to the road and a small avalanche of coal tumbled away from its retreating wheels.

Marek's handsome cheeks were sunken and his eyes bleary. He picked up a glass and rinsed it under the cold tap, his hand shaking. He poured himself a slug of vodka from a bottle on the draining board.

One of the removal men appeared.

'Excuse me,' said Marek, 'but do you think you could leave and come back later?'

'Sir?'

'My wife. She is sleeping upstairs. I do not want her to be disturbed. I intend to take her to our new house when she awakens. Can you return at four o'clock?'

The man hesitated, confused. 'Yes, sir. Whatever you say.' He went out to tell his mate.

Marek drank the vodka and poured himself some more. He put the brimming glass on the table. He stared at the heaps of unwashed plates and cups, the empty bottles, the crusty saucepans, alongside the sink. With one sweep of his arm he dislodged the lot and it fell crashing on to the floor. He kicked a large jug. Spilling cooking fat, it skittered towards the hall before breaking into pieces against the door jamb.

Kathleen stood in a queue in the chemist's. She waited whilst people collected their prescriptions, discussed cough medicine and cures for warts. Her eyes strayed to a stacked heap of sanitary towel packets on the end of the counter. Embarrassed, she picked up one and hugged it to her chest.

When her turn came she pushed the packet towards the pharmacist, her eyes downcast. She could feel herself blushing. He

blew into a brown paper bag and wrapped the item, discreetly.
'No school today?'

'No.'

He pointed at Da's Box Brownie. 'You've come for your
photographs?'

'Yes.'

'Just a minute.' He disappeared into the back.

Kathleen picked up the brown package and shoved it into the
front of her coat. The pharmacist returned with her envelope of
prints. 'Do your mother and father know you've been taking
these?'

Kathleen nodded, reached out and took them from his hands.
Quickly, not looking at anyone in the queue behind, she paid
him and left.

She passed by Gallini's. Averting her head she refused to look
inside but she guessed they'd had the juke box fixed. She could
hear clearly the Beatles again, singing 'Love Me Do' with a
heavy bass beat.

Back in her attic room, in First Street, Kathleen hid the blood-
stained handkerchief under the bed, with her pyjama trousers.
She struggled to attach a sanitary towel to her knickers with
safety pins. It was too long and it was uncomfortable. She
contemplated the reality of this, every month until she was fifty.
I can see why it's called the Curse, she thought. She lay on her
stomach, on the bed and opened her envelope of photographs.

Despite everything, the top print was a shock. It showed
Gloria's body, half submerged under the water. One of her
hands and the sleeve of her jacket were very clear and she looked
stiff and waxy, like an abandoned shop mannequin. The second
photograph was of the stretcher bearing Gloria's body to the
ambulance. She was merely a white mound under the hospital
blanket but her feet, in her new shoes, stuck out stiffly from the

end. Kathleen swallowed, reminded of the horror. Poor Gloria, she thought. She was so nice and kind. She should have been my mam. Again her eyes filled with tears.

The third photograph hadn't come out well. Kathleen turned it this way and that, but it was nothing but a glare of excess light. She then examined a print of Mr Koninsky, crouching down at the side of Gloria's Mini, using the reflection from the wing mirror to comb his hair. He was on his way to meet Auntie Joyce and he looked both handsome and cruel. Kathleen remembered what poor Petra had said about him hitting his wife.

The Duty Constable at Jinny Hoolets was in focus. He was fat cheeked and jolly, his hands on his hips, his helmet tipped back at a slightly jaunty angle. Beside him, Nosey smiled, his tongue lolling out and Petra looked haughty, despite her foolish shoes, which were white and sinking into the mud. In the far distance, small but distinguishable, Mr Koninsky and Auntie Joyce were shrugging on their coats and leaving the owl's ancient tumbledown barn, hand in hand. Poor Petra, she thought again. Poor Nosey. Poor Gloria. Poor, poor Petra.

The sixth print was puzzling. It seemed to be of a low wall. What's that? Kathleen asked herself. The rear end of Nosey had been captured, disappearing out of the frame. Only his tail, his bottom and one leg were visible. Kathleen then remembered. She stroked a black shapeless stain in the centre of the shot. It was Gloria's raincoat, the one that had been 'borrowed' by Petra, draped over the boundary of the Koninskys' property. I'd forgotten I'd taken that, she thought. I took it because it was poor Gloria's coat, after Nosey had found it. And it was all that was left of her.

Kathleen slid the glossy prints back through her fingers. She took the old photo of Nosey, propped up on the chest of drawers and placed it with the others. She stared at Nosey, at

Petra, at Gloria's feet. I'm glad I took these, she thought. A
least I've got these pictures to remember them by.

She spread out the photographs across the bed. Of the two
last pictures, one was of Mrs Koninsky and it had been taken
from the window of the parlour, downstairs. Kathleen pon
dered. That was the time I followed her to the left footers
church and got frightened by those awful nuns. Kathleen almos
smiled, until she remembered the Blue Danube waltz. Tha
stupid dancer, in her stupid dancing dresses. One thing's certain
she doesn't look very glamorous *here*. She held the photo close
to her eyes. Nadezhda Koninsky was untidy and a cigarette
burned between her fingers. She was wearing a man's coat, the
hem of her dress was torn and she held a bunch of dead weeds in
an exaggerated gesture, as if they were a beautiful bouquet.

Kathleen took this photo, plus the one of a scowling M
Koninsky by Gloria's car, tore them both in half, then in hal
again, stood on her bed, opened her skylight and released the
pieces into the damp afternoon air. In her mind, they were
carried away on the wind. Leadgate, she remembered. That's
where they're headed. Poor old Leadgate better watch out
that's all I can say.

She lay back down on the bed. Her stomach had started
hurting in a new way. It's the Curse, she thought. Petra once
told me that it aches. She told me, and even though I heard her, I
didn't believe her because I hardly ever believed anything she
ever said. She picked up the final picture. It was a landscape shot
of Jinny Hoolets from the top of the bank. Kathleen remem
bered why she'd taken it. Just as she expected, the house nestling
among the heaps, its chimney smoking gently alongside the
placid pond, recreated as it was – in a monochrome photo
graphic image – looked ironically like a country cottage in the
depths of rural England. What a joke, she thought. She was on
the point of tearing it up, when something caught her eye. It was

a figure, small but perfectly within focus, to the side and behind the house, near Petra's bedroom window. Kathleen stared. She cleaned her glasses and rubbed her eyes. The funny man! she thought. She felt her heart lurch. The funny man whom she'd refused to believe in. The one Petra kept going on about! She examined the figure more closely and let out a slow noisy, breath. No, she thought, I know who this is. She sat upright, holding the photograph. She held a lens of her spectacles close to it, enlarging the image. She squinted. She moved it further away then nearer her eyes. Her pulse was racing.

Downstairs, in the parlour, Inspector Glen perched uncomfortably on the edge of the settee, turning his hat in his hands. Bulky and purple-faced in his overcoat, he seemed too big for the room. Da sat opposite, sucking on his pipe. As he exhaled he almost disappeared, becoming dim and indistinct in a shroud of smoke which fragranced the cold air. Light rain pattered on the windowpane. Joyce bustled in and out, rattling teacups on a tray. She was still wearing her violet uniform and she'd not removed her hat. 'Oops!' she muttered nervously, her hands shaking as she pulled out a small table. 'Forgotten the sugar!'

Nana sat stiff and domineering in the other chair, stroking the wrinkles out of her skirt, down her long thighs. She was tight lipped, tense and nodding to herself as if a conversation was taking place inside her head. She'd removed her housecoat and turban but her hair was still damp from laundering the clothes. Her walking stick leaned against her knee.

Joyce poured the tea.

'Don't overfill them!' said Nana sharply.

The Inspector accepted a cup and blew into it discreetly. Da shook his head, resignedly. He seemed tired and remote and one of his hands was bandaged. He was wearing his suit and his black armband but, unusually, he hadn't put on a tie. Nana placed her cup and saucer on the floor and stared straight ahead. Joyce returned to the kitchen.

'Never mind the biscuits,' shouted Nana, harshly. 'This isn't a tea party!'

Joyce returned and stood just inside the doorway, unwilling to join the policeman on the settee.

'I'm not clear,' said Inspector Glen. 'I thought I was but I'm not.'

Da repeated, 'Gloria was my daughter by my first wife—' His voice was weak.

Nana interrupted. 'Joyce is my daughter by my first husband. Not that it's any of your business, I must say.'

The policeman coughed into his hand. There was a silence. He drank his tea quickly, then handed the cup to Joyce. 'Thank you, my dear.'

'Gloria and I weren't sisters,' Joyce declared. 'Not real sisters.' She moved from one foot to the other. 'We never even knew each other until we were both quite old.'

The Inspector scratched his head. 'I see. Or at least, I think I see.' He hesitated. 'And Kathleen? What about Kathleen?'

Kathleen came downstairs cautiously. She heard voices in the parlour and listened for a moment. Joyce saw her around the door jamb and started, taking a little step to one side.

'We can hear you, madam!' Nana shouted. Her voice was aggressive and full of venom.

Kathleen peeped around the door, hiding the photograph behind her back. Immediately her eyes met those of Inspector Glen. He made a 'thumbs up' sign but didn't smile. He looked perplexed.

'Hah!' exclaimed Nana.

Kathleen withdrew hastily and went through the kitchen where damp laundry hung on a clothes-horse, blocking the fire

288

Acting on impulse, she crossed the yard and went into the wash house. She half closed the door.

The concrete floor was flooded with water and foam and the atmosphere was dim and steamy. There was a smell of soap flakes undercut with bleach. A mop stood propped in a bucket, and there was a tin bath full of washed bedlinen, folded and waiting its turn to be dried in front of the kitchen fire. Kathleen coughed. She polished her glasses and replaced them. The wash house smelled pleasant but it reminded her of Nana and this made her fearful and wary. She looked around. Da's long rain-coat hung on a nail on the back of the door. Kathleen felt it. It was wet. Not just damp. Wet. She groped in a pocket and again found Da's rolled cap, his penknife and Nana's prescription sunglasses which up until recently had been wrapped in a duster in the sideboard. Her eyes wandered around the small space, taking in a watering can, old paint pots, a chair, a disused rabbit hutch full of joinery tools, an empty wicker laundry basket. Nana's galoshes, which she wore to do the washing, were neatly together on the floor. Next to them was a pair of shoes. She went over and examined them. They were Nana's brogues, old but in good repair. They were wet and dirty. They were smeared with black slimy mud, which could have come from only one place. 'Jinny Hoolets,' said Kathleen aloud. She sniffed them. There was no doubt. They smelled of the coal-polluted pond. Kathleen's mind was in turmoil. 'And we all thought you never went out,' she murmured, shocked. 'We all thought you hadn't left the house for more than three years.'

At that moment the door creaked on its hinges, the room brightened a little and Kathleen felt a breath of cold air on the backs of her legs. She turned. Nana stood in the entrance, tall, wide shouldered, one arm folded across her bony bosom, the other leaning on her stick. With the light behind her, her expression was unreadable.

Kathleen was still holding the soiled shoes. She froze. The two of them regarded each other for what seemed like a long time. In the silence Kathleen was aware of her own heartbeat, the sound of a train shunting by the pit, a neighbour's baby crying, and a voice, muffled, in the house. 'Your tea's going cold, Nan,' it called sounding worried. Auntie Joyce was distant and out of reach. Kathleen wanted to shout out to her but knew in an instant that she was incapable of taking the necessary breath.

Suddenly, Nana took a step backwards and the door slammed shut with a crash. Kathleen was plunged into darkness. She heard the decisive rattle of the key turning in the lock.

When Nan was thirteen years old her education ceased. Because she was a good singer and had taught herself to play the battered piano in the school hall, her teacher tried to persuade her mother to allow her to continue her studies, but her drunken father was on short time and the family had scarcely enough to eat.

Nan really wanted employment with the florist in Lanchester. Attracted by the bright blooms she'd ventured in there one day and the heavy scent, the dim light, the glinting metal buckets, the exoticism and luxury of the interior made her almost faint with desire and happiness. In the back, the owner, a broad-shouldered woman with huge fingers, was delicately weaving a funeral wreath of white lilies.

'Is there an opening?' Nan had gasped.

'There might be.'

'Can I . . . can I . . . learn?'

'Come back when you've left school.'

Nan's mother was adamant. 'Over my dead body!' It turned out that there was some scandal surrounding the florist in Lanchester. She wore men's clothes, smoked cigarettes and lived with another woman. She had peculiar city friends who danced the Charleston. Without being specific, Nan's mother hinted at depravity, notoriety and licentiousness. 'I'm not having *my* family's name dragged through *that* kind of mud,' she'd declared.

Instead of arranging bouquets, Nan was sent into service with the doctor on the village's farthest edge, away from the mine. Whenever Nana remembered those days she thought of polish – silver polish, brass polish, beeswax polish, black lead, floor polish, vinegar mix for shining windows – and the unpleasant smell of the slops and the mop bucket first thing in the morning. The doctor was kind but his house was large and Nan was a maid of all work, which meant she had to open the door to patients and be presentable at certain times as well as carrying coal and water, laundering, ironing, cleaning, cooking and performing scullery duties. She started work at five and finished at nine and her short evenings were spent mending, darning and sterilizing returned medicine bottles, which were left in a special elephant's foot container in the hall. She slept in a cupboard-like room with a real skeleton on a stand until one morning she was so upset whilst serving breakfast she felt compelled to tell the doctor of her nightmares. Laughing, he removed the skeleton to the stable.

Nan had one Sunday off a month and spent this with her mother who grabbed her wages in a desperate but not ungrateful way. When she was fifteen, one bright Sunday in June, Nan met Arthur May at her mother's house. He was a young pitman; undersized, blond-haired and cheeky. They went for a walk and he picked her some wild flowers. He was not allowed to call at the doctor's house but because the nights were light and the weather fine, Nan sometimes sneaked out and met him late in the evenings at the end of the lane. Quickly, they became engaged and Arthur explained that this meant they could do more than kiss behind the hedgerows amongst the lush cow parsley and bright buttercups.

Three days after she told him a baby was on the way, little Arthur May suffocated in the mine. Her mother sent her the news in a note and because the engagement had never been announced, she wasn't allowed the day off to attend the funeral. Distraught and silent, Nan continued to polish, lug coal, wash bedclothes in the big metal poss tub, mop floors, greet patients, cook three meals a day and all the rest of it. The scullery smells made her sick and her uniform began to tighten. One day she examined the coloured bottles and sharp instruments in the walk-in cupboard behind the surgery but fled at the doctor's approach.

When she was sent home there was a terrible row. The final months of her pregnancy were spent shut in the attic room in her parents' colliery house in First Street, where there was no window but a skylight, freezing with one thin blanket, out of sight of the neighbours. Her baby was born without assistance and it was a strange colour. Nan begged for the midwife to be called but no one in the house would help. After a few hours it died in her arms and her parents, grandparents, aunts and uncles all agreed that this was the Lord's will, a blessing and a relief and no one need be informed. She never forgot the baby. It was a girl and it had blonde hair, like its father.

Nan accepted her shame and misfortune and blamed herself and Arthur May, who, as it turned out, had a real fiancée in Lanchester, with a ring and a trousseau and a proper studio photograph of the two of them, in a frame.

Nan got a job in the Co-op drapers. Despite all the rumours and whispering, she kept quiet about the baby and tried to hold her head high. Her mother died, then soon afterwards her father, she married the first man who asked her, she left work and was joined by her new husband in her parents' house when she was just nineteen.

Nan was not destined to be happy with men. Her husband was a fast talker with qualifications but he was also light fingered and couldn't keep a job. He'd been sacked from his post as wages clerk at the pit. He was sacked from the office at the Co-op. Nan became pregnant again and she begged the colliery manager to let them stay in the house. After Joyce was born in 1934, her husband started selling brushes from a suitcase, door to door, then later he took orders for vacuum cleaners from a catalogue. The work took him far and wide and the gossip became more and more vicious – he was a philanderer, a bigamist, the father of a not-so-young wealthy widow's twins. Nan tried to close her ears but eventually, when it became too much, she confronted him. The rows began. She started going through his pockets, sniffing his shirts, steaming open his letters, following him in the street. Nan lost her mind and never found it again, even when her husband ran away with a waitress to Australia.

An innocent woman with a rigid disposition, Nan unwittingly found herself disgraced and tainted by scandal for the whole of her life. Joyce's pregnancy was the final straw. Kathleen became the living symbol of her inability to conform, her ostracism, her embarrassment, her bad luck, and her failure. When she punished Kathleen, when she was angry with Kathleen, she was merely demonstrating her feelings about her own personal history.

She became angrier and madder as the years passed. She had rarely been outside the village and had no conception of a wider world. Nothing or nobody could help her.

Kathleen stood in the darkness, completely dismayed. She's locked me in, she realized. Nana's locked me in here and I can't get out. She's used that key she keeps in the tea caddy on the kitchen mantelpiece.

She placed the dirty shoes together on the floor at her feet and tucked the photograph carefully inside one of them. She knew that shouting for help would be useless. With the door shut, no sound carried through the double, reinforced concrete thickness of the windowless, bomb-resistant walls.

There was a rush of air then an insistent hissing sound, almost high enough to be a whistle. Kathleen was startled. She stepped back from the boiler, horrified, but not in time to escape the gagging, poisonous billow of fumes. She's turned the gas on, Kathleen admitted with amazement. She's turned it on from the tap on the pipe outside. The true meaning of this unfolded in her mind. She's turned the gas on. She's trying to murder me. Kathleen felt a flush of panic, which seemed to rise naked from her heart and engulf her. She trembled and her knees knocked together.

The vision of a desperate local housewife took shape in her memory. 'She put her head in the gas oven,' everyone had said, sadly. 'Her man found her just in time.' Kathleen had imagined a greasy cooker and the woman's sad wrinkled stockings.

Several people in the village had done this, over the years, Kathleen knew. Coal gas was the favoured method of suicide in these parts. It was far more popular than drowning. She recalled that most of these victims of self harm had been found alive. Asleep but alive. But one, or possibly two had died.

She groped on the shelf for matches but found none. She overturned a packet of soap powder and it showered down. Nana keeps the matches in her apron pocket, she remembered. I can't light it. I can't light the gas. It's going to kill me. She cleared her throat and tried to hold her breath. Her head swam as if she was about to faint. She's gassing me, she thought in terror. Nana's gassing me because I found the shoes. She pressed her body against the wall at the farthest point from the boiler. She closed her eyes, feeling her chest would burst. She covered her face with her hands.

After a few seconds of unreasoning terror, Kathleen forced herself to think. She concentrated on her arms and legs, willing them to function. Coughing and spluttering, she moved forward and was engulfed by the terrible smell. She grabbed a wet pillowcase from the pile of clean laundry and tied it around her face. Coal gas is heavier than air, she remembered. It will be settling on the floor, displacing the oxygen in the room. Her eyes were becoming accustomed to the gloom. She glanced around, desperately. She wondered if she could somehow block the fumes. She considered trying to crush the pipe, which was delivering death into the confined space. Trying to take only tiny breaths, she examined it helplessly. It was leaden, thick and unyielding. She dragged a wet sheet from the laundry and stuffed it in the space between the jets and the base of the boiler. The sound of the gas was quietened but she knew it wasn't stopped. It would be continuing to build up, relentlessly filling the enclosed space, driving out the breathable air. She ran her hand down a wall. The concrete everywhere appeared entirely solid. The door she knew was heavy, the lock oiled and firm. The roof . . . She blinked and focused her eyes above. A small patch was lighter in colour on the grimy ceiling. Da had made a hole in the flat roof years before, before she was born, after the war, when the air raid shelter was first converted to a wash house. This was to accommodate the chimney of the original boiler which had been heated by a coal fire. The old boiler was long gone, but up one wall of the room, its disused, cast iron flue was still in place. This passed through a rectangle of hardboard, which Da had wedged in the hole to leave the ceiling weatherproof.

Kathleen overturned a bucket and stood on it. Sweating with

terror she stood on her toes, craning upwards. She understood in a moment that this was the one weak point in the entire structure of the wash house. This rusted old chimney passed through a relatively flimsy piece of wood to meet the sky outside.

Kathleen made an effort and gathered her wits. Behind the door, she rummaged in the pocket of Da's raincoat and found his penknife. Her chest exploding she dragged out the disused rabbit hutch, overturned the tin bath and heaved it on top, placed a rickety chair on this then finally balanced the bucket. Holding on to the old flue for support, she climbed up this tower. Near the ceiling the air was breathable. She pulled the pillowcase from her mouth and gulped greedily. She picked open both the blades of the penknife and began running the small sharp one around the edges of the hardboard. The wooden rectangle, she could tell, if dislodged would create a small area only just big enough for her to squeeze through. It was caked and stuck fast with dirt and ancient glue. It seemed immovable. Frustrated, almost sobbing, she stabbed at it with the blunter bigger blade then even more desperately worked the smaller one again and again around the joins. Eventually and aware of the foul gas mounting higher and higher, leaving only a tiny layer of uncontaminated air, she felt the makeshift panel began to give. It wobbled slightly then as she struggled harder, it started to loosen. She struck it ineffectually with her fist then butted it with her head. 'Come on!' she gasped. 'Come on, come on!' Finally, the bucket and chair beneath her feet teetering, she pushed the board with both hands and it moved upwards, dislodging the roofing felt, uncovering a bright and blessed square of daylight, a rush of sweet air, the free sky. Disengaged, the old metal chimney clattered to the floor. The hardboard, now entirely unfastened slipped outwards and to one side.

Carefully, and first taking a deep swallow, Kathleen climbed back down into the invisible but choking coal gas that now entirely filled the wash house. She picked up Nana's shoes and knotted the ends of the laces together, hanging them around her neck. Gingerly, she climbed back up the precarious structure and grasped the edges of the roof. Her bucket slipped from under her feet and the chair toppled.

For a moment Kathleen hung in space, half in, half out of the roof. Her arms were almost numb with pain. Then with a strength she did not know she possessed, she heaved herself clear from the hellish stench of her prison below. She lay on the top of the air-raid shelter for a minute or two, gasping and coughing. She retched a few times and tried to be sick. She sobbed but refused to concede to tears. She stood up, found the drainpipe at the end of the building and slid down to the ground. As she did so, she caught her skirts and ripped the alice blue gown. She looked down. Her hands, her legs her dress were filthy. She turned off the gas at the outside tap and went back into the house.

Kathleen listened at the door of the parlour, which was almost closed. With one grubby finger, she nervously traced a pattern made by damp on the wall.

'I told you all this at the police station,' Da was saying, quietly. 'I told you and the Sergeant. You wrote it all down. I was there all morning, answering questions, after they let me out of the hospital. I told you exactly what I saw.'

'Can you explain this?' It was a man's voice and he sounded very serious. 'Can you explain what your husband saw?'

Friendship Seven's still here, realized Kathleen, thankfully. She was relieved. Her mind was racing. Friendship Seven's continuing his inquiries. He knows that the death, maybe both of those deaths were suspicious. He's not useless, even if he hasn't got any backing. He understands. He's questioning Nana. He knows.

There was a silence and a rustle. Kathleen could sense Joyce's presence, immediately behind the door. She leant against the wall, suddenly exhausted and dazed, unable to listen. She closed her eyes.

'My husband was mistaken,' Nana eventually replied. 'He couldn't have seen me. I never, ever leave this house.'

'But you were angry with your stepdaughter?' Inspector Glen was less aggressive than he might have been, but his tone contained the same persistence, the same degree of accusation and the same imperturbability he had used against Billy Fishboy.

Nana snorted. 'Hah!' she said. '*He* was angry with her too.' She means Da, Kathleen realized. 'He was angry when I told him his precious daughter was walking out with that dirty foreigner, Koninsky. Weren't you just? Eh? Weren't you?'

'Tell me why *you* were angry with her.' The policeman's voice was unrelenting. 'Tell me why again.'

'What, again?'

'Yes, please, if you would.'

Nana thought for a moment. She inhaled, furiously, audibly 'That hussy? Oh, she thought she was *so modern*. Oh, yes, s○ *modern*. She did what she liked, not what she was told. When ○ was a girl, I did as I was told. But not her! Never!' She graspe○ her walking stick in one hand and banged it on the floor, thre○ times.

In the passage Kathleen straightened up and recovere○ herself, alerted by her grandmother's anger.

Nana continued. 'She stopped our Joyce from getting marrie○ by talking about the . . . her daughter. Our Joyce could hav○ married that nice Mr Dobbs from the rent office if Glori○ hadn't—'

Kathleen could picture her expression. Her eyes will be scar○

he decided. She'll look mad. All the knuckles in her hands will
e sticking out.

'Yes, all right,' Joyce interrupted. She sounded frightened of
what might be coming, as if there was a tantrum brewing. 'Let's
ot go through all *that* again.' She spoke to the policeman in a
leading way. 'Do we have to . . . ?'

Nana raised her voice at this point, and spoke quickly, almost
pitting out her grievances. 'She blackened this family's name to
ll and sundry. More than half the women in this village were
oing through that fancy salon and all she ever did was talk.
alk talk, tittle tattle. Laughing at us, when she was doing their
air. Perms and shampoos and sets, and all the while slandering
his family, and laughing, as if we're a joke. Me? A joke. This
art Joyce here, this *beauty queen*? A joke. My so-called
usband, who's the talk of the neighbourhood because he can't
eep his hands off that woman down at Jinny Hoolets . . . ? He
vas a joke too.'

Kathleen wanted to put her hands over her ears, but she
idn't.

Nana was in full spate. 'Slandering us. Then she moved out of
ere. She moved out of here and started living in a flat! On her
wn! Who did she think she was? Just *who* exactly did she think
he was? She did as she pleased . . . said what she liked. She even
alked about us to that filthy beggar from Jinny Hoolets. He
vas told *everything*, that night. I heard them talking on their
vay down the track. She was laughing, as usual. *Everything* was
unny to Gloria.'

'What night?'

There was a silence.

'She saw you, did she? Gloria? Down by Jinny Hoolets?'

Nana did not reply.

The policeman's voice was urgent, uncompromising. 'And the
rl?'

'Girl?'

'The . . . foreign girl.'

Nana's response was instant. 'She drowned my dog.'

Kathleen held her breath. There was another rustle fro[m]
Joyce. She heard Da sigh and light his pipe. Joyce then sniffed [as]
if she was on the verge of tears.

Nana repeated herself, more slowly. 'She . . . drowned . [. .]
my . . . dog.'

The Inspector became quiet, but menacing. 'And how, may [I]
ask, do you know that?'

Nana raised her voice again. 'She was a dirty little slut, j[ust]
like her mother!' She began shouting. 'She couldn't keep h[er]
clothes on, could she? Ask my *husband*! He knows all about t[he]
*mother*! They don't know how to behave, these foreigne[rs.]
The mother was always outside my windows signalling with h[er]
fancy scarves. Wasn't she?' Her voice was crazily raised on the
last three syllables. She was yelling at Da. '*Wasn't she just?*' S[he]
gasped, then her breathing slowly subsided.

No one said anything. Kathleen could hear Da blow o[ut]
smoke from between his lips. He didn't answer. Standing in t[he]
chilly passage, she felt sweaty with fear. She's going to have [a]
turn, she thought. Any minute now, she's going to start a prop[er]
turn. She'll break things with her walking stick. And to thin[k I]
blamed Mrs Koninsky. I said *she* was mad. But she's not mad [at]
all, she's just sad and lonely. Kathleen rubbed her brow a[nd]
adjusted her glasses. The full realization of her mistake w[as]
suddenly upon her. It *is* my Nana who's the raving lunatic, j[ust]
like Petra said. Petra was *right*. She clutched the shoes in o[ne]
hand and felt her heart with the other. It was beating very fast[. I]
just couldn't see it, she thought. I wouldn't face it. Becau[se]
I didn't want to drag this family's name through the mud. S[he]
stared at the mud, smearing the shoes in her hand.

'You saw her drown your dog?' Curiously, the Inspecto[r]

authority seemed to undercut Nana's temper. The emotional explosion Kathleen anticipated didn't come. 'You saw her? Can I be clear? Is that correct?'

Nana was subdued. 'I never leave this house.'

Kathleen pushed against the door and Joyce stepped aside, letting her enter. She moved to the centre of the room, feeling small and dirty and vulnerable. She tried to see Da behind his smokescreen but he was a blur. She looked at Joyce but her face was hidden in her hands. Her eyes skimmed over Nana who was almost certainly straight backed, staring, clasping her walking stick. She took a step towards the policeman.

'Friendship Seven?'

He nodded.

'These are my Nana's shoes,' she said clearly. 'They are mucky from the pond. This is a photograph of my Nana, wearing my Da's coat and cap, and a pair of sunglasses, next to the house at Jinny Hoolets. I took it on Wednesday.'

The policeman accepted the shoes, examined them and placed them on the floor. He picked up the photograph and held it to his eyes.

Kathleen looked at Nana. She was staring back intently, with her one cloudy eye and her one short-sighted eye, but her expression was not one of hatred. Her face was full of understanding and recognition.

'So,' said Nana. 'So.'

Kathleen held her gaze. 'Why did you go to Jinny Hoolets, Nana?'

'I had my reasons.'

'What else have you got to say?' Inspector Glen asked.

Nana's eyes remained on Kathleen. 'Only that I killed them.'

'Both of them?' The policeman's voice was quiet.

'Yes. One for gossiping and being above herself. The other for drowning my dog.' She smiled, horribly. 'And this one—' She raised her stick and pointed it at Kathleen. 'This one too. But she's a clever madam. Cleverer than she looks. I didn't manage to kill *her*.'

Inspector Glen called for assistance from the uniformed officers who were waiting in their car, outside. Kathleen noticed that a lot of neighbours were peeping out from behind net curtains or front doors, astonished by the sight of a police vehicle, parked in their street. Nana got into the car quietly, holding up her head, opening and closing her eyelids, looking neither left nor right.

Kathleen refused to see the doctor. She went into the kitchen and washed her hands, face and legs at the sink. She moved the washing from in front of the fire. It was dry, so she folded it and put it in the ironing basket, except for a clean, unironed dress, which belonged to her. She took off the torn alice blue gown and put this on. I was wearing this when I found Auntie Gloria's body, she remembered. It got all dirty, from Jinny Hoolets.

She could hear Joyce and Da talking quietly in the parlour. She threw a bucket of coals on to the dying embers, opening the damper. She was conscious of performing tasks, which would normally be carried out by her grandmother. She looked at the wall clock and turned on Nana's wireless just in time for the start of the news.

*The Cuban missile crisis is over,* announced the newsreader, a tiny inflection of excitement in his voice.

Kathleen was startled. She sat down in Nana's chair, her eyes fixed on the dark smoke which climbed up the chimney.

*President Khrushchev has agreed to remove all Soviet missiles from Cuban soil under United Nations supervision.*

She lay back. 'Phew!' she said aloud. She picked up one of Nana's cushions and hugged it to her stomach. She listened carefully. The announcer explained that President Kennedy had

reed to lift the blockade as a result of the Russian climbdown.
e went on to detail the American show of force. The US
esident Mr John F. Kennedy had apparently deployed one
ousand four hundred and thirty-six bombers, an eighth of
hich had been in the air at all times. He had mobilized one
undred and seventy-two intercontinental ballistic missiles and
nt one hundred thousand infantrymen to the East Coast.
orty thousand marines and their navy fleet were returning to
se from the Caribbean and the Atlantic. For the last week, all
them had been awaiting nothing but a 'go' signal from the
hite House.

Kathleen swallowed hard. I can stop worrying about it, she
ought. It's over. There isn't going to be a war. We're not going
be blown to bits by a nuclear bomb. Not this time, anyway.
e brushed away a relieved tear.

She listened to an interview with the American Secretary of
ate, Dean Rusk. That's a strange name, Kathleen thought. It
unds like baby food. He was jubilant. *We were eyeball to
eball and I think the other fellow just blinked.*

ter Joyce, wearing her dressing gown instead of her uniform,
a fire in the parlour, which was something Nana never
owed normally, unless it was a special occasion.

'Let's all sit in here,' she said. 'It's nicer.'

Da sat in the same armchair as he'd been in earlier, smoking
s pipe. He'd taken off his jacket and, surprisingly, his
mband. He looked informal, in his shirtsleeves. Joyce closed
e curtains then reclined on the settee, without her shoes,
ting up her legs. Her nylons rasped. Kathleen sat in the chair
hich Nana had occupied, before she was taken away. No one
id anything for a while.

Eventually, Da laid down his pipe on the hearth. 'Kathleen,
yce and I have been talking.'

Kathleen felt trapped. She wanted to go up to her cold roc like she usually did. It's funny being in here, when it's Christmas, or anything, she thought. It's funny without N telling us what to do.

'We've decided to send you to a different school. It's a gc school in the city of Durham. You'll have to take an exam.'

'You're sending me away?'

'No, not away. You can go every day on the train.'

'Why?'

'Because you're a clever girl and you deserve a chance.'

Kathleen was pleased but she kept her face straight. imagined an old building with elegant playing fields and girl blazers, like the ones in *Princess* magazine, who said 'jolly gc show!' Inside there were well-equipped laboratories and sp sterish women in black gowns, holding pieces of chalk.

Her heart quickened. I'm getting out, she thought. I'm on way out. In her mind, the timeless unchanging streetscape the village with its rows, smoking chimneys, cobbles, hea clanking trains and looming pithead began to retreat. She tured the scene becoming smaller and smaller. This place stay in the past, she thought, but it'll be nothing to me. I'll b my own future and it'll be a new world. She couldn't s herself from grinning. Lucky, lucky, lucky, she thought.

Joyce smiled.

Da continued. 'There's something else you ought to know.

Kathleen looked at Joyce. 'I think I know already.'

'I'll tell her,' Joyce said quickly. She met Kathleen's e 'You've been brought up to think I'm your auntie, but rea I'm your mother.' Her voice came out in a rush. She lookec Kathleen, anxiously.

'Yes.' Kathleen felt a lump in her throat.

'This has all been a shock—' said Da.

'I'm your mother. I had you when I was very young, I wasn't married and—'

'It was very difficult,' interrupted Da.

'Yes,' Kathleen repeated. She grasped the arms of the chair. She wanted to stay in the room and she wanted to run away upstairs. She felt both impulses together.

'I was always going to tell you, one day. Nana didn't want you to know. I don't know why, but she insisted you weren't told. Anyway, I've told you now.'

'Do I have to call you Mam?'

Joyce looked nonplussed. Her lips parted but no word came out in reply.

'When you're ready,' said Da gently.

'Can I go upstairs now?' She was at that moment conscious of something missing in the room. She looked at the grandfather clock. It had stopped.

'No,' said Da. 'There's more.'

'More?' Kathleen's mouth was very dry. She looked from one to the other. Da's face and demeanour showed the stresses and strains of the last week. He sat up straight in his chair. He's crying, she thought.

In contrast, Joyce looked younger. It was as if, despite everything, Nana's disappearance had set her free. Kathleen fixed her eyes on some plastic tulips in a vase on the mantelpiece.

'You've been deceived Kathleen,' said Da. He paused. Deceived in a way that is unforgivable. Your Nana always said it was for the best. I never thought so.'

Kathleen waited.

Da bent and picked up his pipe. He fingered it but didn't light it. Kathleen could tell he was struggling to speak. 'I'm not your grandfather. Or your step-grandfather, or anything else you might have been led to believe.' He paused. 'I'm your father.'

She felt a shock like a lightning bolt. It hit her in her chest

then raced through her body. She was unable to speak. Sh
stared at Da, then at her mother, then back again.

'It's true,' murmured Joyce.

'I've never been proud of myself,' explained Da, 'at least
wasn't. Then I realized what a fine girl you are and I started t
feel proud, in a funny sort of way.'

Kathleen tried to speak. A croak issued from her throat.

'It only happened once,' said Joyce, embarrassed. 'I mean, w
weren't having an affair or anything—'

'It was a desperate and weak moment on my behalf,' agree
Da. 'But it happened, once, and you . . . were the result.'

'And Nana—' stammered Kathleen.

'She knew,' replied Da. 'She never forgave me. She neve
forgave either of us. She insisted on keeping it a secret, bu
Gloria—'

'Gloria told people.'

'Apparently, yes.'

Kathleen looked at them both in turn. Joyce was worried no
and Da seemed ashamed. 'So,' she said, recovering her voic
'I've been living with my mam and dad all along. They hadn
run away. They were here. Only I didn't know it.'

Joyce answered immediately. 'We couldn't give you awa
Kathleen. Nana wanted to, but you were ours.'

'Our responsibility,' agreed Da. 'Our clever girl.' He pulle
something out of his pocket. It was a fold of paper. He handed
to Kathleen. She opened it carefully. It was her birth certificat
She read it, her hands shaking, and passed it back.

Kathleen took off her glasses and polished the lenses on th
hem of her dress.

Joyce tried to smile at her again. She was nervous. 'Can yo
forgive us?'

Kathleen thought about the way she'd spent her whole miser
able childhood on her own. It was over now. The blood betwee

her legs meant she'd become a woman this morning so it was too late to try and go back. Her childhood was over and that was that.

'I can remember,' she said, 'when I was very little. I was sitting high up on a man's shoulders and there was a lady with a picnic. He was wearing a white shirt. We went up a very big hill. There were a lot of people coming up the hill and we sat on the grass. We ate the picnic. I knew those people were my parents. But I couldn't remember who they were.'

There was a brief silence. 'That was us,' said Joyce.

Da looked puzzled for a moment, then smiled. 'Pontop Pike, 1954,' he agreed.

Joyce sighed, almost happily. 'It was the eclipse. We went up to the top of Pontop Pike for the eclipse. To watch it. There was quite a crowd.'

'You had a red plastic shopping basket,' said Kathleen.

'We took you with us,' continued Da. 'Your Nana stayed at home. It was spectacular. The occultation of the sun by the moon.'

'I was wearing a white sun hat and there was a bee on a clover.'

'We had these special dark-green plastic squares to look through,' remembered Joyce, 'to protect our eyes.'

'And we sat on a tartan rug,' added Kathleen.

'You were very small,' smiled Joyce.

'I had a bag of peanuts and raisins.'

'It was partial, of course, this far south,' said Da. 'It was totality only off the northern coast of Scotland. It was still remarkable, though. The moon moved over the sun and it was like a gigantic eye, closing then opening again.'

'How dark did it get?' asked Kathleen, interested. 'I don't think I remember the darkness.'

'Oh, it was dark,' exclaimed Joyce. 'It was strange. Sort of a pearly grey colour. Not like normal darkness at all.'

'And it got cold,' said Da. 'And all the birds stopped singing, and some of the flowers up there shut their petals because they were confused. And the animals were frightened. But it was magnificent. Totally magnificent. Then everything gradually returned to normal and the birds started singing and the dogs barked madly. It was like a kind of ... renewal. Like we'd all been reborn.'

'It was exciting,' agreed Joyce. 'We were all quiet and ... sort of impressed and then it was over and everyone cheered.'

Kathleen thought about this and her own memory became clearer. She closed her eyes. She remembered the man lifting her confidently down on to the grass and he suddenly came into focus, with Da's young face, and the lady, as she spread out the tartan rug was of course Joyce, in a blue flowery sundress with a removable bolero.

She opened her eyes and looked at them both. 'The eclipse.' She sighed. 'The eclipse, of course! Thank you for taking me,' she said, her voice formal. 'I'm very glad I was up there, watching.' She blinked. She considered her words for a moment and deliberately softened her tone. 'I'm very glad we were there together.'

# The Center for Extreme Ultraviolet Astrophysics
## UCLA Astronomy Department,
## The University of California

Kathleen sighed as the young, fresh-faced reporter nodded to her, capped his pen, closed his notebook and with one last look at both her postcard of The Angel of the North and her framed letter from John Glenn, left her office.

She smiled. The personal angle. He was more interested in the personal angle than he was in my work. She shook her head. Here I am, she reflected, furnishing one of the last pieces in the cosmological puzzle, the last unexplored spectral window in astrophysics, and that young man wanted the personal angle. She smiled. I think he got rather more than he bargained for. He'll never use it.

She looked at her watch, took off her white lab coat and turned out the fluorescent light. Instead of moving into the Science Operations Center outside her room, she crossed to the window and opened the venetian blind.

Outside, the generous sky was a vivid orange. Kathleen took off her glasses and polished them on the handkerchief she kept in her sleeve. Blinking, she put them on again. Another Californian sunset, she thought. She sighed. It was, as usual, flamboyant, spectacular and altogether necessary. In the background, a row of palm trees rose into the singing air, even now as exotic as pineapples. Somewhere in the distance, a swimming pool glinted. Below, in the quad there was a painter's palette of bougainvillea, rose acacia and hibiscus. I'm warm through to my bones, she decided.

Kathleen moved back to her notice board. Gently s
unpinned the postcard and turned it over. Joyce's arthritis w
bad, she read, and it was raining hard, but she'd won ten poun
on the lottery. She'd signed the brief message, With love fro
your Mam. Kathleen returned the card to its place and focus
again on the luminous American heavens. The recollection
her childhood had been disturbing. She leant against her de
and let the memories slip away. She stared and stared at t
sky and concentrated instead on her telescope, enclosed with
that distant, elegant spacecraft, her own love child, spinning a
turning in pure uncontaminated space, its penetrating spectr
scopic eyes unblinking, probing the cores of distant galaxies.